FRACTURED *night*

STONE BAY SERIES

BOOK TWO

USA TODAY BESTSELLING AUTHOR

PERSEPHONE AUTUMN

BETWEEN WORDS PUBLISHING LLC

FRACTURED *night*

STONE BAY SERIES

BOOK TWO

USA TODAY BESTSELLING AUTHOR

PERSEPHONE AUTUMN

BETWEEN WORDS PUBLISHING LLC

Fractured Night

Copyright © 2023 by Persephone Autumn and Between Words Publishing LLC

www.persephoneautumn.com

All rights reserved.

This book is a work of fiction. Names, characters, establishments, organizations, and incidents are either products of the author's imagination or are used fictitiously to give a sense of authenticity. Any resemblance to actual events, places, or persons, living or dead, is entirely coincidental.

If you're reading this book and did not purchase it, or it was not purchased for your use only, or it was purchased on a site I do not advertise I sell on, then it was pirated illegally. Please purchase a copy of your own on a platform where the author advertises she distributes and respect the hard work of this author.

ISBN: 978-1-951477-79-0 (Ebook)

ISBN: 978-1-951477-86-3 (Paperback)

ISBN: 978-1-951477-88-2 (Special Edition Paperback)

ISBN: 978-1-951477-87-5 (Hardcover)

Proofreader: Rosa Sharon | Fairy Proofmother Proofreading

Cover Design: Abigail Davies | Pink Elephant Designs

BOOKS BY PERSEPHONE AUTUMN

Lake Lavender Series

Depths Awakened

One Night Forsaken

Every Thought Taken

Devotion Series

Distorted Devotion

Undying Devotion

Beloved Devotion

Darkest Devotion

Sweetest Devotion

Bay Area Duet Series

<u>Click Duet</u>

Through the Lens

Time Exposure

<u>Inked Duet</u>

Fine Line

Love Buzz

<u>Insomniac Duet</u>

Restless Night

A Love So Bright

<u>Artist Duet</u>

Blank Canvas

Abstract Passion

<u>Novellas</u>

Reese

Penny

Stone Bay Series

Broken Sky—Prequel

Shattered Sun

Fractured Night

Fallen Stars

Stolen Dreams

Raptured Souls

Standalone Romance Novels

Sweet Tooth

Transcendental

Poetry Collections

Ink Veins

Broken Metronome

Slipping From Existence

Poisonous Heart

Beneath Wildflowers

<u>PUBLISHED UNDER P. AUTUMN</u>

Standalone Non-Romance Novels

By Dawn

For all the souls struggling to stand up for themselves and speak their truth. For everyone that straightens their spine and puts on a brave face so the world doesn't see your scars.

CONTENTS

PROLOGUE
DELILAH

Past—Nine Years Ago

My curtain of black hair hides me from the room as I continue the drawing in my sketchbook. Two dancers on stage, spines tall as they face the audience but look at each other, arms fully extended and hands barely touching. Bust modest, her black-and-silver tutu flares with jagged edges over dark tights and pointe shoes. Topless, his black performance tights hug his muscular legs like a second skin, black ballet slippers on his feet.

Shoes clap and occasionally squeak against the linoleum, followed by the distinct scrape of chair legs. Groans over waking up early for the first time in months and not having enough caffeine before returning to school are the chorus of the day. Hints of pine, ash, citrus, and earth linger in the air.

The short ring of the one-minute warning bell echoes through the halls.

Straightening in my seat, I close my sketchbook and stow my pencils back in the case. On a quick scan of the room, I note the majority of the seats are filled, but a handful remain unoccupied, including one at my table. As the seconds to the final bell tick by, more students rush the room and hustle to the first empty chair they find.

And just when I think I will have the entire table to myself this semester, one last person bolts in the room a second before the late bell.

Phoebe Graves.

"Damn," I mumble under my breath and swallow.

Vibrant, auburn, bouncy waves frame her creamy, freckled skin. A light smoky eye makes her Nordic-blue irises pop more than usual. Red lipstick—her signature since freshman year—perfectly painted on her supple lips. Snug on her frame, the *V* of her burnt-orange dress exposes more cleavage than appropriate at school.

Will the school staff reprimand her? Will she be asked to change clothes?

Not if the staff want to keep their jobs.

Two words easily sum up Phoebe Graves—fire and ice—not just in looks but also personality.

But knowing as much doesn't stop my breath from hitching or pulse from soaring.

Stupid freaking hormones.

I blame romance novels for perpetuating my crush on Phoebe. For sustaining the endless fantasies I've had for years. Damn enemies-to-lovers trope always giving me hope.

Phoebe says something to Ms. Napoli, and the teacher points to the vacant chair on my left. Icy eyes stare at the empty seat for a beat until they meet my gaze. In a blink, the hint of annoyance in her expression morphs into borderline fury as she makes her way to the table.

But I brush it off with a subtle smile.

I have never taken Phoebe's hostile demeanor and behavior personally. The girl wouldn't know what a close friend is if one bit her in the ass. And since no one walks the halls with her, strikes up conversations with her or laughs with her, I refuse to hate Phoebe Graves like most of the student body at Stone Bay High.

Because everyone deserves a chance.

"Hey," I say, lifting my hand in a half-hearted wave as she takes the seat on my left. "I'm Delilah."

Eyes aimed at the teacher, her lips form a tight, synthetic smile for half a second before indifference consumes her expression. "Don't really care."

A low tone vibrates throughout the room and conversations cease as the class turns its attention to the front of the room. Rubber mallet in her hand, Ms. Napoli circles the outside of a crystal singing bowl with slow, even movements.

I close my eyes and let the soft frequency settle in my bones and clear my mind. I find peace within myself at the start of the day and a new school year, shaking off every ounce of negativity.

Seeing as my parents own the only metaphysical shop within a hundred miles, I am familiar with all things love and light and divination. This also means I am familiar with naysayers and cruelty, whom I do my best to ignore. Why waste my energy or voice?

"Fucking ridiculous," Phoebe mutters, garnering a laugh from nearby tables.

Ms. Napoli sets down the mallet, the low vibration fading into silence. "Good morning, class. Welcome back. I trust your summer was much more enjoyable than being here."

Titters float through the air as she faces the dry-erase board and writes.

"But at least your day starts with art and not math." She caps the marker, sets it on the tray, and spins around to scan the tables. "I'm Ms. Napoli and this is Painting I.

Some of you may be here to earn that final, pesky art half credit. Others may be here because art runs in their veins." She presses her palms together in prayer and shares a gentle smile. "Either way, I'm glad to have you in my classroom."

Beside me, Phoebe groans as she flips a spiral notebook open and uncaps a fountain pen. With a practiced flourish, the metal tip of the pen glides over the paper, black ink spilling from the tip. From the corner of my eye, I peek at the elegant letters on the page. It isn't often you see cursive-style writing nowadays. Some might say it is a dying art.

But Phoebe sweeps the ink tip over the page with ease. As if writing with such finesse and refinement was taught to her early in life. And when she reaches the end of the line, she moves to the next and writes the same thing.

Phoebe Aspen Graves, Editor-in-Chief, Stone Bay Gazette

I bite the inside of my cheek so as not to laugh. The impulse is not due to Phoebe's ambition to be on top. More the opposite, actually.

Anyone who knows anything about the Stone Bay Seven—the town's founding families—knows Phoebe Graves is definitely her father's daughter. A Graves, through and through. A bloodhound, thirsty for the next juicy story.

Unfortunately for Phoebe, she won't write anything controversial or remarkable until given a desk at the Gazette. Years from now.

"The seats you're in now will be your seat for the semester," Ms. Napoli announces. "And today, I want you to get to know your tablemate. Introduce yourself and make a new friend for the year." Light chatter fills the room and Ms. Napoli softly snaps her fingers over and over. "I'll give you ten minutes, then we're diving into part two of knowing your tablemate—drawing them."

Phoebe groans again as she caps her pen and stows it in her bag.

"Showcase your skills and draw a detailed, nonprovocative part of your tablemate. Their hand or fingers as they work. Perhaps their eye and brow." Ms. Napoli waves her hands in the air. "You get the idea. Just keep it appropriate for school. Consider this a refresher from Drawing I before we dip brushes in paint and add it to paper or canvas."

Ms. Napoli settles in her seat behind the counter at the front of the room.

At each table, students face each other and spark hushed conversations. Wanting to follow the assignment as instructed, I spin in my seat and meet Phoebe's profile. But she doesn't move, doesn't engage, doesn't give an ounce of effort.

So I put on my brightest smile and reintroduce myself. "Hi, I'm Delilah." I offer my hand to shake. Her eyes fall to my hand, a slight curl to her upper lip. "Delilah Fox," I clarify. "And you're Phoebe, right?"

At my last name, she angles her body toward me. "Fox, you say?"

I trail my finger over the spiral binding of my sketchbook. "Yes."

She hums. "As in the Fox founding family that thinks they're too good for the rest of the founding families?"

The Fox clan isn't oblivious to the gossip surrounding our family. Some think my grandparents stopped attending town meetings and elite events decades ago for egotistical reasons. Others whispered Zachariah and Amelia Fox couldn't handle the responsibility that came with being part of Stone Bay's high society.

We ignore the townsfolk's hushed rumors, knowing they don't hold a modicum of truth.

Cocking my head, I plaster on a smile and tell myself to kill her with kindness. "No." My cheeks sting as I stretch my smile wider. "As in the Fox founding family that just wants to live a happy life." I fold my hands in my lap. "Doesn't the Graves family want a happy life?"

"Ah." She crosses her arms over her chest. "So you know who I am." Her head tips to the side, somewhat matching my pose. "And happiness is overrated," she grumbles as she spins to face the front of the room.

"Says the grouchiest girl in Stone Bay."

A mastered snarl curls her top lip as she glances in my direction. "People call me a bitch," she says with too much ease, straightening her spine. "Doesn't hurt my feelings. In ten years, those same people will still be at the bottom of the food chain while I sit comfortably at the top."

Is this truly how she feels? Does Phoebe actually believe she will unlock some superior status in a certain time frame, all because of her last name? Because her ancestors and mine founded this town and built it from the ground up? Because she is Stone Bay "royalty"?

How sad.

"Sounds lonely," I say. "But if that's what you want…"

"Whatever." She takes out her phone and opens a news app. "We know enough about each other. Talking time is over."

Fine by me. Though I never want to give up on anyone, I also know when to step back and detoxify.

Taking my pencils back out, I flip my sketchbook open and turn to a blank page. Without shame, I study Phoebe's profile, the column of her throat, the slight protrusion of her collar-bones peeking out of her dress, the length of her thin biceps and forearms, the bend of her knuckles and the flawless red paint on her nails as she types on her phone.

Of all the options, I choose to draw her lips. Not the snarl she has flashed more than once. Instead, I opt to draw her lips soft and kind, with a slight upturn at the corners. A nice side of her that probably exists in the privacy of her own company.

This smile may never grace her lips, but I picture it there anyway.

Phoebe may wear the thickest armor over her heart and soul, but that means she has more to lose if there is a chink in her only form of protection.

I respect her but also grieve for her for the immeasurable pressure put on her shoulders by previous generations. For the life she will miss out on because of the shoes she is expected to fill. And for the love she deserves but refuses to accept.

She may hate me because my family chose love and joy over status and privilege, and that is her choice. But as my parents and grandparents taught me, I choose to be a good person over everything else. To do right by others and love with my whole heart.

And when the time is right, my person will come along and want all I have to offer.

Secretly, I still wish for it to be Phoebe Graves.

ONE

PHOEBE

Present

SWEET ALMOND AND VANILLA BLEND WITH A HINT OF MUSK AND nuttiness as I walk through the front door of the Stone Bay Gazette. I stomp my heeled boots on the mat and shake off the last of the snow as I unwrap my scarf.

"Good morning, Ms. Graves," Gladys greets from her reception desk, voice raspy. "Looks like we're getting a break in the snow."

I meet her cheery, wrinkled smile with my professional one. "Thank god." I pass her and head for the kitchen, desperate for caffeine. "Maybe people will actually get some reporting done today."

In the kitchen, I deposit my leftovers in the fridge and grab the hazelnut creamer. Sliding a glass under the drip, I press grind, wait for the portafilter to load, then press the proper brew button.

A few years back, I convinced Father to buy this state-of-the-art barista machine for the office. Made for people who like coffee shop beverages but not the lines or price tags, this machine makes all the fancy coffee drinks. Naturally, Father complained I was the only person in the office who wanted something other than lukewarm coffee that'd been in the pot half the day. I told him he was wrong.

First day this baby was operable, everyone in the damn office lined up for a freshly brewed cup. When Father walked into the break room, I cocked a brow, a silent *told you so* on my tongue.

Loading my favorite tumbler with ice, I pour the espresso in, add four pumps of liquid turbinado sugar, and fill the rest of the cup with hazelnut creamer before securing the lid in place. After my body sighs from the initial sip, I clean the machine then exit the break room.

Stowing my purse, I shrug out of my coat and hang it with my scarf on the rack near my desk.

With a shake of the mouse, I wake up my computer, type in my credentials, and sift through emails and coveted resources for newsworthy stories. Most emails are recycled news, but I scroll through for hidden gems.

One of my favorite resources… a back door into the Stone Bay Police Department.

In my line of work, it pays to be one of the Stone Bay Seven.

Who cares if I obtained the log-on details from my father's file safe without his consent? Father should do a better job at hiding his safe codes.

I open the Stone Bay Seven database, a police database set up for the Seven's eyes only—well, all of the Seven over age thirty because of some idiotic bylaw—and scan the screen. Noise complaints regarding Dalton's Pub at nine last night. An older resident concerned about the bear she's seen on her lawn every night for the past week. Grievances about rowdy teenagers stealing porch decorations and toilet papering plants and trees.

Essentially, it's all trash.

Fingers on the keyboard, I'm one button away from closing the database when it refreshes with a new entry.

Confidential All-Points Bulletin: Body discovered by Stone Bay Ski Resort employee during morning routine checks in Bay Cliff Mountains, roughly two miles south of resort. Units maintaining low profile are responding now.

"Jackpot." My blood heats as a victorious smile tips up the corner of my mouth.

I close the database, rise from my seat, straighten my spine, square my shoulders, and march toward Father's office. Knocking on his cracked door, I plaster on a bright smile before he looks up from his monitor.

"Good morning, Father," I greet when his bright-blue eyes meet mine.

Unlike my older siblings, I have features and characteristics from both my parents. Father's vibrant blue eyes and steely determination. Mother's fiery-red hair and icy demeanor. A little of both their body shapes.

With medium auburn-brown locks, a stocky frame, and sharp jawline, there is no mistaking my oldest sibling, Tyler, is Tobias Graves's son. And when Hayleigh stands poised next to Mother, most men in the room ogle her trim waist and prominent curves far too long before glancing up at her lengthy red locks and mint-green eyes.

In my formative years, I envied my brother and sister. Before I came into the picture, my parents had the perfect family. Two flawless, moldable heirs. Children who they were proud to show off in town.

I disrupted the whole "ideal" Stone Bay family. The *perfect* family. At least in my mother's eyes.

Far too early in life, I hardened my heart as a defense mechanism. Though my parents never outright stated they didn't love or want me, they also never doted on me the way they did Tyler and Hayleigh.

Even as a child, instinct doesn't lie. Kids know when they aren't loved. Not in the way they should be.

"Phoebe," he addresses. "I trust your weekend was well."

I live in a separate wing from my parents in the main house on the Graves estate. Taking this into consideration, one may think we would see each other sometime over the weekend. During a meal or walking from point A to B. But I never see my parents. Not unless they want me to see them.

On occasion, I spot Grandfather Talbert near the fireplace with a newspaper in hand and a stack of global newspapers beside him. Grandmother Gwendolyn spends most of her waking hours tending to plants in the garden or greenhouse, depending on the time of year. Elegant, poised, and well-respected, she is the least snobbish in the living Graves line. Unfortunately, she didn't rub off on Father.

"Yes. And you?"

"Yes. Your mother and I had a wonderful dinner with Hayleigh and Sawyer at Calhoun's Bistro. Much to discuss about the wedding."

As if anyone could forget about Hayleigh's overzealous wedding next month.

"Without a doubt." Wanting to nip this farce of a conversation in the bud, I change the subject. "I want to cover the new murder story."

"Case was closed when Emerson shot the man."

Nice try, Father. "Not the murder near the Barron property. The *new* murder."

Father narrows his eyes. "What new murder?"

The corner of my mouth twitches, eager to kick up in a smirk. I bite the inside of my cheek and resist the urge. "Near the ski resort."

Rubbing a hand over his smooth jaw, he shakes his head. "Not sure how you gained access to something not meant for you," he states, frustration thick in his voice. "The answer is no, Phoebe."

I step farther into his office, close the door, and cross my arms over my chest. "Excuse me?"

His eyes shift back to the computer, his way of ending the conversation and silently dismissing me.

Unlucky for him, I am equally stubborn and unwavering. "Why?"

Bored expression firmly in place, he doesn't meet my gaze. "Why what, Phoebe?"

"Why are you telling me no, *Father*?"

"Always the petulant one," he mutters before giving me his attention again. Lips pursed and arms folded across his chest, he tilts his head and stares for a moment. "Truth?"

I regard him like a bug to crush. "Is that a legitimate question?"

"Fine." Rolling his chair back, he stands and grabs his empty *Stone Bay Gazette* mug off his desk. "You're not ready for a story like this—mentally or emotionally."

"Are you serious?"

He moves past me, opens the door, and exits his office. I follow in his wake, disregarding the stares of others as we pass and head for the break room. Alone again, he continues to ignore me as he presses buttons on the barista machine and brews a fresh cup of coffee.

Seconds turn into minutes as he pays me no attention. He fetches his full mug from under the drip and spins around, eyes aimed at the door.

But I won't let him leave. Not without an answer.

I block the doorway and plant loose fists on my hips. "This is your answer, the silent treatment?" I cock my head and smirk. "So be it. But I'm still looking into it."

"I said no, Phoebe. Don't test me."

The only way I get an inkling of attention or recognition from my family is by pushing boundaries with my parents. Even then, what I get in return is a mere fraction of what they dole out easily to Tyler and Hayleigh. Scraps, if you will.

"All feelings aside, this is huge. Two dead bodies in just over two months. We have a responsibility to notify the towns-people, Father."

He sets his mug on the six-seater table, plants his hands on his hips, tips his head back, and huffs at the ceiling. A beat passes before he levels me with an icy stare.

"No, Phoebe. The last thing we need to do is cause more pandemonium in town. And that's exactly what your story would do… wreak havoc."

Heat crawls across my skin as my nostrils flare.

"Since when did we become the bland news source for Stone Bay?" I hold my hands out in front of me, palms up, then gesture to the room around us. "Generations of Graves have run this paper and delivered notable news for decades. Fires and expansions and community features. A blend of daunting news and feel-good stories." On an audible exhale, I lift my chin. "Now you want to throw all that away? Abandoning the truth for some fluff piece so the town doesn't freak out." I shake my head. "Not sure you deserve the Graves name anymore, Father."

He steps closer, fire lighting his eyes. "Watch how you speak to me, young lady. Show some respect."

That's it. Get angry. Feel something. Then maybe you will actually do *something.*

"I'm covering the story whether I have your approval or not."

"You have no idea what a story like this will do—to you and the town."

"True," I admit. "But letting dead people lie"—*too soon for that one?*—"only tells the responsible party it's acceptable to keep murdering Stone Bay citizens." I lift a brow and hold his gaze. "Do you really want future deaths on your conscience?"

"Solving murders isn't in our job description. The police officers in this town are generously paid for that reason."

"Did I say I wanted to solve the murder?"

Not that it sounds like a horrible idea. Maybe then, I would be revered as something other than *the other Graves daughter.* Maybe I'd finally be regarded with significance.

"No. You didn't need to." He picks up his coffee and takes a sip. "I know you. Writing a story about another murder and nothing more won't give you satisfaction."

I purse my lips and shrug. He isn't wrong.

"If I had confidence you'd write an exceptional story without causing an uproar, I wouldn't be so hesitant."

"Gee, thanks, *Tobias.*"

On a heavy, exasperated sigh, he shakes his head. "Will you be mature for a damn minute?" He shoves a hand in his pocket. "Use your journalism degree for good. Show me that you're capable, and *maybe* I'll let you write a larger-scale story."

"I'll write something else for this week's paper, but I'm still investigating the murder," I assure him. "No one gets this story out before Phoebe Graves."

Gaze falling to the tile, his knee bounces over and over. "If I get a single complaint from *anyone*"—fierce blue irises lift and lock me in place—"I will have you at your desk every working hour and someone on your tail every other hour." The muscles of his jaw tic. "Understand?"

A triumphant smile stretches my cheeks painfully. "Got it."

"I don't have time for games or foolishness."

I win. No need to stand here and go toe to toe with my father another second.

Spinning on my heel, I saunter back toward my desk and call over my shoulder, "Thank you, sir."

Seated at my desk, I open the Stone Bay Seven database again. Sift through every detail entered over the last six months. Look for something, anything, out of the ordinary before either murder was called in. A domestic disturbance call, perhaps. The same citizen reported multiple times. The slightest tip to lead me down an untraveled path. A faint detail someone else missed.

When my eyes go buggy, I turn to the phone. I call the ski resort, pretend to be a tourist looking to visit and ask questions about how safe it is at the resort. Unfortunately, the woman on the other end is far too chipper and won't shut up about how much she loves Stone Bay.

Ugh.

Needing a break from my desk, I fetch my lunch from the fridge and park at the table in the break room. People come in and try to spark conversation, but I tune them out and mull over all the things I've read online.

Several sheets of my legal pad are scribbled with notes on the first murder. The story of the woman in the woods was cut and dry. No evidence at the scene pointed to any one individual. Yet, the police department closed the case when a local man abducted another woman in town with strikingly similar features.

I didn't know the townie deemed responsible, but his tendencies with Kirsten Sparks did not match that of the previous murder victim.

Yes, the man was sick and needed help. Yes, what he did to her in the Emerson bunker may have been the start of something much worse.

But this twinge in my gut says the man who abducted Kirsten isn't the same person responsible for the woman in the woods this past November. This flutter beneath my diaphragm —the one I get when a deeper story exists, when I need to dig further—says someone else is still holding the knife. And that same someone let a crazed, obsessed man take the fall.

"Need to talk to the people," I mutter.

Wood grates tile as I shove my chair back and move to the sink. Rinsing out my container, I stow it in my bag and brew a fresh latte.

With a loaded cup of caffeine, I shrug on my coat, secure my scarf, shoulder my purse, and head for the parking lot. On my way out, I remote start my car and tell Gladys to forward calls to my cell.

Minutes later, I turn on Granite Parkway and scan the sidewalks and storefronts. A light dusting of snow blankets the earth but doesn't keep Stone Bay citizens from enjoying a day in the heart of the town. Wrapped tight in long wool coats, people smile as they move from store to store.

I locate street parking between Rosenberg's Deli and Toasty Bagels. With the car in park, I riffle through my purse, pull out my lucky pen, and close my eyes.

"There's more to this story. I just know it."

As I stow the pen, I exit the car and stroll the sidewalk. I don my brightest professional smile and approach the occasional friendly face. Without causing an uproar, as my father so blatantly put it, I identify myself and where I work. Then I ask how safe they feel in Stone Bay after the recent incidents.

Some blow me off and shuffle to the next store on quick feet. Others remind me of the damn woman from the ski resort and won't shut up. But all of them have one thing in common. Not a single person seems alarmed by the woman in the woods, which is somewhat disturbing.

Why does everyone seem peachy fucking keen so soon after a murder in their backyard?

Did the Seven slip something in the town's water supply?

I may be emotionless at times, but I am far from naive or blasé about people being murdered in my town.

Exiting the nail salon with nothing but a chemical high, I cross the side street and eye Sage Whisperer Metaphysical. Laughter bubbles in my chest and I lift a hand to my mouth as it slips out.

"Maybe someone will tell me my future inside," I jest.

Crystals, tarot cards and incense cones fill the window display. Signs on the glass mention psychic readings and all kinds of woo-woo bullshit. If these people predict the future, why hasn't anyone figured out who is really responsible for the murders?

Clearing my thoughts and curving my lips into a friendly smile, I open the door and step inside.

Some weird smell wafts up my nose within seconds and I scrunch my face. The light tinkle of chimes floats through the air, mingling with soft, melodic music. Floor-to-ceiling book-shelves line the left wall, overflowing with books about witch-craft and chakras and who knows what else. Throughout the rest of the store are cube-style wooden shelves with crystals—in every imaginable color, shape, and size—goblets, bowls, herbs, and a bunch of foreign-to-me items.

A woman with jet-black hair pinned up in a messy bun rounds the checkout counter and smiles in my direction. "Love and light," she says, clasping her hands in prayer and dipping her chin briefly. "What brings you into Sage Whisperer today?"

I don't identify myself—there is no need. Most of the town is aware of the founding family members, just as I know the woman before me is Aurora Fox. Though she married into a founding family, she keeps secrets locked up like the rest of us. And where secrets lie, a story begs to be written.

I clasp the strap of my purse, straighten my spine, square my shoulders, and brighten my smile. "Have you had any *unusual* customer interactions recently?"

TWO
DELILAH

June and I catch up as we sort a new delivery of crystals in the back room of Sage Whisperer. The last few shifts I've worked at the store, June wasn't working or had just left. Not that I didn't see June at least once a week. But it has been almost a week and I miss my sib.

"Dee Dee, you should've seen Jet and Shanti yesterday," they say, a dreamy look coming over their face. "The way they moved around the dance floor…" Arms in a circle in front of them, June twirls around the room and does their best imitation of Jet, our brother and their twin. Soft giggles float in the air when they stop and grip the organizing table. "I wish they'd both just admit they're in love with each other already."

Our brother, Jet, has danced from the moment he figured out how to walk. Mom saw his love for dance and enrolled him in classes when he was four. Ballet, tap, hip-hop… the list is a mile long. And he has mastered every style of dance with finesse.

In his junior year of high school, Jet was accepted to Juilliard. The family was so excited and proud of his accomplishments. Shanti, Jet's dance partner of almost ten years, didn't receive the same letter from Juilliard, unfortunately. And instead of leaving her behind in Stone Bay, he declined the offer from the top dance school and opted to stay.

If that isn't love, I don't know what is.

"When the time is right, one of them will speak up," I say. "Until then, we cheer them on."

"Guess you're right."

Loud conversation trickles into the back room from the main part of the store. June and I freeze, lock eyes, and lean closer to the doorway.

"Why won't you give me a straight answer?" an all too familiar voice asks.

My eyes widen and June mouths, "What?"

Lips in a flat line, I shake my head, set down the crystal in my hand, and weave through boxes for the door. With each step forward, I hear her louder and clearer.

"No doubt this place attracts all the crazies," Phoebe states as she waves a hand at the room. "If this isn't enabling people to do—"

"Hey," I bark out louder than I expect. "Watch what you say next."

Phoebe Graves.

The woman gets more heartless and shrewd with time. Doesn't help that her family is equally cold and judgmental. Though she should choose to rise above the ugly, she elects to embrace it.

Yet somehow, my heart still races at the sight of her. My breath still catches in my throat. And I don't understand why. She has done nothing to deserve even a sliver of my heart.

Phoebe scoffs. "Or what, Delilah? Going to cast a spell on me?" She holds her hands up and wiggles her fingers. "Going to make me pay for asking questions?" Her lips pucker and brows pinch together. "Ooh, I'm scared." She waves me off. "Why don't you go read a book?"

Seriously, how can I still want good things for her?

Because you are a good person.

Inhaling deeply, I remind myself that people behave as they are taught. Most people who grow up with happy, smiley parents that shower them with love and praise don't become assholes. Being a pretentious twit is a learned behavior—whether from family or peers. So is being kind and generous.

We all have the power to rise above being a twat. For whatever reason, Phoebe chooses to embrace her inner cunt. With a wicked smile on her face to boot.

But I won't put up with it. Not here or anywhere. Not today. And certainly not anytime in the future.

"You're not worth a spell, Phoebe Graves." I give a noncommittal shrug. "Karma will gift you with everything you deserve."

Expression turning serious, she cocks her head to the side and steps closer. "Is that a threat, Fox?"

Crossing my arms over my chest, I chuckle. "I know better than to threaten people, Phoebe." I nudge my mom with my elbow. "Good parents teach you that."

Irises colder than the Arctic flare before shifting to my mom. "So you haven't had any skeevy perverts buying ritual knives or love potions?"

I open my mouth to tell Phoebe how absurd she is but don't get the chance. Mom holds up a hand and shuffles closer to Phoebe.

"Sorry to disappoint you, Ms. Graves." Mom gifts Phoebe the kindest smile. A smile she doesn't deserve. "But I wish you well on your journey and hope you sniff out who it is you seek." Lifting her hands, Mom rests them on Phoebe's shoulders. "May love and light surround you and keep you safe."

After a quick squeeze of her shoulders, Mom releases Phoebe, spins on her heel, and walks over to the four-foot piece of selenite. She rests her hands on the opaque crystal, closes her eyes, and inhales deeply.

Mental reset.

Yeah, I will need one of those too, once Phoebe walks out.

"Thanks for stopping in Sage Whisperer," I say, the practiced line I use after bagging purchases. I clasp my hands over my heart. "Love and light." And then I meet Mom at the selenite and cleanse my mind.

A grumble hits my ears a moment before the tiny bell over the door tinkles. The energy of the store resets back to its blue-green aura, and within seconds, serenity blankets me from crown to root.

"Unfortunate young lady," Mom whispers. I glance at Mom and take in her pained half smile. Shoulders caved slightly, she sighs and shakes her head. "But she has to want to be better." Mom twists to face me, lifting her hands to hold me at arm's length. "All we can do is wish her well, my delicate dove."

With a gentle nod, I say, "I know, Momma. And I do. Promise."

Mom wanders back behind the checkout counter while I visually inventory what crystals we have on the sales floor. As I reach the shelf closest to Mom, she waves me closer. Opposite her at the counter, I straighten the small sign in the basket of hematite rings.

"What do you need, Momma?"

"I wanted to wait until Phoebe was gone a while..."

My hands freeze as I face the chakra "touch" stones. I lift my gaze to meet Mom's steely eyes. And for a moment, she appears to be somewhere else, far from Stone Bay. I rest a hand on hers and she blinks back to the present.

"Wait for what?"

Mom peeks over my shoulder at the door, then over her own shoulder toward the back room. Leaning over the counter, she inches closer. "A message was sent to the Seven this morning," she whispers.

My brows bend together. "A message?"

Anytime something notable occurs or is upcoming in Stone Bay, message updates are sent to the Seven. Unfortunately, if you are part of the youngest generation in each family—well, under age thirty or not working in a governing job—the message skips your inbox.

"Please don't share this, Delilah. Not with anyone."

My eyes dart to the back room and Mom shakes her head.

"Dad and I will share with June and Jet. That isn't your responsibility."

"Okay…" I agree, dragging the word out.

Mom brings her hand to my cheek and cups it, her thumb stroking softly as she speaks. "Please be vigilant around town. Listen to your instincts. And if possible, don't go places alone. If it's unavoidable, let someone know when you leave and arrive."

I rest my hand over hers on my cheek. "Momma, what's going on?"

"Phoebe came in asking investigative questions because she must've already heard." Mom pins me in place with the gravest look in her eyes. "Another body was found. Not far from the ski resort."

A cloud of confusion swirls around me and warps reality. "No." I shake my head. "That's not possible." Kirsten pops into my thoughts, her traumatic experience with a crazed stalker still fresh and healing. "The man that abducted Kirsten is dead."

"Well, we don't have details on the new victim. They

could've been in the snow a while before being discovered." Mom toys with my hair, following the action with her eyes. "Either way, until we know more, I need you safe."

Mystified by the news, I nod in slow, clipped movements over and over. "Always, Momma. And I'll let you know when I work at the bookstore too."

Stretching across the counter, she presses a kiss to my forehead. "Thank you. Now go, my delicate dove. Help June in the back."

On a step back, I take a deep, cleansing breath and aim my feet toward the back room. Just as I reach the threshold, I pause and peer over my shoulder. "Love you, Momma."

Her glowing smile brightens all of Stone Bay as she looks my way. "Love you too, delicate dove."

THREE
PHOEBE

Too many days have passed with zero answers since news of another dead body hit the database. Regardless of how many times I refreshed the screen over the last week, nothing new flashed on the monitor. Not who was found. Not if they died with the same marks as the previous victim. Not a single word. As if another dead citizen wasn't found in the frozen tundra of the Bay Cliff Mountains.

"Time to dig deeper."

Grabbing my red lip stain, I lean over the vanity, pucker at my reflection, and swipe the wand over my lips.

"Time to get real answers."

Flipping off the light, I exit the bathroom and cross my suite toward the bed. Foot propped on the tufted leather bench at the foot of my bed, I slip on black satin thigh-high stockings. Swap my silk robe for a red, off-the-shoulder cashmere sweater and black, wide-leg dress slacks. Sit on the bench and slide on my black So Kate Booty Louboutins.

After a quick once-over in the mirror, I fetch my coat and scarf from the closet, bundle up, and exit my wing of the estate. The click of my heels on the stone floor echoes throughout the main foyer as I descend the stairs. Pulling out my phone, I remote start my car on the way to the garage.

Within minutes, I turn off Graves Road onto Founders Way with one destination in mind.

Poke the Yolk.

Owned by Calhoun-Kemp Industries, the cutesy breakfast-and-brunch establishment is beloved by many in Stone Bay. With its abundant options and friendly staff, there is never a slow day at the restaurant.

But I'm not going for breakfast—though I'll probably order something to maintain appearances. No, I plan to pull up a seat next to the police officer who dines there each morning. And if I play my hand right, I'll leave with answers.

Or at least something to lead me toward answers.

Fuchsia and fire set the bruisy, purple sky aglow as I turn on Chalcedony. Instead of an immediate right into the Stone Bay Gazette parking lot, I steer my car left and weave through an already packed lot at Poke the Yolk.

Shouldering my purse, I lock my car and beeline for the entrance. One foot in front of the other, I scan tables and counters as I pass large floor-to-ceiling windows. Just as my hand wraps around the door handle, I spot my target.

Travis Emerson.

Stone Bay police officer. One of the Seven.

Boyfriend to Kirsten Sparks, the town's most recent headline news.

Spine straight and shoulders back, I weave through the tables for the diner counter. After a few steps, I slow my stride and change direction. Move to a table within earshot of his counter seat and deposit my purse and coat in a vacant chair. Take a seat, unlock my phone, and feign distraction.

"Can I start you with coffee or tea this morning?"

I glance up to the woman, pen tip pressed to the guest check pad in her hand, and lock my phone, setting it face down on the table. With a quick look at her name tag, I give her my friendliest smile. "Yes, Trudie. Coffee would be great. Hazelnut creamer and"—I scan the sweetener packets in the caddy and pluck a brown one—"more raw sugar."

Trudie scribbles on the pad then points to the laminated menus on the table. "Today's special is strawberry Nutella crepes with fresh coconut cream. I'll give you a moment to decide on breakfast."

Promptly, as Trudie once appeared at the table, she now walks off with equal speed.

Keeping up pretenses, I pluck the menu from the holder and look for something light to eat. A crepe sounds delicious, but eating something so heavy at this hour twists my stomach in knots.

Trudie returns with a small carafe, flipping the mug already on the table over and filling it with coffee. She deposits a caddy loaded with only raw sugar on the table, followed by a cream pitcher.

"What can I get you for breakfast, sweetheart?"

Internally, I cringe at the term of endearment. It isn't the actual label that makes my skin itch, more that I always find generic pet names so… disingenuous.

Calling everyone at her tables *sweetheart* doesn't make them special. It temporarily fluffs their mood, so they leave better tips.

Try harder, Trudie.

"Yogurt and granola parfait."

She scribbles it on her pad then looks to me as if I'll add more.

I shove the menu back in the holder. "That's it."

The corners of her lips curve up in an uncomfortable smile. "Alright, sweetheart. Shouldn't be long."

Alone again, I flip my phone over and unlock it. Open the notes app and poise my fingers over the keyboard. Lean slightly toward the diner counter and concentrate on one voice in particular.

"Have I mentioned you look sexy as fuck this morning?" Travis tells the blonde, also known as his girlfriend, Kirsten.

Blech.

Peeking at them from the corner of my eye, I observe them. She swats his hand as her eyes dart around the dining room. Then she leans over the counter and he meets her halfway, pressing his lips to hers.

Double blech.

Their PDA ends with a chaste kiss. *Thank god.*

With a bounce in her step, Kirsten walks off to check on her tables. Loony smile plastered on his face, Travis sips his coffee and stares after her.

Eyes on the vacant seats on either side of him, I scowl. Empty seats mean no one to spark a conversation with him. And no idle chitchat equals no overheard stories.

This is not how I pictured my morning—mediocre coffee, an unwanted yogurt parfait, and not a single lead.

Time to step up my game.

Wood grates tile as I scoot my chair back and stand. Spine tall, I swipe up my coat, purse, and coffee. In three strides, I hang my coat and purse on the seat next to Travis. Set my mug on the counter and occupy the stool.

Smile still curving his lips, Travis swivels in my direction. "Good morn—" His expression falls, and with a shake of his head, he faces forward again. "What do you want, Phoebe?"

"Good morning to you too, Travis." I lift my mug to my lips, hiding my smirk. "What makes you think I want something?"

Travis's head swivels in my direction, lips in a flat line and eyes deadpan. His brows lift in a *prove me wrong* challenge and I mentally growl.

Perks of a small town? Everyone knows just about everyone.

Disadvantages of a small town? Again, everyone knows just about everyone.

Major downside of being in the inner circle of a small town? Privacy is a luxury.

In Stone Bay, the Seven are well versed on who resides in the town's borders. Obviously, the occasional rotten apple makes an appearance, but there have been few over the generations. Due to their positions of power, the Emerson, West, and Langston families have the deepest wealth of knowledge. And of those three, it's easier to interrogate an Emerson officer over the chief of police, town mayor, or local judge.

Unfortunately, some of the other founding families associate the Graves name with disgust.

Horrid people, we are not. For generations, the Graves family has done one thing with perfection. Learn the truth and share it with the townsfolk. If we have to hunt down those truths by any means necessary, so be it. Our citizens deserve to know what is happening in their own backyard.

Bending rules to find those answers comes with the job, and I am not ashamed. Nor am I intimidated. Being at the top of most people's *Don't speak with...* list comes with the territory.

Trudie sets a bowl in front of me and smiles. "Something wrong with the table, sweetheart?"

"Was a bit wobbly," I lie. "Didn't want to spill coffee on my cashmere."

Travis rolls his eyes and mumbles, "Unbelievable."

Sympathetic smile on her face, Trudie lays her hand on the counter between us. "Sorry about that, but thanks for letting us know." She eyes my mug. "Anything else you need right now?"

The corners of my lips curve up in a smug smile. "Not from you, Trudie. Just going to enjoy my breakfast and catch up on town news."

Beside me, Travis growls under his breath.

"Well, you flag me down if you need anything else." Tapping the counter, Trudie walks off and leaves me alone with Travis.

Spoon in hand, I dig into the parfait and bring it to my lips but don't take the bite. "So, Travis," I start, voice low. "Tell me about the dead body." I shove the bite in my mouth and swivel slightly in his direction.

Travis chokes on his coffee, setting his mug down to beat his chest with a fist. All eyes pivot in our direction. Kirsten rushes across the dining room, eyes wide and brimming with concern.

"What happened? Are you okay? What can I do?" Her hand rubs small circles on his back.

Clearing his throat, he faces Kirsten and cups her cheek. "I'm good, sunshine. Just went down the wrong pipe." Leaning into her, he kisses her forehead. "No need to worry."

For a moment, neither of them says a word. They simply stare at each other, all dopey-eyed and lovestruck.

I set my spoon down and forgo the parfait, not wanting to puke it up.

The second she walks off, Travis spins around, death glare

firmly in place. "Sophisticated as you Graves claim to be, you have no couth."

Kirsten appears opposite him at the counter and sets a plate on his place mat. Her eyes dart to me then back to him. Not a word is spoken, but their exchange is far from quiet. Without a doubt, she wants to know why I'm sitting here. What it is I want.

Travis softens his expression, giving her a gentle smile.

Though they probably don't keep relationship secrets from each other, I doubt he shares all the town's skeletons with her. Until you marry into the Seven—and sign several confidentiality agreements—privileged information is under lock and key.

Once she walks away, he loads his fork with eggs and keeps his eyes forward. "Bored at the office?" He shoves the bite in his mouth.

I stir my parfait but don't scoop any on the spoon. "Never a dull day in our quaint town."

"Must be dull if you're writing about solved cases." He side-eyes me then stares down at his plate. "We closed the woman in the woods case last month." With a shake of his head, he scoffs. "If I remember correctly, your name appeared beneath the headline *Murder Suspect Shot During Abduction*."

"True," I say, setting down the spoon. "Keyword in that headline…" I shift my gaze and study his expression as I speak. "Suspect."

He stabs his eggs with a bit more aggression.

Thrill dances in my veins at the thought of being on the correct path. I *know* another body was discovered. He may not outright tell me, but his irritation is validation enough.

"Yeah, I'm aware of the case closure." I lean closer and drop my voice. "But I'm also aware a new case was opened. A different victim discovered in a different place."

He growls under his breath. "Not sure where you get information from, but you may want to find a new source."

I scoff. "So, that's it? You're going to play the oblivious card?" Grabbing my phone, I unlock it and open the database. Then I turn the screen to face him and cock a brow. "My source seems reputable."

Eyes on the screen, the muscles of his jaw flex. Then he drops his gaze and stabs more of his breakfast. "Drop it, Phoebe."

I lock my phone and scan the room for his girlfriend. Several tables away, she takes orders with an effortless, bright smile on her face. The scars of what happened to her mere weeks ago are artfully disguised by good spirits.

Leaning into Travis, I whisper, "Obviously, your girlfriend's abductor wasn't the killer." I sit up straight and tilt my head. "Which means the killer is still walking our streets." I push out my bottom lip and let out a sad hum. "I'd hate for poor Kirsten to find out through gossip. It'd stir up such horrible memories."

Wide-eyed, Travis peers over his shoulder to see if anyone overheard. But no one gives us an ounce of attention.

"Seriously, Phoebe. Let. It. Go." He drops his fork. "Nothing good will come of you searching for a murder suspect." A snarl curls his top lip. "And if you say a goddamn word to Kirsten..." His knuckles pale as his fingers ball into tight fists on the counter.

Validation.

Thrill courses through my veins. "Or... maybe I'll figure out who it is before you. How sad would that be?" I wave a hand in an arch. "The headline will read... *News Reporter Locates Killer Before Police.*"

Swiveling in my direction, he narrows his eyes. "Or it will read... *Nosy Reporter Dies After Ignoring Police Advice.*"

Hopping off the stool, I shrug on my coat, shoulder my purse, and grab my phone. I toss a few bills on the counter for Trudie.

"But at least the truth will be told." I weave through the tables for the exit. "Thanks, Travis," I call out with a finger wave. "Have a great day."

Now, it's time to find this killer.

FOUR

DELILAH

Strong arms wrap around me from behind and hug me tight. I gasp as I'm hoisted off the floor.

The cucumber in my hand falls to the ground. Rebel shoots up off the floor, hissing. *Thank the goddess I wasn't holding a knife.* When Rebel lands on all fours, she gives us a death glare before exiting the kitchen.

I peek over my shoulder, already knowing whose smile I'll see. "Did you have to scare Rebel?" I tease as Jet sets me back on my feet. "She's already mad I didn't bring her a new catnip plant."

Mom and Dad's cat, Rebel, is the feistiest and most terrifying cat.

Weeks before I left for college, Mom came home with the black, long-haired ball of fluff. Since I was taking the next step in my academic career and wouldn't be under the Fox roof for years, Mom wanted someone else to take care of. Not that June and Jet didn't keep our parents busy enough. But Mom was used to tending to three of us. Excited as she was for me to grow and flourish, she would miss seeing me daily.

Insert Rebel.

Mom's exact words to us as she introduced Rebel. *"Such a sweet spirit… until you piss her off."*

Rebel loves Mom and June. As for me, Jet, and Dad… not so much, hence why I bring new catnip plants to family dinner nights. Unfortunately, when I stopped at the Northcott farm stand on the way here, the catnip shelf was empty.

Good thing I don't sleep under the same roof as Rebel. She'd probably claw my eyes out in my sleep.

"She'll get over it," Jet says, picking up the cucumber. He takes it to the sink, gives it a thorough wash, then hands it over. "What's on the menu tonight?"

"Lemon caper fettuccine, garlic bread, and salad." I peel the skin off the cucumber. "June made an apple dessert pizza."

Jet grabs a second cutting board from the cabinet and sets it near mine. "Hope there's enough for everyone." He chuckles as he takes a knife from the block. "Dad home yet?"

While I cut the cucumber into thin half-moons, Jet cuts Roma tomatoes into bite-size chunks. June is out back with Mom, preparing the garden for new crops next week. And Dad is checking on Fox vacation properties before the next renters arrive in town.

"On his way." I toss the cucumber slices on the lettuce in the large wooden bowl. "All but one of the vacation rentals is booked for February."

Jet adds the chopped tomato as I start on radishes. "Seriously?" He takes his board and knife to the sink, cleaning them. "We've never had that many renters this time of year."

Sprinkling the radish slices over the salad, I sidle up to Jet and clean my board and knife. "We've also never had a wine-and-chocolate festival for the two weeks surrounding National Love Day."

"True." His eyes lose focus as he stares out the large

windows facing the backyard. "Do you think they don't know?"

I lean my back against the counter and cross my arms, mimicking his position. Beyond the back porch, Mom and June rest their knees on pads as they prep the soil for new life. June smiles as they dig and churn the earth. Mom, on the other hand, worries her bottom lip.

Her warning about being vigilant repeats in my mind.

"Listen to your instincts. Don't go places alone. Let someone know when you leave and arrive."

I hate that I know something my siblings don't yet. In the Fox family, we don't keep secrets. But Mom and Dad wanted to wait until family dinner night to share the news. Although it'd been days since I'd learned about a second victim in town, Jet only knew of the first and what had happened to Kirsten.

"Not sure. Either they do and couldn't care less. Or they don't because the Seven made sure it didn't leave the town's borders."

Minutes tick by in silence, but the quiet doesn't bother us. Jet and I are alike in this way.

For years, Mom teased I was more his twin—ignoring the obvious five years between us—than June. I disagreed. Although we act and think and feel similarly, I don't share the same connection with Jet as June. I never will, and that is a good thing. Truly, they are yin and yang. Light and shadow. Day and night. In perfect balance with each other in every moment. When one is up, the other is down. But most days, they balance the scales perfectly in the middle.

I love my siblings with my whole heart. But our bond is no match for that with which they share.

Chatter echoes through the house from the foyer a moment before Dad rounds the corner with guests.

I push off the counter and cross the room, wrapping my arms around him. "Hi, Daddy."

"Hey, little dove." Warm arms bundle me up and fill me with love. "Dinner smells good," he says, releasing me and scanning the kitchen. "Where's Mom and June."

Jet steps up and hugs Dad. "Out back, playing in the dirt."

Grandpa Zach chuckles as he steps around Dad and sweeps me into his arms. "Sounds about right."

Of all the hugs, Grandpa Zach gives the best. Strong yet gentle. Affectionate and peaceful. Like all your favorite comforts wrapped into one embrace. His hugs... you can never have too many.

"Don't hog her, Zachariah," Grandma Amelia grumbles. "I'm not getting any younger over here."

Grandpa releases me and turns to Grandma, framing her face with his hands. "You've never been more beautiful, my love." He gives her a chaste kiss on the lips, causing a soft blush to color her cheeks.

Warmth blankets my chest at seeing their open, honest affection. I long for a love like theirs, like the love Mom and Dad share. A fierce yet tender love.

One day. Hopefully.

"Give your grandma a hug, little bird." Arms wide, she steps into me and hugs me with impossible strength. "How's the bookstore?" she asks, inching back and holding me at arm's length. "Any new sexy covers I need to add to my bookshelf?"

Before I could read on my own, Grandma was determined to make me a bookworm. She read to and with me often. And as I matured, so did the books she shared. Now, it is my turn to return the favor. Not only do we share of love for fiction, but we also share an obsession with romance.

"The store is great. We've seen a boost in sales since the

new library addition." I lean in and drop my voice. "I set aside a few spicy gems for you." I wink.

"Best grandchild ever," she proclaims as Mom and June walk in.

"Hey," Jet and June say simultaneously.

"I'm kidding." She holds her hands up in surrender. "Maybe."

Everyone laughs as they move from person to person for hugs.

Aunt Destiny announces she and Uncle Westley brought wine as he holds up two bottles. Mom and June wash up as Jet and I carry food to the table. And before long, we all take a seat at the table and fill our plates.

Family dinner was instituted by Grandpa Zach and Grandma Amelia before I was born. As Dad neared adulthood and life got busier, they insisted on family dinner two or three times a month. A way to disconnect from daily stress and reconnect with the people you love.

I love this simple tradition. A shared meal with my favorite people. Every other month and near holidays, Papa Jeremy, Nana Cassandra, Aunt Jada, and Aunt Camille—Aunt Jada's wife—join us. Hands down, those gatherings fill my heart the most.

Light tinkling chimes through the room and conversation quiets. "Can I have everyone's attention?" Dad sets his fork down and takes a sip of wine. "Some unfortunate news has come to my attention."

The energy in the room takes a nosedive. Grandma reaches for Grandpa's hand on the table, giving it a slight squeeze. *Of course, they already know.* But as my eyes flit from one face to the next, I discern my parents and I are the only others that know too.

"What's going on, August?" Uncle Westley plants his elbows on either side of his plate and leans forward.

"Goes without saying; this stays between us and the Seven."

Jet twists in his seat, his knee bumping my leg. "What stays between us, Dad?"

Sad smile on his face, Dad's gaze moves from one person to the next before landing on Mom at his side. "Another dead body was discovered in Stone Bay."

Ice seeps through my pores, snaking itself around my veins and settling in my bones. The warmth that always surrounds family dinner night is blanketed with an endless, bitter chill.

"Who?" June whisper-asks, their face pale as they stare at Dad.

"Margot Pierce."

"The dental hygienist?" Aunt Destiny covers her mouth with a hand as tears brim her eyes.

Eyes glassy, Dad nods. "The dentist's office reported her missing when she didn't show two days in a row after her vacation ended." He takes a deep breath and searches for the strength we all need in this moment. "Her phone went straight to voice mail and she hadn't responded to texts or knocks at the door."

Uncle Westley slouches in his chair, his brow marred with concern. "Do they have any leads?"

"No, but..."

Mom lays a hand on Dad's forearm and gives a subtle nod.

"It's reported she bears the same cuts and bruises as the woman found in November. So we may be looking for a copy-cat." Closing his eyes, he shakes his head. On a slow exhale, he opens his eyes and audibly swallows. "Or the previous suspect was not the killer." He pinches the bridge of his nose. "There was one difference between the crime scenes."

When Dad doesn't elaborate, Grandpa speaks up. "Go on, son."

Dad meets Mom's eyes, a slight tremble to his chin. "A half-burned bundle of sage was laid on her chest."

Just great.

Funny how a small bundle of herbs meant for cleansing will now thrust Sage Whisperer and the Fox family into the middle of a murder investigation.

So not only will we have Emerson and West eyes on us, but we'll also be badgered by the Graves family.

Time to charge my protection crystals and mentally prepare for daily, intrusive visits from Phoebe Graves.

FIVE
PHOEBE

The room glows in a sea of gold, peach, and cream shimmery balloons, blown in a variety of sizes and artfully strung together. Sprigs of artificial greenery, peach tulle, and white paper flowers are strategically placed between the shiny globes. A massive cluster arches over the heart of the room near two stone-colored tufted sofas. Between the five-seaters, a small bundle of balloons adorns an oak-and-iron table, an elegant antique-gold-and-glass chandelier perfectly centered above it.

Every surface, including the ceiling, is highlighted with the same colors. The colors my sister chose for her wedding theme. Colors that scream wealth and power and purity.

Hayleigh is far from pure, though.

Prim and proper as she leads my mother to believe she is, I heard every time Hayleigh snuck out of the house during high school. I peeked out my door as she tiptoed back to her room, hair disheveled and lipstick smeared. Dress strap loose on her arm and skirt askew.

Has my older sister matured since her promiscuous high school years? Absolutely. In the Graves family, you learn to grow up fast. There is no other option. Not when an entire town scrutinizes your every move. In Stone Bay, if you're a Graves, having thick skin is a necessity.

The bigger question is, has she tamed her ways? Doubtful. Perfectly as Hayleigh plays the good-girl role, she is anything but.

Dressed in gold lace and cream tulle, my mother strolls across the room with Marilyn Langston at her side. Eyes surveying the room, they examine every detail to make sure nothing is out of place.

Nothing but the best for Hayleigh.

When Mother's severe gaze lands on me across the room, I groan.

"Great."

In graceful strides, she eviscerates the distance between us, Marilyn on her heels. Champagne flute half-full, she lifts it to her lips and takes the smallest sip, her eyes never leaving mine.

"Phoebe, darling." Practiced, artificial joy curves the corners of her mouth. "You remember Mrs. Langston."

I cock a brow and shift my attention to Marilyn.

Blonde locks perfectly coiffed, the length secured artfully at the nape of her neck. Smoky shadow and bold liner making her blue eyes pop. A faint dusting of blush accents her high cheekbones, while a rosy stain draws attention to her lips. The deep *V* in her floor-length champagne gown displays more cleavage than expected, small gold leaves and vines embellishing the bodice and winding down the skirt.

Marilyn is in this room for two reasons—her last name and that she owns the building. Otherwise, Mother wouldn't associate herself with the woman. Not after the stunt her daughter pulled last year.

"Mrs. Langston." I tip my head. "How's Kelli?" I bite my tongue before adding, *is orange her new favorite color?*

A well-rehearsed smile highlights her face, not a wrinkle to be found. "Kelli is great, dear. Taking it one day at a time."

Great? Really?

Can't say I've met anyone who would be *great* if sentenced to decades behind bars. Prison isn't some damn retreat with massages and facials. There are no book clubs or tea parties in the common area. No social hierarchies or personal body-guards. And no amount of money will buy you safety or freedom—not that Kelli has money after the stunt she pulled.

Kelli Langston may not have killed anyone, but that woman is far from innocent or charming.

Much of Stone Bay paints me as cold and callous, and I embrace it. I wield their judgment as a weapon and trudge forward. Live my best life with my head held high. A gleaming smile on my red lips.

But the youngest Langston isn't just cold. Kelli is the fucking Antarctic. Self-serving with zero heart. A cesspool of greed and ego and superiority. She abused her status and power in this town and thought her father—a judge—would turn a cheek and grant her immunity.

Unfortunately for Kelli, her father had no say in her case or sentencing. I think that pissed her off more than anything.

Since the clap of the gavel last year, the Langston name bears more revulsion than respect. And every day, Marilyn, Beaufort, and Beau, Kelli's brother, work tirelessly to repair the damage Kelli inflicted.

Perhaps Marilyn wants to picture her daughter in a posi-tive light. No one is proud of their child going to prison for a laundry list of charges, some federal. So maybe Marilyn elects to focus on the good, like what her daughter will learn from this situation.

"Good for her." I sip my champagne, the fizzy bubbles dancing on my tongue.

"Phoebe, mind your manners."

I bite the inside of my lip and swallow down every retort on my tongue.

"This is Hayleigh's bridal shower. Mingle." Her eyes scan countless guests milling about. "Celebrate your sister and quit sulking in the corner."

Mingle. She wants me to mingle.

Before my top lip curls at the notion, an idea sparks to life.

"No more quiet observations. On it." I tip my head toward Marilyn. "Was nice seeing you, Marilyn. Send Kelli our love." My mother doesn't get the chance to scold me before I walk off.

Draining the last of my champagne, I set the glass down and pick up a full flute. In search of someone worth speaking with, I weave between the crowd of men and women. Styled in sophisticated ball gowns and perfectly tailored suits, everyone I pass gives me a polite smile.

When the wedding planner suggested the bridal shower be women only, Mother and Hayleigh immediately shut down the idea. They claimed it was sexist to only invite women. And while I agreed, I recognized the lie for what it was.

Fewer attendees equals less attention. It also means fewer gifts. Not that Hayleigh won't receive more gifts at her bachelorette party and wedding reception.

Materialistic greedmonger

"Mr. and Mrs. Barron," I greet with a smile. "How are you?" I cup Scarlett's elbow. "A little birdie told me you're grandparents now."

Warmth and love radiate off them as smiles light their eyes.

"Our little Cyrus." Scarlett lays a hand over her heart. "He's a burst of love and laughter in the Barron home."

Edwin peers down at his wife, a dreamy glint in his brown eyes. "Especially since he started sleeping through the night," he teases.

Scarlett playfully slaps Edwin's arm and we all laugh. "How are you, Phoebe?" Eyes roaming the room a moment, she sips her champagne. "I assume your family is pushing you to find love as well."

At every turn.

"I'd think them ill if they didn't," I say, laughing. "But we're not here for me and my nonexistent partner."

Softness consumes Scarlett's expression as she rests a hand on my forearm. "When the time is right, you'll find your person, Phoebe. I wholeheartedly believe it."

Glad someone has confidence in my future. My family sure as hell doesn't.

"Enough about me." I wave off her comment. "How's business? Is the firm staying busy?"

One of the top fifteen law offices in the state, Barron Law and Associates is the highest-ranked firm in western Washington. Generations of attorneys occupy the four stone walls near the town hall. Prized for their strong ethics, diverse leadership, powerhouse skills, and endless compassion, Barron Law is more than an office packed with prestigious attorneys. The Barrons are true pioneers in Stone Bay.

On occasion, they flaunt their founding family status, usually when it benefits the town as a whole or a family in need.

I admire this about them.

Edwin chuckles. "Never a dull day. Not in this town."

"Too true." I glance around the room, taking in the smiles, soft chatter, and occasional laughter. "I suppose you've heard the latest news." I turn my attention back to them. "Near the ski resort."

Edwin's expression shifts from easygoing to indifferent. Scarlett's does much the same as she lifts her drink to her lips.

"No sense in denying it." I shrug. "But I would like to find out who's behind it."

"Edwin. Scarlett." Mother sidles up on my right, looping my arm with hers. "Forgive my daughter." She playfully rolls her eyes. "Phoebe hasn't mastered clocking out of her reporter role yet." With a tug of my arm, she steers us away. "Enjoy the shower."

Dragging me through the room, she guides us to a distressed wood door. I'd open my mouth to argue, but don't see the point. In mere seconds, Priscilla Graves is going to lecture me about couth. Won't be the first time. It definitely won't be the last.

Gently closing the door behind us, not a breath passes before her shrill voice echoes through the air. "Show your sister some respect, Phoebe."

I spin on my heels, prop my hands on my hips, and pin her greens with my icy blues. "How did I disrespect Hayleigh?"

"Don't play childish games. It's very unbecoming." Shoulders back and spine straight, her heels clap the marble as she steps closer. "This is neither the time nor place to play reporter. If I hear one more word about murderers, dead bodies, crimes, or news in town during this event or any other for your sister, you can kiss the Gazette goodbye."

Fire roars in my veins. I inch forward and come nose to nose with my mother. "Watch your tongue, *Mother*." My nails dig into my palms at my sides. "Spouting threats you can't fulfill is futile and shallow." Disgust curls my lip. "Careful. You might wrinkle your Botox."

Thwack. Her palm collides with my cheek.

"Speak to me that way again"—she grips my chin hard, her nails digging into my cheeks—"and you'll never leave the estate." She releases and shoves me away. "I may not have been born a Graves, but at least I deserve the name." Glacial green eyes scan me head to heel. "Now, clean yourself up and show your sister you love her."

Facing the floor-to-ceiling mirror, she primps her hair and straightens her dress. Without another word, she exits the bathroom.

"Fucking bitch," I mutter.

Minutes tick by as I seethe over her threats. Leave it to Priscilla Graves to rob me of my only joy. To take delight in whittling me down so her reputation remains intact.

Woman doesn't have a maternal bone in her body.

As the red handprint fades from my cheek, I frame my face with my hair and head for the door. I twist the knob and step out, loud chatter and laughter and glasses clinking hits me all at once.

Grabbing a fresh flute of champagne, I move through the room, carefully avoiding my mother. As I lift my glass to my lips, Grandmother Gwendolyn blocks my line of sight.

"Where have you been?"

I open my mouth to answer her, but she waves me off.

"Never you mind." Soft, delicate fingers take my hand. "Come with me. A gentleman has been asking for you."

Grandmother means well. Truly. But the last thing I need is to be set up with some egotistical snob.

"Here she is," Grandmother says, shifting her stance. "This is my granddaughter, Phoebe."

Dark-blue eyes sparkle as they scan my curves, and I shiver. Not in a good way. If we were anywhere else, if the room wasn't filled with Stone Bay's upper class, I'd knee Beau Langston in the balls for the way he just visually assaulted me.

"Phoebe," he purrs my name as he steps closer. He reaches for my hand, but I yank it back. Unaffected, he continues.

"Wonderful to see you. Gwendolyn has told me so much about you." Beau smiles at my grandmother.

Smile wrinkling the corners of her lips and eyes, she leans in and kisses my cheek. "A fine gentleman," she whispers, so only I hear.

I give her a curt smile before she steps away. If only she could get a glimpse of the real Beau Langston.

"Your grandmother says you're available."

There he is, the real Beau. Prick.

"Unattached, yes. Available..." I curl my lip at him. "Not for you."

"Appease the old woman, Phoebe. Have dinner with me. Maybe a little *fun*."

He steps closer.

Too close.

Bile climbs up my throat as I decipher what Beau means by *fun*. "Hard pass."

His breath paints my cheek and I recoil. "I may or may not know something about recent news in town."

I turn my glare on him, stepping back when my nose brushes his. "Don't toy with my emotions, Langston. Being vague won't get you points."

A sinister smile curves the corners of his lips. "We can talk over dinner."

Do I want answers about the most recent death in Stone Bay? You're damn right I do. Taking the lead on this story, getting recognition for bringing a killer to justice, making headlines outside of Stone Bay... god, what an incomparable high.

But I won't whore my body or soul to the likes of Beau Langston for *potential* answers. Knowing him, he has as much information as I do.

"Was good seeing you, Beau," I lie as I walk away.

I set my glass down, head back to the bathroom, and duck into a stall. Plopping down on the closed lid, I close my eyes and inhale deeply.

Somewhat happy as I may be for my sister and soon-to-be brother-in-law, I have a love-hate relationship with big events. If I could be myself, it would be less agonizing.

But no one seems to like the real me.

Not that I care.

I just want to get out of here and do what I love most. Unearth secrets and write a jaw-dropping story.

SIX

DELILAH

Thump. Th-thump. Thump, thump.

Heart beating against my breastbone, my pulse whooshes in my ears. Lips slightly parted, I sip short gulps of air. A light sheen of perspiration slicks my skin as my body heats. Hotter. Hungrier. The ache between my thighs builds. Higher. Heavier.

Swallowing, I peek up and scan the room. Not a soul in sight.

I flip the page and keep reading.

Slick with arousal, my fingers pump faster in Clarissa's swollen pussy. Peppering kisses down her neck, along her collarbone, over the swell of her breast, I circle her nipple with my tongue once, twice, before sucking it between my lips.

Clarissa tugs my hair. Hard. "Oh god, Harper." My thrusting fingers impale her pussy. "Right there."

"Good book?"

A scream rips from my throat as I toss said book in the air and it lands with a thump on the hardwood. I smack a hand to my chest, my heart in borderline cardiac arrest as I inhale deep, calming breaths.

When my pulse steadies and breaths even out, I glance up to two of the biggest smiles. Skylar masks most of hers with her hand. Kirsten, on the cusp of laughter, has her smile on full display.

I narrow my eyes. "Was that necessary?"

Bending, I swipe the book off the floor and fan through the pages. One thing about reading in the bookstore you work in… you ingrain the page number in your memory after every page flip. Not knowing when I'll have to put the book down, I mentally mark each new page.

When I land in the middle of Clarissa and Harper's steamy sex scene, I remove a Page by Paige bookmark from my store apron. I mark my page and stow the book behind others on the shelf.

"Asking if it's a good book?" Skylar cocks a brow as she uncovers her mouth. "Seems like a legit question in a bookstore."

Kirsten nudges Skylar with her elbow. "By the blush on Dee Dee's cheeks, it's safe to assume it's a good book."

"Ugh." I roll my eyes and turn my attention to the shelves, straightening the already-organized books. "Remind me again why we're friends."

Skylar barrels into me, followed by Kirsten. With hard squeezes, I become the cream in a Delilah cookie sandwich.

"Because you loooove us." Skylar drops a sloppy kiss on my cheek.

I snicker. "Yeah, I guess I do."

After another tight squeeze, they release me and step back.

"We got your text." Kirsten glances over my shoulder, down the aisle. "What time are you off?"

Midway through my lunch break, an ache bloomed in my chest. At first, I thought it cropped up over the scene I'd just read. But when the tension tapered off in the book and the ache remained, I dug deeper for an answer. Closing the book, I ate my salad and let my mind drift. Before I reached the bottom of the bowl, this overwhelming need to have time with my friends hit me square in the chest.

By no means am I a needy human. Growing up in the Fox household taught me you can have love and independence without sacrificing your individuality.

But do I crave companionship? Do I thirst for stronger connections? One hundred percent.

I wouldn't be human if I didn't.

After living with Kirsten and Skylar for years, I am now the sole occupant of the gray house with oxford-white trim on Jasper Court. I relished those first few days of solitude, walking through the house in next to nothing without a care. Not having to worry about what food or drinks in the fridge and pantry belonged to whom. By the end of week one, though, the house was too quiet.

I like the quiet. Just not *this* quiet.

I miss having daily access to my friends.

Kirsten and Skylar fell in love with incredible guys and took the next step in their relationships. Faulting them for this, I cannot. When we moved in together, I had no preconceived ideas about us living together until our hair grayed and skin wrinkled. Romantic relationships are an inevitability, not a possibility.

I simply want more time with my friends before life tugs us in different directions.

"Four." I pluck the lip balm from my pocket and coat my lips. "What about Law and Travis?"

I don't ask about Oliver. Poke the Yolk closed an hour ago. As we speak, he's probably practicing with his bandmates, strumming his guitar solo, or finding a reason to hang with Levi.

"Law wraps up with his final client just before five," Skylar says, twisting the thin band on her left thumb.

Kirsten checks her watch. "Travis should be home in the next half hour." She lifts a hand to her neck, her fingers toying with the rose gold sun and moon charms at the hollow of her throat. "He needs time to wind down. An hour or so."

Taking my phone out of my back pocket, I open the *Inner Circle* group text. My fingers fly over the keyboard, then I hit send.

> Movie night. My place. 6:30

Skylar and Kirsten stare down at their phones and smile. A few feet separate us, but they both respond to the text.

> **K**
>
> I vote we watch something smutty
>
> **SKY**
>
> Charcuterie and wine ✓
>
> Also, I vote yes for smut

I laugh at their responses as my phone vibrates with a new text.

> **OLLIE**
>
> Look guys. I get it, we're close. But are we that close?
>
> I love me some ⬛ 🔪 😈 🔪 movies. Do I want to watch them with you? 😬

"He has a point," I say, rereading his texts with all the sexually suggestive emojis. "Could get awkward."

Skylar snorts as her fingers type out another message.

SKY

Perfect opportunity to invite Levi 😉

"When will he learn?" Skylar teases with a shake of her head.

OLLIE

No pizza for you 😔

LAW

Movie night, yes – smut, also yes

TRAVIS

Good way to end the week. I'm down

Travis's message is a cold slap of reality. I peek up at Kirsten from under my lashes and read her expression. A smile curves the corners of her lips, a sparkle lighting her eyes.

He hasn't told her yet.

With her abduction a little more than a month ago, it doesn't surprise me he's kept the newest discovery to himself.

Low-key as the news needs to be, my friends deserve to know something is amiss in town.

Popcorn, candy, and nonalcoholic drinks on me 🍿

We agree on a movie that isn't mostly porn. Thank goodness.

I have zero hate for porn. As an avid romance reader and single person, I enjoy my fair share of sexually stimulating entertainment. I just have no desire to watch hardcore sex scenes with my friends in the room.

"Thanks for pizza, Ollie," Skylar garbles around the bite in her mouth. "Always tastes better when you bring it."

A smirk dons Oliver's face. "That's cause Dion wants in my pants again."

Carbonation burns my nose as I spit my drink across the room. One harsh cough after another, I beat my chest. Heat climbs up my chest to my neck before it spreads like wildfire across my face.

"TMI, Ollie," I choke out, then sip my sparkling water.

With a wave of his hand, he scoffs. "Not like any of us are virgins." Lifting a half-eaten slice of supreme pizza to his lips, he takes a huge bite. "What? We can't talk about sex 'cause I'm a guy?" He chews the bite and swallows, washing it down with Cherry Coke. "Seems discriminatory."

Open-mouthed, I stare at my friend. "Are you serious right now?"

With a purse of his lips, he shrugs.

"If you need advice or a shoulder to cry on or to get something off your chest, you know I'm here for you." I will always be here for my friends, day or night. Without a doubt, they reciprocate the sentiment. "Me not wanting to hear about your sex life has nothing to do with your penis."

Kirsten snorts while Travis shakes his head.

"It's just me not wanting graphic details of my friends' sex lives. Period." I shove my empty plate away. "Can we talk about something else, please?"

Movie playing in the background, conversation sparks about the new wine-and-chocolate festival.

In time for the season of love, Bales Winery is hosting its first annual event. Several wines will be available for sampling from the vineyard. Chef Beaulieu from Calhoun's Bistro is sculpting chocolate showpieces while coordinating with Angel

Calhoun of Calhoun's Confections for smaller treats for attendees.

Dad says every rental in town is booked during the two-week event. The boost in sales will be great for the town and residents.

I just hope news of the second woman doesn't spread during the influx of visitors.

My gaze drifts to Travis and how close he holds Kirsten. Bubbly as she is, there's not a chance he has mentioned the body near the ski resort.

Stealing her smile is the last thing I want to do. But if someone opens their mouth and takes her by surprise with the news, she'll be hurt, feel betrayed, and won't know who to trust.

The Stone Bay gossip mill is ruthless. Without shame, those old bats talk smack with you in earshot. Hearing about another victim through whispers and rumors will shatter Kirsten. Stir up bad memories that she still works through daily.

Kirsten may no longer worry about the man who abducted her. But learning of a new victim will undoubtedly be a shot of anxiety in her veins. Learning her abductor may not have been the person who killed Julia Quinn may send her into a tailspin.

No one should feel they need to constantly look over their shoulder. No one should live in an endless state of fear.

Kirsten deserves to feel safe. We all do.

When the conversation quiets, I open my mouth to share some half-truths.

"Mom said a lot of bizarre characters have been in the store."

Oliver pops a gummy worm in his mouth. "How is that different than any other day?"

I reach for the Twizzlers on the table, pull one from the big bag, and chuck it at Oliver. "Don't be an ass."

Swiping it up from his lap, he bites off a third of the red licorice. "Quit taking me so seriously." He waves the licorice back and forth. "And thank you."

"Anyway…" I roll my eyes. "Just wanted to pass along the news. Could be nothing, but Mom's intuition is never wrong." I glance at Travis to find him staring at me, the muscles of his jaw tight. "Mom and Dad have me, June, and Jet checking in more often. Might not be bad for us to do too."

Kirsten clasps the charms on her necklace, rolling them between her fingers. "Did something happen at the store?" Her knee starts to bounce. "Is Momma Fox okay?"

The thing about skirting around the truth… it's easier to do when a direct question about the truth isn't asked.

"Nothing happened at the store." I grab a chunk of dark chocolate off the snack spread. "Momma is good."

Kirsten's shoulders relax a beat before she leans more into Travis. He drapes an arm over her shoulders, trailing his fingertips up and down her arm, his eyes never leaving mine.

In those sharp, amber eyes, I see worry, panic and uncertainty. But I also see relief and gratitude. After everything he and Kirsten recently went through, his learning of another dead body had to be a knife to his chest. Keeping that burden on his shoulders to protect her heart… heroic as it is, isn't healthy. And if my roundabout half-truths help him breathe easier, I'm glad I opened my mouth.

Travis and I may see the world from different points of view, but we both have one thing in common. We take care of the people we love. We protect them in whatever way possible.

And not even some demented lunatic will change that.

"Do you have more sage?" An unfamiliar man holds up an empty basket.

My brows pinch together as my eyes dart from him to the basket.

How is that empty already?

Yesterday, that basket was overflowing. Our recent shipment should've lasted another week, if not longer. Sage is one of our hottest sellers, but we've never had to order outside the automatic reorder.

"Sorry." I shake my head. "We'll have more next week."

On a nod, he sets the basket down and continues to browse. I jot down sage on the pad of paper near the register. Reaching beneath the glass display, I take out the cleaner and towel. After a few pumps of spray, I wipe down the counter.

"What are these crystals used for?" The man holds up a large chunk of rose quartz.

"Rose quartz is mainly for love and healing."

"And this one?" He holds up an amethyst.

I want to tell him to *read the damn label on the basket.* But I don't. Instead, I smile brighter. "Protection and purification."

"Will it protect me from ghosts?"

Ghosts?

A strange flutter erupts in my belly. I study his face, looking for an ounce of familiarity in his dark eyes and scruffy jaw. Recall his voice and try to place it with those I've heard before. But I come up blank.

Who is this guy?

"Um, it's not generally used to protect the living from spirits." I take a few steps in his direction, hoping for a better view. "Are you experiencing paranormal activity?"

He sets the amethyst down and shakes his head. "Nothing like that." Giving me his back, he moves farther away, his finger running over the book spines on the shelf.

Rounding the service counter, I follow in his wake and pretend to straighten items on the shelves. "Is there something in particular you're looking for?" I move around the store on slightly faster feet, closing the distance between us.

He glances up and meets my stare.

I brighten my smile. I take one step, then another. But on my third step, he pivots on his heel and bolts for the door.

Mere feet behind him, I dash out the door and look down the sidewalk.

Gone. The man is gone.

As for the odd twinge of awareness in my belly moments ago... it's a full-fledged storm now.

SEVEN

PHOEBE

The morning after my sister's bridal shower, I'd woken to a text.

UNKNOWN NUMBER
Appease the old woman

A low growl had escaped my throat before I'd gotten out of bed. Not how I'd wanted to start my day, enraged and on the cusp of vomiting. But I'd stomped through my suite as I dressed for the day.

The unsavory truth gnawed in the back of my mind. I didn't ask Beau how he got my number. There had been no need. I already knew the answer.

Grandmother may want me happy and in love, but she would never force me into a situation without my consent. Sure, she may nudge a little. Give a gentle push if she thinks it will be beneficial. But that's it. In the end, she lets me decide.

Gwendolyn Graves is the epitome of grace and decorum and would never do something so uncouth.

My mother, on the other hand, is the complete opposite. How my father fell in love with her, I will never understand.

Prim and proper and regarded with such high esteem in public, Priscilla Graves is a ruthless monster behind closed doors. So long as it benefits her, Mother will do as she pleases.

It baffles me how clueless Father is to this side of her. Either she hides it well, or he doesn't care.

Not sure what Mother stands to gain by giving my number to Beau. After the stunt Kelli pulled, the Langston name doesn't hold the same merit or respect it once did. In all honesty, I'm shocked my mother would want the Graves name associated with any Langston.

And when I'd reached the bottom landing, I released my wrath. I expressed my anger at her violation of my privacy with several shouted expletives. She didn't bat an eye.

Tempted to block Beau, I chose to keep open communication with him. The enemy of my enemy and all that. And after his most recent text—an obvious attempt to get on my good side—blocking wasn't an option. Even if he's just spewing bullshit until something sticks, he has details no one else does.

UNKNOWN NUMBER

Ask about sage

Beau's text had been vague. Simple. An unannounced element. Just enough to keep me curious.

I didn't ask for further information. That would've opened a door to conversations I didn't want with him. The last thing Beau needs is a foot in the door. But I will keep him as a last-resort resource.

Parking on the street, I scan the busier than normal foot traffic. Study a mix of familiar and foreign faces. Search for questionable and unsavory characters. Pay close attention to every person walking through the door of Sage Whisperer.

Is Beau Langston leading me on a wild-goose chase? For his sake, I hope not.

Cutting the engine, I unbuckle my seat belt, shoulder my purse, and exit the car. Hands shoved in my coat pockets, I leisurely walk toward the store, eavesdropping on conversations as I pass townsfolk and tourists. Most talk about the wine-and-chocolate festival. The rest is dull and repetitive—weather, children, sports, blah blah blah.

The light tinkle of a bell jingles when I open the door to Sage Whisperer. Incense assaults my nose as wooden flute music floods my ears. An odd sense of calm loosens my limbs and tempers my mood.

Nice as it feels, the sudden shift makes me uneasy. Like I don't have control over my own body, thoughts, or emotions.

Inhaling deeply, I shove away the feeling and put up my defenses.

My eyes roam the store, several people wandering the aisles. An older woman at the far end of the bookshelves, book in hand, as she skims the pages. A younger couple at the display of essential oils unscrewing the bottles and sniffing the various fragrances. A man at the checkout counter, his head down and finger on the glass display case as Delilah points to and removes a piece of jewelry.

Loosening my scarf, I stroll down the closest aisle, peeking over the top of the shelf. I feign interest in the tarot card decks as I monitor the store. As I shuffle to the next shelf, Delilah pins me with a severe stare. The corner of my mouth twitches, my pulse picks up.

She finalizes the transaction with her customer and moves out from behind the counter. Intentionally ignoring me, she attends to actual shoppers, a soft smile on her face. After she thanks the last patron and they exit the store, she crosses the room, lips in a flat line.

"What do you want, Phoebe?" She plants loose fists on her hips.

An unfamiliar tingle sparks to life in my chest and I mentally freeze.

What the hell is that?

Shaking off the sensation, I arch a brow and smirk. "Rumor has it this is the hottest shop in town." I amble down the aisle, finger tracing the shelves, my smile growing as Delilah follows. "One item in particular is flying off the shelf."

Delilah glances around the store, confirming we're alone. The muscle in her jaw tics when her steely gaze returns to mine. "Say what you want to say, Phoebe. Vague isn't good for your complexion."

The tingle returns, flaring with new life. For a beat, I delight in the fiery fizzle. Relish the flicker of warmth. But as quickly as it sparks to life, I shove it aside and trudge forward.

Tilting my head to the right, I place a hand under my chin and look up and left. "You flatter me, Fox."

This elicits a huff from Delilah.

"So sage is the new drug of choice?"

With a roll of her eyes, Delilah shakes her head. "You do know people don't *smoke* sage, right? Please tell me you aren't that misinformed."

My skin heats as I hold her intense gaze. Don't know what it is, but something about antagonizing Delilah Fox sets my blood on fire. And damn, how I love the burn.

For years, people have spoken to me with bitterness on their tongue. An unfortunate side effect of being a Graves in Stone Bay. A fact I've adjusted to with time and developed thick skin because of.

But being on the receiving end of Delilah's acerbity... damn, I want to push her harder. Piss her off more. Provoke her until her cheeks flush and knuckles blanch. Agitate her until she inches closer and we're toe to toe.

"I don't know," I tease. "People do light it on fire and waft it around the room." Shuffling closer, I whisper, "Sometimes they wave the smoke over people to *cleanse* them." I raise both my brows. "Sounds like *smoking*."

Narrowing her eyes, she purses her lips. For a moment, we stare at each other in silent challenge. Delilah, pissed off, and me, intoxicated by her irritation.

Without a word, she spins on her heel and walks off, muttering something unintelligible.

"What's that?" I dart around a large wind chime and follow her footsteps.

A foot from the checkout counter, she stops and takes a few deep breaths. Tips her head skyward and probably prays for me to leave the store. And then she faces me again, fingers pinching the bridge of her nose. A sardonic smile curves her lips and twists my insides.

Arms crossed over her chest, she steps in my direction. "What a waste of time. That's what I said."

My skin blazes for an entirely different reason. Though bickering with Delilah energizes my soul, I won't be disregarded. Not by her. Not by anyone.

"As if you have anything better to do." I scoff and step within inches of her. "Allow me to get to the point."

"Should've started there," she retorts.

My hands ball into tight fists. "Since you're Seven, you've heard about the latest death." I pause and she nods. "Well, Fox, it's come to my attention sage played a part." I inch impossibly closer and stare down at her. "And since you're the only store to supply the area…"

"Are you accusing—"

"Delilah." Aurora enters from the back room and sidles up to her daughter. A gentle smile tugs up the corners of her mouth as she meets my stare. "Phoebe would do no such thing. Would you?"

I match her smile with one of my own. "Not at all, Aurora."

Delilah drops her hands to her hips and rolls her eyes.

Aurora stares over my shoulder and beyond the front windows. Pensive, the corners of her mouth and eyes twitch every other second. The music transitions from one song to the next. Still, she remains silent.

Is this a tactic? Shut me up with silence masked as an ill-fated promise of answers.

I open my mouth, more questions poised on my tongue. But I don't get the chance to ask one.

"Margot Pierce," Aurora says as her eyes focus back on mine. "Did you know her?"

"The dental hygienist?" I shrug. "Of course. Most of the town knows her."

"She's the woman they found near the ski resort."

I'm sorry, what?

How the hell do they know the name of the victim and I don't?

Since the initial report in the database, no updates have been added. Even with countless distractions the past few days, I checked the database no less than ten times a day. Hell, I opened it thirty minutes ago, before I left the Gazette for Sage Whisperer. Zero new entries.

"How do I not know this?" Folding my arms over my chest, I tilt my head. "Nothing's been updated in the Seven database."

An indistinguishable smirk graces Aurora's lips for a half second. "August said it'd been compromised. New channels are being used."

It's on the tip of my tongue to ask if Tobias reported the leak. I wouldn't put it past my father. He doesn't know how I gained access to the database, but it pissed him off.

So he took action. Without batting an eye, Father shut

down my main source for juicy stories in Stone Bay. This one swift move is his way of telling me to back off and move on.

Tobias Graves should know his daughter better than that. Small bumps in the road never stop me.

I try to appear unfazed by the news. "Hmm. I'll speak with my father."

Lost in thought, Aurora stares past me again. "I just want my quiet town back," she whispers. Delilah rubs a hand up and down Aurora's arm. When Aurora's deep blues focus and hold my gaze, her eyes widen. "What if…"

Rapt with what she might say, Delilah and I stand frozen and mute, waiting for her to continue. Yet, minute-long seconds tick by without a word.

Delilah hooks her arm in the crook of Aurora's elbow. "What if?"

Fondness softens the lines of Aurora's face. Resting a hand on Delilah's forearm, she peers down at her daughter. Love, pride and reverence radiate off her as if first nature.

My muscles stiffen as a hot blade pierces my gut. I look away from their easy, unsullied affection. Take a deep breath and quell the irrational spasm of jealousy beneath my diaphragm.

Love is a weakness.

"What if you join forces," Aurora suggests, snapping me out of my thoughts. Her eyes dart between me and Delilah. "Find a way to make peace with each other and get to the bottom of this."

"Momma, I don't—"

"The town isn't safe, delicate dove." Aurora gives Delilah's forearm a gentle squeeze. "By no means am I appointing you as town vigilantes. It isn't your place to take down a killer."

A ridge forms between Delilah's brows. "Then what are you saying, Momma?"

Aurora spins and holds Delilah at arm's length. "With Phoebe's incredible investigative skills and your uncanny intuition, maybe together you'll find clues no one else has. And maybe those clues will help us get our town back."

The thought of working or spending time with Delilah should grate my nerves. But my mind refuses to focus on that right now. Instead, I keep replaying Aurora's compliment.

Phoebe's incredible investigative skills.

Compliments aren't a foreign concept. But most I've received were regarding my physical appearance. I honestly don't remember the last time someone flattered my intelligence or personality. Whoever it was, it certainly wasn't a family member.

The backs of my eyes sting, but I blink back the surge of emotion. Inhaling a slow, deep breath, I slip my mask back in place. Then I straighten my spine and nod. "The faster we figure this out, the better."

"You mean the faster we get your story, the better," Delilah snaps.

That tingle sparks back to life in my veins and I smile.

"You have your job and I have mine." I shrug. "The sooner we solve this"—*I just said we*—"the sooner we move on with our lives."

Delilah flinches. "Yeah. Sure." She flashes a half-hearted smile. "Sounds great."

I dig in my purse and take out my phone. Opening my contacts, I tap the plus sign and fill in her name before handing her my phone. "Add your number and I'll message you when I get another update."

A smile lights Aurora's face while a grimace shadows Delilah's expression.

Has Delilah been grouchy a day in her life?

In all the years I've known her, I've never seen a sour look on her face. If anything, Delilah Fox always tries to lighten the mood. Be a burst of sunshine in a cloudy sky.

Pout firmly in place, Delilah types her number in my phone and hands it back. As I stare down at the ten digits, an unexpected buzz dances over my skin.

I lift my gaze to hers and swallow. "Thanks," I choke out. "I'll be in touch." Without another word, I pivot, head for the door, and dash outside.

The February chill smacks me in the face and brings me back to reality.

Delilah and I just agreed to be partners, to play crime fighters together. This should piss me off. This should make me want to storm back inside and tell them I work alone. Tell them Delilah will only slow me down while she tries to steal my glory.

Instead, my eyes lose focus on the store across the street. A curious flutter erupts beneath my breastbone. My breaths come in brief inhales. And for a moment, I allow myself to get lost in the sensation. Let it bloom in my chest and swallow me whole.

Whatever this is, I love and hate how it consumes my soul.

Someone brushes against me as they pass, then apologizes. I blink out of the trance but miss the opportunity to snap at whoever walked by. Pedestrian chatter and the purr of car engines filter back in. Hoisting my purse higher, I aim my feet in the direction of my car and walk.

"Focus, Phoebe," I chastise myself. "Keep your head in the game."

EIGHT
DELILAH

Solitude has never been bothersome. I relish time to myself in the same way I do time with friends and family. It's an opportunity to mentally reset and digest everything going on in my life.

But as I stare at the vacant chairs neatly tucked at the dining table, a gray cloud floats over my heart.

I miss seeing my friends at this table during the week. The occasional shared breakfast when our schedules aligned. Takeout spreads in the middle as we piled plates high and talked about our day. Those random weekend afternoons when one of us decided we wanted to do a puzzle or crafty project.

A little more than three months ago, Lawrence asked Skylar to move in with him. They'd been dating close to six months, but it was an immediate yes from her. Days later, her room was packed up and we shared our last pizza night as roommates.

Not living with Skylar had been an adjustment. The house was quieter in the morning. Our girls' nights were less frequent. But Kirsten and I adapted and planned regular gatherings with our friends.

Then Kirsten's romantic life took center stage as two men fought for her attention and affection. Well as I knew Kirsten, I assumed she'd drop them both and remain happily independent. Have her fun with them and move on.

Wrong.

As Travis and Ben vied for heart, some creep following her around town had other plans. As Kirsten's heart teetered between her childhood best friend and the hot cop she had flirted with daily for years, the deranged lunatic left ominous notes and twisted gifts. The situation got worse before it got better. In the end, though, it hadn't been difficult for Kirsten to decide.

Weeks later, her room was packed up and I officially lived alone.

Being alone never bothered me *until now*.

I eat the last of my breakfast and take my dishes to the sink, washing them. Back at the table, I flip open my journal and thumb through the pages until I reach a clean one. Uncapping my pen, I date the top of the page and scribble down my thoughts.

As I wrap the strap around the vegan leather, my phone vibrates on the table, Phoebe's name next to the text icon.

Put on your sleuth hat, Fox. Detective duty starts today.

I close my eyes and shake my head. "Why did I go along with this?" On a deep inhale, I open my eyes and type out a response.

Beanies only 🕵 Where should we meet?

Send your address. I'll pick you up.

My fingers hover over the keys, hesitant.

Why does she want to pick me up? Yes, we agreed to covertly investigate the newest murder in Stone Bay. But we didn't agree to anything else. Driving myself means calling it a day at any time. If things get heated, all I need to do is drive away. With Phoebe behind the wheel, it puts me on her schedule and at her mercy.

But if I don't let Phoebe assume control, it will make this whole situation a hundred times worse.

Today, Fox

By the end of this investigation, it might be me behind bars for murder. The headline of the Stone Bay Gazette in a bold, thick font for all to read.

Graves Found Dead; Fox Guilty.

"One breath at a time," I coach myself as I type out my address and hit send.

15 mins

Pushing back from the table, I take my journal to the bedroom and set it on my nightstand. Then, I spend the next ten minutes deciding what to wear.

Phoebe whips into a parking spot facing the entrance of the Stone Bay Ski Resort and cuts the engine.

Nestled in acres of forestry, the grandiose luxury resort is just north of the Bay Cliff Mountains on the eastern side of Stone Bay. With close to a hundred guest suites, several restaurants, and endless activities on site, visitors of the resort can remain on the grounds their entire stay and be thoroughly entertained. Skiing, hiking trails, swimming in the warmer months, ice skating in the colder months, full-service spa and wellness center, and a host of other amenities.

Hands in my hoodie pocket, I peer at Phoebe from the corner of my eye.

Wool coat past her knees, her heels click on the stone drive as we approach the entrance. Dressed in navy slacks and a cream button-down, the top few buttons undone and her ample cleavage on display, Phoebe enters the resort with her head held high. Everything about her screams wealth and power.

Although my family is revered as highly as hers in Stone Bay, although our bank accounts and investments are equally padded, if not more, some residents regard the Fox family with different eyes and temperament.

Years ago, the alienation from being one of the Seven, yet not one, gnawed at my self-esteem. By both the Seven and average citizens, I felt like an outcast. I had no place of my own.

But as time passed and perspective kicked in, gratitude replaced the dark thoughts. I found my place.

The Fox family has wealth and power like the rest of the Seven. But we have one thing they don't. Freedom to be ourselves without shame, guilt or consequence. And I love that freedom the most.

"Let me do the talking," Phoebe mutters as we approach the expansive concierge counter.

"Sure thing," I agree without hesitation. "Think of me as your sidekick."

Pausing a few feet back, she narrows her eyes, her lips in a flat line. "Wait here."

As I nod in agreement, the clap of her heels echoes off the thirty-foot ceiling.

Lips stained her signature rouge, Phoebe smiles brightly at the man behind the counter. Not close enough to hear what she says, it's easy to see her charming him into letting us roam the grounds. Cheeks flush, he mirrors her smile with one of his own. She leans toward him, forearms on the counter, cleavage practically in his face. His gaze falls for two breaths before meeting hers again. On a noticeable swallow, he nods and fumbles with something on his side of the counter.

My fingers curl into tight fists in my hoodie as Phoebe continues to flaunt the swells of her breasts. My blood simmers beneath my skin as she rests a hand on his when he reaches across the counter. But it isn't until he rounds the counter, joins her, and she hooks her arm with his that I almost crack a tooth.

"Delilah, this is Will, our tour guide for the day. Will, meet Delilah."

Her artificial saccharine tone grates my nerves, but I extend my hand anyway and shake his.

What am I doing here? If Phoebe has Will to play guide around the resort, she doesn't need my help. I sure as hell don't want to play third wheel to some flirt fest.

Yet, I unstick my feet from the polished stone and follow them through the resort. I stare at the red soles on Phoebe's heeled boots and wonder why the hell she wore such expensive shoes to romp in the snowy forest.

Will opens a door and leads us down a hall. The clap of our shoes bounces around the endless corridor. As I open my mouth to ask where we're going, we reach another door. Will unlocks it and we step inside. Lights flicker on, the room equivalent to a ten-car garage and overcrowded with all-terrain carts.

Pointing to a cart, Will says, "Need to grab the keys, but we'll take that one."

Phoebe takes the passenger seat, leaving me to sit on the back bench. Will hops in the driver's seat, turns the key, and starts the cart. After a press of the automatic door clicker, we exit the garage and sail across the thin layer of snow.

Rather than focus on how much Phoebe annoys me right now, I get lost in the sights around us. The snow-dusted evergreens and white-capped mountains in the foreground. The sporadic deer and chipmunk as they scavenge for food. The crisp piney air as I inhale deeply. Letting it settle in my lungs and soothe my soul.

Phoebe asks Will question after question as we drive down a freshly plowed trail near the tree line, the ski lift overhead. I tune out their conversation, staring through the trees to the rock face. Anything they discuss of significance, Phoebe will brag about once we leave the resort.

Honestly, I feel bad for Will. Every time he flashes his bright smile at Phoebe, she returns in kind. With Phoebe's flirtatious laughter and sporadic touch of his arm, Will undoubtedly thinks this visit will end with him scoring a date. A night with a beautiful woman that ends with a kiss *or more*.

Clearly clueless as to who Phoebe is, it won't take long for the disappointment to set in. In time, he'll learn he is a pawn in her quest for superiority and nothing more.

The cart veers left and I grip the handle as we cross to the mountain base on the opposite side of the lift. Will drives slower as we weave between clusters of trees and wild shrubs. Daylight fades to a faint glow as the tree canopy shadows the forest floor.

"We're here," Will announces as the cart stops.

Phoebe hops out of the cart, her eyes examining the trees,

rocks and earth. I ease off the back bench and follow on slower feet as I take in the scene.

Hands in her coat pockets, Phoebe pauses near an evergreen. "Where exactly did they find her?"

Will sidles up to her, lifts a hand and points. "About fifteen feet from here." He steps forward, Phoebe on his heels. "Police discreetly marked the closest tree, not wanting to freak out visitors on a hike."

I roll my eyes. "Goddess forbid we alert tourists to another murder in town," I mutter, voice fading as quickly as my puffy white breaths.

But of course, Phoebe hears every word. Smirk firmly in place as she peeks over her shoulder.

"This is it." Will points at the ground, nothing visually notable.

Phoebe reaches for Will, fingers curling around his forearm, her brightest smile on display. "Do you have tools on that nifty cart of yours?" Her fingers slip down to his and I grind my molars. "Anything that'll help us look?"

A faint dusting of pink colors Will's cheeks. "I-I'm sure I have something." After a quick squeeze of her fingers, he releases her hand. "Be right back." Permanent smile on his face, he jogs back to the cart.

Once he is out of earshot, I sidle up to Phoebe and shake my head. "Shouldn't lead him on."

Dropping down in a low squat, Phoebe scans the forest floor with scrupulous attention to detail. "Is it a crime to flirt?"

I scoff. "Maybe it should be if you're knowingly using someone."

Phoebe rises to her full height, crosses her arms over her chest, and cocks a brow. "Because you're so righteous, Fox?"

"Never claimed to be." I mirror her posture. "But at least I don't mislead people. What they see is what they get."

Her lips part, a witty retort on the tip of her tongue. But it never meets my ears.

"Best I can do," Will says, a shovel in one hand and garden hoe in the other.

Phoebe flashes him that dazzling smile, laying a hand on his for a beat before taking the hoe. "Perfect," she purrs. "Thanks for all your help, Will."

"Any time." He blinks a few times, the Phoebe-induced haze clearing from his eyes. "What're we looking for?"

"Not sure." Phoebe shrugs. "Anything the police might've missed. A gum wrapper. A cigarette butt. A piece of fabric."

Hands in an awkward grip on the handle, she scratches the surface of the snow with the hoe blade, barely moving the powder. I bite my tongue and fight the urge to laugh.

Phoebe wouldn't know the first thing about manual labor if it slapped her in the face. Pretentious as her mother is, the Graves children probably grew up with servants and gardeners and personal chefs. I doubt she's lifted a finger her entire life.

She may be intelligent, but Phoebe still has much to learn about the world.

While she and Will clear the thin layer of snow from the earth, I scour for anything out of place. As the needle-filled patch of brown grows larger, Phoebe plows faster, harder. Her eyes on the ground, searching for anything to tell her this trip isn't pointless.

The blade of the hoe spears the earth as a loud huff fills the air. "Delilah, would you mind taking over for a minute?"

I clamp my lips between my teeth, then snort-laugh.

Phoebe narrows her eyes, her nostrils flaring. "What's so funny, Fox?"

"Tired after five minutes," I tease and take the hoe from her. "Should work on that stamina." My eyes dart between her and Will. "If you want things to last longer than a minute."

To my surprise, Phoebe leans in and drops her lips to my ear. "My stamina is just fine."

A shiver rolls up my spine a beat before cool air licks my skin. Phoebe inches back, a tilt to her head, her signature smirk in place.

Before I have the chance to decipher her words, her gaze darts away. Brows pinched at the middle, she leans forward and takes a tentative step. Then another.

"What is that?"

I follow her line of sight but see nothing. "What is what?"

"Will, stop." She holds up a hand.

One foot in front of the other, she closes in on whatever caught her attention. At the edge of the snow-free circle, Phoebe squats and reaches for something. Leaning the hoe against a tree, I step up behind her and peer over her shoulder.

"What is it?"

In her glove-covered palm is a small piece of colored paper. Pinkish-purple with a hint of a swirl pattern. She flips it over, the same color and swirl on the other side.

"Not sure." Eyes on the piece of paper, Phoebe slowly straightens to standing. "But it has to be something." She pulls her phone from her pocket, opens the camera app, and snaps a picture of the colored paper. "There's no reasonable explanation for this to be here."

Although I don't care to admit it, Phoebe is right. Buried beneath the snow, if that paper had been here since fall, it would be in worse condition. Disintegrating or buried in the soil by animals. It isn't much to go on, but it is a clue.

"Now what?"

I only joined this investigation because Mom suggested it.

Though I read a lot of books, I don't have the faintest idea of what actual private detectives do when they make a discovery.

Does Phoebe have a secret room with notes, pictures and maps tacked to the wall? Is there red string connecting clues to pictures of people or places? Is there a dry-erase board with random oddities scribbled down, waiting for a clue to tie it to this case?

A room like that would be the messiest place in Phoebe's life. A place no one but her has access to until the case is solved.

Her eyes flit to mine. "Now we talk to the one person with answers."

My expression scrunches with confusion.

"Emerson," she calls over her shoulder as she walks off.

Great. Now Kirsten will know I'm working with Phoebe.

NINE
PHOEBE

Travis wasn't at the police station when Delilah and I arrived early yesterday evening. The man at reception offered another officer's help, but I insisted on working with Emerson. Not only had he worked the previous murder case a few months back, but he was also one of the Seven.

And with this new development, I want to work with someone I trust to not disregard me or what I discover.

Which is why I am up with the sun and driving toward Poke the Yolk.

Aside from the typical early risers, Stone Bay is quiet this time of day. Town workers do sweeps of the sidewalks and streets, clearing debris, unloading full trash and recycle bins, and tending to plants. The occasional jogger in the pedestrian lane.

I steer the car into the lot, the glow of the restaurant lights brighter than the early sun. Scanning the cars, the one I want to see isn't here yet. Parking near the entrance, I shoulder my purse, exit the car, and beeline for the diner counter.

Peeling off my coat, I take the seat next to Travis's usual

spot. Within seconds, Kirsten stands opposite me, hands on her hips.

"Too soon to start calling you a regular?"

I snicker. "Definitely."

"What can I help you with, Phoebe?"

Leaning forward, I clasp my hands on the counter. "Coffee, extra raw sugar, hazelnut creamer."

Deadpan, her eyes dart between mine. "What else can I help you with?"

The corner of my mouth kicks up. I never make a point to hide who I am, what I'm doing, or what I want. Not when it comes to seeking the truth. Not when it comes to the story.

"Need to talk with Travis."

"About?"

"Police business." My smile widens at the fact neither Travis nor Delilah has shared the latest town news with her.

With a roll of her eyes, she spins around and fetches the coffeepot from the warmer. Flipping over the mug on my place setting, she fills it with coffee, then reaches beneath the counter and procures additional sugar. "Be back with the creamer." And then she walks off.

Packet after packet, I dump them in the coffee and stir. As a small container of creamer is set in front of me, Travis slides into the seat on my left. Kirsten pours coffee into his mug, sets the carafe on the counter, and flits her attention between us.

"To what do I owe the displeasure, Phoebe?"

I swivel my chair in his direction and push out my bottom lip. "Do you greet everyone with such disrespect?"

He twists to pin me with his glare. "Only those who lack respect for others." Not taking his eyes off me, he says, "I'll have an omelet, sunshine."

With a nod, Kirsten props her hands on her hips. "And you, Phoebe?"

Nothing is what I want to tell her. But if I want any sort of conversation with Travis, I need to play nice.

"One egg, scrambled, no milk, and fresh fruit."

Reluctantly, Kirsten steps away and goes to the order kiosk at the end of the counter. Her eyes flit to mine every few seconds and I simply smile.

Eyes on the counter, Travis sips his coffee. "I have nothing to say, Phoebe."

"You might change your tune." I pull my phone from my purse and go to my photos, tapping on the one from yesterday. "I found something at the crime scene near the ski resort."

A long, heavy sigh leaves his lips. "There's a reason you're not a cop." His thumbs trace the rim of his mug. "Quit sticking your nose where it doesn't belong."

I slide my phone across the counter and point to the torn piece of paper in the picture. "This was beneath the snow where the body was found."

"Lower your damn voice," he hisses, eyes shifting to the photo. "And I have no clue what this is." He pushes the phone back in my direction.

I lock my phone and stow it back in my purse. "It's thick like cardstock." Reaching for the creamer, I pour until the coffee almost spills over the mug rim. "More colorful than the picture." Unraveling my silverware, I stir my coffee then sip the mediocre brew. "Maybe a piece of a business card." Mug inches from my lips, I hum. "Or a calling card."

Travis sits in silence, staring at the back of the server alley, the muscles of his jaw clenched. He sips his coffee and does his best to ignore my presence.

By now, he should know I don't give up that easily.

"Something paired with the bundled sage," I muse. "Something ritualistic in nature." I lean in his direction. "Did you find sage near the first body?"

Jaw clenched and lips in a flat line, Travis levels me with an icy glare.

I open my mouth, ready to push him harder for answers, but get cut off as Kirsten sets our breakfasts in front of us.

"Need anything else? Ketchup, hot sauce, more sweetener?"

My face twists in disgust. "If I didn't want to taste my egg, I would've ordered something else."

Travis rolls his eyes. "I'm good, sunshine. Thank Max for me."

Kirsten leans across the counter and Travis meets her in the middle for a kiss.

Blech.

"Be back in a few to check on you."

I spear a strawberry and pop it in my mouth. Give Travis a moment of reprieve and let him eat his breakfast. Let him think I've dropped the subject.

Halfway through his omelet, the radio on his shoulder crackles a second before a voice comes through.

"Attention all units. Possible ten fifty-four near the Freeman estate. Who is responding?"

I rack my memory, sifting for the police code. Close my eyes for a moment and think, think, think. Before Travis reaches for the radio button to respond, my eyes pop open and widen.

Possible dead body.

Holy shit.

"Officer Emerson responding. Fifteen minutes out." Travis wipes his mouth with a napkin and rises from his seat, grabbing his wallet and dropping money on the counter.

I fumble through my purse for my wallet and drop a twenty on the counter. Swivel out of my seat, shrug on my coat, and shoulder my purse. Throwing Kirsten a saccharine smile, I wave and follow Travis out the door.

Five steps toward my car, Travis spins around and jabs a finger in my direction. "Back off, Phoebe," Travis barks.

Hands up, I step back. "No need to yell."

"I mean it, Phoebe. I don't have time for your bullshit." His eyes roam the parking lot before coming back to mine. "This isn't a game." He inches closer. "People are fucking dead," he whispers.

"Fine." I nod. "I'll back off."

Relief washes over his face. "Thank you." And then he jogs to his SUV, jumps in, and speeds out of the lot.

"I'll back off for about an hour," I mutter as I slide behind the wheel of my car and push the ignition.

Setting my purse in the passenger seat, I take out my phone and type out a text to Delilah. Early as it is, I don't expect her to respond immediately.

> Driving to the Freeman estate in an hour.
> Another body was found.

I connect the phone to the car and scroll through my music, settling on the pop radio channel. Before I put the car in reverse, my phone pings with a new text.

> FOX
>
> Headed to work soon. Keep me posted. Meet up later?

An unfamiliar cocoon of warmth surrounds me as I read her message. Like Travis and my father, most would tell me to leave it alone. To leave it to the police to solve this killing spree in our small town.

But not Delilah.

Much as I've frustrated and irritated her, she still manages to treat me with a level of respect and kindness. And if I'm honest, no one has regarded me with such esteem. No one has made me feel like I truly matter. No one has believed in me.

Delilah, though… she always sees the good. She has confidence in what I do. And it's such a foreign feeling.

Will do and yes. Dinner?

TEN

DELILAH

Mom jokes I was born with a book in my hand. Funny as it is, I don't doubt it for a second. Not a single moment of my life has existed without books, either read by my parents or grandparents to me or read on my own once I learned how. At every age, I have loved the magic in the pages of a book. Loved that every story takes me on a journey, mentally and emotionally. Loved getting to glimpse someone's imagination and fall in love with it.

Except today.

I round the end of the bookcase and start cleaning the F through J romance books. Pulling the duster from my apron, I wipe the books and shelves. Straighten the books and face some of my favorite authors' titles. Pluck a store notecard and pen from my apron, jot a quick, catchy phrase to grab readers' attention, and slide it into a card holder beneath the book.

But before I reach the bottom shelf, I pull my phone from my back pocket. Unlock it and go to my text history with Phoebe. Scan her messages for the umpteenth time since I punched my time card at Page by Paige.

PHOEBE

Headed to the Freeman estate now

Parked near the northeast curve. Walking the
rest of the way.

This is bad

Meet at Da Phở at 5?

Not wanting to blow up her phone while she tiptoed through the woods near a crime scene, I responded only once.

Da Phở at 5 is perfect

I lock my phone and stare at the time on the screen: 2:39.

"Quit daydreaming," I chastise myself. "Just focus on work. It'll be four soon."

As if the goddess hears me and sympathizes, a customer rounds the opposite end of the shelf. When they see me, the lines of frustration between their brows smooth out.

"Oh, thank goodness." A smile lights their face. "Would you help me find a title?" They playfully roll their eyes. "It's for book club and a friend said you had several copies. But I can't seem to find them."

"Which book is it?"

"*In Knots for You.*"

I bite my bottom lip, fighting my wicked smile. "Good choice." I pass them in the aisle and they spin to follow. "Due to popularity, we recently moved some titles." I weave toward the front tables in the store and head for the *So You like it Spicy* display. I pick up the erotic short story and hand it to them. "Here you are."

Taking it, they glance down at the vivid, provocative cover. "Never would've thought it'd be at the front of the store."

A smile lights my face as I stare at the other titles and covers on the table. "Most booksellers want modest or discreet covers in their stores to not ruffle feathers." I tidy the risqué-covered books. "But Paige believes all books deserve space on the shelf. Yes, we have discreet covers. But we also want to give space to the provocative covers."

"Paige deserves an award for being inclusive."

I glance across the store to see Paige erecting a new display. "She really does."

"Thank you for your help." They wave and walk toward the checkout. "Enjoy the rest of your day."

"My pleasure, and you as well."

Smile plastered on my face, I wander back to the aisle I was cleaning. And just as I reach the end of the *J* section, the clock strikes four.

Da Phở tricks you with its somewhat small storefront, but the owners, Nga and Quý Tran, did an impeccable job making the restaurant feel open and alive and larger than life. Expansive windows in the dining room brighten the tables and counters during the day and add a romantic vibe at night. Greenery hangs from the ceiling in the middle of the restaurant and brings a touch of nature. Light brick is offset by cream walls, long wood tables, and a mix of black, white, and rose gold chairs. On the wall opposite the entrance, the kitchen is visibly open to the guests, with separate cook stations set up for the menu's variety.

I love all food, but Vietnamese sits high on the list. Phoebe suggesting Da Phở for our catch-up spot is kismet.

Weaving through the tables, I spot Phoebe at a two-top

near the back of the restaurant. Head down, she types vigorously on her phone. I peel off my coat and hang it on the back of the chair, sitting across from her, and she peers up.

"Hey, Fox." She lays her phone face down on the table. "I have so much to share. But first"—she picks up a menu—"let's order. I'm starving."

Is it me, or is Phoebe acting nice?

Bizarre, but miracles do happen, I suppose.

I pick up the other menu on the table and scan the appetizers first. As my stomach growls, the server sidles up to the table. We order appetizers and drinks, but I ask for a few more minutes. Eyes on the menu, I ponder between two of my favorites. By the time the server returns with drinks, I decide on the tofu and vegetable phở, and Phoebe orders the grilled pork bún bowl.

Soon as the server steps away, Phoebe rests her forearms on the table and leans in my direction. Thrill dances in her Nordic blue irises as elation highlights her aura. I mirror her posture, pulled in by some invisible and undeniable enchantment. A magnetism I've always felt near Phoebe, but never with this much intensity.

Even if I had wanted to, I refuse to look away. Seeing this side of Phoebe—enthusiastic, candid and amiable—feels like one of those once-in-a-lifetime moments. If you blink, it will be as if it never existed.

Phoebe glances around at the nearby guests then levels me with her gaze. "Stone Bay may have its first official serial killer," she whispers almost inaudibly, her brows inching toward her hairline.

My eyes lose focus as I replay her supposition.

"Stone Bay may have its first official serial killer."

With each pass, her words sink in deeper. Take root and

chill me to the bone. Making my stomach flip and breath stutter.

Without permission, my mind drifts to the serial killer documentaries Skylar loves too much. The way she watched them with intrigue, curled on the couch with her favorite blanket as she munched on chips or licorice. Periodically, she'd point to the screen and tell me and Kirsten, *"Someone like that could be anywhere. Even here."*

I always waved off Skylar's notion of serial killers and stalkers being in every town.

Now, though I hate to admit it, she may be right.

The commotion of the restaurant hits me full force as I snap out of my foggy state. "You really think so?"

Phoebe opens her mouth to answer, but pauses when the server steps up with our appetizers.

Momentarily distracted, I dip my fresh spring roll in peanut sauce and take the first bite. A soft moan vibrates my chest when it hits my tongue. I don't miss the pause of Phoebe's hand as she mixes her pork, shrimp, and shredded cabbage salad.

Halfway through our appetizers, Phoebe sets down her chopsticks and folds her forearms in front of herself on the table. Her expression more sober than I've seen on her. "Not sure what's happening in our town, Fox, but yes, I really think we have a serial killer in our midst." Lips pursed, her fingers drum the table a moment. "What I don't get is why this is being kept so quiet."

I wipe my mouth with a napkin and move my empty plate near the edge of the table. "Do you not remember the hysteria after everyone heard about the woman in the woods?" I lean back in my chair and tuck some hair behind my ear. "Shelves in the grocery store were emptied. People all but barricaded their homes. Granite Parkway and most of the stores and restaurants were desolate." I shrug. "Maybe they don't want everyone to freak out again."

Phoebe finishes her salad and sets the small bowl on my empty plate. She dabs the corners of her mouth with her napkin before setting it in her lap. Then she hits me with those glacial blue eyes, the sharp angles of her jaw highlighted by her purposeful expression.

"I get not wanting the townsfolk to lose their shit." She leans back in her chair and crosses her arms over her chest. "But people *should* be worried. People *should* be cautious and skeptical."

"I don't disagree."

The server sidles up to the table, bright smile on their face as they set down our meals. Promising to check back soon, they walk off.

Squeezing hoisin into the broth, I stir my phở and slowly add the fresh ingredients. Phoebe dumps a copious amount of peanut sauce on her bún bowl, coating every ingredient with the thick brown sauce. Silence falls over the table as we eat the first few bites, both of us in our heads.

After an audible slurp of soup, I continue my earlier thought. "I don't disagree," I repeat. "But maybe they have their eye on someone. Maybe they're keeping it quiet so they *can* catch the killer."

Phoebe's chopsticks freeze midway between her bowl and mouth. "That makes no sense, Fox."

Swirling the broth, I capture a tofu chunk with my chopsticks. "By not creating a frenzy, everyone is acting normal. Including the killer. Maybe by not announcing this, they're looking for certain markers as they ride around town or go into stores or eat their meals in public." I shrug. "Kind of like hiding in plain sight."

Popping a bite in her mouth, Phoebe mulls over my theory.

Chopsticks pointed at me, she cocks her head. "Novel concept, Fox." Her eyes lose focus for a beat. "I just..."

I wait for her to finish her thought, but she doesn't. So, I nudge her. "You just..."

Placing the chopsticks in her bowl, she props an elbow on the table and rests her chin on a fist as she leans forward. "I just can't picture the chief wanting that." She shakes her head. "That man loves results. He loves closing cases and receiving recognition for a job well done. Not actively hunting down the town's first serial killer—"

"Shh," I admonish, eyes wide.

Phoebe rolls her eyes and leans closer. "It's bad police work," she says, quieter. "The body from today"—she takes a deep breath—"that's the first crime scene I've seen *in the moment.*" She futzes with her chopsticks in her food. "Granted, I wasn't up close and didn't arrive early on, but I had my binoculars and camera with the telephoto lens." A ridge forms between her brows. "It's bad, Fox." Mesmerizing, concerned blue eyes lock me in place. "Whoever's doing this..." She swallows. "They're seriously fucked in the head."

I set down my chopsticks and drop my hands in my lap. "Maybe we should back off."

Face twisted with obvious confusion, she shakes her head. "Not a chance in hell." She picks up her chopsticks and pinches a heap of noodles between them. "Just means we're more vigilant as we dig deeper." She lifts the bite to her mouth but doesn't take it. "I won't lose this story, Fox. People deserve to know the truth and I plan to deliver."

"Phoebe, I don't—"

"Back out if you want. Your call." She shrugs. "Or tell me if you're free tomorrow."

I reach for a lock of my hair, wrapping the end around my finger. On a sigh of resignation, I cave. "I'm off tomorrow."

The brightest smile lights Phoebe's face. "Perfect. I'll pick you up at eight." Then she shoves the monstrous bite in her mouth and ends the conversation.

Though he wasn't one of the Seven, Old Man Freeman owned the largest parcel of land in Stone Bay. On countless acres of land, a weathered two-story, seven-bedroom home and barn sit unoccupied. Widowed decades ago, when Leo Freeman passed a few years back with no children, the deed to his land and home was signed over to the town.

Rumor has it the property was left to someone. But only select Seven know the name and have kept it locked up tight while they search for them. Although I can't be certain, I assume Emery Barron—the lead property attorney in town and one of the Seven—oversees the property and hunts for the new owner.

Seems the Seven aren't the only ones with secrets in this town.

Sipping her coffee, Phoebe drives the long, winding, sole road leading to the Freeman house. Sunlight peeks through the trees, but the road remains shadowed by thick, tall evergreens crowding either side of the private road. The road curves to the right and I flip down the visor. Two songs later, the road curves right again. After what feels like several miles, Phoebe eases off the accelerator and parks on the shoulder.

My stomach twists and I immediately scan the forest, the road, the side mirror for someone lurking nearby. Phoebe, on the other hand, is cool as a cucumber as she sets her coffee in the cup holder and opens her door. After one more inspection of the forest, I exit the car and cross the street to meet Phoebe at the tree line.

"Obviously, they cleared the body. But I want to search the surrounding area. Maybe we'll find another clue the cops missed."

Shoving my hands in my coat pockets, I follow in Phoebe's wake as we enter the woods. A thin layer of snow crunches beneath our shoes as we weave between trees. Branches rustle nearby and I spot a chipmunk as it scurries up a tree.

Eyes scanning the forest floor, the memory of us finding the piece of paper under the snow pops into my head. "Did you bring a shovel?"

Phoebe pats her coat pocket. "Grabbed my grandmother's small garden shovel before I left the house. Was easier to throw in the car."

In the distance, I spot a tree with a bright orange X on the trunk. Considering no other trees are marked, I assume it's the heart of the crime scene. As we approach, Phoebe takes more calculated steps as her eyes scan the forest floor. I step farther from her and survey the ground with scrupulous eyes.

Hour-long minutes pass as we circle the area. I decide to take pictures of the area, wondering if any of the crime scenes have anything in common. Phoebe squats down on occasion and moves thicker sections of snow. But after a couple hours, we discover nothing new.

Face red and jaw tight, Phoebe's irritation is beyond evident.

Something has bothered me since Phoebe texted me about this new murder. All of them bother me, but this one hits differently.

"Do you know who found the body? Who called it in?"

Phoebe straightens to her full height and brushes nonexistent dirt off her coat. "Someone from the property maintenance company the town hired to keep up the land." She tips her head toward the road and starts walking. "News has been hard to uncover, but I pieced it together with a few vague answers from my father."

As we walk in silence, I battle with what to say or do next. Though Phoebe and I have become cordial recently, in no way do I consider her a friend. Yet. But I get the feeling she could use a friend. Someone she can count on.

Do I want to be that person for her? I haven't decided yet.

"Sorry we didn't find anything here. Want to go back to my place and brainstorm?"

The trees thin and the car comes into view.

Phoebe glances at me and smiles—and not that *I'm smiling out of courtesy, but I really hate you* smile. "Yeah. Sounds good."

After a tight U-turn, we navigate off the Freeman property and toward my house. Phoebe cranks the radio and drives well over the speed limit. I rest my arm on the center armrest seconds before Phoebe reaches for her coffee.

An irrefutable spark shoots up my arm as her fingers brush my hand. I suck in a sharp breath as she jerks her hand away.

"Sorry," she mutters, eyes fixed on the road. Her knuckles blanch and a faint squeak echoes through the car as her fingers curl tighter around the steering wheel.

"It's okay," I whisper as I peek at her from the corner of my eye.

And just like that, frigid Phoebe returns.

ELEVEN

PHOEBE

Clenching the steering wheel, I will away the buzz in my fingers, my hand, up my arm. The current that refuses to fizzle out. The crackle that seems to expand and spread and twist my thoughts.

Accelerator practically smashed to the floorboard, I weave through town back to Delilah's house.

Minutes ago, she asked me to hang out and brainstorm. Without hesitation, I agreed. At every turn, this case is growing more complex. More baffling. Too many things aren't adding up. Having a second set of eyes on the clues, a second mind to puzzle the pieces together in a different way may open new doors.

But now…

After the accidental brush of her hand and this damn hum that refuses to fizzle out and die, hovering over photos and clues side by side in her house *alone* doesn't sound like the best idea.

I grip the wheel tighter. Mentally demand the constant thrill in my body to dissolve into nothing. Tell myself over and over it's a fluke, an oddity, an offbeat moment that would happen with anyone.

It has to be.

Because whatever the hell this is, it can never be… anything. I don't *want* it to be anything.

A block from Delilah's house, the warmth on my skin and spark in my veins grows hotter, more intense. The air in the car turns thick and heavy and pulsing with the same electric fire.

I suck in a sharp breath and force myself to focus on the street, on each house we pass, the kids playing in the light layers of snow.

Navy, cream, pine, earth.

I list the colors of the houses in my head as we pass them. Anything to distract myself. Anything to keep me from looking at or speaking to Delilah.

Gray.

I pull into her driveway, not bothering to throw the car in park. "Actually, I just remembered my mother needs me at home. Something to do with my sister's wedding," I lie.

The last place I want to be is anywhere near my mother or Hayleigh. But the fib is easy to believe.

Out of the corner of my eye, Delilah nods and yanks on the door handle. "Okay."

The door swings open, cool air whipping through the car cabin. If only it'd tame the heat on my skin.

"I'll be home all day," she shares, her voice soft, timid. "If you get time and want to work on this…"

Eyes aimed at the windshield, I mutter, "I'll let you know."

Delilah exits the car with a quiet "Later" and closes the door.

Once she steps away from the car, I throw the gear in reverse, whip out of her driveway, throw it in drive, then speed off without a backward glance.

I opt to take the scenic route on the way home. I coast along Granite Parkway, my eyes trailing the streets, the sidewalks, every pedestrian I pass. With the new wine-and-chocolate festival starting next week, visitors are arriving today and throughout the weekend. In a matter of days, the town will be inundated with unfamiliar faces.

Turning down the music, I flip my blinker on as the stop sign comes into view. After a left, I bypass Chalcedony and instead take the next left on Garnet. Road quieter, I slow down and peer out the passenger window. Gaze at the strong and mighty evergreens that line the eastern coast of the town's namesake, Stone Bay. Through the occasional break in the trees, the water glitters with the sun overhead.

And for a moment, I let the world fade away. I forget about everything. The stress of figuring out who this killer is so I can write an award-winning story. The pressure my family purposefully lays on my shoulders to be this perfect figure for the townsfolk as well as find a "suitable" man to marry. The incessant weight bearing down on me to be all things to all people all the time.

The trees thin as a small sign comes into view. Hung similarly to a realty sign, the large plank of live edge wood is stained a warm brown. Burned with precision, it reads, *The Fox family welcomes you. Fox Cabin 1*, the street address in small script at the bottom.

A humorless laugh bubbles in my chest and spills from my lips. "Everywhere, Fox. You are everywhere."

The rest of my drive on Garnet is spent well over the speed limit. When the road curves and merges with the more popular part of town, I slow to safer speeds.

Although it's the last place I want to be, I aim my wheels toward Founders Way and the Graves estate. The Gazette is always an option, but if I can avoid my parents for a few more hours at the house, I'll take the reprieve. It will grant me time to mull over the three murders. Give me time to find some link to these dead women.

I may not have seen the actual body of the most recent victim, but I glimpsed long brown hair on a lean feminine frame. Considering the first two murders were women, it's safe to assume the same of the third victim.

"Three women," I mutter as I turn on Graves Road. "What do you ladies have in common?"

As I sift through the possibilities, the main house comes into view… and too many damn cars for the middle of the day.

Fucking great.

I ease my GLE Coupe into my bay of the garage, pressing the button to lower the door once inside. Reaching in the backseat, I fetch my purse and shoulder it. And then, I inhale a deep breath, trying to center myself before I face the onslaught of animosity.

Cutting the engine, I exit the car and straighten my spine. Hold my head high and aim my feet toward the door. *Clip-clap. Clip-clap.* My heels clack the concrete and echo off the walls as I reach the door. One more deep breath and then I twist the handle and step in the house.

Cacophonous chatter smacks my eardrums, Hayleigh's shrill tone piercing the air louder than anyone else's voice. Sweet almond wafts through the air and up my nose and my stomach grumbles, reminding me I haven't eaten in hours.

With quiet, measured steps, I exit the small hallway between the garage and main house and round the corner of the open kitchen. Lucy, the current Graves personal chef, stands at the counter between the cooktop and wall ovens. She cuts thin slices from one of several unfrosted cakes and sets them on dessert plates. Smile on her face, she sets them on a tray, spins on her heel, and carries the tray to the dinette.

Sitting at the smaller, informal table are Mother, Father, Hayleigh, and Sawyer—Hayleigh's fiancé—Grandfather Talbert and Grandmother Gwendolyn. Spines tall, chins high, they sit poised and stoic as Lucy sets a plate before each of them.

I shift toward the staircase and tiptoe on light feet. So long as they don't look this direction, I should be able to make it up the stairs undetected. If I'm lucky, the columns on either side of the wet bar may keep me hidden from view.

Unfortunately, luck isn't on my side.

"Phoebe, join us," Mother calls, authority in her tone.

Dammit.

More confident than I feel, I cross the open space, stopping halfway between the wet bar and dinette. "I'd love to, Mother, but I have work to do."

Mother's top lip curls in disgust. "What on earth could be so important? Sit." She points to one of two vacant chairs at the table. "Help your sister decide which cake to have at her bachelorette party."

As if Hayleigh wants or needs my help. No, she'd rather I steer clear of anything to do with her upcoming nuptials. The only thing I'm *needed* for is disingenuous family photos and to help display the Graves family as an unshakable unit during an ostentatious ceremony.

"I thought bachelorette parties focused on booze and strippers," I state, impassive. "Why is there cake? We just had cake at the bridal shower. We'll have cake at the wedding in nine days."

Scowl firmly in place, Mother pushes back in her chair and stands to her full height. "Come sit at this table, Phoebe." Again, she points to the chair, directing me as if I'm still a scared little girl who cowers to her mother.

Though my mother still unnerves me, I am no longer a

frightened little girl. I am older, stronger, smarter, and dammit, I have purpose and passion. None of which include tasting bullshit cake for a sister that gives no fucks about me.

"No, Mother. I have work to do." I spin on my heel and head back to the staircase. But before I take the first step up, Father inserts his opinion.

"Leave it alone, Phoebe," he demands, voice low and definitive. "You aren't some vigilante crime fighter. Let the police handle this."

Molars grinding and eyes narrowed, I peek over my shoulder. "Yeah, Father. Sure. Because they did such a bang-up job with the first murder." I shake my head. "They assumed it had to do with Sparks's stalker. You know what they say about assuming, don't you, Father?"

His chair kicks back, hitting the window ledge as he rises. "I said leave it alone, Phoebe," he barks out.

I laugh without humor as I stare into icy eyes that match my own. "If anyone else had taken this on, if anyone else at the paper walked in your office and said, *I'd love to write a story on these murders, Tobias*, you would say it's a great idea. You'd encourage them. You wouldn't interfere unless they asked for help. You'd cheer them on as they uncovered clues and pieced together the biggest news story this town has ever known."

I tip my head back and count to ten before meeting his gaze once more.

"But because it's *me*..." The backs of my eyes sting, but I fight off the tears. He doesn't deserve a single one. "When will I ever be good enough? Too nosy for the paper. Too prissy for the socialites. Not dressed right for the event." My voice grows louder as each thought is given a voice. "I haven't dated enough or found a man suitable to be connected with the Graves name. I talk too much. I eat the wrong foods. My lipstick makes me look like a whore." My arms fly up, then slap the sides of my thighs. "Sorry I'm the fuck up."

"Watch your mouth," Mother snaps.

"Oh, please." I snort. "What are you going to do, Mother? Hit me? Or is that only saved for when we're alone?"

My father turns his icy glare on her. "What's she talking about, Priscilla?"

Fire lights her green eyes as anger spills off her in waves. "Nothing, Tobias. Phoebe is just being Phoebe. Dramatic and always clamoring for attention."

That's right, my thoughts and feelings don't matter to this woman. In her eyes, everything I do is for show, to piss her off and dim the light that shines on her throne.

But I'm tired—of her bullshit, of not being heard, of not being seen, of my family treating me as if I'm more of a burden than anything else.

"Just me wanting attention." I cross my arms over my chest, shake my head, and scoff. "So I imagined you dragging me into the bathroom at Hayleigh's bridal shower and scolding me like a child? I imagined you slapping me across the face so hard I had to shift my hair to hide your fading handprint?" I shift my gaze to my sister and her fiancé. "I'm sure no one will like my cake choice. Choose the one that makes you happy. Whatever you pick, Mother will surely approve."

Giving them my back, I take the stairs two at a time, ignoring the new argument on the first floor. I cross the loft, storm across the bridge that looks down on the foyer and indoor terrarium, and enter my wing on the second floor.

Slamming the door, I pace the room, growling with each turn in the opposite direction. One deep breath after another, I locate a modicum of calm. With each pass of my pristinely made bed, my head clears a little more.

I pause and sit on the tufted bench at the foot of my bed. Take out my phone and go to the messaging app. Tap on the chat with Delilah and type out a new text. Staring down at the screen, I take a deep breath and hit send.

Sorry about earlier. Mind if I come over?

TWELVE

DELILAH

Half-awake, I stumble into the bathroom, hand over my eyes as I flip on the light. Little by little, I let my eyes adjust to the sudden brightness. Let my mind wake up slowly, peacefully. Mornings may be my favorite time of day—when the world is quieter and resetting itself—but it isn't often I wake up before the sun.

Foregoing a shower, I go about the rest of my morning routine. As I apply moisturizer to my face, an idea pops into my head. I rush through the rest of my regimen, exit the bathroom, and dart into my closet. Dressed in layers, I swipe up my keys and the cream backpack I use in place of a purse and head for the garage.

Minutes later, I turn off of Jasper and aim my tires toward my favorite spot in town.

Twinkling lights and the soft glow from the lampposts greet me as I drive past closed stores and restaurants in town, not a soul on the sidewalks. Splashes of red and pink on windows attract patrons inside for romantic gifts or meals. The peaks of the Bay Cliff Mountains silhouetted by nautical twilight in the distance.

At the only traffic light in town, I turn right and head west. In less than a mile, the landscape shifts. Buildings are replaced with countless trees. The hint of light from downtown fades the farther I drive.

I crack the window and breathe deeply. Let the crisp, piney air fill my lungs and soothe my soul. And it isn't long before I ease my foot off the accelerator. Before I flip my blinker on and turn onto a winding gravel road. Before I park in the driveway of one of several Fox family rentals in town.

Thankfully, this house is vacant until later today.

Leaving my backpack on the passenger floorboard, I exit the car and go to the hatch. I dig out the blanket I keep for such occasions, then lock the car. Leaves, needles and twigs crunch beneath my sneakers as I pass the house and head for the rocky peninsula at the waterfront border of the property.

I trek up the hill, following the foot-worn path until the trees thin and the bay comes into view. A few tall evergreens skirt the rocky cliffside, but the view is otherwise obstruction-free.

"Perfect," I whisper, the soft word catching on the wind and floating out to sea.

Shaking out the blanket, I cocoon myself in thick cotton and lower to the ground near the cliff. I hug my knees to my chest, resting my chin on them. Unhurried, my eyes drift along the horizon.

On the western side of the bay, boats bob in the water near the marina. Farther in the distance, the lighthouse sits tall at the mouth of the bay. An endless line of tall trees and rocky points border the remainder of the bay.

As dawn approaches and night fades, the sky no longer blends with the bay. Hints of coral, peach and marigold peek between the clouds and reflect on the water. Minute by minute, the sunrise grows brighter, bolder, more breathtaking.

And as I get lost in the sights, my mind drifts to the last two days.

Not long after the accidental hand brush in Phoebe's car, she asked to come over. The way she'd shut down, I didn't expect to hear from her so soon. If anything, I expected days to go by without contact.

When she walked through my front door hours later, a large tote slung over her shoulder and determination set in her expression, all thoughts of the hand touch vanished. Something else had upset her. Something bigger than me or us or what happened in the car. Although I wanted to pry, I didn't ask questions.

If she wants to tell me, she will in her own time.

Murder case notes and images spread across the dining room table; we ate takeout from boxes and studied every detail for hours. Still, we were no closer to figuring out who was behind the deaths of three Stone Bay women.

Just before midnight, Phoebe stowed everything back in her tote and said goodnight. Part of me wanted to offer her one of the spare beds, but we weren't there yet. Barely friends, we still had a way to go before we did something other than fight crime together.

Would we be in this position if Mom hadn't suggested we work together?

Would Phoebe have warmed up to the idea of friendship with me at any point in the future?

Since I met Phoebe, this undeniable need to connect with her has lived in my veins. No matter how hard I try, I can't explain the feeling, the drive, the pull. It's just... there, existing.

Maybe this is my opportunity, my way in.

Maybe we both had to experience ups and downs before

we reached this point—bordering enemies and friends. Not that I've ever considered Phoebe my enemy.

I sit on the cliff a little longer. Wrap the blanket tighter around my body and bask in the glow of the morning sun. Let it warm my chilled cheeks and energize my soul. For a little longer, I ignore life and soak up nature.

All too soon, I bid farewell to my favorite place in town. Rising from the cliff, I fold the blanket and amble back to the car. Take in the view one last time as the car warms up.

As I drive away from the rental, I shove all thoughts of Phoebe aside and focus on my plans for the day. Breakfast at Poke the Yolk. Maybe a stop at Sage Whisperer to hug Mom. And later, lunch with the twins.

First to arrive at RJ's for lunch, the hostess greets me by name and seats me at a table for four. She tells me today's specials, then wanders back to her spot near the door, checking in with patrons on her way.

Before I swipe up a menu and peruse the long list of mouth-watering goodness, Jet pulls out the chair across from me, peels off his jacket, and drapes it over the back. I rise from the bench and he meets me halfway for a hug.

"How was your morning class?"

He releases me and we settle in our seats. "Good. Never thought we'd have so many in the studio before noon." Poised in his seat, he runs his fingers through his hair. "But Aurelio was optimistic."

"Glad it's been a positive change." I stare down at the menu but don't read a word. "How's Shanti?"

In my periphery, I notice the slight shift in Jet's posture, though he tries to mask it by picking up the menu.

Since the day Shanti Mahal walked into Rhythm and Flow, Jet has been a goner.

For weeks, all I heard about was Shanti. How easily she learned the dance moves. How smart she was for a kindergartner. How she had the prettiest hair.

As other kids their age dropped out of dance, Jet and Shanti stayed. Two years in, they started dancing as a duo, though they still danced solo. And by the time Jet entered high school, they were absolutely inseparable.

Shanti is Jet's person, his best friend, and I don't doubt he fills the same role for her. The big question is, is she as in love with him as he is her? Remains to be seen.

"Shanti is well." He gives a subtle nod. "We're co-teaching the first years starting next month." He flips his menu over and swallows. "So we'll be busy at the studio."

For a moment, I picture seven-year-old Jet in his black leggings, fitted white T-shirt, snug white socks, and black ballet shoes. Even at such a young age, Jet was regal. Being one of two boys in the ballet class didn't deter him. If anything, it made him want to prove he could do it more.

Dance is in his blood, in his soul, and passing that on is the next step in his long journey.

"That's wonderful, Jet." I reach across the table and rest my hand on his. "So proud of you."

His cheeks redden a beat before June pulls out the chair next to him. "Hey, sibs. Sorry I'm late."

I wave them off. "You're fine. We haven't even ordered drinks yet."

The table quiets as we decide on lunch. After we place our order, Jet wraps an arm around June's shoulders and tugs them to his side. "What's new with you, twin?"

June shrugs then rests their head on Jet's shoulder. "I'm so over all these unhinged people coming into the shop."

"There's been more?" I ask.

Unlike me, June works at Sage Whisperer full time. To help lighten the load, I help out a couple evenings a week for two to three hours and one morning a week when I'm not scheduled at the bookstore. Since Mom suggested Phoebe and I team up and search for some homicidal maniac, I've been at the shop less.

"At least one a day." They take a sip of water. "The weirdest thing…" Eyes darting between me and Jet, they twist the water glass on the table. "I filled the basket of sage yesterday morning and it's already empty." With pursed lips, they shrug. "I asked Momma if someone bought the whole supply at once and she said no. It was mostly regulars buying a few at a time so they wouldn't run out. But there was one person…"

I inch forward in my seat, rest my forearms on the table, and lean toward them. "One person…" I silently nudge June to continue.

"Momma said she'd never seen them before." June mirrors my posture and lowers their voice. "This man in a black suit bought a dozen bundles of sage. She tried to make conversation and ask them questions, but she said they kept quiet. Deadpan and mute. Her words, not mine." They sigh. "I was in the back, so I missed seeing them."

In moments such as this, I wish the shop had additional security cameras. Mom and Dad wanted to protect their assets, so cameras were installed to monitor certain parts of the store. The cash register, the safe, the jewelry cases, the section of the store with the larger, more expensive crystals, the back door. But there are none near the bookcases. None on the front door. None focus on the general part of the store. Mom didn't want to disrupt the energy in the store or invade privacy unnecessarily. And anyone checking out at the register could easily avoid being filmed by the security cameras.

"Nothing you need to worry about, little June Sun."

Our lunch arrives and the table quiets as we dig in. I use the reprieve to mull over this new information.

Sage Whisperer has been a staple in Stone Bay for twenty-seven years. From the day Mom and Dad cut the grand opening ribbon, the store has never had a bad day or year, *not until this past month*. And there are only bad days now because some disturbed individual is buying all our sage and doing who knows what with it.

Is it our sage being left with the murder victims?

Phoebe and I don't know much because we haven't seen it firsthand, but sage was found at the crime scenes. To think it might have been *our* sage makes me sick.

"So..." Jet dunks his grilled cheese in tomato soup. "How's things with Phoebe?"

Though I didn't expect either of my siblings to bring up Phoebe, I should have anticipated it. Like Jet has crushed on Shanti for years, he and June both know I've had a crush—albeit minor until recently—on Phoebe since junior year of high school.

Things with Phoebe are unpredictable, but good is what I want to say. But I keep that to myself.

Instead, I say, "Busy. We've been trying to figure out what this small piece of paper is—"

"Not what I mean," Jet teases under his breath, chuckling.

A heavy sigh deflates my chest. I dip a fry in barbecue sauce and swirl it around again and again. Eyes on my plate, I nod. "Yeah, I know." I drop the fry on my plate and meet his waiting stare. "But I can't think about that right now."

"Why?" June chimes in.

I love and loathe how unified my twin sibs can be.

Leaning back in my seat, I tip my head and lose focus on the ceiling. "Because our hands accidentally touched the other day and she freaked out."

"Over a hand touch?" Jet scoffs. "That's a bit much."

It wasn't the actual contact that sent Phoebe running. No one does a one-eighty like that unless they're rattled.

If she felt what I did, if that undeniable zing danced over her skin and heated her blood, I don't fault Phoebe for pulling away. Though I've wanted a connection with her for years, I was taken by surprise when our hands touched.

Phoebe is undoubtedly bewildered and taken aback by it. Uncertain about what it means—for her or us.

We've spent time together since the incident, but we don't speak about it. She's present, ready to take on Stone Bay and capture this killer, but that damn touch keeps her distant. Has her mindful of every single move she makes.

Lips pursed, I level my gaze with his. "It is, but that's Phoebe."

Closed off. Uptight. Mysterious. Aloof.

Most of all, not mine. Not my friend. Not my enemy. Not anything.

THIRTEEN
PHOEBE

"You're wearing a champagne silk top?" Mother plucks the hanging top off the wall hook next to my closet and inspects it with scrutinous eyes.

With a roll of my eyes, I lean closer to the mirror and line my eyelids with kohl. "Goes with her wedding colors."

"Yes, it does." Her fingers trace the neckline, the lack of sleeves, the bottom hem. Lips in a flat line, she hangs the top back on the hook. "But I thought you'd wear something less…"

I should have known there was a but in there. That she would not approve of my choice of outfit. Because not a soul this evening should dare look better than Hayleigh. But I've seen my sister's bachelorette attire—a cream and gold, shimmery floor-length dress with a revealing bust and slit up her thigh to her hip, exposing her entire leg—and I'd be utterly shocked if anyone paid me a modicum of attention.

"Less what, Mother?" The question leaves my lips with a bite as I swap eyeliner for mascara.

"Mind your tongue, Phoebe."

Mascara wand inches from my eye; I flick my gaze to her in

the mirror and narrow my eyes. Jaw clenched, molars grinding, heat claws up my neck and reddens my cheeks. Lips sealed, I hold her stare for one, two, three strained breaths before meeting my reflection in the mirror.

"Less attention seeking."

I shove the wand into the tube and drop it. Twisting, I prop my hands on my hips. "Why is everything I do wrong?"

"Don't be dramatic, Phoebe." She spins on her heel and strolls to the door. "Be ready to leave in an hour."

Before she exits the room, I spill more of my truths, my buried insecurities. "Tyler and Hayleigh have never been perfect. They've messed up as much as me over the years. Yet you gift them your smile. You encourage them. You praise every single thing they do." My hands fall from my hips, my shoulders sagging forward. "But not me." Saliva pools in my mouth as the backs of my eyes sting. I swallow and blink away the imminent tears. "As if I'm the unfortunate third child you never wanted."

In the threshold, she twists and meets my gaze. "Don't be ridiculous."

"Why do you do that?"

Straightening her spine and squaring her shoulders, she lifts her brows. "Do what, Phoebe?" Annoyance laces her tone.

I scoff. "As a psychologist, I'd think you'd know when you're trying to gaslight someone." I fold my arms across my chest. "But maybe that's one thing you reserve only for me."

She purses her lips, gives me her back, and steps out of the room. "Be ready in an hour."

Crossing the room, I shut my doors and flip the lock. I close my eyes and take a few deep breaths. On the final exhale, I move back to the mirror and finish my makeup.

Once my signature red lipstick is in place, I peel off my robe and remove the strapless and semi-backless top from the hanger. I lift the collar to the base of my throat and reach around to tie the silk in a loose knot at the back of my neck, letting the length drape down my spine. Then, I secure the other two straps at the middle of my back, leaving my midriff and full back on display.

Tempted as I am to leave so much skin exposed to piss off my mother, I plan to don an off-white coat that matches the high-waisted slacks I'm wearing with the top.

Dressed, I study my reflection in the full-length mirror. I center the top and shift a few wayward locks of hair. Slide on my Rolex and lock the clasp near my wrist. Step into my glittered, light silk Louboutin heels, the toes peeking out beneath the hem of my slacks.

One last glance at my reflection, I tip my head to the side and arch a brow. Sexy yet sophisticated.

The corners of my mouth twitch as Delilah crosses my mind.

Checking my watch, my smile grows. With time to spare, I swipe my phone off the charger and open my text history with Delilah.

For days, we've brainstormed the murders via text. With Hayleigh's bachelorette party and wedding prep, Mother has made it her mission to keep me close. Not sure why. I literally have nothing to do except insert my unpopular opinion and be berated for every idea.

Delilah told me her family's metaphysical shop sold out of the recent shipment of sage in less than twenty-four hours. One man bought the majority of it. Aurora said the man wasn't anyone she'd seen before. She described him as tall, stalky, and tight-lipped with an unsavory, dark aura. And somehow, the man knew how to hide himself from the few cameras he passed in the store.

The more Delilah and I work on this case, the more I get to

know her and the Fox family—not that I know them *well*—the more I crave their simplistic lifestyle. Though they still interact and make decisions with the Seven, they otherwise disengage from the other founding families. They steer away from the drama. They refuse to flaunt the millions in their bank accounts.

I will never admit it aloud, but I envy Delilah Fox. Envy how effortless she lives her life. Envy the love, admiration and gentleness bestowed upon her by her family.

Please tell me your day is better than mine.

Eyes on the screen, I aimlessly wander toward my closet and fetch my coat, shrugging it on and leaving the buttons unfastened.

FOX

If you count hitting the end on my favorite new romance book, then yes.

My fingers fly across the screen, my head shaking.

Is that what you do at the bookstore? Read all day

One of the perks of the job. Someone has to read the books to recommend them.

My mind flits to the Gazette and the perks of my own job. Aside from being the voice of Stone Bay, there isn't much else I'd consider a perk. The weekly news source highlights note-worthy news, a few feel-good stories in town, juicy tidbits for the gossip lovers, a full page of comics, and far too many puzzles and word games.

Wonder what Father would think about adding new

features? What if the Gazette had a book recommendation section with different categories? What if we added an advice column?

Not only would the town love those features, but it'd boost the Gazette. A win-win.

Happy reading. I'm off to bachelorette party hell. Wish me luck

Good luck

In a private room in Calhoun's Bistro, several of the same faces from Hayleigh's bridal shower crowd around her, offering glasses of champagne and endless congratulations on her upcoming wedding. They fawn over her and she glows under their constant attention.

Bachelorette parties aren't something I'm very informed on, but this one seems lame. It's basically her bridal shower with fewer people. Call me clueless, but aren't these supposed to be fun? Her last hurrah before she's legally attached at the hip to Sawyer.

Where are the sexually suggestive named drinks? Where are the half-dressed men with hard bodies and gyrating hips? Where are my sister's screaming friends, encouraging her to do every bad thing in the book?

Far from here is the answer to all of the above.

Again, lame.

"Let's play a game," one of Hayleigh's bridesmaids suggests. The way she says it, it sounds as if we're playing a child's party game.

Tucked in the corner, I sit on the red, tufted suede couch and sip my third glass of champagne. So far, it's been socializing and light appetizers. While eavesdropping on several conversations, I've enjoyed the latter. I pray the main course comes soon and everyone will ignore me further.

The bridesmaid reaches into a bag and retrieves a big black box with bright pink letters on the face. She holds the box over her head and shakes it. The other bridesmaids and the maid of honor hoot and holler.

"What's the game?" Hayleigh asks, tucking hair behind her ear, then untucking it.

"Think of it as Cards Against Humanity for brides."

This catches my attention. Maybe the party won't be so bad after all.

As the game is organized, Mother asks a restaurant employee to move chairs and couches. I nibble on prosciutto-wrapped shrimp and sink deeper into the corner.

Grandmother approaches the couch, a gentle smile on her face. She sits next to me and stares at the bustling room. "Not joining the game?"

I wipe my hands on a cloth napkin. "No." Setting the napkin on the table, I pick up my almost empty flute of champagne. "Party games aren't my thing."

"Could be fun."

Peeking at her from the corner of my eye, I shrug. "Could be. But my guess is it'll be more entertaining to watch than participate."

A server comes to the table and asks if we'd like more to drink. Grandmother asks for Hayleigh's specialty drink, a pink concoction of alcohol and fruit juice. Rather than add to my champagne buzz, I request sparkling water with lime.

When the server walks off, Grandmother sets a hand on my leg near my knee. "How are you, darling?"

Loaded question.

Though Grandmother Gwendolyn isn't as pretentious as the rest of the Graves, she's lived this life for a long time. The influence of my great-grandparents and their parents rubbed off on her for decades before I entered the world.

"Currently, I'm bored. As for life…" My mind drifts to the case, then to Delilah. "Life is good."

"What about your romantic life?"

My shoulders cave as my lungs deflate on a heavy exhale.

What is with the sudden interest in my love life?

With Tyler happily married and Hayleigh walking down the aisle in five days, she probably wants to see me equally in love.

But love, *true love*, isn't something that should be rushed. It shouldn't be forced upon you. Not if you want it to last. Not if you want it to be real and adventurous and enthralling. Love is more than money and a "good" bloodline.

I refuse to settle to appease my family. I'd rather die alone than waste my life with someone I don't care for.

"BOB and I get on just fine."

Her forehead wrinkles as her brows pinch together. "Bob?" And then, with a shake of her head, she rolls her eyes. "Phoebe, please tell me you're not speaking of personal pleasure devices."

Personal pleasure devices.

I snort. "Alright, I won't tell you."

On a heavy sigh, she pats my thigh. "Why don't you go on a date with that young man from the bridal shower? Beau Langston. He was quite the gentleman."

My lip curls in disgust. "You may think him a gentleman, Grandmother, but he is far from it."

The server delivers our drinks and clears empty dishes from the table.

"No man is perfect, Phoebe. In fact, we're all flawed." She sips the fruity concoction. "It's only a matter of finding the person whose flaws complement yours."

Persistent, I will give her that. But at least she isn't like Mother. At least she cares about *me* and wants me to find happiness.

"I promise that I'll find someone." I stare after my sister and her bridesmaids as they play the silly game. "When the time is right, when I find my person, I'll fall in love."

Perspiration dampens my skin as a shiver rolls up my spine. Something snakes around my heart and constricts the rapidly beating organ. My chest burns as I stop breathing.

Hand shaking, I lift my drink to my lips and swallow half the glass. Try to stave off the ball of anxiety swelling beneath my breasts.

Why does the idea of falling in love scare the shit out of me?

Maybe because I've never really known love. Not real love. In any capacity.

FOURTEEN

DELILAH

After a long day, all I want is a bubble bath, mindless television, and a huge bowl of umami goodness.

Months ago, coming home after an especially grueling day would've been different. Skylar would've shoved me down the hall, making me take a bath while she picked out a movie and snacks. Kirsten would've been on takeout duty, ordering enough for us to eat for days. And then we'd all gather in the living room, load our mouths with too much food, and talk over the movie the entire time.

I loved those nights.

I miss those nights.

But there's something to be said about coming home and not worrying if you're disrupting someone else's evening. There's something to be said about leaving the bathroom door open, roaming the house naked, or stinking up the space while I cook.

I miss seeing my friends every time I walk through the door, but I have a new love for solitude.

Bubbles sit inches from the lip of the tub as I cut the water off. Stripping off the day, I step into the tub and hiss as I lower into the steamy bubble wonderland. I open up my favorite instrumental playlist, press play, set my phone on the shelf, then lie back and close my eyes.

Close to an hour later, when the water turns tepid, I unstop the drain, step out, and towel off. I don my coziest pajamas and amble to the kitchen to make dinner. As I add pan-seared tofu and mushrooms to my ramen bowl, there's a knock at the door.

My eyes flit to the clock on the range and my brows pinch together. Just after eight. Not late, but late for unannounced visitors at the door.

Turning off the burner heating my broth and soft boiling my egg, I grab my phone from the counter and unlock it, ready to call for help if some lunatic is on my porch.

Then I roll my eyes. "Crazy people don't knock, Delilah," I chastise myself.

Peeking through the peephole, I stop breathing when I spot Phoebe on the porch. A thick cloud of confusion muddles my thoughts as I continue to stare at her.

Why is she here?

From one day to the next, I never know what to expect from Phoebe. One minute, she's closed off and cold and focused solely on work. The next, she cracks the door to her heart and mind open and gives me a glimpse of who she is when not under someone's thumb.

Friends ask why I don't give up on Phoebe—on trying to be her friend, on the mysterious crush I've harbored for years. And the truth is, I don't know why.

As cruel as she's been to me at times, this small piece of me refuses to let go. Phoebe isn't a project or conquest I want to claim defeat on. There's always been something about her. A nameless connection just out of reach. An invisible impulse beckoning me closer. An irrefutable tether keeping me in her orbit.

Although I'd happily exist in her orbit without anything in return, a sliver of hope on the edge of my heart begs her to let me in.

Unlocking the door, I ease it open and offer her my smile. "Didn't expect to see you. Everything okay?"

She tugs her coat tighter around her middle, her fingers tapping her arm as she looks past me into the house. "Yes." Lines mar her forehead. "No." On a heavy exhale, she shakes her head. "Can I come in?"

I shuffle back from the door and open it wider. "Of course. Sorry. Was just surprised to see you."

In all honesty, the past few days have been a shock.

Distant, stony Phoebe is who I prepare myself to see and speak with during every interaction. After years of practice, I'm well-equipped to handle her glacial side, as are most townsfolk.

But over the past few days, I've glimpsed a new side of Phoebe Graves. I won't be so bold as to call it her warm side. It'd take a hell of a lot to melt the decades of ice encapsulating her heart. But her showing up on my doorstep without an invitation or warning text is very un-Phoebe-like.

"Ugh," she huffs as she removes her full-length coat and hangs it on a hook in the foyer. "So done with all this bullshit." She shrugs out of the cream pantsuit jacket and hangs it beside her coat.

Heat blooms in my chest, the flush crawling up my neck and spreading across my cheeks. My pulse soars as my eyes scan every inch of her exposed skin. I swallow and blink up to meet her waiting gaze.

"What—" Voice raspy and nearly inaudible; I clear my throat. "What bullshit?"

"Are you cooking?"

Brows bending at the subject change, I process her question and snap back to reality. "Shit. Yes."

I spin around and wander back to the kitchen. Although I cut the burner before answering the door, I don't want my egg overcooking. Ladling out the egg, I set it on the cutting board to cool, then pour the broth into my ramen bowl.

Phoebe enters the kitchen, propping a hip on the counter and peering down at the bowl. "Smells and looks good."

The corner of my mouth curves up slightly. "Thanks." I thinly slice scallions and carrots, adding them to the center of the bowl. As I check if the egg is cool enough to peel, I speak without thinking. "Want me to make you a bowl?"

The air gets sucked from the room as we stand in silence. I don't look up. Don't meet her gaze that burns my profile. Instead, I keep my eyes down on the egg. As if the question is no big deal.

Were it Kirsten, Skylar or Oliver next to me, my question wouldn't be out of the ordinary. It's customary for us to make each other food or pick up takeout for more than ourselves, especially on movie nights. That's what friends do.

But Phoebe and I aren't there—the friendship zone. At least, I don't think we're there yet. When it comes to Phoebe, it's difficult to discern where you stand.

"You don't have to." Her fingers grip the edge of the counter, curling slightly.

Not a "no."

The corner of my mouth twitches, and I bite the inside of my cheek to resist smiling. I lift my gaze to hers and lock onto her brilliant, addictive blues for one jagged inhale. "It's no trouble."

My tongue darts out and wets my lips. And for a split second, her gaze drops to lock onto the action. Before I'm able to revel in it, her eyes are back on mine.

"Sure." She nods. "That'd be nice."

Who is this Phoebe?

I get to work on her bowl. Since I often eat rice and noodle bowls, most of the components just need to be warmed up. Broth in the pot on the burner, I add frozen corn, diced mushrooms, and tofu. While those heat, I grab the container of precooked noodles from the fridge, as well as scallions, carrots, and fresh mint. I peel the egg, cut it in half, and set it aside for last.

As I slowly add the ingredients to a bowl, I *feel* Phoebe's eyes on me. Watching my every move with piqued interest. Considering my family is the only of the Seven to not flaunt their money and founder status, it wouldn't surprise me if Phoebe has never seen someone other than a chef cook for her.

A warm hum dances beneath the surface of my skin at the idea of being the first person to cook for her not out of obligation.

Pouring the broth, mushrooms, and tofu into her bowl, I top it the same as I did my own. Then I add half an egg to each bowl and sprinkle both with gomasio. Fishing chopsticks from the drawer, I hand her a pair before taking my bowl to the dining room table.

Silence stretches out between us as we dive into our bowls. And for a moment, I allow my mind to drift. Fantasies of more time like this with Phoebe flit to the surface. A friendship I've always wanted with her slowly becoming a reality. Smiles and endless laughter as we joke about the latest gossip in town. Late-night conversations and movies in the dark as we spend more time together and grow closer. Her fingers on my skin and my lips pressed to hers as we cross the friendship line and become *more*.

Lost in my daydream, I swallow without chewing enough and a piece of corn goes down the wrong pipe. Choking on the rogue kernel, I cough hard, smacking my chest violently to dislodge it.

Phoebe drops her chopsticks, shoves back on her chair, and sidles up to me with wide eyes. "Shit." She lifts a hand, poised to smack my back. "Can you breathe?"

I nod.

Her frame sags infinitesimally. "What can I do?"

I hold my hand in front of my mouth and motion as if taking a drink.

Phoebe bolts from my side into the kitchen, whips open the fridge and grabs a can of flavored sparkling water. Popping the tab on her way back, she hands it to me, the can shaking slightly in her grip.

Between harsh coughs, I sip the drink. And as the cool liquid soothes my throat and lulls the cough, I look at Phoebe through a different lens.

Everyone in Stone Bay regards Phoebe Graves as this glacial, heartless bitch. With her frequently curled lip, signature sneer, or frigid stare that'd easily terrify children on a sunny day, she makes it easy for them.

But somehow, I've always seen past her cold exterior.

It's no secret the majority of the older generations of the Seven are ruthless and dead inside. More than a century ago, even several decades ago. I somewhat understand why they'd need to be aloof and assertive. In the early 1900s, the world was a different place.

Though I don't agree with how my ancestors—and those who formed the Seven—took the land from the local Indigenous, I can't change history. All I can do now is learn and grow and do right by others going forward.

The cold disposition from more than a century ago still fuels several of the Seven today, including the Graves family.

But since Phoebe and I were thrust together to unearth who is behind the murders in Stone Bay, I've glimpsed a new side of her. Dare I say a compassionate side?

As my coughing fit settles, it dawns on me she never shared her reason for stopping by. Setting my half-full can down, I clear my throat.

"What bullshit?" The question comes out raspy, scratching my irritated throat.

"What?"

I bring a spoonful of broth to my lips and sip it slowly, letting the warm liquid coat my throat and ease the discomfort. "Earlier, you said you were done with all the bullshit. What happened?"

Phoebe stirs her ramen with the chopsticks, round and round in the bowl until she captures a mushroom. But she doesn't bring it to her mouth. Eyes going unfocused, she holds it between the chopsticks above the bowl.

"Do you ever feel like your life is a lie?"

Blinking up, she meets my gaze, a deep worry line between her brows.

"Yes and no." I give her a sympathetic smile. "Since my grandparents took a step back from the *what it means to be a founding family* way of life, I was raised differently." I shrug. "Yes, we're still in the loop of what happens in town. Yes, we're still part of the decision-making process for important matters in town. That will never change."

Lifting a hand, I toy with the end of my hair.

"But we choose to live like everyone else in town. Simply."

I wrap a strand around my finger then unravel it. "Considering we *aren't* like everyone else in town, yes, it does sometimes feel like I'm a wolf in sheep's clothing. But then I remember who I am." Laying a hand over my heart, I tap it. "It's what's in here that matters most."

"God." The single word is breathy on her lips. "I wish it was that easy for me." She drops her chopsticks, leans back, and crosses her arms over her chest. "I wish I could just say I'm done with all this hierarchy shit and live my life however I choose."

I push my bowl aside, drop my forearms on the table, and lean in her direction.

"What would that look like? You living life your own way."

Her eyes drift up and lose focus as she pictures this made-up existence. While she imagines it, I try to envision it too. But I don't get far.

Out of nowhere, her chortle fills the room. In seconds, it morphs into boisterous, disbelieving laughter as she throws her head back.

And for a blip in time, I unabashedly stare at Phoebe Graves. Take in this unfamiliar sight and stow it in my memory. Earmark the sound of her laughter and snap a mental picture of her buoyant smile.

When she quiets, sadness shadows her expression. "How tragic is it that I have no clue what my life would be like if my family wasn't at the helm?"

Herein lies one of the dark sides of being a founding family member. Most of the Seven don't have a say in their future. They're all steered down a premeditated path. They all have ridiculously high standards to live up to. All except the Fox family.

"Wish I could sympathize." I give her a soft smile. "You don't need to figure it all out now. You don't need all the answers today." An idea sparks and my smile widens. "Being a writer, maybe that's what you should do."

Confusion creases her brow.

"Brain dump in a journal. It doesn't have to be monumental. Just get what you're feeling off your chest." I shrug. "Can be electronic or paper, whichever you prefer, but write it down. If you see something you want in or out of your future, put it in the journal."

A rare, gentle smile curves up the corners of her mouth. "Such a smart Fox."

Heat crawls up my neck at her compliment. "Thanks." I rise from my chair, pick up my bowl and drink. "Enough with the heavy talk. Let's chill on the couch and watch trivial television."

"Erm…"

Beside her, I pause and meet her hypnotic blue eyes. "When was the last time you sat on the couch and channel surfed?"

Her cheeks flush, and my heart flutters at the sight.

She winces and says, a breath above a whisper, "Never."

My jaw all but hits the floor. "Never?"

Lips tucked between her teeth, she shakes her head.

"Well, now you have to."

I wander toward the couch, set my bowl and drink on the coffee table, and grab the remote. Waking up the television, I scroll through several series I've watched and pick one. Before pressing play, I head for the kitchen, grab another drink and several binge-watching snacks. The entire time, Phoebe sits at the table, watching me move from one spot to the next.

Arms loaded, I meander back to the living room, eyes on the television. "Come on, Graves. Get your ass on the couch."

A soft chuckle filters through the room a beat before she meets me on the couch. I hit play on the remote, pick up my ramen, and finish eating while we get lost in mindless television.

A few episodes and several half-eaten snacks later, Phoebe rises from the couch and yawns. "I should go."

Nervous energy buzzes like a hive of bees in my belly as I press pause on the remote. "You can stay." I swallow and scoot to the edge of the couch, training my eyes on the empty bowls on the table. "Two empty beds with clean sheets, all for you."

What are you doing, Delilah?

Phoebe showing up out of nowhere tonight was an anomaly. Asking her to stay over and her actually doing it would be miraculous.

When she doesn't answer for a beat, I peer up at her. To my complete and utter shock, it looks as if she's considering the idea.

Not wanting to push it, I gather some of the wrappers on the table. I shove them in my bowl and rise off the couch. As I reach for her bowl, Phoebe does too. I grab the bowl in the same place she does, my hand over hers, and we both stop breathing.

A static charge fills the air as we remain rooted in place.

Slowly, I lift my chin and meet her gaze. Neither of us says a word. My eyes drop to her slightly parted lips, and her tongue darts out to lick them. An inferno heats every inch of my skin before swirling and converging between my thighs.

Inches apart, I peer up to find panic-stricken eyes on mine.

Sucking in a sharp breath, she yanks her hand away and shuffles back a few feet. "No, I should go. Busy day tomorrow."

Welcome back, closed-off Phoebe.

"Yeah. Okay." I drop everything on the table. "Let me walk you out."

Phoebe bolts for the foyer, slipping on her heels. "No need." Back to me, she dons her pantsuit jacket, then her coat. "I don't need help."

When she flips the dead bolt and reaches for the door handle, I reach out and lay a hand on her shoulder. Her flinch at the contact speaks volumes.

Though I don't owe her an apology, I give her one anyway. "Phoebe, I'm sorry." I drop my hand. "It was an accident."

Again and again, she nods. "It's fine." She whips open the front door and steps out.

Barefoot, I follow her out, arms banded over my chest. I watch her as she speed-walks to her car, unlocks it, and slips behind the wheel. Squint as her headlights glow to life and brighten the front of the house.

As she backs out of the driveway, I wave goodbye. "Night," I whisper.

I can't see through her darkly tinted windows, but I know, without a shadow of a doubt, Phoebe doesn't return the gesture because that accidental touch moments ago spooked her. Just like the one in the car the other day.

I wonder if it will always be like this with Phoebe—one step forward, several steps back.

I hope not.

After seeing a new side of her, a freer, happier side, all I want to do is crack her hard exterior. Show her what it's like to live without the chains of our forefathers. Give her a safe space to land when she finally decides to stand up and put her foot down.

If I've learned anything since this whole investigation started, it's to expect the unexpected. And if I'm honest, I should apply the same when it comes to Phoebe.

I may have wanted more than her animosity for the past decade. I may have known another side of her existed beneath all the harsh words and cold stares. But it isn't my place to tell Phoebe how to live her life. She has to figure it out on her own. She has to find her bearings and fight back when she's ready.

And if that new version of Phoebe's life doesn't include me, I will respect her choice. Even if it cuts me in two.

FIFTEEN

PHOEBE

 the swell of my breast, up the column of my throat, and curl around the nape of my neck. I gasp, my back bowing off the bed as her lips pepper kisses along the line of my jaw.

Before my next breath, her lips drift up to mine.

Gentle.

Warm.

Coaxing.

Her tongue darts out and licks the seam of my lips.

Teasing.

Taunting.

Seeking entrance.

I part my lips and our tongues tangle on the next breath. A moan claws its way up my throat as I fist the sheet. Her relentless kisses and ravenous tongue ignite a fire low in my belly. Her desperate need for me is a shot of dopamine and adrenaline to my bloodstream.

Lost in the kiss, lost in her, the world around us disappears. The noise, the expectations, the scrutinous eyes, all of it vanishes.

My arms band around her supple curves, the fingers of one hand ghosting up the ridges of her spine as I grip her waist firmly with the other. Hips rock against mine, the top of her thigh grinding against my center. An amorous cry spills from my mouth into hers and she deepens the kiss. My fingers dive into her hair and fist the locks, my other hand palming the thick curve of her ass and pinning her to me as I lift and grind against her.

She yanks my head back, breaking the kiss, her breath hot on my lips. "Are you wet for me, Phoebe?" She nips my bottom lip.

"Yes."

I tremble beneath her, eager for her touch, her mouth. Her.

Fingers trail up the inside of my thigh, eager yet unhurried. Inch by slow inch, she makes her way to the apex of my thighs, her pace delicious torture.

The ache between my legs grows heavier. Throbbing. Pulsing. Desperate. As my lips part, a plea for more on the tip of my tongue, her finger drags up the center of my pussy.

"Mmm." She flattens her tongue on my lips, licking the seam. "So damn wet."

Sucking my bottom lip between hers, she dips a finger in my pussy. I moan and circle my hips.

"Such a needy girl." She adds a second finger. "I love it when you're greedy."

Slow and rhythmic, she pumps her fingers, curling them slightly. Hitting that spot deep inside. I rock my hips, meeting her thrust for thrust. Fire expands low in my belly, crawling its way up my chest, my neck, and pinking my cheeks.

Her mouth takes mine in a hungry kiss, driving me wild. Sweat slicks my skin as I fist the sheet and grind harder against her hand.

She breaks the kiss, nipping my bottom lip, my jaw, the column of my throat before dragging her tongue across my collarbone. Painting my flesh with fevered kisses, her tongue traces the swell of my breast before circling my nipple. And then she sucks. Hard. Her teeth clamping down on the peak of my nipple.

I hiss, and she smiles.

"Like that, don't you?"

A dose of pain with my pleasure... "Yes," I confess, breathy.

She releases my nipple with a pop, *kisses her way across my chest, and pays equal attention to my other breast. And then she moves down, down, down my body. Lips kissing, teeth nibbling, tongue tasting as she drifts lower and lower.*

My breaths come faster, my legs twitching as she kisses the trimmed tuft of hair on my mound.

Her fingers pause inside me, and I drop my gaze down my body. Hovering just above where I want her most, lust-filled eyes hold my stare.

"Please," I beg, voice croaky.

Eyes locked on mine, her tongue darts out and flicks my clit. I jerk at the contact, then lift my hips in a silent plea for more. Slowly, too damn slowly, she eliminates the space between her mouth and my clit.

Then all I feel is her. *Her fingers, her lips, her tongue. Thrusting, consuming, edging.*

My walls constrict around her fingers and she moans. Pumps faster. Sucks my clit harder.

I comb my fingers through her hair and make a fist at the back of her head. Hold her in place. Jerk my hips up and impale myself on her fingers, her face, again and again.

Fiery energy expands, ignites, spreads throughout my body. I gasp for breath, soft whimpers leaving my lips as I crush her face and hand with my pussy. And then all that fire converges between my thighs. Swirling. Tightening. Detonating.

Stars prick my vision a second before I shatter, my limbs shaking uncontrollably.

I shoot up in bed, breath ragged and fingers slick between my thighs. "Fucking hell."

Yanking my hand away, I rip the covers off of me, swing my legs off the bed, and fist the edge of the mattress. Pain shoots up my forearms, the fabric of the mattress groaning as I curl my fingers tighter. Heart banging violently against my rib cage, I close my eyes and inhale a lungful of air, hold it until my chest burns, and then exhale slowly through my mouth.

What the fuck is wrong with me?

Bringing my attention back to the room, I push up and off the bed, amble toward the French doors, whip back the curtains, and swing the doors open on to the balcony. The bite in the February air is a welcome balm for my overheated skin. I pad over to the railing, rest my hands on top, and tighten my hold until the gritty concrete scrapes my palms.

For endless minutes, I stare beyond the manicured lawn and immaculately pruned garden. Lose focus as I gaze at the forest surrounding the main house to the edge of the Graves property. Let go of every preconceived notion of what it means to be a Graves and founding family member in Stone Bay.

A simple touch, that's all it was. Something that could happen between any two people. An accident.

But it wasn't simple.

And after the second touch a couple nights ago, it never will be simple. It's not possible.

"I'm not gay," I whisper, the words floating away with the breeze.

I utter the words aloud, giving them life, but they still hold no conviction. Not an ounce. And the truth of it twists me up inside.

I clutch the rail harder. Punish myself physically for what my mind refuses to let go of.

Simple human contact—something that could happen in passing—that is beyond simple.

Much as I want to cast it aside, much as I want to blame her, neither is possible. Being forced to work together isn't

Delilah's fault. Spending more time with her than I have with anyone else in years isn't her fault.

Plus, I'm not attracted to women. Not sexually.

Or am I?

"Ugh!" My groan bounces off the house and fizzles out before it hits the trees.

Releasing the rail, I spin on my heel and storm through the French doors. I stomp over to the nightstand, yank open the top drawer, and stare down at the contents.

Boring staple items fill half the drawer. Cough drops, lip balm, lighter, travel tissues. A small notebook, pen, digital recorder.

The other half of the drawer, though... Two nonvibrating dildos. Different sizes and shapes. A vibrator wand and clit stimulator. A pocket vibrator for on the go. And near the back, a bottle of lube I haven't touched in months and a couple condoms that are undoubtedly past their expiration date.

I slam the drawer shut, followed by the balcony doors, and head for the bathroom.

Cranking the water hot as it'll go, I strip off my nightie and shimmy out of my panties. And for a brief moment, I stare at my reflection in the bathroom mirror. Visually trace the flare of my hips and slight dip at my waist, the swell of my breasts and peaks of my nipples, the length of my throat and angle of my jaw.

Goose bumps erupt on my skin as an image from my dream pops into my head. I clamp my thighs together as my fingers twitch at my sides, eager to slip between my legs to alleviate the sudden ache.

When I finally meet my own gaze in the mirror, I stop breathing. Eyes dilated, jaw slack, my pulse thrums behind my ears. Steam from the shower fogs the mirror and conceals me from myself. Steals the sight of my stiff-peaked nipples, of the arousal glistening at the apex of my thighs.

"Are you wet for me, Phoebe?"

Her question from my dream echoes in my mind.

I dip my fingers between my legs and moan as they glide through my evident arousal. Without a second thought, I circle my clit with two fingers again and again. Unabashedly, a moan falls from my lips. Not that anyone will hear it. I prop a foot on the shelf beneath the vanity counter, rock my hips, and add more pressure.

Faster, harder, I circle my clit before dipping my fingers inside and finger fucking my pussy. I grip the counter, my toes curling on the shelf and bathroom rug as I pump in and out over and over. Delilah from my dream comes to mind and I imagine it's her fingers between my thighs. I imagine her lips on my lips, on my throat, on my breast, teeth clamping down just enough to sting.

That final thought triggers my orgasm. I come harder than I have in years. Hell, maybe ever.

But as the high fades and reality sets back in, I ridicule myself. For letting my mind get swept up in fantasies, for allowing myself to indulge in lies. For creating more problems I definitely don't need in my life.

I wipe the fog from the mirror and stare at my blurry reflection.

"Don't be a fuckup, Graves."

As the mirror clouds again, I inhale deeply, spin around, and step into the shower to wash away any and all fantasies of Delilah Fox.

"Where do you think you're going?" Mother barks as I descend the stairs into the foyer.

Leather creaks as I clutch the straps of my bag tighter. "The Gazette." I continue past her and toward the garage. "It's Thursday. Where else would I be going this early?"

"Cut the attitude, Phoebe. Your incessant disrespect is exhausting."

I freeze midstride, my foot falling back to the floor as I look over my shoulder at her. With a slight shake of my head, I scoff. "Maybe if you didn't want me to be such a bitch, you shouldn't have taught me how to be one." My heels clap on the floor as I walk off on faster feet.

But she is right behind me, spewing more venom my direction. "No one at the paper needs you, Phoebe. The gossip rag can wait. You have other priorities. More important matters to attend to."

Her acidic words wiggle their way into my brain and stop me again. Why can't this woman let me *live*?

"The Gazette isn't a fucking gossip rag, Mother. It's the Graves legacy. Our family may have gotten its wealth from farms and vineyards, but that paper"—I step closer to her and jab a finger in her direction—"is what carries the Graves name now." I wave a hand down her body. "Do you think anyone would give a shit about Priscilla *Marx*?" I hiss her maiden name. "No." I inch closer, anger burning white hot in my veins. "All you'd be is another gold-digger bitch trying to make a name for yourself."

Thwack. Her hand connects with my cheek.

"There she is." Cupping my cheek, I laugh without humor. "Without Father, or anyone else bearing the Graves name, all you'd be is a sad, uptight attention whore."

The muscles of her jaw flex and her cheeks redden. "Don't test me, Phoebe."

"Or what?" I step back and put distance between us. "What could you possibly do to me that you haven't done already?" Lip curled, I look her up and down. "Death would be too kind." Straightening my spine, I turn away from her and continue to the garage.

"Your sister gets married in three days."

Her voice is too close for my liking, so I pick up speed. I open the door and enter the mudroom between the main house and garage. She's hot on my heels, but I ignore her. I twist the handle on the next door and enter the garage, beeping the locks on my SUV.

"You should spend time with Hayleigh before she moves out."

Her argument is pathetic. I want to laugh, but I bite my tongue.

I open my car door and toss my bag inside. But before I slip behind the wheel, I meet her glare over the car door. "Don't worry, Mother. Hayleigh won't go far after she marries Sawyer. Just as much as you, she needs to feed her ego and be told her maliciousness is acceptable." My lips curve up in a mocking smile. "You're two peas in a pod."

Before she gets a word out in response, I hop into the driver's seat and shut the door. I crank the music, press the garage door opener, click my seat belt in place, and exit the garage.

As the garage door closes and I lose sight of her, I take my first real breath in minutes. And when I turn onto Founders Way, I open the mirror on the visor and study the red mark on my cheek.

Hate is just as powerful and reckless as love. Some would argue it's not possible to feel one without the other. I disagree. Because I have zero love for Priscilla Graves, but I harbor a lot of damn hate for her.

"Is something in fucking retrograde?" I grumble to myself as I sift through piles of pictures and paperwork, not an ounce of progress in sight.

"Actually, Uranus is."

My fingers curl in the papers on my desk as I avert my attention to Dale across the aisle. "Excuse me?"

"You asked what's in retrograde." He presses the hot pink straw in his iced coffee to his lips and sucks down a fourth of the drink—his second of the day. "Uranus is in retrograde."

Tipping my head back, I inhale deeply. As I level him with my gaze, I give him my tight, *fuck the hell off* smile. "Great. Thanks, Dale."

He reciprocates my smile with a genuine one. "Uranus is a good thing, though."

I'm not a fan of random conversations with people I have no interest in. But somehow, Dale is setting a new bar with all his blather about asshole planets.

"It's an awakener," he continues the lesson I didn't ask for. "Like a poke in the butt to wake you up and confront things."

Fuck. Someone stop me from feeding into this. "Is that so?"

He slurps down the rest of his coffee, then rattles the ice in the cup. "Yep. Your focus is better, so it's the best time to release and deal with struggles and egos."

My focus appears to be in complete opposition to the blessings of Uranus's retrograde. Naturally. "Good to know."

Dale continues to prattle on about the benefits of Uranus, but I zone out and shift my attention to the mess on my desk. Eyes skimming notes and pictures, I land on the colored corner of paper we found by the ski resort. I pick it up and bring it closer to my face. Study the colors and faint lines.

This has to mean something. A calling card, maybe?

With the calling card front of mind, I push away from my desk, lock my computer, and rise from my seat. Donning my coat, I stuff the clue in my bag and shoulder it.

"See," Dale says. "Uranus is already working its magic."

I give in and laugh, shaking my head at Dale. "Bless Uranus."

Exiting the Gazette, I slide behind the wheel of my car and crank the engine. While the engine warms, I pull the paper from my bag and study it.

Astrology may not be something I pay attention to, but perhaps Dale's tirade was exactly what I needed. A distraction to get my mind off the perpetual cycle of nonanswers. A chance to let my mind wander in different directions.

I should buy his next iced coffee.

Pulling out of the lot, I take the short drive from Opal to Granite. Within minutes, I park in front of the Stone Bay Police Department. It's been a week since I've badgered Emerson about the case and he got called away to another crime scene. Maybe if I play my cards right, I can convince him that it'd be better if we worked together. As a cop, he has connections. But so do I.

Straightening my spine and squaring my shoulders, I strut the path to the entrance. Hot air blasts me in the face as I cross the threshold. Burnt coffee lingers in the air. Day-old donuts stain the box on a table in the waiting area.

The man behind the desk greets me with a forced smile. "Ms. Graves. What can I do for you?"

"Is Emerson in?"

"Which one?"

The one that might actually give me answers. "Travis." It's a rare day if I ever ask for Chief Emerson. That man is a fortress of secrets and suspicion.

"Have a seat. I'll see if he's available."

I cross and rest my forearms on the counter, leaning forward. "I'll wait here." I flash him a tight smile.

"Whatever," he mutters as he walks off.

My fingers tap the counter as I follow him with my eyes. He weaves between desks and disappears behind a partition. Seconds tick by painfully slow as I wait for Travis to make an appearance. After what feels like hours, Front Desk Man returns, his expression bored.

"Officer Emerson has a break in his schedule. You have five minutes." He presses a button on his side of the counter and a growly buzz echoes in the air before a door off to the side opens.

"How lucky I am." My lips stretch in a flat line. "Must be Uranus." I pass through the door and wander through the bullpen to Travis's desk.

"What?"

I laugh under my breath.

Travis shuffles papers into folders as I approach his desk. He flips them over and rests his hands on top of them, lacing his fingers.

"To what do I owe the pleasure, Phoebe?"

I pull out the chair across from him and sit. Removing the paper, I slap it on his desk and get right to the point. "I know this means something. What is it?"

His knuckles blanch in my periphery, the muscles of his jaw flexing as he fights answering. "It's nothing, Phoebe. Leave it alone."

Shoving his nameplate aside, I rest an arm on his desk, lean forward, and invade his space. Eyes locked on his, I stab the paper with a finger. "It's something. I know it is." I push it closer to him. "Telling me to leave it alone only fuels my desire for answers."

Propping his elbows on the desk, he hangs his head and huffs. He threads his fingers through his hair, tugs the strands briefly, then straightens in his seat. His eyes dart around the room a beat before meeting mine again. With a subtle shake of his head, he whispers, "I can't."

I scoot closer and lower my voice. "Helping me helps you."

"Not if you publish shit in the paper." He pinches the bridge of his nose. "Shit can't get leaked." His eyes drop to the paper. "We're hoping someone will slip up. Mention details we haven't shared. Or the gossip mill."

The story of a lifetime remains my key motivation. But I'm not an idiot. Writing up a story prematurely, especially about a serial killer on the loose, puts a target on my back. And I'm too important and pretty to die this young.

"Swear I won't speak or write a word of anything you say until this person is caught." I draw an X over my heart.

Travis scoffs. "Childish promises won't protect you. Not from this sick fuck."

"True." I smirk. "My personality is weapon enough. The day people don't grumble or shrink away from me is when we should all be shocked or concerned."

"Can't disagree with that." He covers his mouth with a hand, a wide smile plumping his cheeks. "Seriously, though." His expression sobers. "Psychos hiding behind religious figures is disturbing enough."

My brows tug in as I stare at Travis. "Religious figure?"

"Shit," he mutters, dropping his hands to the desk and balling them into fists. "Fuck, fuck, fuck."

I swipe the paper off his desk and stare down at it with fresh eyes.

A religious figure.

The last time I stepped inside a church was when Tyler and Monica married five years ago. I spent more time interested in the intricate architecture than watching my brother's nuptials. Hands folded in my lap, bored expression firmly in place, I sat in silence while everyone cited prayers for their future.

Now, I wish I had paid closer attention. To the prayers. To the setting. To the papers and cards in the rack on the pews.

"Phoebe." Travis reaches across the desk and rests a hand on mine. "You want to help. You want a story. I hate it, but I get it." He pins me with solemn eyes. "Much as I want to, I can't stop you." He subtly shakes his head. "But you need to be careful. Whoever this is, they're angry." Leaning closer, he swallows. "They're getting angrier."

Brave and strong as I am, I won't do anything stupid. I don't have a death wish.

"I'll be careful. Promise." And I mean it. "Who knows... maybe I'll find something you miss and we can get this person put away sooner rather than later."

SIXTEEN

DELILAH

Complete silence from Phoebe Graves would undoubtedly please most Stone Bay residents. For me, her silence the past four days is a slow-building panic attack waiting to explode.

But I refuse to give Phoebe that much power.

In the past three days, I've done more meditation and yoga than I have in three months. At this point, I'm surprised my favorite zen app isn't questioning my mental health or recommending professional help. After years of sneaking glances and pining for someone who has zero interest in me—in any capacity—I am exhausted.

I don't want to give up on her, but I also can't continue living like this. I can't keep feeding an adolescent crush and starving my heart in the process. It isn't sustainable for a healthy and fulfilling life.

Difficult as it is, I need to let go of all my Phoebe Graves fantasies. Even those of friendship.

Skylar leans into my side and rests her head on my shoulder. "Doing okay?"

I drop my head on hers, close my eyes, and take a deep breath. "Not really." On the exhale, I open my eyes and stare across the garage at Oliver and his band as they practice. "But I'll get past it."

"I'm here." Skylar loops her arm in mine and hugs me closer to her side. "Always."

The corner of my mouth twitches and I awkwardly nod against her crown. "Thanks, Sky. Love you."

"Love you, Dee Dee."

I twist and kiss her hair before straightening in my spot on the couch. "Tell me something good. How's work? How's Law? Is domestic life everything you thought it'd be?"

Pulsating, low thumps of the bass drum echo through the garage a beat before Oliver's sticks connect with his drums and kick off the next song. Trip plucks a couple chords on his bass guitar before Hailey, his girlfriend, adds the brutal tone of her electric guitar. All three of them bow over their instruments, the song pouring out of their souls and commanding attention. Hailey steps up to her mic and pelts out lyrics in her raspy, seductive voice.

And for a moment, I lose focus. I let my mind wander as I tilt my head and watch her.

Hailey Hart is nowhere near my type, but her gravitational energy lures me in effortlessly. The smile she flashes Trip as she looks to him, her lips pressed to the mic, only adds to her allure. Like he's the reason she smiles.

I want to be the reason someone smiles. Not the only reason, but maybe the biggest reason.

As the song nears the end, Skylar twists in her spot on the couch, tucking her feet under her, and toys with the length of my hair. "I got a promotion and raise."

I spin and mirror her position. "Seriously?"

She nods.

"That's awesome, Sky. When?"

"Yesterday, actually." She laughs. "Job isn't much different than what I was doing. A few more tasks on my to-do list. But the extra income is no joke."

I fall forward and wrap her in my arms. "So happy for you," I mumble into her shoulder.

When we break apart, the biggest smile brightens her expression. "Law's good. Finally putting all the shit Kelli Langston and his former coworkers stirred up to rest."

Last year, one of the biggest financial crimes in Stone Bay came to light. While preparing for a meeting with a client, Lawrence noticed inaccurate figures in the financial profile. Uncertain why the numbers were off, he hired a friend to look into the matter. What they unearthed was the first domino in a major scheme. Since the discovery, Lawrence has worked tirelessly to restore Stone Bay Financial's reputation and its relationship with the wealthiest people in town.

"Thank goodness." Giving the gossip mill one less thing to chat about is always a good thing. "And living with Law. That's going well?"

A noticeable blush pinks her cheeks a breath before she leans in closer. "Probably TMI, but I've never had so much sex in my life."

I want to tell her it's not too much to share the parts of her life that bring her happiness. I won't dull her shine because my love life is dismal at best.

But am I a tad jealous that my friend is having incredible sex more than once a day? One hundred damn percent. College was my last relationship, the last time I shared a bed with someone.

I met Blu Hendricks at the start of junior year. Blu had this almost ethereal vibe about her. This mystical energy I veered toward without a second thought.

We spent endless hours studying together those first few weeks. Became fast friends as we bounced design ideas off each other over dinner, sharing more about our families during movie nights in my apartment or hers. I shared my love of romance books with her. In return, she smiled and said it'd been years since she picked up a book that wasn't required. She asked for a list of my favorites and I jotted them on the back of a takeout receipt. On my next visit to her apartment, a well-loved copy of my all-time favorite romance sat on the table in her living room.

Dressed in Beetlejuice costumes—Blu in a super short, sexy as hell black-and-white-striped dress with matching thigh highs and heels; me in a red, satin and tulle dress, red fishnets, black Mary Jane's, and my hair teased and doused in hairspray —Blu and I shared our first kiss at a Halloween party on campus.

I still remember the way my body buzzed when she backed me into the corner. When she trailed her fingers up my thigh. When she cupped my cheek and crushed my lips with hers.

By Thanksgiving, we were practically inseparable. Neither of us went home during the long weekend. Instead, we shared our first holiday as a couple.

A month later, when I took her to the airport at the start of winter break, she told me she loved me before getting on a plane for New York.

For two years, I loved Blu Hendricks.

After graduation, she asked me to follow her to New York. I asked her to move to Stone Bay. Neither of us budged, and it was the tragic end of something beautiful.

When I returned to Stone Bay, I mourned the loss of my relationship with Blu. Cried myself to sleep for months. Spilled my pain to Kirsten, Skylar, and Oliver as they held me tight.

In the end, it was Mom that soothed my broken heart with wise words and everlasting hugs.

"Maybe Blu was only meant to show you how incredible love can

be. So when you find it with your forever person, your heart will know the difference between first love and eternal love."

Now, almost three years later, a small piece of me still loves her—the woman who made me feel more comfortable in my own skin. The woman who showed me what it means to love and be loved in return.

When I think of Blu, good memories are all I see and think of.

As Skylar daydreams over her feverish sex life, my thoughts ping from one point to another and land on Phoebe once more.

I let my mind wander. I let myself wonder what it'd be like to kiss Phoebe. What it'd be like to fist her hips, haul her closer, and deepen the kiss. What her skin would feel like against mine. What she'd taste like on my tongue.

"What's got you all hot and bothered?"

I startle out of my lusty, wayward thoughts and meet Skylar's stare, a devious smile on her lips. Dropping my gaze to my lap, I give a subtle headshake and swallow. "It's nothing."

Skylar lightly tugs the end of my hair. "The blush on your cheeks says otherwise."

With a huff of resignation, I face Skylar. "No matter what she does or how hard I try, I can't stop thinking about her."

"Phoebe?"

Lips pursed, I nod.

"Wish I had the right answer to make it better."

"Thanks, Sky. You're a good friend."

She rests her hand on my shoulder, her thumb moving back and forth in soft, comforting strokes.

"I don't know what it is that won't let you let go of her, Dee Dee. You've always had this way of seeing the good in everyone. It's one of my favorite things about you."

Her hand on my shoulder gives a slight squeeze.

"But you need to learn when to stop giving your all to someone who does nothing but take and give nothing in return. You need to let her go."

Harsh as it is to hear, her admission bears nothing but the truth. I feel the honesty of it deep in my bones.

Regardless of the truth, regardless of how Phoebe treats me, my heart refuses to let her go. Every time I try, a random memory sneaks in.

Phoebe's late-night, unexpected knock at my door.

Our texts that have nothing to do with finding the killer.

The occasional softness in her expression when she meets my gaze.

Her continued desire to work with me on this case, although she is more than capable of doing so alone.

What if all Phoebe needs is someone to take a chance on her? What if all she needs is someone to choose her first? What if her shitty attitude is her version of armor?

I should let Phoebe Graves go. I should forget about her.

But what if I am the only person keeping her afloat?

SEVENTEEN

PHOEBE

I'VE BEEN CHAMPING AT THE BIT SINCE TRAVIS'S SLIPUP THE other day.

When I exited the police station with renewed hope, my plan was to drive to the church and interrogate the pastor. But as I slipped behind the wheel and cranked the engine, Father called and demanded my presence at home. Told me *playing* investigator would have to wait. That the Gazette was only running fluff pieces the week surrounding Hayleigh's wedding so the Graves family could celebrate stress-free.

The past few days have been nothing short of obnoxious and soul-sucking.

Scowl firmly in place, anyone looking my way may think me bitter toward Hayleigh and Sawyer. Toward the attention they're receiving. Toward the supposed love they share.

Faults and all, in my own way, I do love my sister. But the last thing I am is jealous.

What I am is exhausted by all the pomp and circumstance. The constant parade of flashy gowns and noses pointed high. Of the holier than thou attitudes and persistence my life be one way only.

Seeing as I've lived my entire life this way, does it make me a hypocrite that I now despise every minute of it?

Either way, I do not care.

"Walk your grandmother to her seat and take yours," Mother orders, not bothering to glance in my direction.

Stepping up to Hayleigh at the full-length mirror, Mother frames her shoulders and stares at her with a level of love I will never know from her.

"My darling girl, you are stunning," she says to Hayleigh with obvious affection. "Sawyer is lucky to call you his. Never let him forget it."

Turning away from them, I leave the bridal suite and find my grandmother in the next room. Dressed in a vintage, gold, floor-length gown, the shimmery overlay embellished with countless jewels, she sits tall on a plush couch, sipping champagne.

I take her in and the easy comfort she has in her role as the Graves matriarch.

In her younger days, Gwendolyn Graves turned many heads. Not only did she stun everyone in the room with her beauty, but she also had this uncanny ability to shock people speechless with her wit.

Of all the women in my lineage, she is the person I aspire to emulate most. Beautiful and charismatic. Intelligent and a force all her own. Timeless and compassionate. Someone others envy, look up to and seek out for advice.

"May I escort you, Grandmother?" I move toward the couch and offer my hand.

Setting her now empty champagne flute on the table, she rises from the couch and takes my hand. "Thank you, Phoebe." She hooks her arm in mine.

We exit the room and wind our way through the crowd. Several people stop us along the way to congratulate our

family. As I guide us into the wedding ceremony room, we pause every few feet when people say hello to Grandmother. While she smiles and shares brief, cordial conversations, I take in the room.

Imitation grass blankets the floor, giving an earthy energy to the space. White roses, brown thistle, dried pampas, and bunny tail grass wrapped in gold satin sit at the end of each row of chairs, the aisle speckled with loose rose petals. Hundreds of gold chairs crowd the room, off-white cushions on the seat with matching tulle artfully woven through the back and gathered at the base. More tulle swoops down from the ceiling, short strands of fairy lights dangling throughout the room and creating an ethereal, starry look. At the focal point of the room, a wooden arch blanketed in flowers beckons your attention.

After what seems like hours, we make it to our seats in the front row. People continue to swarm us with fake smiles and artificial conversation. Grandmother handles it with more grace than I ever will. Were it up to me, I'd deliver my fuck-off smile and glare until they walked away, tail tucked between their legs.

After schmoozing with the elder generation of the Seven, Grandfather takes his seat. He hooks his arm with Grandmother's, the corners of his eyes softening as he holds her gaze.

In their prime, my grandparents were undoubtedly a force to be reckoned with. Now, their gentle embraces and subtle glances give me hope.

The ostentatious ceremony begins. Each mother is walked down the aisle and seated before each of the dozen bridesmaids and groomsmen follow. Before my sister enters the room with our father, before a single vow or I do is spoken, I'm ready for this day to be over.

"Quit fidgeting," Mother snaps in a whisper beside me.

With as long as this is taking, you'd think we were a highly religious family. If only. At least we'd be in the church and I could nonchalantly work. But no, Hailey and Sawyer wanted the ceremony at the social center and reception at the vineyard.

The music shifts and everyone rises from their seat as the doors swing open and Hayleigh and Father enter the room. Soft gasps and whispers of how beautiful she looks float through the crowd. And they aren't wrong.

Flustered as I am with so many things in my life, a smile pushes up my cheeks as I take in my teary-eyed sister.

Our family may be dysfunctional; we may bicker and slam doors and give each other the silent treatment more often than not, but they are my family. Although we're constantly at each other's throats, I still love them in my own way.

Well, most of them.

When they reach Sawyer, Father lays Hayleigh's hand in his and whispers something no one else can hear. Sawyer gives a curt nod, mouthing, *"Yes, sir."*

The ceremony passes with words of love and eternal devotion, promises and the occasional fallen tear. Faster than anticipated, Hayleigh and Sawyer kiss as the crowd explodes with cheers. Faces alight with undiluted joy, they face their family and friends for a moment before walking down the aisle and exiting the room.

Chaos erupts in the room as people clamber to leave their seats and follow the newlyweds. Mother and Father tell me they'll meet me and the rest of the family at the vineyard after the wedding photo shoot.

My grandparents and I weave through the throng of people and make our way to valet. Within minutes, we are whisked away in a town car and driven miles up the road to the vineyard.

Soon as I enter Bales Winery, a staff member offers me a

glass of wine. I take two and ignore their subtle surprise. Considering I'm expected to stay at the reception the next three to four hours, I need something to take the edge off.

The first hour passes in flashes—of cameras, rehearsed speeches, and trivial conversations. Meals are delivered to our tables and more wine is poured. Music and chatter clash, the volume in the room growing insufferable.

"It's that time, folks," the emcee announces from their booth in the corner of the room. "The newlyweds first dance as husband and wife."

Cheers boom through the room.

"Let's welcome Mr. and Mrs. Bales to the dance floor."

Sawyer rises and proffers his hand to Hayleigh. Seconds later, he twirls her into his arms as guitar strums float through the room. Her fingers lacing behind his neck as his arms wind around her waist, "Dance in the Starlight" by Josh Nuzum playing as he rests his forehead on hers.

Cameras flash, hands cover mouths, and eyes water as everyone watches on.

Applause bounces off the walls as the song fades and a new, more upbeat song starts to play. The emcee encourages others to join the newlyweds on the dance floor. Grandfather asks Grandmother to dance, but she declines and suggests he dance with me instead.

With every fiber of my being, I want to refuse. But I won't. It isn't worth the argument.

We reach the dance floor and Grandfather spins me quickly before framing my hip and taking my hand. As we glide through the crowd, people move aside and watch us in awe. At seventy-three, Talbert Graves dances as if he were decades younger. His poise and energy are so infectious I can't help but smile.

When my parents talk down to me, it's moments like this I

think of. My grandparents may have unattractive qualities—every Graves does—but at least those tendencies don't outshine their charm.

"May I cut in?" The deep voice is familiar and too close for comfort.

Before I get the chance to say no, Grandfather releases me from his hold and offers my hand to Beau Langston. "By all means, Mr. Langston."

The moment my grandfather turns away and Beau pulls me close, I curl my lip and try to yank my hand free.

But he doesn't let me go so easily. His fingers tighten around my hand and waist as he leans in and drops his lips to my ear.

"There's no escape, Phoebe," he purrs as he presses the length of his body to mine. "Not when I've spoken at length with your family about *us*."

I jerk back and glare at his smug face. "There is no *us*, Beau." Nose scrunched in disgust, I look him up and down. "And there never will be."

Brow cocked and shit-eating grin in place, he subtly shakes his head. "No one's told you, have they?"

What the fuck is he talking about?

"And I thought my family was shitty."

"Your family is shitty," I grit out, over his whole egotistical puffed-chest act. "And told me what?"

Lips fighting a smile, he twirls me around the room. He regards me like a trophy, a prize handed over for a job well done, as he flaunts me in his hands to the crowd.

The longer he remains quiet, the more nauseous I become. One scenario after another pops into my head. The longer I hold his mischievous gaze, the more an unspoken truth settles in my gut and chills me to the bone.

In the past month, Grandmother has *pushed* me in Beau's

direction more than once—physically or verbally. His name has been nonchalantly mentioned in conversation by either my grandparents or parents while we organized Hayleigh's big day. At every possible opportunity, I am forced to spend time with him.

No. No, no, no, no, no.

"Ah, she's putting the pieces together," he coos.

Again, I try to yank my hand from his, try to step out of his grip. His hands clasp me harder, painfully, as he pins me to him.

"Let me go," I growl. "Now."

"Quit being such a bitch, Phoebe. Everyone is watching."

My eyes dart around the room and sure enough, countless people are staring at us. "I'm going to throw up."

"Always so fucking dramatic." He shakes his head. "Grow up. This has been in the works for years. But after the bullshit with my sister last year, your family thought it best to wait until the news died down."

"I'm not doing this."

Once more, I try to pull away. It only eggs him on, and he clutches my hand and hip so hard I stifle a cry.

"They can't make me do this. And neither can you."

"Like it or not, Phoebe, you are mine."

This time, when I yank my hand, I slip free of his hold. I step back and shake my head. "Never."

And before he attempts to pull me back in, I bolt from the dance floor. I dash by the table, grab my clutch, and sprint for the bathroom. My grandmother calls after me, but her words are white noise as I escape the room. People smile and reach for me as I pass, but I ignore them.

Rather than use the closest bathroom, I opt for one farther away from the party. The last thing I need right now is for my mother to walk in and berate me on how I'm ruining my sister's big day.

Pushing through the door, I go to the farthest stall, step inside, and bolt the door. The moment the lock clicks in place, I take my first real breath in minutes. I close the toilet lid, drop down on the seat, and wring my clutch in my hands.

Anger bubbles in my chest, expanding into a firestorm, ready to explode. An eager, hellacious scream impatiently waits at the back of my throat, but I don't set it free. Not here. Not where someone may hear me and send for help.

Instead, I fist my clutch tighter and beat the stall door with it. Open my mouth and silently scream at the universe for putting me in this shitty situation.

I am far from righteous, but I don't deserve this bullshit. No one does.

Knee bouncing, I pull my phone from my clutch and tap the screen until I reach my chat history with Delilah. It's been five days since we last spoke. Five days since I lost my shit because her hand touched mine and I felt something *more* during those timeless seconds.

It's sad to admit, but I've never had friends. Not real friends. Every *friend* I've had has either been a child of my mother's socialite acquaintances or someone told to be nice to me, even when I treated them like shit.

Ashamed, I admit I've treated everyone like trash. It's what I know. What I was taught by my mother as she regarded me as such.

But no matter how much of a bitch I am to Delilah, she always treats me with respect and kindness. As if she knows goodness exists inside me and is simply waiting for it to bloom.

I should leave her alone. Should continue ignoring her and

let her live a better life. One that doesn't include a wretched *friend* named Phoebe Graves.

But I don't want to leave her alone. I don't want to ignore her. More than anything, I want Delilah Fox and all her beautiful humanity in my life.

Without second-guessing myself, I type out a message and hit send.

> Sorry about the other day. I freaked out.

The fingers of my free hand tap my thigh as I stare down at the screen. As the bubble pops up to indicate she's typing, the screen dims. Biting my bottom lip, I wake the screen up with a quick poke.

> I figured. Don't worry about it.

She isn't mad?

I all but ran to my car and away from her. For almost a week, I've ignored her.

Delilah isn't the type to throw fits or scream her anger to the world, but I expected some form of wrath. Maybe a *"Fuck you. I never want to see or speak to you again."* Possibly the silent treatment for life.

By now, I should know to expect the unexpected from Delilah Fox.

> Why are you so nice to me?

> Everyone should have at least one person be nice to them. If I'm that one person for you, I'm glad.

The backs of my eyes sting as I stare down at the screen.

Fingers trembling above the keyboard, I slowly type out the next message.

> I need to get out of here. Can I come over?

For a beat, nothing happens. No dancing dots in a gray bubble on the screen. No response. Nothing.

The screen dims and my stomach churns. The sting behind my eyes morphs into an irrefutable burn. A thick swell of emotion in my throat makes it difficult to breathe. Tears prick my eyes and the screen blurs.

Before I blink away the tears, the phone vibrates in my hand. Quickly, I wipe beneath my eyes and read her text.

> I'm not home. I'm at one of the rentals.

Her next text is the address to said rental. A rental mere minutes away.

Closing my eyes, I inhale deeply, holding the breath until my lungs burn and beg for release. On the exhale, I peer down at the screen, swallow, and type.

> Be there soon.

I exit the stall and meet my reflection in the large mirror over the sinks.

Grabbing a towel, I blot the faint tear stains beneath my eyes, then toss it in the dirty basket. Before I tuck my phone back in my clutch, I order a ride, then freshen my lip stain. Fix a few wayward strands of hair. Shift my dress back to rights after Beau manhandled me.

Satisfied with my appearance, I grip the handle, ease the door open, and peek out of the bathroom. When I find the hall empty, I step out and take the long way toward the exit. As I near the front entrance, I scan the few people nearby, relieved to see no one familiar.

Rather than take the ride to the rental, I give the driver my address.

With most of the town at the reception, we make it to the house in half the time. I thank them, exit the car, and beeline for my own car.

On the road, I pass the winery minutes later. I flip my blinker and turn on a gravel road. Ease off the accelerator and stare out the windshield at the inky night sky. Tap the steering wheel with my thumb over and over as the quaint cottage by the water comes into view.

"What am I doing?" I mutter as I park behind Delilah's MINI Cooper.

The answer... For the first time in my life, I have no clue.

But it feels *right*.

EIGHTEEN
DELILAH

My Vans softly clap the hardwood as I pace the room and wait for Phoebe.

After days of silence, I assumed our temporary friendship hit a dead end. I let my conversation with Skylar sink in and did my damnedest to let go of my disillusions.

This morning, I felt more myself when I woke up. Today, Phoebe wasn't my first thought.

It was refreshing that she hadn't crossed my mind for hours. Not until I started reading my current romance, which pissed me off.

By the time my anger fizzled out, I headed to Mom and Dad's for Sunday dinner.

June, Jet, and I helped Mom in the kitchen, making a feast for the family. Hours of slicing, dicing, smashing, and mixing distracted me from the world beyond the Fox estate.

It wasn't until we sat down for dinner and Grandpa mentioned the Graves-Bales wedding that my mind drifted to Phoebe once more. Then, unbeknownst to her, Mom rubbed salt in my Phoebe-shaped wound when she asked if Phoebe and I were making progress with our investigation.

With a shake of my head, I downplayed the lack of headway on Phoebe not having time the week leading up to her sister's wedding.

Everyone bought the lie, and I've felt slimy since.

The truth is simple, though. When I touched Phoebe the other night, she felt the same charged buzz I did. The subtle shift in her expression and body language said everything her voice wouldn't. Instead of embracing the connection, she ran— far and fast.

Her silence the past five days spoke volumes, and I didn't expect to hear from her again. Which is why her text a half hour ago was a complete shock.

I wanted to ignore the text, but the small piece of me that's always held onto hope for Phoebe wouldn't let me.

Headlights beam through the cottage windows and I stop pacing the room. Facing the door, I suck in a jagged breath and shake out my hands at my sides. Bounce in place as I wait for her to knock on the door.

And then it comes, a soft rap of knuckles on wood.

"No expectations," I mumble before ambling toward the door.

I lift a hand and unbolt the lock. Inhale one last deep breath before I grab the handle and twist. Exhale and open the door, then stumble back as I take in the sight of her.

I'm fucked.

"Hi." I barely hear her greeting as her lips curve into an indiscernible smile.

Dressed in a floor-length gown, Phoebe sparkles and shines like the night sky. Thick straps of ivory satin glide down her shoulders to hug her voluptuous breasts before framing her waist. The skirt flows off her hips and elegantly falls to the floor. Over the satin, thin sheer fabric embellished with intricate gold flowers and vines shimmers.

Phoebe Graves is a goddess, and I would gladly worship at her feet.

"H-hi." I swallow down the nervous lump in my throat. "You look…" I want to tell her she looks beautiful, but I bite back the compliment, not wanting to scare her further.

"Like I just came from some rich-girl party." I don't miss the slight tease in her tone.

I shrug. "Not what I was going to say, but it works."

"Can I?" She points to the inside of the cottage.

Snapping out of my stupor, I move aside. "Yeah. Sorry."

She visibly shivers as she passes, her dress sweeping the floor and my feet.

"Are you cold?" I rush to close the door and dart across the room before she answers. "Here." I whip a blanket off the couch and hand it to her. "Not sure what else we have in the cottage."

A noticeable smile plumps her cheeks as she takes the blanket and wraps it around her shoulders. "Thank you. Hadn't noticed I was cold until you said something."

Fingers itching to touch her, to warm her, I shove my hands in my hoodie pockets and ball my fingers into fists. "How was the wedding?"

Phoebe tightens the blanket around herself and hugs her middle. Crossing the room, she enters the open kitchen, moves to the sink, and stares out the window at the darkened bay.

Silence stretches between us, but I don't interrupt it. Badly as I want to follow in her footsteps, wrap my arms around her, and take away every ounce of hurt, confusion and false ideology she's been taught her whole life, I remain rooted in place.

"Why are you here?" she asks, a breath above a whisper.

Alright, she wants to avoid the wedding. Got it.

Ignoring my own advice, I enter the kitchen and sidle up to

her by the sink.

"When I need to clear my head or get away from the noise, I come here." I point out the window to the rocky cliffside. "Near the water is a huge evergreen. At the base is a boulder that's been there longer than our families." I drop my hand, mindful not to touch her. "My family said it belonged there. That it wasn't up to us to move it. On that boulder and near the cliff are my favorite spots to sit and think."

"Will you show me?"

I shift to gaze at her silhouetted profile and swallow. "Another time. When it's light."

Eyes still on the window, she nods.

"What happened, Phoebe?"

Her eyes close as she takes a deep breath. On a slow exhale, she opens her eyes and turns her gaze in my direction. "Sorry I bolted the other day."

"I get—"

She holds up a hand and cuts me off. "Please, let me finish."

Tucking my hand back in my pocket, I face her fully and dip my chin.

"I've never had friends," she confesses, chin dropping to her chest and wobbling slightly. She rolls her lips between her teeth then swallows. "When you're raised by an ice queen, raised to believe everyone is beneath you…" She lifts her gaze and shrugs. "I didn't care if anyone liked me. I didn't care that everyone called me names. At the time, in my eyes, I was superior to anyone not in the Seven."

Fists clenched, I fight the urge to reach out, take her in my arms, and console her—as a friend or something more. Phoebe's life is already chaotic; I don't need to make it worse.

Her brows bend at the middle, her eyes softening at the corners as she holds my stare. "For years, I've been a bitch to you." Tears rim her eyes. "And you've only ever been nice in return." She worries her lips between her teeth. "You're the only person I'd call a friend, and I'm not sure if we actually are friends."

I inch closer but keep my hands in my pockets. Shove away what I really want to say and try for something lighter. "I am your friend, Phoebe. If you want me to be."

At this, her brows bunch tighter and a crease forms at the middle. "Why?" She shakes her head. "Why don't you hate me?"

Because for some stupid reason, I'm in love with you. That's what I want to say.

Instead, I say what's easier for her to hear. "Because beneath your hard exterior is a good person." I lick my lips and swallow. "And I'd like to know that Phoebe."

She hugs the blanket tighter to her chest and averts her gaze. "I'm not gay," she whispers.

I open my mouth to tell her that's okay, but don't get the chance.

Phoebe renders me speechless when her Nordic blue eyes slam into my gunmetal blues. "But I like you."

She likes me? In what way?

My tongue darts out to wet my already damp lips and her gaze drops to follow the action. A beat later, she blinks away. And it's with that single action I have my answer.

Phoebe wants me as a friend but is terrified to admit she wants me as more than a friend too.

I won't push her to own her truth. Accepting this part of yourself looks different for everyone. Some choose to deny it their entire life, worried what others will think of them.

As one of the Seven that's had expectations drilled in her head for two and a half decades, her concerns are easily tenfold.

"I like you too," I confess, leaving my response as vague as her admission.

Phoebe shuffles closer, the skirt of her dress brushing my jeans. "This feels so juvenile." A smile grazes her lips a beat before she laughs. "Like we're in grade school and meeting for the first time."

Inching forward, I chuckle. "Want to borrow my crayons?" I tease.

Her laughter floats through the cottage and my chest warms at knowing I've lightened the mood a little.

"Stick figures are my specialty. Don't ask me to draw anything else."

"I'll remember that." I tap my temple twice before my expression softens. "Does liking me scare you?"

"Yes."

This answer, I expect. Doesn't stop me from wanting to know the reason behind her fear. "May I ask why?"

Her entire frame locks up as she looks over my shoulder.

"You don't have to tell me anything. I was just curious." I inch impossibly closer to her. "But if you do want to tell me, I'll listen. Without judgment. Without expectation." I fist the inside of my hoodie pocket. "If you need to get things out, if you need someone to listen or give advice, I'm here."

Again and again, she shakes her head. "Why?"

"Isn't it obvious?"

She swallows. "Yes, but I still don't understand why."

If I ever want Phoebe to be comfortable sharing herself with me, I need to share a piece of myself in return.

So, I decide to go big. Spill a truth that could bring her closer or send her running.

"I remember the first time I saw you." I lean against the counter as the memory flashes behind my eyes. "We were eight, and all of the Seven gathered to discuss the Founder's

Day event. While our parents discussed boring stuff, the kids were shuffled into a separate room with several forms of entertainment. Everyone was distracted by electronics or art supplies or one of the countless games in the room. But not you." I shake my head and laugh. "You sat perfectly straight at a table, a calligraphy pen in your hand as you wrote on a lined piece of paper."

A smile brightens her face and I mirror her expression.

"I looked up to you in that moment. Imagined you writing a novel." I chuckle. "Even then, I loved to read. And whatever you were writing, I wanted to read it."

Phoebe shakes her head. "I don't remember that."

"That's okay. I'll remember for both of us." I wink. "The boys in the room started teasing you. They said you didn't know how to have fun. I told them to shut up."

Her forehead wrinkles in confusion. "You defended me?"

"I did."

"We didn't even know each other. Not really."

I shrug. "Doesn't matter. They were being shits, and something about you not acting like every other kid our age made me like you."

"So you've liked me all these years because of that?"

I tip my head side to side. "Not just that." I meet her waiting gaze. "Do you remember being my tablemate in high school art?"

She squints, her lips scrunching together. "Kind of."

"Standoffish as you were to me in class, I couldn't take my eyes off you," I confess.

"Oh," she mutters.

"You were the inspiration for much of my art that year."

"I was?"

"Yes. And the more you blew me off, the more I wanted to know you."

"Why?"

I inhale a shaky breath and hold it. "The heart wants what the heart wants." I lift a shoulder in a half shrug. "No matter what anyone said, I still wanted you."

"As a friend?"

Rolling my lips between my teeth, I slowly shake my head. "More than a friend."

She scoots closer, her knee bumping my leg. "And now?"

The air charges between us as I hold her waiting gaze. I don't dare move. Don't take another step—literally or figuratively.

But fuck, I want to kiss her. I want to show her how much I want her. How much I've always wanted her.

"Still more than a friend," I whisper.

She swallows a beat before her hands peek out from under the blanket. And then she reaches for my hoodie, clutches it in loose fists, and slowly banishes the space between us.

I don't question her or what she plans to do. I don't utter a word or take a breath, fearing anything I do will break the spell. Beneath my rib cage, my heart hammers a vicious rhythm, my pulse whooshing in my ears as I wait for her next move.

Inch by painstaking inch, she pulls me into her orbit. But it's when her eyes fall shut, the heat of her breath ghosting my lips, that I know this is real.

Phoebe Graves is going to kiss me, and I can't fuck it up.

As my eyes close, warm lips press mine. With that single chaste kiss, I am a puddle of goo. Putty in her dexterous fingers. When her tongue darts out and licks the seam of my lips, I forget how to think or breathe or exist outside this moment.

With one kiss, Phoebe Graves owns me. And without hesitation, I will gladly worship her.

NINETEEN

PHOEBE

I fist her hoodie harder. Step impossibly closer. Crush my body to hers and punish her mouth with mine. Shove my tongue between her lips and devour her sweet taste. Moan unabashedly when her hands clutch my hips and pin me to her.

The blanket falls from my shoulders, but I no longer need it. With each swipe of her tongue, Delilah heats every inch of my skin. Drives my pulse higher and higher. Has me needy and desperate and hungry for more.

More of her lips, her tongue, her taste. More of her body pressed to mine, equally insatiable.

Her hands trail up the curves of my waist, past the swell of my breasts, the length of my throat. Delicate fingers curve around my neck as she cups my jaw. Tilting her head the other way, she deepens the kiss. Digs her fingers in the hair at the base of my skull.

And then her lips drift from mine.

Tugging my hair, she tips my head to the side, kissing and licking and nipping her way down my neck. Pulse deafening in my ears, wildfire licks every inch of my skin. Ravenous desire thrums between my thighs. Expansive, voracious and aching. My thighs clench and rub together, craving some form of relief.

As if she senses my need for relief, Delilah licks her way up to my mouth and nips my bottom lip.

"Expected the fire." She takes my mouth in another heated kiss but breaks away far too soon. "Not the sweet, though."

Something about her words has me dropping my hands and taking a step back. My pulse skyrockets for an entirely different reason, and I take another step back.

"And she shuts down," Delilah mutters.

I drop my gaze to the floor and shake my head over and over and over. Hands at my sides, I ball my fingers into fists until my nails bite my palms. The backs of my eyes sting, my breaths come in short, unfulfilling bursts.

I'm not gay.

My heart beats so fast and hard and relentless in my chest it's painful.

I. Am. Not. Gay.

"Okay," Delilah says softly.

I lift my head to meet her gaze. My brows bunch together as I discern the sympathy in her expression. "What?"

Delilah inches closer, lifting a hand but not touching me. "You're not gay." A soft smile tips up the corners of her lips then falls as quickly. "It's okay."

Tears rim my eyes and I avert my gaze. My heels clap the hardwood as I cross the cottage and sit on the couch. I drop my head in my hands, shaking my head a beat before I fist my hair.

Poison in the form of panic filters through my bloodstream, seeping into my limbs, my heart, my bones. And ever so slowly, it morphs into humiliation. Swallows me whole and shames me for craving something I shouldn't want.

On my next breath, a different brand of heat floods my veins. Anger.

"Phoebe?" My name on her tongue is hushed, delicate, uncertain. It only serves to piss me off more.

I bolt up from the couch, meet her concerned blues, and fist the skirt of my dress. "I'm not fucking gay, Delilah," I scream.

She jerks back and lifts her hands in surrender. "Never said you were."

The fact she doesn't fight back, she doesn't scream and tell me to calm the hell down, lights another fire in my chest. The backs of my eyes burn as I fight the tears rimming them. "But you want me to be," I bite back.

One foot in front of the other, she slowly crosses the room. "No, Phoebe." She shakes her head. "I want you to be yourself."

"A bitch?"

She scoffs. "You do have your moments."

Her gentle tease temporarily lightens the mood, and I chuckle under my breath.

With a shrug, she moves in closer. "Kissing women, wanting more than friendship with a woman, doesn't make you gay. You can like whoever you choose—men, women, nonbinary—and still not label yourself."

"You're gay." I fold my arms over my chest and give her a pointed stare.

"Lesbian." She nods. "And you're not."

"No, I'm not."

"But you like kissing me." She cocks a brow, so sure of herself. It's kind of sexy.

"Does it matter?"

"Yes."

With another step in my direction, she's within arm's reach.

"I will never pressure you, Phoebe. Ever." She shoves her

hands in her hoodie pockets. "If you never want to kiss me again"—her brows twitch—"just tell me." Tucking her lips between her teeth, she rolls them a few times. "We can be friends and nothing more."

A sharp, persistent pain steals my next breath. My hand spasms at my side, desperate to press my breastbone and smother the pang. But I don't reach for my chest. Don't move an inch or acknowledge anything she said.

Instead, I revert to what's familiar. Hate. Disdain. A frigid exterior while I slowly die inside.

"We aren't friends, Fox." I back away from her and move for the door. "We aren't anything." Peering over my shoulder, I soak her in with one last glance. "Never will be."

I rip the front door open and slam it as I storm down the walkway for my car. The breeze off the bay mingles with the February evening chill and has me lengthening my stride.

Within seconds, I'm behind the wheel, cranking the engine and blasting the heat. I throw the car in reverse, whip out of the driveway, and kick up gravel as I speed for the end of the road.

As I roll up to the stop sign, my hands start to shake. I slam my foot on the brake, take a deep breath, and stare down at my hands on the wheel. The tremble worsens, rippling up my arms and invading my chest.

I shove the car into park, ball my fingers into tight fists in my lap, and then scream at the windshield until the pain in my throat begs me to stop. Over and over, I slam my fists on the steering wheel. Absorb each blow, each ounce of hurt, because I deserve nothing less.

Tears blur my vision as my blows to the steering wheel lessen. My anger from moments ago softens and molds into something new, something more complex. A swirl of hate and sadness, fear and guilt.

Laying a hand over my rapidly beating heart, I clutch my chest and let my feeble control go. A sob rips from my throat as a torrent of tears spills down my cheeks.

For the first time in my life, I am purposely weak. I allow myself to *feel* whatever comes. Allow myself to be honest and vulnerable without worrying about other people's opinions.

Eyes puffy, my tears dry up. I wipe my cheeks and stare at the stop sign. My rational mind says to drive home and never look back. But my impulsive side says I can't leave things with Delilah like this—upside down and shaken.

Before I give it too much thought, I put the gear in drive and turn around.

My heart is a wild beast pounding against my rib cage as gravel crunches beneath the tires. When the headlights brighten the face of the cottage, I stop breathing.

How can she not hate me now?

"I'd hate me," I whisper as I put the car in park and cut the engine.

Minutes pass as I remain glued to the seat. Eyes on the cottage, I shake for an entirely different reason.

Before I walked out the door, I doused her in ugly words, struck the match, and turned my back as I set us ablaze. With one irrational act, it's quite possible I ruined everything.

Delilah says we can be friends and nothing more *if that's what I want*. But what if I have no idea what I want?

I exit the car and head for the door, hesitant. Before I reach the porch steps, the front door opens.

Spine straight as she fills the doorway, her veiny eyes and trembling chin say more than words. A rogue tear spills down my cheek as I stride up the steps, cross the porch, and stop within inches of her.

"Sorry," I whisper with a subtle nod. "Please don't hate me."

Delilah looks over my shoulder, out into the dark of night.

And while she mulls over what to say, I study her. The perfect lines and angles of her jaw. The slight slope of her nose. Her dark, indistinctly curved brows that make the smoky-blue color of her eyes pop. Those damn kissable lips, the bottom fuller than the top. The thick, long, black strands framing her face and begging for my fingers.

Women have never been on my radar, but damn do I want her. Her skin under my fingers. Her mouth pressed to mine. Her taste and moans and need on my tongue.

"I can't—" She shakes her head. "No, I *won't* keep doing this, Phoebe."

My brows tighten and she reads my confusion.

"Wait around for another blow." Her eyes fall shut, her chest rising and falling once before her eyes meet mine again. "I avoid drama for a reason. I look for the good in everyone for a reason."

"Fox…" I inch closer, fisting my dress to avoid reaching for her.

"No, Phoebe," she chokes out with another shake of her head. "You don't get to yell at me, storm out, and then come back like nothing happened. You don't get to pretend like what you said didn't hurt." She slaps a hand to her chest and fists her hoodie. "It hurts, Phoebe. *I* hurt."

My vision blurs as my chin wobbles. I glance to the side and fight the emotion begging for release.

"Hurt is all I know," I confess, then meet her gaze. "All my life, I was taught to bear it or inflict it." I drop my gaze to her hand still clutching her hoodie. "I don't want to hurt you"—my watery blues meet hers—"but I don't know how not to."

"It takes time, but if anyone can do it, it's you."

Her confidence in me is a shot of dopamine to my system. Without thinking, I step into her, frame her face with my hands, and kiss her. We stumble into the cottage and the door shuts behind us. Her arms band around my middle, pull me closer, hold me to her.

As our lips dance and tongues tangle, I note the difference in this kiss from the first. While I spill my apology into the kiss, she gifts me her forgiveness. And I can't help but pull her closer, crush her mouth to mine and take more.

Her absolution is my addiction. Her mercy is my freedom.

She breaks the kiss, her panting breaths painting my lips as she hovers close. "We should stop."

I tip her head back and drop a chaste kiss to her lips. "What if I don't want to stop?"

A wide smile plumps her cheeks. "Never said I *wanted* to stop, only that we should." Her fingers dance over the exposed skin of my back. "Don't want to scare you off again."

I rest my forehead on hers and close my eyes. "Glad one of us is thinking."

As the haze of the kiss fades, reality trickles back in and I tense.

"What's wrong?"

Why is everything a fucking roller coaster? I barely have time to enjoy the high before I fall into the pits of hell.

My hold on her face tightens as I swallow past the growing ball of nervous energy in my throat. "No one can know."

She tries to pull back, but I'm not ready to let her go. My eyes open and find hers waiting.

"About us?"

I nod. "About anything—how close we've gotten, the kiss, none of it."

This time, when she pulls away, I let her go.

"I won't lie to people, Phoebe. Especially my family."

Sweat dampens my skin as dizzy energy swirls through my body. "They can't know."

Her gaze drops to the floor as she rocks back on her heels. My pulse whooshes in my ears as I wait for her to look up, to promise me she won't tell anyone about this, about us. It's on the tip of my tongue to beg again, but she speaks up before I get the chance.

"I won't come out and tell anyone."

I sag in relief.

"But if my family outright asks, I won't lie to them. I trust them, Phoebe. If I ask for their discretion, they'll keep what I say between us."

"What about your friends?"

She steps back into me and brings a hand to my cheek. "They've asked about you for years. They know how I feel about you. Skirting around the truth with them is a bit easier."

"Thank you."

Delilah inches forward and presses a chaste kiss to my lips.

"Accepting this part of yourself when the world wants you to be someone else is hard. Unfortunately, it never fully goes away. But I've learned how to be happy with who I am and cast away the ugly. It takes time, and there's no rush. You say when each step happens."

If only it were that easy. If only I didn't have my family breathing down my neck.

Taking a step back, Delilah reaches behind her neck. Before I get the chance to ask what she's doing, something shimmers in the faint light of the cottage. A silver necklace with a small bird at the center.

Without a word, Delilah's hand moves to the nape of my neck. After some finagling, she secures the chain around my neck, the bird resting inches from my heart.

Eyes on her, I brush my fingers over the simple charm. In one swift and easy move, Delilah has given me the greatest gift.

A token. A piece of herself.

"What's this for?" The words come out garbled.

"Think of it as a reminder."

Of her? I don't need a piece of jewelry to remind me of Delilah Fox.

As if she hears my thoughts, she gives a subtle shake of her head.

She rests her hand over mine on the charm. "A reminder that you have wings. A reminder that you can spread those wings whenever you're ready." She lifts her hand to cup my cheek. "And that you'll always have someone on your side."

The backs of my eyes sting. "Even when I'm horrible?" I whisper the words, terrified of her answer.

A gentle smile tugs up the corners of her mouth as her thumb strokes my cheek. "Even then."

I sniffle. "I'll fuck up."

Her eyes never leave mine. "So will I."

My chest warms at her admission. "Thank you, Fox."

"For what?"

"Being you."

Delilah pushes up on her toes and presses her lips to mine in a chaste kiss. "Right back at ya."

TWENTY
DELILAH

Secrets and lies are a virus. An infection my family worked hard to eradicate for future Fox generations. And for several years, their strenuous efforts paid off.

Until now.

Because days ago, I willingly agreed to not tell the whole truth about my relationship with Phoebe to anyone, including my family. If my family outright asks about Phoebe or our relationship, I won't lie. But in my heart, I know I won't give them the full story either.

Worse than that… I am clueless as to what our relationship actually is.

In such a short period, we have gone from adversaries—Phoebe's perspective—to allies. It never crossed my mind to look at Phoebe as my enemy, but she cannot say the same. Before Phoebe and I spent considerable time together, everyone was her enemy. The notion was imprinted in her DNA and force-fed into her psyche for decades.

Now that we've eradicated the nonexistent enemy boundary, now that we've crossed a line I never thought we'd traverse, I have no idea what I am to her. An acquaintance with sporadic kissing benefits? A friend she's attracted to and kisses on occasion? Her right-hand partner as we puzzle out the murders happening in town?

Her secret…*something* with a token of my affection latched around her neck?

How long will this last? Will it end when the killer is behind bars?

I wish I had answers. I wish I knew what the future holds. But when it comes to Phoebe, everything is up in the air. Everything is uncertain.

The biggest what-if that keeps me up at night… Will things between us fizzle out once the mystery is laid to rest? Once the adrenaline rush of hunting down the killer fades, will she stay?

I want her to stay.

But not as a secret. In the end, secrets and lies ruin everything.

"Everything okay, Delilah?"

I simultaneously slap a hand to my chest and suck in a sharp breath. Looking to my right, Paige stands feet away with an apologetic wince on her face.

"Sorry." She steps closer and rests a hand on my shoulder. "You've moved the same two books for the past few minutes." Her hand falls away, her smile shifting to one of sympathy. "Can't say I've seen you this distant before. Was just worried."

Ugh. Now I have to lie to Paige.

Damn, I hate this.

"Everything's fine." I shove my hands in my pockets and give what I hope is a believable smile. "After I read the synopsis for that new dance partner romance we got in, I keep thinking of Jet and Shanti."

Paige softens, a gentle smile tugging at the corners of her mouth. "Those two are a slow-burn romance waiting to be written." She snickers, then sobers. "You sure that's all? The past few days, you haven't been yourself."

"Reading all the books on the clock?" I tease, hoping to skirt the subject.

With a roll of her eyes, she chuckles. "Always an odd day if I don't catch you reading." She inches closer and wraps gentle fingers around my arm. "But seriously, you don't seem yourself." Her thumb brushes the cotton of my shirt in small strokes. "It's okay to not be okay. And I'm always here if you need to get something off your chest."

"Thanks, Paige." Without warning, I wrap her in my arms and hug her tight to my chest. "I appreciate it." As she strengthens her hold, I let go and step back. "If I need to talk, I'll reach out."

Lies.

Phoebe made me promise not to tell anyone, and I hate myself for saying yes. I hate that all it took was her kissing me for me to break all my own rules. My crush on her will be the death of me.

"Good." Her gaze shifts to the alien romance books I was futzing with moments ago. "You read those yet?"

I shake my head. "On my TBR."

A heated, dreamy look takes over Paige. "So good. I'd volunteer for abduction any day of the week."

I snort-laugh. "Oh my…" I grab a book from the shelf and swat Paige's arm. "You're ridiculous."

Brow arched, she shrugs. "True. You still love me, though."

"Yeah, yeah." I set the book back on the shelf. "Go get your jollies in sci-fi and let me get back to work."

Paige saunters off and leaves me alone with my thoughts. Naturally, they bounce right back to Phoebe. This time, though, it's not about our kiss or vowing secrecy. My mind drifts to the investigation.

More than a week has passed since we scrutinized facts and evidence. It's been much longer since we've made any progress. And seeing as Phoebe has all the printouts and pictures, I'm twiddling my thumbs as I mull over what I remember.

The weirdest part of it all... the town is somehow still oblivious. Same for the horde of tourists we had for the wine-and-chocolate festival.

The Stone Bay gossip mill is a committee of ravenous vultures eager and waiting for any juicy news in town. The fact they haven't heard a thing about two additional murders is beyond bizarre. Somehow, the Seven have kept the newest murders colder than the victims on the ground.

I get that they don't want to cause an uproar. When the woman in the woods was discovered in November, the residents went berserk. Businesses shut down early. Groceries were emptied from the shelves within days. Residents only left home if absolutely necessary.

Stone Bay went from booming to a ghost town in a matter of hours. Witnessing the eerie, vacant sidewalks and storefronts is not something I'll soon forget.

And perhaps that is why the Seven—more specifically, the Emerson officers—have kept the news under lock and key. I don't doubt Phoebe's father is working overtime to keep the news from hitting the Gazette as well.

Bzz. Bzz.

I front a super sexy alien romance cover on the shelf then reach for my phone in my pocket.

"Speak of the devil," I mutter as a text from Phoebe fills my screen.

After parting ways at the cottage four nights ago, I wanted to change Phoebe's name in my phone. She asked for discretion and I wanted to gift her as much privacy as possible. Most of our texts are innocent and about the case. But now that we've crossed a line, I don't want her name to flash on the screen with possibly sinful content and be seen by anyone.

For hours, I pondered what nickname to give Phoebe. I wanted something that fit her personality but not something anyone would easily figure out. I didn't want a cute term of endearment easily associated with a lover. Mentally, I thumbed through some of my favorite romances and recalled random pet names other than *baby* or *honey*. Not that I don't like those, I do. I just can't use them with Phoebe.

The longer I spent trying to figure out a name, the more frustrated I became. So, I went another route. I listed Phoebe's traits on a blank note in my phone. It was when I typed out *fiery* that it hit.

Firefly.

It's too perfect. Fireflies get their name for their luminescence—early discoverers thought of fire when they lit up—but they emit cold light. Fiery, bright, and cold... fits Phoebe. At least, the Phoebe of weeks ago.

Bottom lip between my teeth, I stare down at the screen as she types out a response.

Tell you in person. Pick you up from work?

Paige won't care if I leave my car in the lot, but I'd rather have it at home. Last thing I need is more questions, and leaving my car here after shift would stir up several.

My place is better. Should be home by 4:15 at the latest.

Be there at 4:15. Wear something church appropriate.

What?

Rather than ask for details, I react to her message with a thumbs-up.

Could today get any stranger? I turn my attention back to the bookshelf.

Truth is, anything is possible in Stone Bay. More than a century after the town was founded, we've barely glimpsed insanity in our borders. We have our share of secrets, but life has been peaceful and charming in our small town. Luck has been on our side.

But if the past year is any indication, our luck is running out.

We have yet to see how dark life can get in Stone Bay, but I sense a shift in the air. See the gloom in the atmosphere that stays longer than usual. Witness the anxiety that lingers with some of the residents after the woman in the woods.

Obviously, the Emersons and other Seven families see it too —vile people weaseling their way into Stone Bay. I just wish they'd be a little more vocal about it. I wish they'd find a gentle way to make the residents aware.

One of the worst parts of all of this, the townsfolk aren't prepared. They have no clue of the evil lurking in the shadows.

TWENTY-ONE

PHOEBE

Delilah's silence is maddening.

Minutes ago, as I pulled into her driveway, she exited her house before I put the car in park. With a quiet *"hey"* and half-hearted smile, she slid into the passenger seat, buckled her seat belt, and faced forward as I backed out.

She's been on mute since.

A thick cloud of uncertainty and unease looms over us. Heavy and oppressive and intent on drowning us until we come up for air. I hate the feel of it, the way it separates us.

I want to ask what has her so reticent. I want to ask if she's okay. More than anything, I want to ask if she's told anyone about us.

But I don't.

Instead, I bite my tongue, grip the steering wheel until my knuckles scream, and drive the short distance to the Stone Bay Community Church.

"Why are we going to the church?"

Finally, she speaks.

"Last week, I paid a visit to our favorite police officer." I smile, happy with the news and at having a reason to talk with

Delilah. "He held his own for a bit, but frustration and sleep deprivation worked in my favor."

Sometimes, those small victories are my favorite. It's no secret I'm persistent. But when it pays off, the reward is worth every future look of disgust thrown my way.

"I showed him the colored paper again and he tried to blow me off. Didn't last long." I peek over at Delilah and arch a brow. "You know how tenacious I am."

"Do I ever," she mumbles.

I chuckle. "Anyway, I must've asked at the right moment." Flipping the blinker on, I slow and enter the church parking lot. "He said it's part of some religious figure card." I gesture to the massive Victorian Gothic stone structure. "What better place to ask questions than the church?"

Silence fills the car cabin as I steer into a parking space and cut the engine. Delilah leans forward and studies the colossal structure with curious eyes.

My guess is she's not set foot inside the temple claiming to welcome all but mainly practicing Christianity.

Seldom does the Graves family enter the church. Usually, only when a wedding or death is hosted within its walls. Knowing my mother, she undoubtedly thinks religion is beneath her. Knowing my mother, she also only attends those events so she is seen as *caring*, which is a joke.

Delilah's family likely avoids the church and organized religion because they follow other ideologies. As easygoing, optimistic and affectionate as the Fox clan is, I picture them revering any principle promoting good karma. *Do unto others as you'd have them do unto you*, or whatever.

"Let me ask the questions," I suggest.

Delilah sits back and unbuckles her belt with a nod. "Absolutely."

I chuckle in the hopes of easing her discomfort. "It's not as bad as it looks."

I reach across the console and rest my hand on her forearm. An uncontrollable hum skitters through my fingers and up my arm. Rather than fight the feeling, I inhale deeply, count to three, exhale, and let the sensation boost my confidence.

"While I ask questions, you observe."

She dips her chin and stares at my fingers on her skin. A gentle smile tugs at the corners of her mouth then disappears as she meets my gaze. "Who you're talking to?"

"Them, the church, all the small details." I reach into the backseat and grab my bag. "I'll have my eye on things too but may miss something you catch. No detail is too small."

"On it."

We exit the car and cross the lot for the entrance. Quiet beside me, our stride slow but steady, Delilah studies the exterior of the church. Following her line of sight, I visually roam the property with fresh eyes.

Pristinely landscaped, young yet tall evergreens reach for the sky from mulch beds between the bumper lines. Earth-tone boulders, fiery red shrubs, pale grassy bushes, lavender stems, and flowering plants artfully fill in the empty space. Strategically placed feeders stick out of the ground to attract hummingbirds, butterflies and bees. More mature evergreens shadow the church near the sidewalk leading to the entrance but sit far enough from the building to let natural light shine through the countless stained-glass windows.

Elegantly carved obsidian frames, granite walls, Gothic windows, and a wide double-door entrance. A Rosetta window centered high above, a series of life-size granite statues adorn either wall of the doors, welcoming all who walk inside. On either side of the steps leading up to the portal is a tall buttress, one with a spire reaching for the heavens, the other with a high yet shorter spire and pinnacle.

As we take the first step up, Delilah mutters, "Absurd."

"Just a little ostentatious."

Snort-laughing, I turn a few heads. Unfamiliar churchgoers meet my gaze, then quickly look away.

"Wait until you see the inside."

Iron handle in my grasp, I tug open the heavy door. My heels clap on the ornate tiled floor as we cross the threshold and enter a whole new world—a place filled with strong convictions, relentless worship, and unparalleled trust.

My generation is the first in the Graves line to not be an ever-present fixture at the church each week. A true man of God—whatever that means—Grandfather Talbert insisted his family dress in their finest attire and attend church no less than three times a week. He and Grandmother were the most loyal of the Seven to the town's church, and they enjoyed the attention doted upon them. Father, Uncle Winston, and Aunt Angelica smiled and greeted the town during each visit but didn't love the church and God like their parents.

During those formative years, my aunt and uncle played their part. But when the opportunity to leave for college arrived, they jumped at the chance to drive away from Stone Bay. Everyone assumed they would return after their studies, but neither did.

Uncle Winston met the love of his life in his junior year of college at a party. A year behind him, he stayed until she graduated. Without a word to the family, Uncle Winston packed what belongings mattered, moved to Tennessee—where Aunt Farrah was from—and began teaching middle school math. Aunt Farrah, middle school English.

As for Aunt Angelica, she earned her business degree then let it collect dust. Her senior year of college, from what Father told me, she spearheaded a food-and-gift drive for those in need. After seeing the impact of helping others, Aunt Angelica made it her mission to feed, clothe, and help as many people as humanly possible. While traveling the globe, she met Uncle Johan. Their shared love to lift others up and give them a better life has kept them together more than two decades.

Neither my aunt nor uncle subscribe to the politics in Stone Bay. They don't care that a descendant of our family helped found this town. They don't care that the residents of this town consider them a form of royalty.

Both check in around holidays, birthdays, and a few random times between. Other than that, they live happy, unencumbered lives far from Washington.

As for my parents, they still make random appearances at the church—on the rare Sunday and during charity events. But it's more for show than having a relationship with God.

"Such a waste," Delilah mutters, her voice bouncing off the high vaulted ceiling and garnering my attention.

Eyes on her, I observe as she takes in the vestibule. The flashes of gold on fixtures, walls, and floors. Elaborate paintings of deities and people deemed worthy of worship over the centuries. Intricate lines curved into granite and precious stones to form a grand arch leading into the nave. Four-foot tall, jewel-encrusted candelabras stand on either side of the nave entrance, the candles lit. Directly above the center of the vestibule, an antique-gold-and-glass chandelier hangs from the ceiling.

Several places within Stone Bay's borders scream wealth. Town hall and the courthouse. The country club and performing arts center. Even the post office and library. Each cost hundreds of thousands to build in their time.

Still, none of them flaunt affluence quite like the church, which feels wrong in more ways than one.

"The cost of everything in this room could feed the entire town for weeks, possibly months." Delilah shakes her head. "For a church welcoming all beliefs, they sure have a lot of Christianity on their walls."

I do my damnedest to restrain myself but am unable to hold back as laughter bubbles in my chest. An unbridled cackle echoes throughout the vestibule and makes me laugh harder, louder. Good thing it isn't Sunday. Not only would I garner nasty stares from half the town, but I'd also never hear the end of how I'm an embarrassment to the Graves name.

"Don't worry," I say as my laughter fizzles out. "It gets better the farther we go." With a tip of my head toward the entrance of the nave, I lead the way. "Come on."

Delilah's eyes bug out of her head as we enter the nave. Can't say I blame her. I've been here several times and the opulence overwhelms me each time.

Colossal stained-glass windows behind thick granite pillars curving into decorative, pointed arches frame aisles on either side of the nave. Above the aisles, a gallery walkway and more windows. Countless pews fill the nave, each capable of seating at least ten faithful followers. At the focal point of the room, the chancel begs for your attention with pops of red and blue accented with too much gold, a series of two-story stained-glass windows, and a large granite altar.

Five pews into the nave, a nun appears out of thin air.

"Welcome to Stone Bay Community Church." The corners of her mouth tip up in a strained smile. "For where two or three gather in my name, there am I with them."

I narrow my eyes in confusion, unsure how to respond to her obvious scripted Bible quote. Beside me, Delilah shoves her hands in her pockets and purses her lips. I bite the inside of my cheek to not laugh in this nun's face.

With an exasperated huff, the nun clasps her hands in front

of her waist. "Matthew 18:20. Would appear you ladies need to work on your scripture."

Not today or any day in the future.

Lips curving up in my practiced fuck-you smile, I say, "Another time, perhaps. We actually stopped by with some questions."

Tilting her head, the nun studies us for a beat. Seemingly satisfied, she offers her hand. "Sister Rebecca, and I'll be happy to answer any questions you have…"

I slip my hand in hers and mentally cringe as her icy grip makes my joints ache. "Phoebe."

Sister Rebecca twists and offers her hand to Delilah. But Delilah hesitates. It isn't for long, but I notice her slow reaction to introducing herself. The delay has me curious.

A breath passes before Delilah takes her hand, not hiding the shiver rolling up her spine. "Dove," she says.

Why the lie?

A question I stash away for later.

"What a beautiful name, my child," Sister Rebecca says, practically cooing. "A symbol of peace."

Delilah gifts Sister Rebecca a synthetic smile before shoving her hand back into her pocket.

"Phoebe, Dove, what questions do you have for the church today?"

What an odd way to phrase it, but whatever.

"We recently stumbled upon the corner of what I'm told is a religious figure card." I rummage through my bag, retrieving the copy of said corner and offering it to Sister Rebecca with a practiced smile. "We'd be eternally grateful for more information on a card such as this."

Lips pursed, Sister Rebecca takes the paper and studies it. She lifts it closer to her face and examines the lines and colors on the page. While the nun is distracted, I peek at Delilah out of the corner of my eye and note her eyes scanning the church. She pauses on each new item and, one by one, takes mental snapshots. The pews and card holders. Specific lines of scripture painted on the wall. The confessional booths on either side of the chancel.

I revert my attention back to Sister Rebecca as she shakes her head and meets my gaze.

"Looks like part of a prayer card." She draws the sign of the cross over herself. "Upsetting to see a piece of God defiled." Sister Rebecca hands back the paper. "I can't be certain which card it is with such a small piece. With the colors, it may be Saint Joseph."

May or may not. Either way, it's more information than I had before walking in the door.

"Do you offer prayer cards like this in the church?" I tuck the paper back into my bag.

Clasping her hands at her waist once more, she shakes her head. "Only in times of great need." Her eyes dart between me and Delilah, her lips in a flat line. "Most people purchase them off the internet, like anything else."

Sister Rebecca appears a little irritated. Is she anti-internet and advanced technology? Maybe she dislikes the idea of people finding support online rather than coming to her or the pastor. Maybe she detests people creating online communities rather than begging her for help and boosting her ego.

"Wonderful," I say, my voice laced with honey. "I'll look it up online when we leave."

With a slight curl of her top lip and a light flare of her nostrils, I have my answer.

"You've been a great help, Sister Rebecca." I rest my hand on Delilah's shoulder. "Did you have anything to add, *Dove*?"

Delilah shakes her head. "You pretty much covered everything."

"Perfect." I flash Sister Rebecca a saccharine smile. "Again, thank you for your help."

I pivot on my heel, Delilah mirroring my action, and take a step toward the door.

"We'll see you on Sunday, ladies."

Fuck-you smile firmly in place; I peer over my shoulder and meet Sister Rebecca's waiting gaze. "Wouldn't miss it."

Walking three times faster out of the church than when we entered, we clear the main entrance in seconds. But I don't stop on the steps or sidewalk. I trudge forward, putting as much space between us and the church as possible.

Unlocking the doors, I slip behind the wheel, crank the engine, and let my head fall back on the headrest. After a few deep breaths, I swivel my head to look at Delilah. "Thoughts?"

Eyes narrowed, she studies the outside of the church. "Didn't see anything out of the ordinary." She turns her gaze on me. "But overall, I don't like the vibe of the place." Losing focus, she shakes her head. "Something isn't right inside those walls."

"Agreed. Definitely some creepy inculcation in those walls." I scoff. "Probably because they're not as open to all beliefs as they claim to be."

Delilah shrugs. "Isn't my place to cast judgment." She bands her arms over her chest and shivers. "If we need to come back here, I'd rather not."

"No problem." I yank on my seat belt and buckle myself in. "How about dinner and some internet perusal at your place?"

"I could eat."

A genuine smile curves my lips. "My stomach's been growling for RJ's all day."

"Mmm... don't judge me for eating my weight in mac 'n' cheese."

I reach across the console and take her hand in mine. "Only if you don't judge me for the same."

Her answering smile floods my chest with pulse-pounding warmth.

In this moment, I care a little less about writing an award-winning story for the Gazette and more about spending time with this woman. Yes, I still plan to write a kick-ass story. One the town won't soon forget. But it's no longer the *only* thing I care about.

For the first time in my life, I see more than my status, privilege and wealth. Now, I see happiness and laughter and the promise of something bigger than myself or my last name. I see a life well lived.

All because of her. Delilah. My Fox.

TWENTY-TWO

DELILAH

Whispers over the past week have caught my attention.

Residents have started to question the recent, lengthy disappearance of two more women in Stone Bay. Disbelief swirls in vicious circles around the rumors that both women have taken extended time away—a falsehood perpetuated by the Seven and the police department in order to keep the town calm. Several townsfolk are curious if people are dying at the hands of a new crazed lunatic. A large-scale panic seems imminent as more people question if our town is safe.

But with no evidence to back their postulation, the questions and speculation have fizzled to a low murmur. With the Seven feeding the perpetual narrative they want residents to hear, the whispers become less and less.

In no time and with little effort, life in Stone Bay is as it was a year ago—charming, carefree and cheery. As if someone wiped the suspicion from their minds and replaced it with synthetic joy and artificial memories.

Discussion of the murders continues between the Seven. Daily brainstorming sessions on what the Seven can do to protect the community. Deliberation on the Seven's secret forum on how to apprehend and lock up this sicko before they hurt someone else.

They will never lie to us, but I see the way my parents tiptoe around the subject. Anytime conversation veers toward the murders or me and Phoebe looking into them, it gets steered in another direction. Though it was Mom's idea we investigate them in the first place, they try to hide how they feel about the whole situation. I pick up on the fear in my parents' voices.

The more time that passes without answers, clues, or someone in handcuffs, the more Mom says she needs help at Sage Whisperer. Now that I live alone, she continually finds ways to keep me close so she knows I am safe. June and Jet too.

And to my complete lack of surprise, since our visit to the church eight days ago, I've seen less of Phoebe. Every two or three days, she texts with an update on her research—which has again hit a dead end. Other than that, nothing. No calls. No random visits at the bookstore or Sage Whisperer. No late-night appearances at my front door.

In the past eight days, I've seen Phoebe once, and it was a complete accident as we crossed paths for takeout. To say it was an awkward passing of two people that've been mildly intimate would be an understatement. I smiled and lifted a hand to wave. She started to smile, glanced over my shoulder, schooled her features, then moved past me as if I had never existed.

Back to square one.

Deep down, I knew this would happen. Either Phoebe will walk away because the case closes, or she'll walk away because there is no real reason—for her—to spend time together.

Phoebe has been my crush for years, but I've been nothing

to her until weeks ago. Expecting anything of or with Phoebe is foolish. Still, my heart holds on to hope.

Flashes of her pressed to me, her lips crushing mine, her need for me on her tongue... Now more than ever, it will be hard to let go of Phoebe Graves.

I love and hate the constant ache in my chest. I love and hate the way my heart beats uncontrollably anytime I hear her name or think I see her on the street. I love and hate that I can't think of anything or anyone else because she's got me in an emotional stranglehold.

"I need a distraction," I mumble under my breath as I straighten crystals on the shelf in Sage Whisperer. The same crystals I've been *cleaning* and *organizing* for the past—I check my watch—twenty minutes. "Fuck my life."

Scanning the store and finding no one nearby, I grab my phone from my pocket and tap on the messaging app. For a moment, my finger hovers over my chat history with Phoebe. More than once, I almost tap her name. Almost type out a generic message, just so she doesn't forget about me.

But then my inner authority figure puts her foot down, plants her hands on her hips, and shakes her head.

Make Phoebe come to you. It's time for her to step up. She needs to make the next move.

On a deep inhale, I instead tap the chat with Skylar and Kirsten.

Plans tonight?

I glance up and survey the still-empty store as my phone vibrates.

K

Travis is neck deep in some supersecret case
I'm free

My pulse soars for a different reason.

Travis hasn't mentioned the new murders to Kirsten, which I get. Police business is confidential until they decide to make it public knowledge. They've kept things quiet to not cause panic.

The decision by the Seven and the police department to keep the murders quiet means I have to lie to my best friends. And since lying isn't my strong suit, it's best if I steer conversations in other directions. Still feels gross.

SKY

Checked with Law. No plans on my end.

Thank goodness.

Girls' night at Dalton's?

K

Tell me when

SKY

Yes please

Meet in an hour?

SKY

Perfect

K

See you

I shove my phone into my pocket and weave through the store. Do one last sweep of the shelves with the duster and straighten anything out of place. Count the till and drop the extra money in the safe. Parting the curtain between the main store and the storage area in the back, I smile at Mom as I enter.

"Anything you need me to do before I leave?"

Mom gifts me a smile that is equally soft and kind yet loaded with fear and uncertainty. "I appreciate your help, my delicate dove." She sets down the large amethyst geode she was inspecting. "Headed home?"

I nod. "For a few. Then I'm meeting Kirsten and Skylar at Dalton's."

The lines at the corners of her eyes and between her brows deepen. "Please be careful."

I cross the room, invade her aura, and wrap my arms around her middle. "Promise I will be, Momma. Always."

Her arms band around my shoulders and tighten with unmatched ferocity. "You, June, and Jet are my world," she mumbles against my hair. "I'd be lost without any of you."

"What about Daddy?"

Light laughter shakes her frame. "Him too, but you know what I mean."

"Yeah." I give one last, breath-stealing squeeze, then release her. "I do."

"Have fun with your girlfriends. I love you, my delicate dove."

I grab my bag from the desk and shoulder it. "Love you too, Momma."

"Why is life so complicated?"

Kirsten snorts, plucks a chicken wing from the basket in

front of her, and shoves it in her mouth. Lips twisted, Skylar shrugs then lifts her Dr Pepper to her mouth and hides behind the glass.

"Better yet, why is *love* so complicated?"

"Love?" Skylar and Kirsten question in unison.

Whoops.

Time to backpedal. And slow down on the drinks.

Grabbing a fry, I saturate it in barbecue sauce, cram it in my mouth, and wince when I basically consume a mouthful of the smoky condiment. Once I swallow down the saucy fry, I drain the rest of beer number two.

Under normal circumstances, I'm not much of a drinker. I make an exception for special occasions and nights out with friends. Even then, I do my best to remain somewhat lucid. I don't enjoy not having control over what I say or how I behave. Not that I'm a control freak. I just prefer to not make an ass of myself, especially in public.

I wave off their joint inquiry. Ignore their raised brows and intrusive, unrelenting stares.

"Not *actual* love."

I roll my eyes. Pinching a fry between my fingers, I squeeze until the end separates and the insides squish out.

"Finding love. Feeling things for people that obviously don't reciprocate."

I drop the fry, wipe my hands on the napkin in my lap, then huff out my annoyance.

"Sometimes, I wish there was a way to hit delete on certain memories. To let them go and forget the moment happened."

A little less inebriated than me, Kirsten and Skylar reach across the table, each of them laying a hand on mine. Their touch is a slight balm to the swirling ache beneath my breastbone.

With my friends, the frustration, hurt and confusion ease a

little. But it's their individual gazes that hit me hardest. In their eyes, I glimpse the hint of sadness, the shadow of sympathy, the flare of strength, and the flash of protectiveness. I see their fierce love and willingness to fight anyone who dares to disrupt my happiness.

Gratitude and displeasure swim in my veins at the sight. Two halves of a whole. Yin and yang. Light and shadow. Pleasure and anger.

I love that I have such incredible friends. People who will drop whatever they're doing to spend time with me if I need them. Friends that cheer me on. Lift me up, and go to bat, even if unnecessary. Friends that lend their shoulder and listen to me blather on while I drink too much or soak their shirt with tears. Besties I can spill my heart to and know they'll keep every word a secret.

In a heartbeat, I'd do the same for them.

Unfortunately, the secrets I harbor, the secrets tearing me up inside, aren't mine to share.

"Same, girl." Kirsten strokes her thumb over the top of my hand. "That shit in December…" She inhales a deep, audible breath, holds it as the seconds tick by, then finally releases it. "I'd delete that a million times over."

A new pang forms in my chest. Guilt. Thick and expanding and suffocating.

I invited my friends out for a girls' night so I could release my pent-up frustrations over greasy food and too much alcohol. And not for a single second did I consider their feelings or what may be going on in their own lives. All I thought about was myself.

Phoebe ghosting me is juvenile and inconsequential compared to the horrendous things Kirsten endured a little more than two months ago. Hell, it's been less than a year since Skylar was held hostage.

And here I am, crying into my empty beer glass over a damn woman.

My forehead tightens as my face scrunches inward. "Sorry." I flip my hand over and take hold of hers. "Wish I could erase that for you too."

The server sidles up to the table, a beaming smile on his face as he scans the table. "Another round, ladies?"

I should say no, but I'm past caring. "Please."

He collects the empty glasses and baskets. "You got it." Weaving between the tables, he disappears behind the bar.

Eyes on the basket in front of her, Kirsten reaches for another wing but doesn't bring it to her mouth.

"Here's what's weird, though." Her lips twist a beat before she looks up and meets my and Skylar's gazes. "As much as I'd like to forget it all"—her eyes glass over as she swallows—"I also want to remember it."

She drops the wing and reaches for a napkin from the stack.

"Shitty as it was, I'm trying to focus on the good that came out of it." The corners of her mouth curve up in a soft smile. "Travis, for starters. And I don't think things with Ben would be where they are without those days at the cabin."

She balls up the napkin and tosses it on the table.

"Most of all, it opened my eyes. I'm more careful about who I gift my trust to now. More aware of my surroundings."

Fresh drinks are delivered, the table going silent a moment as we guzzle our drink of choice and slowly empty the remaining baskets.

Thoughts swimming in far too much beer, I scan the crowd in Dalton's. Search for the one person I want to see but know is nowhere near here. The one woman my mind refuses to let go of, no matter how much I beg it to.

When my gaze reaches the end of the bar, I startle in my seat.

Partially hidden by the dim lighting in the corner, a sizable man sits far too still as he openly, unabashedly stares at me. The pint in front of him full, the glass blanketed in condensation, the beer foam nonexistent. A chill rolls up my spine and I visibly shiver. At this, his lips tip up in a nefarious smile.

Who is this guy?

Were I not so intoxicated, I may actually have the wherewithal to sort through my mental database of townies. As it stands, I'll be lucky to remember my own name by the time I get home.

"Hello?" Skylar waves a hand in front of my face.

I blink and shift my gaze in her direction. "Sorry, what?"

Chuckling, Skylar leans back in her seat. "I said that I'm always here if you want to talk about Phoebe or anything else weighing you down."

"Me too." Kirsten takes a swig from her water glass. "Just because we've been through shit doesn't mean you can't talk to us about yours."

Vision a bit hazy, my gaze crawls from Kirsten to Skylar. "I love you guys."

"Ope." Kirsten smirks. "Looks like the beer is taking over."

"Beer?" The word comes out in slow motion as my face screws up.

With a slow blink, I drag my eyes back to the end of the bar. The stool with the beefy man sits empty now, the beer glass gone.

Bewildered, I shake my head, then stop when the ground wobbles beneath my stool legs.

I fight the urge to lift my hand and point across the pub at the empty seat. I *know* he was there. A moment ago, he stared at me with his beady, black eyes on his big, round head. I'd swear my life on it.

Am I drunk out of my mind? Without question. It doesn't happen often, so it doesn't take much for me to lose all sense of thought or direction.

Do I have an active imagination? One hundred percent. Blame it on growing up with an open mind and desire to create.

But did I conjure up a creepy, suspicious man in the bar? Did I fabricate a dubious person, a suspect? Did my mind do this so I'd have a reason to reach out to Phoebe?

Phoebe.

"Let's get you home, Dee Dee." Skylar flags down the server and asks for the check.

I dig into my pocket and pull out cash. With clumsy fingers, I sift through the bills and hand Skylar two twenties. "Is this enough?"

"Plenty."

"I'll text Travis." Kirsten's fingers fly over the screen. Before I argue and suggest ordering a ride, a wide smile brightens Kirsten's face. "He'll be here in a few." She slides off the stool and offers me her hand. "Up you go."

We weave through the bar and exit into the crisp night air. It sobers me slightly, but not enough to make the world stabilize.

I pull my phone from my back pocket and open the chat history between me and Phoebe. My unfocused gaze studies the screen as my fingers hover above the keyboard.

"What're you doing?" The sharp bite of Kirsten's question has me hugging the phone to my chest.

"Nothing."

Kirsten chuckles. "Let me rephrase. What were you about to do?"

My whole face tightens. "Nothing."

Tugging at my phone, it doesn't take much effort for Kirsten to pry it from my fingers. Her eyes dart to the screen but don't linger long enough to read the messages. She shakes her head. "No, Dee Dee. Do not text whoever that is. Not like this."

"Why not?" I reach for my phone and take it back. "Not like she'll answer. She hasn't talked to me in days." I blink down at the screen, slightly aware I'm oversharing. "Probably blocked me."

"I agree with K," Skylar chimes in as Travis pulls up. "Wait until the morning. If you still want to text her, then do it with a clear head."

"Ugh."

We climb into Travis's truck, the cab too warm. Travis asks about our night. Kirsten highlights the sober moments before I mentioned love. Skylar leans forward in her seat next to me and suggests we all get together soon at her and Lawrence's house.

And while they chat, I unlock my phone and type. Before Travis pulls into my driveway, I hit send *for the umpteenth time*.

TWENTY-THREE

PHOEBE

NO MATTER HOW MANY TIMES I READ HER TEXTS FROM LAST night, my heart spasms anew. My lungs scream and beg for air. My eyes burn with a mixture of anger, frustration and devastation.

Buried in a heap of useless information as I searched for answers on the religious figure card, I lost track of the time, the day. When my eyes wouldn't stay open, I slept. When my stomach twisted in pain, I tiptoed down to the kitchen, loaded up a tray of food, and brought it back to my suite. For over a week, I ignored my phone and the world as I scanned thousands of images online for the one matching our clue.

The result? Not a goddamn thing.

Unless you count me unintentionally ghosting Delilah. And occasionally arguing with my parents. Those I accomplished effortlessly.

FOX

Got drunk to forget you

Didn't work

Why's it sooo easy for you to forget me???

I hate that I can't forget you

Just tell me you're done with me so I can move on

Ignore the last text

Please let me know you're not dead from the cereal killer

*serial

I think I saw a creepy guy at the bar

But he disappeared

But not like you

I miss you.

The double doors to my bedroom suite fly open. My mother stands in the doorway with her hands propped on her hips. Lip curled in disgust, her eyes scanning the room I haven't let the maid clean for several days. Avoiding eye contact, she crosses the room and rips the curtains open. Sunlight beams throughout the room and I wince at the sudden invasion.

"Is there something you need, Mother?"

From the bed, I follow her with my eyes. She evades looking in my direction.

"This has gone on long enough, Phoebe. Get out of bed." She lifts a hand to her nose. "For God's sake, shower. Dress in suitable attire and come downstairs."

"For what?" My bark bounces off the walls.

At this, she spins around and pins me with a glare that

makes grown men falter. But I am flesh of her flesh, and I don't cower to her vitriol.

On the next breath, she flashes her well-rehearsed, artificial smile—the same one she taught me as a child. "Since you've been locked in your room for God knows how long, you've obviously forgotten the date."

Much as I want to tell her I don't give a fuck what day it is, I bite my tongue. Instead, I give her a blank stare.

"Such a child," she mutters before giving me her back. "Your date is tonight." She peers over her shoulder. "Do not embarrass me or your father. Be ready in two hours. Beau is arriving early to have drinks in the parlor."

I swing my legs off the bed and storm across the room.

"Don't want me to act like a child." I step within reaching distance of her. "Quit fucking treating me like a child." An inferno ignites in my chest, liquid fire spreading in my veins. "Quit trying to marry me off. I'm not some fucking child bride."

Fists clenched at her sides, she whirls around and inches forward. Revulsion radiates off her like a cloud of poison. The love and adoration she so easily gives my siblings is nowhere in sight. All I see when Priscilla Graves glares at me is hatred, disgust and regret.

Distracted, I fail to see her next move. Fail to catch her before her fist makes contact with my cheek.

The burn hits first, radiating from the point of contact. Sharp pain mingles with a dull and constant ache throughout my skull. Incessant ringing, ringing, ringing as I stumble backward and clutch my head. The room spins and wobbles as the backs of my legs hit the bench at the foot of my bed.

"Phoebe, I—"

"Get out!" I scream, then wince as pain pulses behind my eyes.

She clears her throat and squares her shoulders. "Two hours."

"Get. The. Fuck. Out."

Knobs in her hands, she backs out of the room slowly. Doors inches apart, she pauses. "It's past time to grow up, Phoebe. Time to cast aside your feelings and do what's right for this family. Your family."

I meet her dead eyes with my glacial blues. "That's all we are… titles and money." I drop my hand from my face and slowly straighten my spine. "I'd rather die than be Beau Langston's whore." Planting my hands on the bench, I rise to my full height. "I'd rather be *no one* than marry someone for status."

"Too bad it isn't up to you." She cocks a brow. "No one loves you as you are. They love you for who they think you are. And even then, love is a stretch."

She pulls one door shut but keeps her eyes on me as she hammers the last nail in the coffin.

"You're unlovable, Phoebe. Always have been. Always will be."

The door closes with a quiet click, but it might as well be the bullet piercing my heart.

For the next hour, I curl in on myself on the shower floor. Cry and scream and smack the bottom of my fists against the tile. Let it all out and watch as it swirls down the drain.

"You're unlovable, Phoebe. Always have been. Always will be."

If I'm so damn unlovable, why did Delilah message me a dozen times last night?

After ignoring her for over a week, she should hate me. But she doesn't.

I miss you.

It's her final text that wraps itself around my heart and keeps it beating. It's those three words that root in my marrow and make me stronger as I dab makeup on the blooming bruise on my cheekbone. It's the image of her in my mind's eye that reminds me to take my next breath as I dress for the date I never asked for.

Normal first dates involve two people. Alone. At a restaurant. Or perhaps, an intimate setting in public.

But because my mother is insistent and intrusive and iniquitous, my arranged date with Beau is at the Graves estate, in the formal dining room, with not only my parents but also my grandparents. Predinner drinks as an excuse for those with dicks to measure them, while those with vaginas pretend to be enthralled.

After Mother's hook to my cheek, I only have the strength to offer my indifference.

Naturally, Mother has to flaunt the Graves' wealth during my date; that's not really a date. The dinnerware and silverware we generally reserve for flashy holiday events are out on display. Every Graves household employee is on duty—pouring wine and serving food with white gloves on and cowering every time my mother opens her mouth.

Dinner has been much the same as the predinner drinks—schmoozing and bullshit.

Grandfather and Grandmother sit at either end of the lengthy, hand-carved walnut table. Grandfather speaks up on occasion and asks Beau uncomfortable questions, which I quite enjoy. Grandmother plays more of the observer, her scrupulous gaze not missing a thing.

Across the table, Mother sits like she has a stick up her ass, eating the smallest bites with her pinkie stuck out.

Fucking ridiculous.

Father puffs his chest out and plays nice guy to Grandfather's inquisition. But Father isn't fooling me with his good cop to Grandfather's bad cop facade.

When you've been a reporter more years of your life than not, everything you do is with intention. You observe, listen, pick up on every little detail in the room.

My father has always been an incredible journalist. He always saw things others missed. Reported the hard stories and received accolades for stepping outside the box.

So I can't help but wonder why he is okay with this whole charade.

Why would Tobias Graves accept a slimy man like Beau Langston into his fold?

How can he not see who Beau really is? A deceitful weasel, just like his imprisoned sister, with a repugnant taste for illicit activities.

I know Beau's secret. That he's been caught with underage girls. And it makes me sick to my stomach.

Wine glass in hand, I bring it to my lips as conversation around the table quiets. "How's prison treating Kelli?" I take a sip then set my glass down, picking up my fork and moving food around my plate. "Anyone try to shiv her yet?"

Jaw tense and lips in a rigid, flat line, Mother's face reddens. Murderous green eyes pin me in my seat across the table.

I simply cock a brow and move potatoes around on my plate.

Most of my life, I've loved the wealth and status my family and I possess in Stone Bay. For decades, I've flaunted it with my callous nature and expensive attire. Expected people to respect me because my last name entitles me in this town. For years, I saw myself as a goddess amongst the inconsequential townsfolk.

Then I spent time with Delilah.

Without effort or intention, Delilah opened my eyes to the world. She gave me the wake-up call I didn't ask for but desperately needed. She allowed me to see life from a different vantage point without coercion or deception. Let me experience something other than emptiness and bitterness.

Being in this room, sitting with people that are family by blood but don't give a shit about me, has me eager to find the closest escape. Has me anxious to drive across town and bang on Delilah's door.

I am sick of the lies. Exhausted by the constant display of artifice.

All I want is something real. A fulfilling life with someone who sees the real me and wants me to stay.

Obnoxious laughter echoes through the room a beat before a hand lands on my thigh beneath the table. My body turns to stone for one, two, three heartbeats before I blink away the shock, reach beneath the table, and force Beau's hand off my leg.

"Do not touch me," I growl.

This only makes him laugh harder. Adding insult to injury, my entire family joins in on his laughter.

"Kelli is a big girl. I'm sure she has a shiv of her own." The way he makes a joke out of it, the way everyone around the table—with the exception of Grandmother—smiles, as if Kelli being in prison for financial crimes is preposterous and insignificant, makes me nauseous.

I set my fork down and reach for my wineglass again. "Sure. What's a little murder after theft, fraud, and embezzlement?"

"That's enough," Mother scolds. "Mind your manners."

Her gaze shifts to Beau. "Our apologies, Beau. Not sure what's gotten into Phoebe recently."

Tilting my head, I lift the glass to my lips and swallow the last of my wine. I slam the glass on the table, lean forward, reach up and lightly stroke the makeup-caked bruise on my cheek. Heart hammering in my rib cage, I meet the lifeless eyes of my mother.

"What's gotten into *me*? Are you fucking kidding me right now?"

I shove back my chair and rise from the seat, fingers curled into fists at my sides.

"You're such a fucking joke. Just put a price tag around my neck and sell me to the highest bidder." I shake my head. "That's what you really want. To be rid of me." An unladylike snort-laugh escapes and adds fuel to the fire. "And it pisses you off that neither your words nor your fists can beat me into submission."

"Phoebe," Father mutters. "We already discussed this."

I pin him with an arctic glare. "Well, Father, I think we should discuss it every time she hits me. Today was more punch than slap, if you care."

I shift my bitter gaze to Mother.

"I hear orange is in this spring. Maybe we should get you a jumpsuit like Kelli. Emerson owes me a favor."

Neither Travis nor his father owes me anything, but my family doesn't know that.

Right now, Priscilla Graves needs a dose of her own poison. And I'll gladly inject her with every damn drop.

"Tobias," Grandfather growls from his seat at the head of the table. "A word in the parlor."

Without another word, Father and Grandfather exit the dining room.

Beyond done with this evening, this situation, and the

endless bullshit, I spin on my heel and head for the stairs. No one stops my escape. No one follows me to my wing of the house. No one bothers me for the remainder of the night.

And until my eyes grow heavy, I read Delilah's texts over and over.

"Tomorrow, Fox. Tomorrow."

TWENTY-FOUR
DELILAH

"I need something that'll make my husband go all night if you catch my drift."

Oh, I catch your drift, unfortunately.

Plastering on what I hope is a bright, genuine smile, I point toward the display of essential oils. "Let's see what we can conjure up over here." I lead her to the display and sift through the options. Read the labels and pray one or more of them say something about the male libido.

"You youngsters don't have to worry about such things," she says as she studies the oil diffusers. "Losing umph in the bedroom."

Ugh. Please stop.

"In our twenties and thirties, all I had to do was wear a pretty dress or add a spritz of perfume and"—she snaps her fingers—"my Stanley was hard as a rock."

Please, Goddess, help me find this woman some damn erection oil.

"Every decade since our forties, it takes more work to get his soldier at attention."

I pick up a bottle of carpolobia oil and read the label.

Known to affect male sexual performance.

I add it to her basket as she openly and loudly carries on in the store about her husband's penis. The next bottle on the shelf—eurycoma longifolia—is another winner, so I add it to the basket as well. Then I move on to general aphrodisiac scents, ones I'm more familiar with—rose, clary sage, sandalwood, bergamot. And since she is basically sharing her husband's erectile dysfunction with the entire store—and by the end of the week, the entire town—I add all of them to her basket.

"Did you find a diffuser you like?"

"Oh, erm…" She studies them again, then plucks one from the shelf. "This one's nice. Looks like a vase."

"Perfect." I turn on my heel and walk toward the register. "Let's get you checked out and back home to Stanley."

"You've been such a help, dear," she says as we reach Mom at the register. "Aurora, you have the most wonderful family."

Mom takes the items from the handbasket and starts ringing up her purchases. "Thank you, Barbara."

While Mom finishes with Barbara, I take the basket to the stack at the front of the store. Then I do my best to steer clear of Barbara until she exits the building. In the last thirty minutes, I've heard way more than I ever wanted to about Stanley, his penis, and Barbara's obvious need for it. I pray to never see them in town. Ever.

Two or three times a season, Sage Whisperer hosts events to bring in the townsfolk or tourists. With the spring equinox a couple weeks away, today's event is about saying goodbye to winter and preparing for the return of spring, out with the old and in with the new.

As with all the celebrations, Sage Whisperer has a massive influx of patrons. But unlike every event, some gatherings bring out the more eccentric. As spring approaches, those interesting folks always emerge.

"Thank you for putting up with Barbara, my delicate dove." Mom rests a hand on my shoulder as I straighten a shelf of crystals. "I would've taken her had I not been with someone already."

I pat her hand on my shoulder. "Is she always so... vocal about her personal life?"

Mom chuckles. "Yes. Barbara's never had a filter."

A couple enters the store and Mom steps away to greet them. While she informs them of the sales and readings, I weave through the shop and check on the customers that've been browsing a bit. Remind them that Isla starts tarot readings in thirty minutes and Yash starts palm readings in an hour.

As I turn down the next aisle, I spot a lanky man at the opposite end, scanning the store with too much interest. Clothes ill-fitted for his frame, hair disheveled and in need of washing, eyes constantly looking for something or someone, hands twitching at his sides.

Mom and Dad taught us to never judge someone by their appearance. Some of the kindest souls don't give much energy or effort to their outward impression. Some of the wealthiest people don't care to flaunt their abundance. Life is a constant cycle of change. What may be great for one person may be dismal for another. You never know what someone is going through, so it's a best practice to treat everyone equally and with love.

So, I approach the man with an open mind and heart. "Is there something I can help you with today?"

The man startles and shuffles away, his eyes everywhere but meeting mine. "No, no." He gives me his back and walks away. "Was just curious about..." He rounds the end of the aisle and nearly knocks a woman over.

Warning bells go off in my head, an odd twist forming in

my belly.

I follow him as my hospitality shifts to concern. Ducking around the woman at the end of the aisle, I flash her an apologetic smile.

The bell over the door jingles and a burst of fiery-red curls comes into view. The man squeezes past Phoebe and bolts out the door.

"Excuse you," she calls after him. "Asshole." A second later, she spots me and softens. "Hey."

But I don't reply.

Instead, I inch past her and step out onto the sidewalk. Look left then right for the dodgy man, but don't see him on the walkway teeming with eager shoppers. Push up on my tiptoes and look again, coming up empty.

"Everything okay?" Phoebe asks as I walk back inside.

Eyes still on the sidewalk through the door, I nod. "He was just acting strange. Then he bolted." I huff out a breath and turn my attention to Phoebe. "But he's gone, so..."

Store patrons bustle around us, quiet conversation and music and chimes float in the air alongside the faint aroma of ylang-ylang incense. Isla sets up her table for tarot readings. June rings up a customer while Mom chats with another.

The whole world continues to move around us, but we remain utterly still.

Flashes of my drunken texting spree flit in my mind and I inwardly cringe. The string of texts was the blathering work of an inebriated fool, but I meant every one of them. And when I unlocked my nearly dead phone and saw them on the screen yesterday morning, I told myself I would never get drunk again, at least not with my phone nearby.

And since I all but told her I loved her in those texts, the ball is officially in her court.

"Fox, I'm..."

She shoves her hands into her coat pocket, tips her head back, and audibly exhales. Fifteen erratic heartbeats later, she levels me with her gaze.

"I'm sorry," she whispers. "I got sucked into this dark hole looking for that damn card online. Then my parents set me up with Beau Langston."

I jerk back, my heart rapid-firing in my chest as a light sheen of sweat slicks my skin.

Phoebe inches closer and lowers her voice. "I don't want him, Fox." She shakes her head. "And I made it abundantly clear to my family." Hidden by her coat, warm fingers graze my forearm. "I'm not trying to make excuses for the last week and a half." She releases me and steps back. "I got lost in work."

Lost in work.

The words roll around in my head over and over. I'm no stranger to getting lost in something—a project, a great book, a movie marathon. I've had my share of days where I curled up on the couch with a book and didn't come up for air until eight hours later.

But eight hours is vastly different than ten days. And I don't quite know how to feel about it.

Will it always be like this? Will her need for information and the next big story always steal her time?

For nearly a decade, I've been low-key fascinated with Phoebe. Regardless of how she treats me, the invisible, inde-structible thread keeping me bound to her holds strong. And as much as I want the tether to remain intact, I also question if it should.

After knowing what it's like to be hers, even if only a little, is it worth risking my mental health to *stay* hers? A piece of my heart, my soul, says Phoebe will always be worth it. That beneath her callous exterior is a woman who needs someone willing to stand up for and with her.

Now that I've seen her warmth, her fire, her hunger, it's not something I'm sure I can live without.

I open my mouth to ask if we can meet up after my shift but am cut off when the door flies open and Dad walks inside, worry creasing his forehead, his brows, the corners of his eyes.

Unease blankets me as I follow him with my eyes to where Mom is talking with a customer. Dad gives the patron a polite but forced smile, then tips his head to the side when he locks eyes with Mom.

"Delilah," Dad calls, then tips his head for me to follow too. I don't miss the slight stutter in his voice.

"Be right back." I give Phoebe a half-hearted smile before crossing the shop to Dad. "What's going on?"

His expression somewhat composed, he leads us to the doorway between the storefront and the backroom.

"News just came in from the Seven."

Dad averts his gaze, studying every inch of Sage Whisperer before he continues. With the exception of Phoebe, no one pays us any attention.

"There's been another murder," he whispers, barely audible.

A chill blankets me in an instant. My hands and arms tremble at my sides. Folding my arms over my chest, I tuck my fists tight beneath my elbows. My pulse whoosh, whoosh, whooshes in my ears. My lungs burn and remind me to breathe.

Dad continues to speak in soft tones, telling us he'll tell the rest of the family. "Emerson thought maybe they'd moved on. It's been a month of quiet and dead ends."

"Where?" My single-word question comes out scratchy.

"Near the train yard. Northeast corner of the tracks and Obsidian Pass, at the base of the mountains."

I meet Dad's gaze, tipping my head toward Phoebe. "I'm telling her."

Dad glances across the store, where I know Phoebe is intently watching our exchange. He gives a single nod. "Please be careful, little dove." Warm, large hands capture my shoulders a beat before Dad pulls me into his chest. "Whoever this is…" A tremor ripples through him and he hugs me tighter. "They can't find a pattern amongst the women. Please, little dove."

I hug him with equal fervor. "Promise I'll be safe, Daddy."

"Love you"—he kisses my hair—"so much."

"Love you, too."

After a moment of hesitation, Dad releases me and turns to Mom. Framing her face in his hands, he kisses her tenderly. "No one works alone."

She nods.

"You enter and leave in pairs."

Mom covers his hands with hers then rests her forehead on his.

"If anyone looks remotely suspicious…"

"I'll call you and Emerson immediately," she whispers.

"Love you, baby."

Mom presses a chaste kiss to Dad's lips. "Love you, Auggie."

One foot in front of the other, I remind myself to breathe as I close the distance between me and Phoebe. I meet her gaze and read the awareness in her eyes. Phoebe is no imbecile. Something major has happened and she is on alert.

Swallowing, I tip my head toward the door and walk past her for the sidewalk. The cool, early March air paints my exposed skin, but it is nothing compared to the bone-deep chill that's settled in my marrow. A few feet out of the store, a warm hand wraps around my bicep and stops me.

"What happened?"

I move to the storefront window, out of foot traffic and earshot. Looking up and down the sidewalk, my stomach cramps at the thought it could be anyone on this sidewalk killing people. Maybe it's the man from the bar. Or perhaps the dodgy man from earlier.

"Fox." Phoebe grabs my shoulders and gives me a slight shake. "You're freaking me out."

I lift my gaze to hers, my chin wobbly. "Another murder."

Phoebe instantly stands taller. Her worried gaze drifts from mine to the pedestrians and assesses everyone within eyeshot. "Where?"

"Train yard," I mutter. "Mountain foothill, north of the tracks."

"We should go. Now."

I reach for and clutch the sleeve of her coat, my head shaking. "Something about this one feels different." I tug her closer. "And I can't leave. Not until the end of my shift." The backs of my eyes sting. "You shouldn't go alone."

"We're in too deep." Her brows cinch together. "I have to go. The cops will be there. I won't be alone."

"Still don't like it."

"Meet me there. After your shift."

The cramp in my stomach twists and churns and has me on the cusp of puking. "I don't—"

"Please, Fox." Phoebe inches close. Too close for public. "Can't do this without you."

Of all the people I should cave for, Phoebe Graves should not be one of them. Every time I give in to my feelings or her persuasion, I end up on the losing end.

Yet, I still submit to her.

Time after time, I surrender to whatever Phoebe asks or wants. Even when I know it's the wrong decision.

"Okay." I relent. "I'll text you just before I leave."

The most genuine smile to grace Phoebe's lips shines back at me. With a wink, she steps back, pivots, and dashes for her car.

As for me, I'm a swirl of fear, panic, excitement, and confusion, standing alone on the sidewalk for the whole town to see.

TWENTY-FIVE
PHOEBE

THE FIRST SET OF FLASHING LIGHTS APPEARS ON THE NORTH SIDE of the four-way stop at Bloodstone and Obsidian. An officer stands beside his parked car blocking northbound traffic, large paper cup from Beyond Beans in one hand, his cell phone in the other as he mindlessly scrolls.

I ease off the brake and steer the car left, mentally crossing my fingers that he'll ignore my car. But the moment my tires aim north on Obsidian, his sunglasses-covered eyes leave his phone and meet mine through the windshield. Stowing his phone in his pocket, he steps farther into the street and blocks me from driving past.

Foot on the brake, I plaster on my best reporter smile and roll down the window as he approaches.

"Road's closed, Ms. Graves."

I twist and lean out the window slightly. Rake my eyes down his frame and arch a brow on the way up. Give a subtle smirk when my eyes meet his again. "You and I both know the road isn't closed…" I glance at the last name on his tag. "Officer Sumner."

With a cock of his head, his lips bunch as if fighting off

laughter. "This flirting act of yours"—he waves in front of me —"may work with other guys." He shakes his head. "But it does nothing for me."

"I wasn't flirting." *I was flirting.* "I was simply appreciating the fine officers of Stone Bay."

A snort of laughter rips from his throat. "When I was posted here, they warned me you'd show up. I may be new to Stone Bay and the department, but I've been apprised of the founding families and the lengths some go to for a story."

Sitting forward in my seat, I stare out the windshield at the sea of red and blue lights. Stare at the gateway to the next clue in a case that needs to be closed.

Do I want to write the best damn story of my life centered around this serial killer? You bet your ass I do. To finally be recognized as someone more than a nosy journalist or the youngest child of Tobias and Priscilla Graves is all I've wanted for years. To be seen more for my talents and less for the surface-level bullshit I inherited, it feels like a desperate dream.

And this prick of a cop... I won't let him rob me of what's mine.

This man thinks he knows me because his fellow officers *warned* him. He doesn't know shit.

Eyes forward, jaw set, I let the acid in my voice do all the talking. "I tried playing nice, Sumner." I turn my head and glare through his dark lenses. "But playtime is over." My nostrils flare as I grip the base of the steering wheel. "Be a good boy and let me pass..." I tilt my head and ease a brow up. "Or I'll have your job by tomorrow morning."

Thick arms across his chest. "Are you threatening me, Ms. Graves? I doubt Chief Emerson takes kindly to blackmail, especially of an officer."

Smug smile firmly in place, I shake my head. "And I've

known the chief since I was in diapers, little boy. He may detest manipulation, but he has secrets like the rest of the Seven." My smile widens as his frame starts to cave. "And the thing about we Seven… no matter how much we despise one another, no matter what slimy shit happens behind our closed doors, we protect each other first."

I turn and face forward once more.

"If you'd like to keep your cozy job in our quaint little town, I suggest you let me pass. Now."

"Fuck," he mutters.

Good boy.

"Oh." Lifting a hand, I point his way. "Almost forgot. In a bit, my friend Delilah is meeting me here." I peek at him from the corner of my eye. "Delilah Fox. Another of the Seven. Long black hair, cute nose, drives a blacked-out MINI Cooper." Tipping my head his way, I wink. "Be a good boy and let her pass too."

The muscles of his jaw flex in obvious irritation. "Anything else?" he grits out.

Good to see I haven't lost my touch. "That's it for now." I roll up my window, dismissing him.

He takes a few steps back and gestures for me to pass on the southbound lane.

I steer around his police cruiser and eat up the distance to the train yard in no time. Several yards back from the station building, cop cars line either side of the street—Stone Bay police and county officer vehicles—a few denoting K-9 units.

I park on the shoulder. Fetching my phone and fob, I exit the car and trek the rest of the way on foot. Though the actual crime scene is a half mile or more away, I scan every inch of earth between my car and the body. Look for the slightest clue, anything remotely out of place.

The train yard isn't a place often visited by residents, with the exception of those who work here or businesses picking up supply orders. Most of what comes through here is lumber, stone, and farming supplies. The transportation method is somewhat antiquated with all the other available options, but Stone Bay, along with several other towns and cities in the region, still uses the rail system. So it stays.

As I near the tracks, dogs bark in the distance. An officer looks over the shoulder of another as I approach, indignation hardening the line of her jaw and set of her eyes.

"Ms. Graves, you need to leave."

Squaring my shoulders, I lift my chin. "Hmm. Let me think about it." I tap a finger to my chin. "No."

"This isn't a game, Phoebe." Stepping around the other officer, she comes toe to toe with me. "Turn around and leave." Her voice is sharp. Lethal.

But I don't bow to the likes of her.

Crushing the toe of her boots with the red sole of my heels, I peer down my nose at her. "Respect your founders, officer." I gift her my fuck-you smile. "Best you step back and remember who you're speaking to." I crowd her further. "Besides, I've been working with Officer Emerson to catch this killer. You know, since you all seem incompetent to do so."

Her nostrils flare as she inches away. "Fucking bitch," she mutters.

Cocking my head, I lift a hand to my ear. "Sorry. What was that?"

She returns my fuck-you smile with one of her own. "I said, let me walk you to the crime scene."

I pat her shoulder like a dog. "That's what I thought I heard."

Obedient but pissed off, she leads me to the fourth murder victim in four months in our small town. Gravel crunches beneath our shoes as we cross the tracks. Within seconds, the evergreen canopy shades us from the sun. And with each step forward, with each twig snap, the energy around us morphs from distressed to frantic.

Dozens of uniformed officers and K-9s crowd the base of the mountain. Chatter and commands bounce off the stone and echo through the woods as they capture hundreds of photos and sift through tree debris on the ground. Bright-yellow crime scene tape screams not to pass. EMTs stand off to the side, a large black bag empty and waiting on a gurney.

"No." Travis storms between the trees, his K-9 at his side. "Not today, Phoebe."

"Good luck," my escort singsongs as she walks off.

"I'm not leaving, Travis." My hands go to my hips. "Let me help."

"This isn't a game." He stops a foot away and peeks over his shoulder briefly. "This isn't some fiction piece for the Gazette."

"Have I published anything about the murders in the paper?"

A low growl rumbles in his throat as his jaw rocks side to side.

"No, I haven't. And I won't. Not until we catch this psycho."

"*We?*" He shakes his head. "There is no *we*, Phoebe."

"I'm not leaving," I repeat. "I've been on this case as long as you. I've invested just as many hours looking for answers." My hands fall to my sides. "Let me be a part of this. Let me help," I all but beg. "I'll stay out of everyone's way."

Knee bouncing, he tips his head back and groans. I take it as a good sign.

"Who knows?" I continue to push. "I may think of something you don't."

He lowers his chin and levels me with a narrowed gaze.

I tap my temple. "Reporters don't think like cops. We're trained to dig until we find what we want."

Sheer annoyance mars his expression as he folds his arms over his chest.

With a roll of my eyes, I clarify. "Meaning, everything isn't black and white to us. We aren't bound by the same rules as you. If we need to commit felonious acts to get what we want" —I shrug—"we do what it takes."

A literal growl fills the air. "I did not just hear that."

"Hear what?"

On a heavy exhale, he jabs his hands my way. "Not a word, Phoebe."

I mentally throw my arms up and do a little victory jig.

"You stick with me and don't share a damn thing about this with anyone."

I wince. "Erm…"

Travis huffs. "What?"

"Delilah's meeting me here after work."

"Fox?" His brows bend inward. "Why?"

"Aurora thought it'd be good for us to work together. To help catch whoever this is faster."

"For fuck's sake." Travis pinches the bridge of his nose. "Anything else?"

"Nope."

Travis pulls out his phone, types on the screen, then pockets it again. Lifting the crime scene tape, he steps back, saying something in another language, and the K-9 at his side stands taller. "Told the officers to let Dee Dee through." He drops the tape and dips his chin to the dog. "This is Pepper. Do not talk to her. Do not touch her. She's a working officer. Understood?"

"Like I want anything to do with your dog."

Travis walks ahead, leading the way toward another life

lost at the hands of some lunatic. Several sets of eyes bounce between Travis and me as we approach, no one speaking up and asking why I'm in the middle of the crime scene. Irritation evident in the way they stare me down; I simply smile and continue forward.

Smug and confident as I am, nothing prepares me for the sight on the forest floor.

Bare, translucent skin slashed viciously across her breasts, her belly, her thighs. Substantial bruises in the shape of hands on her upper arms and around her throat. Long black hair fanned out around her head. Ghostly white eyes open, staring up to the heavens.

Upon first glance, she bears a resemblance to Delilah. But I shake off the thought, knowing I left Delilah less than an hour ago, safe and well and whole.

I dig my phone from my pocket.

"No photos or video," Travis orders.

Shaking my head, I turn my phone toward him and show him the open notepad. "Just taking notes."

"Yuki Takahashi."

I lift my gaze to his. "What?"

Travis dips his chin toward the woman. "The victim. Her name is Yuki Takahashi. She's a trail guide in town."

My fingers fly over the screen, typing every detail Travis shares.

"Her girlfriend came into the station this morning and reported her missing." His jaw works back and forth. "SBTG said her last scheduled hike was five days ago. They also said it wasn't abnormal for her to go back out on her own after a guided hike and camp for the night."

"When did the girlfriend last hear from her?"

"After the guided hike." Travis inhales a deep breath. "Told her she'd be home early the next morning."

"But the girlfriend didn't report it until today?"

Why wait so many days? Seems odd. Especially if it didn't match her routine and she specified when she'd return.

He nods. "The girlfriend tried finding her on her own. Checked all her usual trails, but came up empty. Called her several times, but it went straight to voice mail." He sighs. "She assumed Yuki was too far out and had poor cell reception."

"So who found her? Not like this is a normal place for people to wander."

Travis points to the woman's hand and it's then that I notice a finger missing. "Station manager called. Said he found what looked like the tip of a finger on the tracks during routine walks of the rails."

Bile climbs up my throat. "Find anything else?"

"Not yet." He shifts his attention to my profile. "Want to search with us?" He gestures between him and Pepper. "There're a couple pieces we have yet to find that've been at the other crime scenes."

This is the first time I've been at a crime scene early on. The first time I'd been welcomed—well, forcibly welcomed—into the fold. As intense and overwhelming as the situation is, I refuse to waste this opportunity. I refuse to leave here without something tangible or new to guide us closer to finding this maniac.

With a wave of my hand, I say, "Lead the way."

And until Delilah arrives, Travis, Pepper, and I scour every inch of earth surrounding the crime scene.

TWENTY-SIX

DELILAH

On the shoulder behind Phoebe's SUV, I throw my car in park and stare at the countless police vehicles.

The last time I saw an officer from the county sheriff's department was during the town's centennial festival fifteen years ago. Emerson was worried the abundance of visitors would be too much for the local police to handle, so he requested county assistance.

Not even the heinous murder of a sixteen-year-old girl when I was in kindergarten garnered outside aid. Day and night, they searched for the person responsible. Barrels of coffee and an endless supply of food and support from the townsfolk kept them going until the killer was caught. Still, no one but the Stone Bay police worked the homicide.

Mom and Dad taught me hard lessons that year. Though we always look for the good in every person and situation, we aren't naive.

"There's love and light in everyone, little dove," Dad says. "But every once in a while, darkness has a way of taking someone's light. It isn't our place to learn why or to judge them. We guard ourselves

from their darkness, hope they find peace, and let the town protectors do their job."

With the number of cops on scene, it's obvious the recent string of murders in Stone Bay is too much for local law enforcement. In a matter of months, our small town went from charming and happy to horrific and bleak. Worst of all, the majority of the residents remain in the dark.

I exit the car, pull my phone from my pocket, and shoot off a text to Phoebe.

> I'm here. Where are you?

Eyes on the screen, I head for the tracks and station house.

> About a quarter mile past the tracks. Base of the mountain.

> Give your name to anyone and they'll show you the way.

Not once have I doubted Phoebe's ability to persuade people. But coercing the entire local and county police departments on scene to do as she says is impressive. And kind of hot.

I react to her message with a thumbs-up, shove my phone in my pocket, and trudge forward.

After some muttered curses by the police at the train station hub, a female officer from the county leads me to the swarm of law enforcement at the foot of the mountain. I thank her, cross under the bright-yellow tape, and tread lightly as I search for Phoebe.

"Fox."

I whip my head left and spot Phoebe several feet away. Eyes constantly darting between her and the ground, I weave around trees and make my way to her. Travis and Pepper meet us in the middle, frustration and exhaustion written in the lines of his face.

Travis catches me up on the situation, omitting the gore. "Right now, we're just searching for the same evidence we've found at the other crime scenes."

"Religious figure card," Phoebe states.

"And one other piece." For a beat, Travis looks smug. As if it brings him pleasure that Phoebe didn't know there was additional evidence at each murder scene. But then his self-satisfaction morphs into a pained wince. "A burned sage bundle."

You have got to be kidding me.

The earth wobbles beneath my feet. My thoughts swirl faster and faster as Travis's words sink in, as it registers that some mentally disturbed person is taking something meant to cleanse and using it for nefarious, despicable acts.

"Do my parents know?" The question is muted and scratchy on my tongue.

Travis nods. "Since the woman near the ski resort." One corner of his mouth tips up in a sympathetic smile. "We asked them not to say anything and to keep an eye on who was buying sage in the shop."

"Oh."

He rests a hand on my shoulder. "We'll talk about it later." Dropping his hand, he exhales an audible breath. "For now, let's find what's here."

Unsure if he feels bad about my lack of insight on the sage situation, Travis divulges details neither Phoebe nor I know about the killings. At each crime scene, they've discovered pieces of the religious figure card and never one fully intact. Their guess is that it's one ripped card and this sicko is leaving puzzle pieces with each body.

After relaying which areas have been combed through, he hands me gloves and a bag in case I find anything.

Phoebe and I map out our patch of earth to search and get to work. Minutes spin into hours as we weed through leaves, twigs and needles on the forest floor. It won't be long before we lose daylight and have to call it quits until tomorrow.

Roughly fifty feet from where the body was discovered, I skirt around a tree and come to a screeching halt. Sitting atop a thick stack of pine needles is a half-burned bundle of sage. A hint of purple flowers visible on one side. A pale-pink strip of cotton wrapped around the base.

Bile claws its way up my throat and burns the back of my tongue.

When Mom first opened Sage Whisperer, the store wasn't as well-stocked with variety as it is now. In the early years, Mom only carried white sage bundles—the most popular. But as time moved on and customers requested more variety, Mom spoke with the small business that supplies our sage bundles. And ever since, Sage Whisperer has offered an assortment of smudge sticks.

Sage Whisperer is the only metaphysical shop in a hundred-mile radius to sell white sage bundled with flowers or herbs. Lavender sprigs, rose petals, statice flowers, rosemary, sweet grass, and several other seasonal varieties. Mom prides herself on offering the town and tourists something no one has available.

The only other difference with our smudge sticks versus others... Mom adds her own touch before they're put on the sales floor. A strip of colorful fabric wrapped around the base three times—for luck—and tied in the perfect bow.

It may be a coincidence, but my gut says it isn't. Whoever is killing these women has been inside Sage Whisperer. They have tainted not only the energy of the store but also the goodness and light we aim to share in the community.

Taking out my phone, I snap a few pictures. Then I pull out the gloves Travis gave me, slip them on, gingerly pick up the sage, and deposit it in the bag. Before I walk off from the tree, I find a large stick and stab it into the ground, marking the location in case Travis needs it.

Inhaling deeply, I peel off the gloves, stow them in my pocket, put one foot in front of the other and continue to search. As my eyes scour the forest floor, my mind sifts through every person I've helped recently in Sage Whisperer. I filter through countless memories of customer interactions and sales, hunting for a single clue as to who this may be.

As my eyes lose focus, I trip over a tree root and stumble forward. I manage to catch myself before I fall face-first onto the ground. Brushing my hands on my thighs, I chastise myself, "Focus, Delilah. Brainstorm later."

And brainstorm, I will. Whatever it takes, I will help find this killer. Whatever it takes, I will not let this crazed lunatic tarnish my family or our business.

Daylight fading more with each passing minute, I wind my way back toward Phoebe and Travis near the tree line. Eyes downcast, treading carefully to not stumble again, I narrow my gaze when something light in color stands out between the leaves and needles.

I dig one of the gloves from my pocket and slip it on. Squatting down, I brush away the foliage. My eyes widen as I take in the torn piece of golden paper.

"Find something?" Twigs and vegetation crunch beneath his feet as Travis approaches.

I nod and pick up the paper, no bigger than my thumb. "A piece of the card, I think." I rise up and pull the bag from my hoodie pocket. "And sage."

Phoebe sidles up to us and we all stare down at the yellow paper. At the bottom, a sliver of golden hair and a halo. Near the top, the edge of a letter followed by "gnes."

"Well, I'm of no help. Religion isn't my strong suit," Phoebe says.

Organized religion isn't my specialty either, but Mom made a point of us knowing bits and pieces from different beliefs as we grew up. Nothing radical. She wanted us to do our own research and feel right about what we chose to put our faith in.

So, while I'm not well-versed in how Christians practice their faith, I do know a thing or two about some of the saints' names. And the only one familiar with those letters is...

"Saint Agnes," I mumble at the same time Travis says, "I think it's Agnes."

Phoebe inches back. "You know who it is?"

I lift my chin and meet her gaze. "Not specifically, but I remember seeing the name years ago during research."

Dropping the piece in the bag, I hand it to Travis. He stabs a small flag on a metal skewer into the ground to mark the location. The three of us walk toward the tracks and out of the tree canopy. Phoebe pulls out her phone and taps on the screen several times. By the time we hit the tracks, she vibrates with excitement.

"Saint Agnes, also known as Agnes of Rome, is—you'll love this—the patron saint of girls, *chastity, virgins*, victims of sexual abuse, and gardeners." Phoebe hums. "Last one seems odd next to the rest." She shakes her head but keeps reading. "Her feast day is January twenty-first."

Travis and Phoebe freeze.

Phoebe looks to him, her brows tugging together as her eyes lose focus. With a blink, she snaps out of her momentary daze. "Wasn't there a murder in the third week of January?"

Though the victim in January was the second woman discovered, maybe the killer was *warming up* for their crime spree.

"Jesus fucking Christ." Travis closes his eyes, takes a deep breath, then opens them on the exhale. "Yeah. Was called in on the twenty-third." He tips his head toward the crowd of officers near the station house. "C'mon. We need to clue them in."

The sun dips below the horizon as Travis relays the news of what we found on the ground and on the internet. With less reluctance, several officers thank us for our assistance and perspective.

As we trek back to our cars, I nudge Phoebe with my elbow. "Takeout and case talk at my place?"

Phoebe glances over her shoulder, her eyes roaming our surroundings for one, two, three steps.

I startle when her hand finds mine and pulls me to a stop. In the middle of the dimly lit street, she inches closer, takes my chin in her other hand, lifts it up, and drops her lips to mine.

Stunned, I don't immediately kiss her back. But it's when her tongue swipes the seam of my lips that I'm jolted back to life. I part my lips, fist the front of her coat, drag her closer, and match her fire with my own.

All too soon, she breaks the kiss. "Your place sounds perfect." She hooks her arm with mine, turns, and starts walking again. "Now for the hard question."

Still high from the kiss, my thoughts are in the clouds. "Hard question?"

Phoebe chuckles. "Pizza or sushi?"

I laugh. "Why not both?"

TWENTY-SEVEN

PHOEBE

EVENTS OF THE DAY FLIT THROUGH MY MIND AS I POP SOY-SAUCE-dipped salmon sashimi in my mouth.

Witnessing a crime scene from the near start is both a rush and horrific.

Never will I be able to unsee Yuki Takahashi's defiled, lifeless body. Undoubtedly, it will haunt me for years to come. Her ghostly eyes. The rage-inflicted slashes on her skin. How impossibly still she lay on the earth.

Never will I be welcomed into the fold the way I was after persuading Travis to let me and Delilah help. He fought me tooth and nail. Gave as good as I did, but his exhaustion got the better of him, and he caved.

At this point, a fresh perspective of the evidence may be what's necessary to crack this killing spree.

And, fingers crossed, never will I be regarded as only a callous bitch hungry for a story.

Yes, I'm still a bitch. But in the past couple of months, it's been on a case-by-case basis, which is new. Yes, I'm still champing at the bit for the story of a lifetime. But not as I was before the serial killer waltzed into Stone Bay.

This killer has left a permanent scar on the town. Once the news is out, residents will either get as far from Stone Bay as possible or band together and be more vigilant over the town they love and call home.

But I'd be a moron to not credit how this killer has impacted my life. Thankfully not firsthand, but definitely in an indirect capacity.

Had this person not stumbled in and wreaked havoc, I wouldn't be sitting cross-legged on the floor beside Delilah, eating sushi and pizza, and studying every detail about St. Agnes. And I wouldn't know what it means to have someone in your corner. A true champion of me as a whole.

In her eyes, I'm not some legacy or socialite or goddess among commoners. For some mystical reason, Delilah sees something no one else does. Goodness. A virtuousness I'm not so sure exists. Not that it matters what I believe. All that matters is what she holds true.

Delilah as an ally is the best high I've experienced in… well, ever. The way she regards me, it's incomparable. Most townsfolk don't take the time to look beneath the surface. If they did, they'd see I have just as many bruises and scars as they do.

But Delilah… the way she looks at me sometimes… I've never felt something so real and pure and addictive.

"Do you think all the women attended church?" Delilah mumbles around half a slice of pizza in her mouth. "Or maybe it's because they *didn't* go to church."

I blink out of my reverie, pop another piece of sushi in my mouth, and shake my head. "Don't think that's it," I say after I swallow. Pointing at my laptop screen, I continue. "Sure, whoever's killing these women leans on religion. Why else would they use sage—something that represents cleansing and purification—and intentionally leave pieces of a religious figure—one known for chastity—at each scene?"

"So we shouldn't heavily rely on the religious aspect?"

My eyes drift to the spread-out papers on either side of my laptop on the coffee table. One by one, I study the small images of the women before their demise. Young, all in their mid-to-late twenties. Beautiful, uniquely so, with vibrant smiles as they stare at the camera. From different walks of life —one clawing her way up from the bottom, another at the height of her career. A lifetime of possibilities at their feet.

At this point, from what I see in black and white, they only have two things in common. All women. All young adults.

"What're we missing?" I scoot closer and sweep my legs under my butt. Stare down at the facts—birthdays, relationship statuses, street addresses. "What ties them together?"

"Is it possible they have nothing in common?"

I suppose if you're a serial killer, you don't have to have one set-in-stone motive other than killing people.

No degrees hang on my wall for detective work or police academy attendance, so I don't have the same rigorous training. But I did grow up in the shadow of truth-seeking journalists. I did spend years at college learning the ins and outs of being a good reporter.

I may not wear a star-shaped badge or carry firearms on my belt, but my pursuit of the truth is equally fierce. And I'll stop at nothing to find this truth.

My brows bend in as my eyes lose focus. Falling back against the couch, I shift my attention to Delilah.

"What if it's not the victims we should be focusing on?"

Delilah tilts her head, confusion written in the lines of her face.

Tipping my head back, I press my fingers to my temples. "What if something happened to the killer?"

I level my gaze with Delilah's gunmetal blues and soak in her curious stare. Badly as I want to lose myself in those hypnotic, stormy eyes, now is not the time.

"What if the killer is a victim of someone else's crime and decided to take it out on others as, I don't know, revenge?"

"Revenge?"

Lips pursed, I shrug. "Someone wronged the killer in the past. Maybe that someone died. Maybe they're rotting in jail. But our serial killer isn't satisfied, so they're taking it out on others?"

Her head teeters side to side as she mulls over the idea. But when Delilah gives me an unconvinced smile, I have my answer.

"I don't know a lot about killers and how they choose victims. But if Skylar's obsession with serial killer documentaries taught me anything, it's that it's always personal. Somebody abused or deceived them. Maybe put them in a precarious position. But at some point, they had no control. No one listened. No one helped. Not until it was too late. So, this is their way of assuming and taking back control." The corners of her mouth turn down. "Or maybe they saw someone else take a life and connected with it. Maybe committing the act gives them this sense of… euphoria."

She picks up an uneaten pizza crust and taps it on the edge of the box. I drop my gaze to her fingers and get lost in the repetitive sound for a moment. Let my eyes lose focus as my mind plugs in these new tidbits.

"The St. Agnes card means something to the killer," Delilah continues. "Maybe the victims confessed something the killer deems sacrilegious. Perhaps they did something the killer deems sinful. If each crime scene has a piece of the St. Agnes card, the killer must think each woman went against what St. Agnes represents."

"Chastity, virginity…"

"Purity."

Holy shit. I whip my head up and meet Delilah's waiting stare. "What if we've been looking at all the wrong people?"

Delilah narrows her eyes, uncertain as to my line of thinking. "I don't follow."

"Reports show the first three women weren't sexually assaulted."

"Okay…"

"Only one was in a relationship."

"Yuki Takahashi."

I nod. "But Yuki was as equally independent as the other women. Maybe more so." Even in a relationship, she went off on her own for days at a time, according to her girlfriend.

"Still not connecting the same dots as you."

Energized by this possible revelation, I sit taller. "What if the killer isn't a man?" I inch closer to Delilah and grab both her shoulders. "Who enacts revenge or spite or hostility better than a woman?"

Delilah's eyes go wide as this possibility sinks in. "You make some valid points, and I want to be on board with this…"

"But…"

"The bodies were moved. No traces of blood, other than what was on the bodies, were at any of the crime scenes."

"You saying a woman couldn't have moved them?"

She shakes her head. "Of course not."

"Then what are you saying?"

Delilah looks over my shoulder, her mind elsewhere as she figures out how to voice her thoughts. But I see the moment it all snaps into place.

Her pupils dilate a beat before she shifts her gaze back to mine. "The slashes and bruises. A clear sign this person is angry. Stripping each woman of her clothes, but not sexually violating them…"

I reach for the length of Delilah's hair and toy with the strands.

"It's like they want the victims to be humiliated. Even in death."

My eyes drop to my fingers in Delilah's hair. Warmth blooms from the center of my chest from the contact, from the way her wisdom, her insight, turns me on. Badly as I want to give into the feeling, I stow it momentarily.

"Summing it up…" Thrill courses through me at this new revelation. "Possible woman with anger issues and a big knife. Not deviant because she believes women should remain pure —whatever that means. Kills victims somewhere else, then moves them. But maybe she doesn't work alone. And for some reason, she leaves them naked in the woods to potentially humiliate them."

"Maybe…"

My fingers drift higher in her hair, grazing her collarbone. Lips slightly parted, she stops breathing.

"Everything is so…" She pauses when I trace the hollow of her throat. "Clean."

"Clean?" I brush her hair from her shoulder.

Swallowing, she nods. "The cuts are vicious, but the bodies aren't covered with as much blood as they should be."

My eyes dart to hers, the pads of my fingers slowly trailing the column of her throat. "Maybe another form of purity?"

Delilah's breaths come in sharp bursts. "Maybe."

"Should go back to the church tomorrow."

Her eyes roll back. "Mmm-hmm."

I lean in, ready to take her mouth with mine but stop a breath away. For whatever shitty reason, last night comes barreling back in. My rib cage tightens in my chest and steals the breath from my lungs.

Smoky blues latch onto my icy blues, soft fingers curling around my wrist. "What's wrong?" The words are so delicate, so warm.

"Sorry to ruin the moment." Every cell in my body urges me to pull back from Delilah, but I remain rooted in place. Connected physically to the only person who makes me feel remotely whole. I tighten my hold at the nape of her neck.

"Never apologize for not doing something you're not ready for."

"It's not that." Fingers still on her skin, I drop my chin to my chest, uneasy looking her in the eyes as the next words leave my lips. "My parents forced a date on me last night. With Beau."

"They forced you?"

In this day and age, the notion seems far-fetched, but I nod.

"Look at me, Phoebe." When several breaths pass without me following through, she adds, "Please."

Inhaling a shaky breath, I slowly lift my gaze to hers. What I assume I'll see and what I'm met with are two polar opposites.

"Talk to me."

"It's fucking stupid, and I handled it, but you should know."

"That your parents are trying to set you up with Beau?"

"Were," I annunciate. "They *were* trying to set me up with him."

"Okay."

I jerk back an inch. "Okay?"

"Let me rephrase." Dainty fingers clutch my shirt. "What they're doing is far from okay. But Phoebe"—she leans in and eliminates some of the space I created between us—"I believe you when you say you handled it."

"You do?"

Her knees bump mine as she nods.

She believes me. She believes in *me.*

My fingers at the nape of her neck grip harder a beat before I haul her forward and crush my mouth with hers. For three erratic heartbeats, Delilah doesn't react. She simply lets me bruise her lips in a bone-searing kiss. The longer she remains frozen, the faster my mortification takes over.

As I'm about to break the kiss and bolt for the door, she sucks in a breath, tugs me impossibly closer by the shirt, and matches my intensity.

Hot and wet and hungry, Delilah kisses me like a starved woman. But I'm just as ravenous. Just as desperate. Just as greedy for her touch, her mouth, her bare, soft skin beneath my fingers. And I tell her as much in the kiss.

Then she shoves my shoulders, my back crashing into the couch. Legs on either side of mine, she frames my face with her hands and crawls onto my lap. With one hand at the nape of her neck, my other drifts around her waist, thrusts her into me, and pins her body to mine.

Time slips away as she gives and takes and stirs this insatiable hunger between my thighs.

And then her lips are gone. Her weight eases from my lap as she stands. I peek up at her, an inkling of that mortification seeping back in. But when she takes a step back and offers her hand, the dread vanishes.

I slip my hand in hers and rise. The corners of her mouth curve up in a tender smile before she turns and faces the hall.

Food and files and the world forgotten, Delilah leads me to her bedroom. She leaves the door open. She leaves the lights on. And then she pulls me back into her.

TWENTY-EIGHT
DELILAH

Am I ready for this? To take Phoebe to my bed and turn one of my countless fantasies into reality?

The fire blazing beneath my skin, the jagged breath in my lungs, and the fitful beat of my heart all scream yes in unison. They howl that it's about damn time.

But… my mind has yet to get fully on board with the idea. It's my mind that circles in an endless loop, asking if this is something Phoebe really wants or if she's just going with the flow.

The buzz from wandering the crime scene still filters through my veins. Without a doubt, Phoebe is high from the day too.

Are her lips on my lips a mere side effect of that high? Are her fingers in my hair and at my waist because that heightened thrill still courses through her?

Or does she want this? Does Phoebe want me?

"Stop thinking, Fox," she mumbles against my skin.

Her lips wrap around the pulse point beneath my ear and suck. It's a direct shot to my core. A switch flipped on and cranked up. One distinct move that shoves away every doubt. An action that brings every single second into hyperfocus.

On my next breath, my fingers are in Phoebe's hair, tugging at the roots and hauling her mouth back to mine. Fire lights beneath my breastbone and spreads throughout my body. Every point of contact spurs me on. Drives me wild. Has me desperate for more. Of her lips on my lips. Of her body pressed firmly against mine. Of her hands in my hair, on my face, tracing my curves.

I tear my mouth away, reach for the bottom hem of her shirt, and shove it up her body. She mimics the move and tosses my shirt on the floor. Both in bras and pants, we stand motionless and study each other's exposed skin.

Part of me waits for reality to kick in for Phoebe. Part of me anticipates the moment her mind catches up and she shuts down.

But Phoebe surprises me at every turn.

She reaches for her waist, releases the button on her slacks, drags the zipper down, and ever so slowly pushes the fabric lower on her thighs. The material pools at her feet as she stands a little less confidently before me. Vulnerable is not a word I'd typically associate with Phoebe, but right now, she is more exposed with me than ever.

And it makes me want her more.

I step into her, lift a hand and trace the soft skin along her collarbone with my fingertips. Goose bumps erupt on her skin as my fingers drift down her side, over the outer swell of her lace-covered breast, the slight dip of her waist, the supple flare of her hip.

Her breaths come in uneven bursts. Her chest rises and falls faster and faster.

As much as I want to peel away her matching lacy undergarments, I tamp the urge, but only for a moment.

Unfastening my jeans, I shimmy them down my thighs and kick them away.

I don't miss the way Phoebe's icy blues darken. Don't miss the way her eyes dilate, hands twitching at her sides. But before she reaches for me and mirrors my action, trailing her fingers over my skin, I reach back and unclasp my bra.

Ever so slowly, the straps slide down my arms and the material falls away. Nipples pert, my small breasts fully exposed, I lock my gaze on Phoebe's face. Watch as her breathing changes and becomes unsteady. Get more turned on as her eyes refuse to look anywhere but at my breasts.

Arousal soaks my panties as I take one breath, then another, and reach for the waistband of my panties. Inch by painstaking inch, I send the fabric down my thighs until it falls on its own to the floor.

Completely bare, I remain rooted in place. Give Phoebe a chance to absorb this moment. Give her a chance to think of her next move. Let her decide what happens next.

With a lick of her lips, she swallows. Her eyes do one last perusal before lifting to meet and hold mine. "I want to touch you."

Restless energy flutters beneath my diaphragm as my heart pounds a vicious rhythm. I inch closer to her. "I want you to touch me," I choke out, the words barely audible.

Slight shake to her hand, Phoebe reaches for me. For a moment, time slows down. The seconds it takes for her fingers to reach my skin is an eternity. My body vibrates with need, thrumming with insatiable hunger. The moment her fingers graze the subtle swell of my breast, I exhale a breath I didn't realize I was holding.

A wave of goose bumps erupts across my skin. Her touch is soft, barely there, but I feel it everywhere. Her fingers do a slow dance as they trail the curve of my breast and then sweep up to circle my nipple. Her delicate touch has me clenching my thighs, my arousal a slick puddle on my skin.

"So soft," she whispers as her fingers drift to my other breast and repeat the same torturous act. "Except here." The corners of her mouth tip up slightly as her finger loops around my hard nipple over and over.

"Phoebe." Her name is a litany on my tongue.

Undiluted carnality stares back at me as Phoebe meets my hooded gaze. With a modest tilt of her head, I see something I never expected from her.

Yearning.

And before my mind catches up with reality, Phoebe's fingers track down my midline, past my navel, and lower. Instinctually, I spread my legs as her fingers toy with the small tuft of hair on my mound. So damn close to where I want her touch, but not nearly close enough.

I don't move. Don't breathe. Don't speak.

I simply wait.

My hands twitch at my sides, eager to touch her, to peel off her bra and panties, to feel her skin beneath the pads of my fingers. But I keep them at my sides and let her explore my body.

And I don't have to wait long for her next move.

Hesitant fingers drift lower and slide easily between my soaked thighs. Her lips part, eyes dilating further as a low moan spills from deep inside her.

"I make you this wet, Fox?" Her question has an edge to it.

"Yes," I breathe out.

Her fingers glide through my pussy lips once, twice, a third time before stopping on my clit. She steps into me, crowds me, pushing me back until my knees hit the mattress. And then her fingers swirl around my clit again and again with the perfect amount of pressure.

The corner of her mouth twitches. "Do you think of me when you touch yourself, Fox? When you tease your clit and finger fuck your pussy, do you imagine it's my fingers?"

The number of fantasies I've had over the years, Phoebe was the star in too many to count. The only time Phoebe wasn't front and center was when I dated Blu and shortly thereafter.

A breathy moan slips from my lips. "Yes."

I widen my stance further. Grip her biceps, lean in, and give her my weight. Part my lips and breathe heavier.

With methodical strokes, Phoebe sparks a fire low in my belly. Drives me closer and closer to the edge of bliss. My nails bite her skin as her fingers move faster. She grips my hip with her other hand and gives it a punishing squeeze.

One, two, three more circles on my clit and my breaths morph from heavy pants to soft whimpers.

Her hand on my hip drifts up my body, her fingers pausing long enough to tug my nipple before wandering farther and wrapping around my throat.

"You're almost there, aren't you, pretty little Fox?"

"Y-yes."

Phoebe closes in on me, the tip of her nose pressed to mine. She grips my jaw with bruising force and tips my head back. Her breath hot and heady as it paints my lips.

My eyes fall shut as my body climbs higher and higher. And just as I tip over the edge, Phoebe crashes her mouth down on mine.

White noise fills my ears as stars dot my vision. Phoebe's fingers don't stop as my body continues to detonate. I dizzy as one orgasm bleeds into another. I tap her arm and try to move out of her touch, but she keeps me pinned in place, trapped between her and the bed.

Unable to take much more, I fall back on the bed and close

my eyes. Phoebe laughs and says something I can't make out.

When the noise quiets and I feel more myself, I open my eyes. I half expect Phoebe to be dressed or slipping on her clothes. So when I find her naked and waiting, her eyes zeroed in on the junction of my spread thighs, her hands palming her breasts, I reach out a hand.

"Come here."

Her eyes dart to mine a beat before she takes my hand. One of her knees slips between my legs and the mattress dips. A second later, she climbs up my body, drops her hands on either side of my face, and cages me in.

But I want control.

Lifting my legs, I secure them around her waist. With a swift tug of her arm, she falls to the side and I flip her onto her back. Laughter floats through the room as I mount her hips, grab her wrists, and pin her to the mattress.

"My turn, firefly."

She opens her mouth, undoubtedly to ask why I called her firefly, but only a moan rolls off her tongue as I dip and wrap my lips around her nipple.

"Oh, fuck," she hisses as her back arches off the mattress.

With a soft pop, her nipple slips from my lips. I rock forward and lock on to her wanton gaze. "Gonna be a good girl if I let go of your wrists?"

One corner of her mouth tips up. "Define good girl."

"A good girl lets me take over this round."

"What if I want to touch you?" She lifts her hips for emphasis.

"Didn't say you couldn't touch me. Just that I want to be in control." I release one of her wrists and take hold of her chin. "Put your fucking hands on me, Phoebe. Put your fingers in me. But I'm in control for the rest of the night." I lower until my lips are a breath from hers. "Understand?"

A wicked grin curves her lips. "Yes, ma'am."

"Good girl."

I release her other wrist and sit up straight. Roll my hips over her bare mound and slick her with my orgasm. Her hands grip my hips, her eyes zeroed in on my pussy as it skates back and forth over her skin.

It's hypnotic... watching her watch me. Such a simple act, yet it has me ready for her.

Reaching between my thighs, I dip and coat my fingers with a mix of cum and fresh arousal. Her pupils dilate further as her tongue darts out to lick her lips.

Pushing up on my knees a little, I give her a better view. Pump my fingers slowly in and out of my pussy. Circle my clit then slip my fingers back inside myself. And she watches on, completely enthralled.

I pull my fingers out and my pussy all but weeps for more. *Soon.*

Phoebe eyes my slick fingers as I hold them between us. On the next breath, I paint her lips with my glossy fingers. Before I back away fully, she meets my gaze and licks her lips. A sultry moan vibrates her chest and provokes my need for her.

Her lips part as she fists my waist harder and rolls her hips. I lower my hand, ready to paint her lips again, but she surprises me by grabbing my wrist, opening her mouth wider, and wrapping her lips around my fingers.

Mesmerized, I stare down at this fiery vixen, nipples hard and skin pink, as she sucks me off my fingers.

I bend over and take her pebbled nipple between my lips. Suck her flesh as if I'll never have the chance again. Add a little teeth and revel in the slight twitch of her body.

And then I pull my fingers from her mouth. Pay equal attention to her other breast. Knead her tits that barely fit in my palm. Trail my way down her body, kissing and licking and nipping her soft, supple skin.

When I reach her mound, she trembles beneath my touch. I lift my gaze and look up her body. Her eyes are fixed on where I hover over her pussy, a nervous gleam in her icy blues.

"Is this okay?"

Her brows tug together for a split second before she nods.

"Use your words, firefly."

She inhales deeply, then swallows. "It's okay."

The corner of my mouth twitches. "Good." I lick my lips. "Because I've wanted to taste your pussy for a long time."

A guttural moan rumbles in her throat as she slowly draws up her knees and spreads her legs.

The prettiest pink pussy stares back at me, soaked with her arousal and begging to be touched. I trail my fingers down her inner thigh from her knee at a torturous pace. She whimpers the closer I get, adding a little rock to her hips.

I lift my gaze from her mouthwatering pussy to her icy blues. "What do you want first, firefly? My fingers, my mouth, or a toy?"

Phoebe bites her bottom lip. "Your mouth."

Soon as the words leave her lips, I drop between her thighs and taste her for the first time. Salty, tangy, and something distinctly Phoebe hits my tongue. An unbridled moan rumbles in my chest, up my throat, and vibrates between her thighs.

I take my time as I lap at her pussy. Savor each swipe of my tongue over her sensitive flesh. Relish in her ragged breaths and soft whimpers as they fill the room.

But when her fingers slip into my hair and fist the locks, I lose all sense of reality. A switch flips inside me—something animalistic—and I go from gentle, teasing lover to wild, feral beast.

Hooking my arms around her thighs, I tug her impossibly

closer to my mouth. Wrap my lips around her clit and suck the bundle of nerves until her hips buck. Releasing one hip, I run my fingers up and down her soaked center once, twice, and then dip two inside.

Her fingers in my hair curl tighter and pull harder. Pain ripples across my scalp, my eyes begin to water, but I don't let up. If anything, it spurs me on more. Makes my fingers pump faster and mouth tease harsher.

The pitch of her cries changes as her thighs shake on either side of my face. Her walls tighten around my fingers and I know she's close. So damn close.

I curl my fingers inside her and add a little more speed to her clit. Seconds later, she spasms around my fingers as she all but rips the hair from my head. Her orgasm drenches my hand, but I don't let up. Not yet. I drag out her orgasm as long as she'll let me.

Light laughter floats through the room as Phoebe's entire body jerks beneath my hands and mouth. She frees my hair and pushes at my head.

"I-I can't…" She shoves a little harder. "You're k-killing me, Fox."

With a quiet pop, I release her. Slipping my fingers out, I sit back on my haunches and bring my fingers to my lips. Stick out my tongue and suck her orgasm off my fingers.

"Mmm." I glance down at her glistening pussy for a beat before meeting her dopey gaze. "Better than I imagined."

Phoebe pushes up on her elbows, reaches for me, then tugs us both down onto the bed. "I could sleep for a year," she mumbles as she rolls onto her side and drapes one of her legs over my body.

A sense of victory burns in my chest at her words.

By no means am I a virgin—that card went out the window in high school. But I've only had two serious girlfriends. And I wasn't in the habit of hooking up with random people back in the day when I went out with Skylar and Kirsten. Though everyone in the area is open-minded and nonjudgmental regarding who anyone loves, finding another woman to share my bed with was a challenge in Stone Bay.

I may have only had two girlfriends, but we were together for years. We learned from each other.

In college, I got a whole new perspective after visiting lesbian bars and clubs. And after a while, I knew how to find a woman's magic button in a matter of seconds. Though not everyone's magic button is the same, I learned quickly.

In the past, sex hadn't been the hard part. It was the after part that I struggled with.

My first girlfriend, Jenny, never wanted to cuddle. Like ever. And it just made everything cold afterward. My second girlfriend, Blu, was super affectionate. As in, she never wanted to let go. I loved being in her arms, but after more than an hour, I developed a sense of claustrophobia.

Does Phoebe want to cuddle? Or does she want to pass out next to me in the bed?

I gently tap her hip and start to turn away from her. "Come on. Let's shower."

She groans and I laugh.

"Promise we'll crash after."

Lazily, she rolls off the bed and follows me to the bathroom. "Only if you swear." She arches a brow.

I lean in and kiss the tip of her nose. "I'm a woman of my word."

And after a shower that lasts entirely too long because we got lost in each other once more, I turn off the lights before we slip beneath the sheets.

For the first time in years, I'm happy. And it's all because of the woman on my right.

TWENTY-NINE

PHOEBE

I ROLL ONTO MY SIDE AND A HINT OF SANDALWOOD HITS MY NOSE. For a moment, I simply breathe in the scent. Let it soothe and settle me in a way nothing ever has.

Eyes closed, a smile tugging the corners of my lips.

Sad truth… I've never been this happy. Hell, I had no idea what *real* happiness was until Delilah.

My entire life, I've lived in some deceptive bubble created by my parents—more my mother than father—and been told countless lies about what love, joy and truth look like.

Mother hoped I'd be as compliant and arrogant as my older siblings. Not a day exists where she isn't disappointed I'm not. Every soul in Stone Bay can attest to my haughtiness, but it'd be a miracle to find someone who'd say I follow the rules.

As for Father, he just wants someone to carry on his legacy —the Graves name and the Gazette. Praise the invisible deities in the sky that my siblings will both have two-point-five kids. Tiny humans that need constant attention, food and care have never been of any interest. The only baby I want is the paper. So long as I get that, I'll be happy.

Opening my eyes, I tuck a hand beneath my cheek on the

pillow. Inhale another hit of sandalwood and bask in the way her scent relaxes every muscle in my body. And for endless seconds, I take in Delilah's features in the predawn hour.

Her long, black hair lies haphazardly on her pillow. The tattoo on the back of her shoulder—four small birds in flight—peeks out near the curve of her neck. Perfectly manicured brows that draw attention to and highlight her gunmetal blue eyes twitch on occasion as she dreams. Her slender nose with a slight flare at the bottom that leads to my favorite feature... her lips. God, her lips are flawless. Not too thin, not too plump. Absolutely perfect to suck on.

I never pictured myself romantically with a woman. If I'm being honest, I never pictured my future with anyone.

But Delilah... now that I've had her, I want only her. Whenever, wherever, however.

It's always the quiet ones that pull you in. That keeps you hooked. They're the ones you least expect.

Going against every instinct and desire in my body, I turn away from Delilah. Gingerly, I peel off the covers, swing my legs off the side of the bed, and sit up. I reach for my phone on the nightstand and check the time—almost six.

As much as I want to curl up next to and sleep with Delilah for a few more hours, I can't. I need to go home, change clothes, and head to the Gazette. Though I'm not writing any noteworthy stories for publication right now, I do love the resources the paper provides while I research. And with all the things we unearthed yesterday, I have a lot of work ahead of me.

I swipe up my clothes and pad to the bathroom, shutting the door. After some basic morning hygiene, I slip on yesterday's clothes. Then I dig through my bag for paper and my lucky pen and write a note for Delilah.

You're so peaceful when you sleep. I didn't want to disturb your sweet dreams. Going home to change, but I'll be at the Gazette all day. I'll text later.

x

P

I fold the paper in half, scribble *Fox* on the outside, tiptoe back into her bedroom, and set the note on the empty pillow. Easing out of her room, I gather my laptop and the case notes and shove them in my bag. Once I have my shoes on, I slip out the front door, lock the handle, and head for my car.

As always, the town is quiet in the early morning hours. The sporadic car passes me on the road as I drive toward the Graves estate, but most of the town is still asleep. And as my tires eat the miles, I drift back to last night, to my fingers on Delilah's soft skin, to her mouth and hands on so many erogenous zones of my body.

My face hurts from smiling as I put the car in park. But the smile is quickly stolen when I spot another vehicle in the driveway.

"It's too early for this," I mutter as I cut the engine. I leave my bag in the car since I'm only here to change for work.

I walk up the steps, key in my code on the door lock, and enter the house. Not five feet in the door, my mother descends on me—ensemble pressed to perfection and hair impeccably styled—disdain written in the sharp angles of her face.

"Where the hell have you been?"

The bite in her tone grates my nerves, and damn, I want to return every ounce of bitterness with a witty retort.

But like the semi-obedient daughter that I am, I curb my tongue.

"I'm a grown woman, Mother. Curfews and sleeping in my own bed every night don't apply anymore."

Okay, I lied. Much as I want to be the civil, respectable person in this situation, it takes too much work to treat my mother with the respect she hasn't earned.

Her powder-pink Prada pumps clap on the floor as she crosses the room. In three lengthy strides, she's within arm's reach and I'm on high alert.

"This asinine behavior of yours needs to stop. You are a Graves. Not only do you have a duty to this town, you also have family responsibilities. And if you wish to continue living on this estate, you will abide by *my* rules."

Is that a threat?

Sounds more like a challenge. One I gladly accept.

"The only person being ridiculous is you, Mother. And seeing as you married into the Graves name, do you actually have the authority to banish me from the property?"

I tilt my head in challenge. Then I start for the stairs, but she steps in the way.

"I'm warning you, Phoebe."

Gaze straight ahead and not on her, I scoff. "Warning me?" With a shake of my head, I spin to face her. "Do you have nothing better to do with your life other than to ruin mine?" I inch closer to her but prepare to pull back quickly. "God, would it kill you to be nice? To genuinely care?"

Her hand twitches at her side and I take a step back. I slowly shake my head as a hint of sympathy squeezes my chest. And I know the second said pity shows on my face because her expression is pure animosity.

She opens her mouth to lash out but is cut off when Father enters the foyer.

"There you are, darling." Father sidles up to Mother and

kisses her temple. "We were wondering what was taking so long." Father meets my gaze. "Good morning, Phoebe."

I smile but don't feel an ounce of joy. Less than a minute with Mother and every bit of happiness in my life is sucked from my soul.

"Morning."

Another set of shoes claps the floor a moment before Beau rounds the corner. "Ah, there's my girl."

Nausea and rage roil in my belly. "I am *not* your girl," I say with as much venom as I feel. I shift my gaze back to my parents—Father's arm around Mother's waist and Mother looking mightier than she actually is—and give a slow shake of my head. "And you two need to quit trying to force me into something I don't want." Eyes still on my parents, I point at Beau. "Beau and I will never be anything other than acquaintances, and that's being generous." Again, I start for the stairs. "The sooner it sinks in, the better off we'll all be."

Spine straight and shoulders back, I ascend the stairs. But I don't make it to the top before Mother opens her mouth.

"I will not tolerate being treated with such disrespect in my own home, Phoebe." An audible huff echoes in the foyer. "You've spent far too much time with that uncouth Fox girl. She has tainted you and the Graves name."

I spin around, ready to go to battle with my mother. And the bitch that she is, she keeps adding fuel to the fire.

"For days on end, you waste precious time with her, acting as if you're Nancy Drew or Sherlock Holmes." She walks to the base of the staircase but doesn't set foot on the first step. "You are neither." She looks me up and down a beat before her lip curls in disgust. "You are nothing but a disgrace."

"Priscilla," Father snaps.

"No, Tobias." She glances over her shoulder. "You will not defend her insolence and disrespect. I won't have it." Wrathful green eyes whip back and hold my blues. "Clean yourself up, put on something presentable, and come down here for breakfast with us and Beau. Ten minutes."

Why hasn't the serial killer taken my mother?

Yes, it's unspeakable to wish ill will or death on others, but I don't care at this point. I'd bear the karma for the rest of my life to not be at the center of Priscilla Graves's wrathful attention any longer.

What the hell happened in her life to fill her with such vitriol? Did her parents not compliment her enough? Was she not hugged as a child? Has no one ever shown her real love?

What a sad life.

Without a word, I climb the rest of the stairs and head for my section of the house.

Locking the doors, I bolt for the closet and pull down two large suitcases. Tossing them on the bed, I return to the closet and start ripping clothes from hangers. In a matter of minutes, I have enough packed to last more than a week. Then I go into the bathroom and grab my toiletries. Once I have all the necessities, I do one last scan of the room. Look for anything else I might need while I figure out how to move forward from this.

Suitcases zipped up and ready to roll, I sling a travel bag over my shoulder. I exit the bedroom and opt for the elevator over the stairs.

When I reach the bottom floor, I hear Mother mutter, "It's about time." I choose to ignore her self-righteousness and head for the front door.

I stow the second suitcase in the back of my car as my father steps outside, but I don't meet his concerned gaze.

"Don't go, Phoebe." His tone is gentle and far too kind for the woman he calls his wife.

When I don't answer, he crosses the distance and meets me at the driver's door.

"I'll talk to her." He rests an arm on my shoulder when I reach the door.

I scoff. "Doesn't matter." I meet his steady gaze. "She has her mind set on shaping me into someone I'm not." The backs of my eyes sting. "My eyes have been opened, and I will *not* be like her." Dropping my chin, I inhale deeply. "Whatever made her like this, whatever made her hate her own child"—I lift my gaze and fight off the tears ready to fall—"she needs help."

"Phoebe, I—"

"Don't." I open the car door and slip behind the wheel. "Do not make excuses and enable her." I reach for the door handle but hesitate. "Our name may mean something to this town, but none of the Seven are superior to the residents of Stone Bay. And she needs to learn and believe that if she wants a future relationship with me."

I close the door, crank the engine, and drive off the Graves property. And with each foot of distance I put between me and my mother, the weight I never asked for but have borne my entire life lifts off my shoulders.

It's barely after seven when I reach the light at Granite and Opal. The light changes from red to green within seconds, and rather than drive straight, I turn left and head for Poke the Yolk.

The morning crowd is here in full force as I step inside. I forego a table and head for the counter, placing a breakfast order to go.

Kirsten narrows her eyes a moment, then drops her gaze to the pad in her hand. "Dee Dee doesn't eat meat." She rolls her lips between her teeth once before her gaze returns to mine. "Eggs and dairy, but no meat."

My pulse soars in my veins as I connect the dots. She knows Delilah and I are *something*. And seeing as I'm ordering too much food for myself, she assumes some of it is for her.

"Okay…" I drag out the word, not wanting to confirm or deny it matters what Delilah eats.

She shrugs. "I'll get this in for you." She shakes the pad. "Shouldn't take long."

"Thanks."

True to her word, the food is boxed up and ready to go in under fifteen minutes. But the drive from Poke the Yolk to Delilah's house, on the other hand, speeds by in what feels like seconds.

I park in the same spot in Delilah's driveway, grab the food and my bag, and exit the car. My stomach flips and churns the entire walk from my car to the door, but I swallow past the queasiness and trudge forward. At the door, I inhale one deep breath, then another, and another.

It's Delilah. She'll welcome you with open arms. She always has.

I lift my free hand and rap my knuckles on the door. Ten pulse-pounding seconds later, the door swings open, a sleepy Delilah greeting me with a smile.

"Hey." She rubs her eye. "Read your note like five minutes ago." Her brows scrunch together. "What's wrong?"

My heart rattles my ribcage as I suck in one last deep breath. "Can I stay with you?"

THIRTY

DELILAH

I didn't sign up for this—to be at Phoebe's beck and call. But with each passing day, I question my decision to welcome Phoebe into my home with open arms.

One minute, she dotes on me with unexpected affection. The occasional and intentional brush of her hand against mine while we curl up on the couch and mull over the same case information. The way she instantly snuggles me after we ravage each other at night. And the seldom soft kisses she gives that say more than spoken words ever will.

Then, without warning, something flips in her mind. It's like she becomes someone else. In those moments, I either blend into the room or am treated more like an annoying roommate.

Phoebe hasn't asked for space, but I've given it to her. Not so much in the physical sense, but more so allowing her time to think without interruption. She's going through so much with her family, undoubtedly bottling up the hurt and anger and years of pent-up neglect.

She may have a tough exterior, but she isn't all glacial stone walls around a black heart. I've glimpsed the warmer, softer side of Phoebe. I've witnessed the woman scared to be vulnerable. All I want to do is comfort her. Tell her I will remain by her side through the good and bad days.

I don't smother her with unwelcome condolences. I don't tell her I'll be there through thick and thin. Although both are true, saying as much may push her away. And the last thing Phoebe needs is to feel like I'm pressuring her or invading what little privacy she has.

Finding middle ground between her fiery and frigid sides would help.

I love her fire, her drive, her relentless need to share the truth with the world. I never want her to lose those passionate qualities.

Those bitter, brutal moments, though... they make me question my sanity. When she throws me that frigid glare, whether intentional or not, I want to shut her out. Run far and fast. And then I want to crash into her and swathe her in love and light and all the things she desperately needs but has never gotten.

Going into this, I knew it wouldn't be easy. But damn, I didn't expect it to be this hard either.

I don't like feeling this... anger, indignation, distress. Like life grabbed me by the ankles and has been holding me upside down for weeks.

"Dinner and a conversation," I mutter as I exit the back room of Sage Whisperer and enter the main part of the store.

I need to let Phoebe know what's on my mind. If it doesn't end well, at least I'll have my answer.

I straighten the shelves and put back things people set down in the wrong place. Mom rings up the final customer of the day and I lock the door after they say their goodbyes.

"Everything okay, my delicate dove?"

Cutting the music, I make sure the incense cones we light

throughout the store have burned out. "Yeah." I shrug. "Things have just been off with Phoebe. Nothing to worry about."

"Well, if you ever need to talk…" She wraps an arm around my shoulder and hugs me to her side.

I turn into her side and squeeze her with equal gusto. "Thank you, Momma. I love you."

Warm lips press my hair. "Love you, too." She releases me from her hold. "Go. Sort things out."

After one last hug, I grab my hoodie from the back, slip it over my head, and exit the store. Mom watches from the door until I slip inside my car.

As the car warms up, I decide to make a quick trip to the grocery store for dinner ingredients. An Italian feast sounds like the perfect intro to a difficult talk.

A chime echoes through the kitchen as the oven timer goes off. I cut the last piece of a baguette, set the knife down, and fetch oven mitts. Silencing the timer, I open the oven door and am hit with a cloud of cheese, basil, and oregano. My mouth waters as I grip the sides of the small casserole dish and move it to a trivet on the counter.

Moving back to the island, I cut tomato, cucumber, and fresh mozzarella and add them to the spring mix in a large wooden bowl. As I blend herbs, olive oil, and balsamic for dressing and bread dip, the front door opens, the telltale clap of Phoebe's heels drifts from the foyer to my ears.

I peek toward the foyer and watch as she removes her coat and hangs it over her arm. I open my mouth, the word *hey* on the tip of my tongue, but nothing comes out.

Phoebe doesn't look my way. Doesn't announce her arrival. Doesn't mention the aroma floating through the house.

She doesn't acknowledge my existence whatsoever.

Almost as quickly as she enters the house, she moves toward one of the spare rooms—the room she has stored her clothes in since asking to stay here two weeks ago.

I want to yell at her retreating back. Say something to make her stop, spin around, and look me in the eye. Anything to make her *see* me in the room, if only for a moment. I want her to admit I am more than a convenience.

Rather than bark out nasty words, I bite my tongue and make up two place settings at the dining table.

As I load my plate with stuffed shells and salad, Phoebe rounds the end of the hallway, eyes glued to her phone as she blindly walks to the table. It's a full minute after she sits in the chair before she locks her phone, sets it down, and looks at the food on the table.

Still, she says nothing.

"Drink?" The single word leaves my lips harsher than usual.

And for the first time since she's walked in the door, she lifts her gaze to mine and consciously acknowledges my presence. Her brows twitch for a split second as she tries to read my mood. When I give nothing away, she nods.

"Please."

I inhale a slow, deep breath, rise from my chair, and shuffle into the kitchen. Retrieving two wineglasses from the cabinet, I grab the bottle of red wine I uncorked while cooking, return to the table, and pour her glass, then mine. I set the bottle aside then lean toward Phoebe to kiss her cheek.

An inch from her skin, she jerks back, her expression twisting from confusion to realization to an edge of regret.

"Am I not allowed to kiss you anymore?" I grind my

molars as I return to my seat across from her. "Or are we saving that for when you want an orgasm?"

Damn, I am a fool.

I've been so desperate for this woman for so long that I turned off my common sense. For months—hell, maybe years—I've ignored my intuition when it came to Phoebe. I've disregarded every red flag, every warning sign that told me to forget about her and move on.

That's what happens when you're a) an idiot and b) so blinded by hormones and this indescribable, invisible pull.

Every decision I've made regarding Phoebe Graves has been rash and impetuous. Now, they're all catching up, piling high, and I'm just… exhausted.

I won't be someone's convenience. I won't be a doormat.

"Don't be like that, Fox."

I *feel* her eyes on my profile, begging me to look up. Instead, I swipe up my fork and stab my salad over and over and over, overloading the tines.

"It's been a shitty day. My reaction wasn't because I don't want to kiss you."

I scoff then shove the bite in my mouth.

She drops her chin to her chest. "I'm shit at relationships," she mutters, then lifts her head. "I've never done this."

"Spend time with people? Acknowledge they exist? Have a conversation about your day?"

"Yes!" She drops her fork, reaches for her wine, and drinks half the glass.

I mirror her, then cross my arms over my chest and take a few deep breaths.

"We were doing those things. Before you asked to stay, we spent time together. You didn't treat me like a ghost that cleans up after you and feeds you." I curl my fingers into tight fists and try to rein in my building temper. "We talked."

I tip my head back, close my eyes, and send a silent message to the goddess. *Gift me strength.* When my eyes open, I level Phoebe with my gaze.

"I have no clue what we are. I don't presume we're girlfriends. I sure as hell won't say as much to anyone. Not when I don't know how you feel. But Phoebe"—I inhale a shaky breath—"I'm done being convenient and expendable. The least I deserve is basic respect."

"You're right. I'm sorry." She downs the last of her wine and adds more to the glass. "Not trying to make excuses, but I have nothing to go off of." She gestures between us with a finger. "My family… my mother… I wouldn't know love or acceptance if it slapped me in the face." She swallows large gulps of wine. "As far as us…"

Several seconds pass in silence.

"As far as us, what?"

"My parents and grandparents have been on a mission for months to match me with Beau. No matter how many times I reject him, no matter how much I express my disinterest in an arranged relationship, they keep pushing." She audibly exhales. "I may feel *something* for you, Fox, but I won't be forced into anything with you either."

I bolt upright and my chair topples over. "Wow, Phoebe." I shake my head. "Just wow."

Without another word, I storm away from the table, dash down the hall, and enter my bedroom. I slip on socks and shoes, yank a hoodie from its hanger, and shove it over my head. Wallet, fob, and phone in my pockets, I exit the room and all but sprint for the garage.

"Where are you going?" There's a slight hitch to her voice.

"Out." I twist the handle on the garage door but pause and meet her gaze. "I don't expect you to know all the answers tonight, Phoebe. But you need to figure out what it is you want." Releasing the handle, the door swings open. "You may not be ready for people to know you're bi, and I accept that, but I at least deserve to know whether or not we have a future."

I step into the garage and shut the door before she responds.

Cranking the engine, I press the button to open the main garage door. While I wait for the engine to warm up, I shoot a text to the group chat with Skylar and Kirsten.

> Friend emergency. Meet up?

Their replies hit my phone in seconds.

SKY

> Sorry 🙁 yes. Where?

K

> Grabbing my keys

> RJs?

SKY

> Be there in 10

K

> omw

I've never been more grateful for my friends than in this moment. Not once have I thrown out the *friend emergency* card, but the moment I do, they drop everything.

In a matter of minutes, I park in front of RJ's Diner and Dive. Seconds after I'm seated, Skylar and Kirsten crowd me on either side and hug the breath from my lungs. And after we order a couple appetizers and drinks, we dive headfirst into my frustrations with myself and Phoebe.

For over an hour, I quietly recant the last two weeks of living with Phoebe and how I've gone from warm and caring to barely lukewarm and borderline resentful. I share the changes I've noticed in myself and this constant ickiness I feel because of it. I tell them how frustrated I am with Phoebe, yet I still want her.

And for over an hour, Skylar and Kirsten let me spill my soul over cornbread-battered onion rings and loaded potato skins, listening to every word and not interrupting.

"Give her time." Kirsten dunks a potato skin in ranch dressing. "I know you've already given her a lot, but she hasn't found her footing yet. Can't imagine that's easy, either. Her family is a bit... over the top."

"I know," I concede before biting an onion ring. Lifting a hand to cover my mouth, I mumble around the bite, "I have to constantly remind myself that she's been dealing with that heaviness all her life."

I also have to remind myself it isn't fair of me to expect Phoebe to be a different person. I have to remind myself that my grandparents chose a different way of life for themselves and their children and so on.

Where I've been lucky in life, Phoebe has not.

Not only has her family continued the antiquated legacy of living like town royalty, but they've also remained shallow and heartless and passed it to the next generation.

"Please don't take this the wrong way," Kirsten says as she rests a hand over mine on the table. "But quit trying to be someone you're not for Phoebe."

My brows tug together in confusion.

"I'm not saying you *are* being someone different, but you haven't really been true to yourself either." Kirsten pulls her hand back and takes a sip of her Coke. "If Phoebe likes you, she likes *you*. Not some fantasy version of you."

This is why I need time with Skylar and Kirsten.

It was necessary I step away from the situation with Phoebe. For over a week, I've been in a shitty headspace. Rationally talking with Phoebe about it is the right move, but clearing my head is priority number one. That and getting sage advice from my friends.

Yes, I need my friends to be an ear and a shoulder, someone I can lean on when life feels off-kilter. But I also need their straightforward perspective and endless support.

"You're right," I confess. "Ugh... I think because I've wanted something with her for so long, my mind is having difficulty differentiating years of dreams from present-day reality."

I want to be myself with Phoebe. But more importantly, I want her to be herself too. Her sharp edges and steely disposition are what I fell for.

Over time, we'll change and become new versions of ourselves. That much is inevitable. But it isn't right for me to want Phoebe to become her future self without walking tough roads and experiencing life at her own pace.

Skylar grabs a potato skin and coats it with an obscene amount of ranch—something so her that it makes me smile. "Don't rush for the finish line, Dee Dee. Cherish the ups and downs in between." She shoves half the potato skin in her mouth. "They're memories you'll look back on and love when you're wrinkly and gray."

"At least I won't have saggy boobs." I chuckle.

Kirsten flicks her balled-up straw wrapper across the table and hits me in the nose. "Everyone gets saggy boobs." She rolls her eyes. "Some look like sad, depleted water balloons. Others like grapefruits in a produce bag."

Loud laughter bursts from my lips and I slap a hand over my mouth. A second later, Skylar's snort-laughs and Kirsten's cackles fill the air. My vision blurs a beat before tears roll down my cheeks. I lift my free hand to my stomach and try to soothe the cramping organ.

God, it feels good to laugh like this. Free and booming and unadulterated. It's the cathartic release I didn't know I needed.

Several patrons in RJ's glance toward our table. We ignore their questioning stares and whispered words. In Stone Bay, someone will always gawk or mutter or point. I'd rather it be because I'm happy.

When our laughter fizzles out, I reach across the table and rest a hand on one of each of theirs. "I love you." I give them both a squeeze. "Thank you."

We lose track of time as we catch each other up on life and work and everything in between. Our appetizer plates empty and our drinks get refilled. The background music in the diner becomes more noticeable as the tables vacate and most of the town's residents go home for the night.

It feels like old times, but not so old. It feels like a year ago when the three of us lived together and shared late nights in front of the television with tons of takeout, sugar and laughter. It feels like home.

Kirsten's phone dings and she pulls it from her pocket, a wince on her lips as she reads the screen. "Shit. Didn't realize how long we've been here."

"Travis?" I ask.

She nods as she types out a response to his text. "Just making sure everything's okay." She stows her phone. "Should probably get going. It's almost midnight and I need to be up in six hours for work."

We finish our drinks and settle our tabs.

Rising from my seat, I pull them both into me and hug them hard. "Seriously, thank you. Don't know what I'd do without you."

"You'd be miserable," Skylar teases.

"Definitely miserable," Kirsten adds.

I squeeze them harder. "Without a doubt." Releasing them, I step back and look to them both. "Love you."

"Love you back." Kirsten tugs my hoodie string.

"Love you too." Skylar reaches for my hand, grips it tight for a moment, then releases it.

I point a thumb over my shoulder. "Need to use the bathroom."

"Want us to wait?" Skylar asks as she takes her phone out of her purse and taps the screen. Probably a text to Lawrence to say she's on her way home.

"Nah." My gaze drifts from Skylar to Kirsten. "Go home to your guys."

"You sure? I don't mind waiting." Kirsten's phone dings with another text as the words leave her lips.

I start walking backward in the direction of the bathroom. "I'll be fine. Go." And before either of them add another word of protest, I spin on my heels, cross the dining room, and walk down the hall toward the bathroom.

After I wash and dry my hands, I pull out my phone and open my text history with Phoebe. Past messages blur on the screen as I recall our fight hours ago.

I hate how irrational and furious I acted. Though my feelings deserve a voice, I should have found a calmer, more mature way to discuss where my head and heart are at.

I blink back the tears threatening to fall and type out a message.

omwh can we talk?

Phone in hand, I exit the bathroom. I wave good night to the server as I pass her. My phone screen dims as I step outside. I wake it back up to see the gray bubble dancing as she types. Eyes on the screen, I toy with the end of my hair as I walk toward my car.

FIREFLY

see you soon

The corner of my mouth twitches up as a bit of the weight on my heart eases up. I lock my phone and lift my gaze as I reach my car. As I dig the fob out of my pocket, something scuffs the pavement nearby. I twist to look over my shoulder but am met with a thick wall of muscle.

Frame twice the size of mine, an arm circles my shoulder before a large hand wraps around my throat and squeezes. Another hand with a rag covers my nose and mouth. Fingers pinch the bridge of my nose as his palm pins my jaw in place.

I try to open my mouth to scream but struggle to move an inch or make a sound. Hints of cut grass waft up my nose as something sweet blankets my tongue. Nausea builds in my belly as I thrash against the stranger. On the next inhale, my limbs grow heavy. The world spins slower and blurs.

I give one last kick, one last elbow into their torso. And then the world goes black.

THIRTY-ONE

PHOEBE

Tap, tap, tap, tap, tap.

My fingers drum my thigh as I reach the couch, spin on my heel, and cross the room for the umpteenth time. Eyes unfocused, I pace the living room as I mull over every angry and upset word Delilah said before she walked out.

"I'm done being convenient and expendable. The least I deserve is basic respect."

Our friendship or relationship—or whatever the hell it is we have—is still so damn new. Oftentimes, I have no idea what to say or do or how to be around Delilah. It's not that I'm intimidated or embarrassed by her. It's not that I don't want her… as a girlfriend.

Because fuck… after our first kiss, all I want is her.

But I don't know how to be with anyone. I don't know *how* to be with her. I don't know if I can leave these four walls and hold her hand or kiss her lips or be close to her out in the open with other eyes on us.

More than two decades of being told how to behave, being informed of my social status, being taught some twisted, false sense of superiority, my parents—more so my mother than my father—have warped my outlook on the world. As I matured, I could have walked a different path. I could have stood up for myself sooner. But I didn't.

Though it'd been right in front of me the entire time, I hadn't absorbed reality. I chose to be willfully blind to my future and the direction my parents were steering it in. I chose prestige and to stare down my nose at everyone else in Stone Bay. I chose to be an ice queen and close my heart off from everyone.

Until Delilah woke me up from my disillusioned fantasy.

Delilah didn't need to open her arms or heart to me, but she did. And I hate how I've taken her heart, her trust, *her* for granted.

I tried to fight what I felt for her. When you've never had a genuine connection with anyone—friendship or otherwise—it's difficult to let someone in. To be vulnerable.

Thanks to Priscilla and Tobias Graves, I have a glacial heart. But with each passing day, with each touch and kiss and ounce of affection Delilah gifts me, the ice encapsulating my heart thaws a little more.

It will take years to undo the damage my parents have inflicted upon me. Will Delilah stand by my side as I discover the new, better version of myself?

"I'm done being convenient and expendable. The least I deserve is basic respect."

"You deserve more than basic respect, Fox."

Delilah deserves love and passion. A life filled with peace and laughter. Nights at her favorite spot by the bay, wrapped in the arms of someone she loves, the stars twinkling above. Rainy nights by the fire and kisses while the sun sets.

Do I want to be her *someone*? If the sharp pang in my chest is any indication, the answer is a resolute yes.

I stop midstep as the realization sinks in further. As it

settles into my bones. As it immerses my soul.

Love is not a familiar concept or emotion. But what I feel for Delilah is deep, scary, and soul-shattering. It makes my pulse race and steals the air from the room. It rips me apart, exposes all my faults and wounds and scars, and then slowly, tenderly pieces me back together.

Delilah makes me whole. When I had no idea I was incomplete.

A yawn draws my attention back to the room and the fact Delilah isn't home yet. I swipe my phone up from the table and see the time—12:53 a.m. Unlocking my phone, I note the timestamp from her last text—12:02 a.m.

"Where are you, Fox?"

I dash to the front door, swing it open, and step out onto the porch. Goose bumps blanket my exposed skin as I stare at only my car in the driveway. I dart back into the house and rush to the garage.

The rational part of my brain knows I would've heard the garage door open. That I would've heard the soft purr of her engine as she parked. That it'd be odd for Delilah to sit in her car for thirty or forty minutes just to avoid a conversation.

But I have to be certain.

I flip the light on and my heart plummets.

No car. No Delilah.

Slamming the door behind me, I pace the living room again as I type out a text.

Did you drive out of Stone Bay lol

After everything tonight, joking doesn't feel right. So I send a quick second text.

> Kidding. Everything okay? It's been almost an hour.

I stare at the screen until my eyes lose focus. Until the screen dims and I tap it awake. Until several minutes pass with no response.

I tap on her contact picture in messages and hit the call button. After one ring, the line connects.

"Hey"—I open my mouth to ask where she is but am cut off by the rest of her voice mail greeting—"you've reached Delilah. I'm either away from my phone, reading a book, or pretending to work. Leave me a message and I'll call back soon. Have a beautiful day."

Perspiration dampens my skin as my heart pounds, pounds, pounds in the confines of my rib cage when I hang up. The little bit of dinner I ate threatens to make a reappearance as our text history fills the screen once more.

Seconds turn into minutes.

I tap my thigh as I stare at the screen and beg for a response from Delilah.

Still no answer.

I have no idea where she went or if she went wherever alone. I have no way of finding out where she is now. No way of knowing if she's safe. If her car broke down. If she got in an accident and is unconscious.

And it's my own goddamn fault.

"Fuck!"

I clench my fingers into fists and take the punishment as my nails bite the skin of my palms.

"Breathe, Phoebe."

Maybe she hung out with friends. Maybe she texted me she was leaving, but they kept her longer. Maybe she's still with them and her phone died.

Please let that be it.

Her best friends used to live here—Kirsten and Skylar. I don't have either of their numbers, but I do have Travis's number, who happens to be Kirsten's beau.

I exit messages and open up calls. After a few taps, I lift the phone to my ear and listen to it ring. "He can hate me later."

Travis picks up on the third ring. "The fuck, Phoebe?"

I ignore his growly greeting and get right to the point. "Delilah hasn't made it home yet."

Rustling and a mumbled voice echo through the line. It's barely discernible, but I hear Travis ask Kirsten if Delilah left at the same time as her. Kirsten's answer is too soft to make out.

"Stupid question," Travis says, voice clear and edged with authority. "Have you tried to reach her?"

I roll my eyes. "Yes, Travis." I don't have time for this bullshit. "She texted at 12:02 and said she was on her way home." Glancing at the time on the stove, my pulse kicks up another notch. "I texted twice, ten minutes ago. Then I called and it went to voice mail. I can't get ahold of her."

"I'm sure everything's fine." More rustling sounds on the other end.

"Don't fucking placate me, Emerson. I'm freaking the fuck out."

"We'll find her."

"What if…"

The backs of my eyes sting as emotion swells in my throat. I don't want to think it, let alone say it. Because if I put it out there, if I give the idea any ammunition, it may be true. And it can't be true.

It can't be.

I don't want to say the words, but they leave my lips in a whisper anyway. "What if she was taken?"

"We. Will. Find. Her." Travis calls for Pepper, his K-9 partner. "You're at Delilah's house?"

"Yes."

"Kirsten and I are on our way. Don't leave."

"Oka—" The call ends before I finish speaking.

I go to the closet in one of the spare rooms, grab sneakers and a coat, and put them on while I wait.

Hour-long minutes pass as I pace the house. I will my phone to go off. Send countless silent pleas to the universe for Delilah to be okay. Beseech the powers that be to bring Delilah home unscathed.

But my phone doesn't go off. And I don't hear the garage door open.

Instead, I hear the rumble of Travis's vehicle as he parks in the driveway. Seconds later, beeping echoes through the house as a code is keyed into the door lock. Kirsten bolts through the front door, panic written in the tired lines of her expression.

"Nothing?"

The sting behind my eyes returns and I swallow. "No," I mumble with a shake of my head. I wrap my arms around my middle, fist my coat, and squeeze. "Nothing."

My vision blurs as Kirsten crosses the room and wraps me in her arms. "I promise you, we'll find her."

"I need something of Delilah's," Travis interrupts. "A shirt or article of clothing she recently wore. Preferably one that hasn't been washed."

Stepping out of Kirsten's hold, I dash down the hall and enter the bedroom—*our* bedroom. A tear paints my cheek and I wipe it away.

"Focus, Phoebe," I scold myself. "Freak out later."

In the closet, I dig through the laundry basket and pull out a couple shirts near the top. I lift them to my nose and inhale deeply. Sandalwood and something distinctly Delilah. Her scent settles my racing heart, but only momentarily.

Returning to the living room, I hand over the shirts.

Travis rolls the shirts together. "Chief will be here shortly to ask you both questions." His eyes lock on Kirsten. "You get an answer from Skylar?"

Kirsten nods. "She'll be here soon. Law, too."

"Good. Let's wait until we have news before calling her family."

Shit. I didn't even think about her parents. Probably because mine wouldn't give a damn.

"I don't have their numbers," I confess.

Kirsten gives me a sympathetic smile. "I'll give them to you."

A loud knock booms through the house and I startle. Travis crosses the room and opens the front door, stepping aside to let his father in.

Chief Emerson swallows the foyer with his size and authority. "Time?"

Travis glances down at his watch. "One hour, twenty-seven minutes."

I check the time on my phone to see it's 1:29 a.m.

When Chief asked for the time, he didn't want to know what the clock said. He wanted to know how long it's been since anyone's heard from Delilah.

Bile climbs up my throat and I cover my mouth.

Now's not the time. Hold your shit together.

"Last known location?"

"RJ's," Kirsten says. "Skylar and I left just before midnight." She taps on her phone a few times. "My last text to Travis was 11:55 when I told him I was headed home."

"Ms. Fox didn't walk out with you?"

"No." Guilt washes over Kirsten's face. "She needed to use the restroom and told us to leave without her."

I rest a hand on Kirsten's shoulder. "It's not your fault."

"We should've waited." Tears well in her eyes. "After everything that happened to me, why didn't I wait?"

Now it's Travis's turn to look guilty.

If Kirsten had any idea of what's happened since her attack, she wouldn't have even gone out so late. She might have suggested hanging out at one of their houses instead.

But she didn't know. So they did go out. And when it was time to leave, it didn't cross her mind to be cautious. She didn't know they should've waited and all walked out together.

To protect Kirsten's sanity, Travis left her in the dark about the recent murders. I don't fault him for wanting to safeguard her mind and heart. But his actions have consequences. And one of those consequences is Kirsten assuming the blame for her missing friend.

But Kirsten isn't the guilty one. I am.

If I hadn't been so closed off with Delilah these past two weeks, if I'd dug up a single ounce of courage to let her in, really let her in, maybe we wouldn't have fought. If I'd not been so obsessed with finding the St. Agnes killer, if I'd given Delilah more of my time, she would've stayed home. We would've finished dinner and talked like mature people in a relationship.

And if I was strong enough, I would've told her how much she means to me. How she, in such a short period of time, has given me hope and affection and purpose.

But none of that happened because I'm a fucking coward.

Instead of acting like an adult and owning my feelings, I hid behind a mask. The same mask I have my whole life. A mask that has done nothing but cause pain.

My emotional spinelessness is the reason Delilah left angry.

I hurt Delilah. I am the reason she walked away to clear her head. I am the reason she didn't make it home tonight. Me.

And if anything happens to her, I swear to every fucking god, I will rain hell on this town. Consequences be damned.

THIRTY-TWO

DELILAH

T HE DEAFENING BLAST OF A FOGHORN STARTLES ME AWAKE. I BOLT upright and immediately wince as debilitating pain ricochets in my skull. Closing my eyes, I press the heels of my palms to my head and beg for an ounce of relief. Instead, a mix of sandpaper and fire burns my wrists.

The foghorn wails again and my hands try to cover my ears but won't move more than a couple inches apart.

Nausea sways in my belly as though I'm on a boat out at sea in the middle of a storm. I twist and drop my hands to the scratchy material beneath me, my fingers curling into the fabric in an attempt to steady my body. But I'm not moving—not physically, anyway.

I inhale a lungful of air—a blend of lemon, pine, and bleach tickle my nose, my windpipe raw, bruised and protesting—and hold it as I count to five. On a slow exhale, I ease my eyes open and look for something familiar in the dark space. A book, a piece of furniture, or a framed photo on the wall. Anything to ground me, to tell me where I am.

But there's nothing. Nothing except the antique-metal-frame twin bed, a stiff mattress, and an abrasive blanket beneath me.

Bright light flickers through the room and I squint. Just as quickly as it arrives, it vanishes.

Think, Delilah. Think.

I drop my head and clutch my temples between my thumb and fingers. Close my eyes and do my damnedest not to focus on the throbbing agony in my head. I take a deep breath, then another, and try to use meditation techniques to focus my attention.

Foghorn. Pine. Lemon. Bleach. Dark. Bed. Bright light.

If my mind were clear, I'd have figured it out minutes ago. And the moment it clicks, embarrassment and confusion seep in.

I'm near the lighthouse.

Am I in the lighthouse?

A shiver rolls up my spine, ripples down my arms, and shoots tingles into my skull. The ache in my head pulses as the nausea in my belly creeps steadily up my throat. With slow, deliberate movements, I swing my legs off the bed and attempt to stand.

Butt barely off the bed, the room spins at a dizzying pace. I fall back on the mattress as the light brightens the room again. The room rolls in waves. Up and down, up and down. I slap a hand over my mouth and swallow the sudden urge to vomit.

Metal creaks a moment before something slides across the floor. A sharp *whack* followed by another creak fills the room.

"Food and water," a gruff, unfamiliar voice says. "Don't suck it down too fast, or you'll puke it up."

"I—" My voice cracks as my throat screams in agony. I lift my hands to my throat and gently massage the tender muscles. "I don't understand." The words come out somewhat garbled and I'm uncertain he heard me.

"You'll be here until it's time."

"Time for what?" My voice pitches higher on the last word as bile hits the back of my tongue.

"There's a bucket near the window."

On unsteady legs, I rise off the bed and stumble toward his voice. "I don't understand." The room starts to spin again and I slam my eyes shut. "What do you want? Why are you doing this?"

"The drugs will wear off in a couple hours. Best to save the food until then."

Why won't he answer my fucking questions?

"What did I do to you? Why am I here?"

The light flashes by and I catch a glimpse of the door. Metal and wide with several bolts and pins. Near the floor, there's a closed cutout about two feet wide and six inches tall. Higher up, there's a similar, smaller cutout. Slid halfway open, I make out the faint, shadowed, partial profile of the man on the other side.

With a scoff, he shakes his head. "You're all the fucking same."

The foghorn howls again and I clench my molars as I wait for the additional throb in my head to pass.

"Sinful fucking whores," he growls out. "Only your sins look different."

This time, when the light passes, I glimpse from his brow to his chin. I make out the rage and disgust in the lines of his face. The undiluted hatred this man harbors.

And I have no idea who he is.

A slight tremor starts in my fingers. With each shaky breath I inhale, the tremor spreads—to my wrists, along my forearms, up my biceps, to my shoulders—until my entire body shakes uncontrollably.

"You want to know why this is happening to you?" Condescension and revulsion lace his voice.

"W-w-why?" My teeth chatter as I stumble back and hit the bed.

"You've forsaken him."

I shake my head, clearly not understanding his answer.

"Stupid fucking whore at that."

Silence echoes between us as my heart pounds beneath my rib cage. I wait and wait and wait for an answer, but he says nothing. The tremors come faster. Harder. And I curl my fingers into tight fists.

"For a whore is a deep ditch; and a strange woman is a narrow pit. Proverbs 23:27."

"W-w-what?" I clamp my jaw shut in an attempt to stop my chattering teeth.

A growl hits my ears a beat before he speaks again.

"Therefore God also gave them up to uncleanness, in the lusts of their hearts, to dishonor their bodies among themselves, who exchanged the truth of God for the lie, and worshipped and served the creature rather than the Creator, who is blessed forever. Amen."

He pauses long enough to take a breath, then continues *louder*.

"For this reason God gave them up to vile passions. For even their women exchanged the natural for what is against nature. Likewise also the men, leaving the natural use of the woman, burned in their lust for one another, men with men committing what is shameful, and receiving in themselves the penalty of their error which was due. Romans 1:20-29."

Rage boils inside my vibrating frame and somehow takes control, calming my muscles long enough for me to lose my shit on this self-righteous asshole.

"God?" I belt out. "You drugged me, abducted me, and plan to punish or kill me because of your fucking god?"

Every nerve ending in my body ignites and I fight off the shakes.

"Where do you get off judging me?" I step toward the door. "So I bed women and have no plans to marry." I scoff. "Who the fuck cares?" I inch closer to the door. "Wake up, asshole. Join reality with the rest of us." Lifting my bound hands, I wave my hands in his direction. "Your *god* was made up by a bunch of scared white men that wanted control." Hands in loose fists beneath my eyes, I twist them back and forth as I stick out my bottom lip. "Boo-hoo. Frightened little men can't handle the pagans and homosexuals and people enjoying life not under their thumb."

A loud bang echoes through the room, either from his fist or foot hitting the door.

"For your sins, you will pay the ultimate price." His voice booms with outrage.

I stare at the visible fraction of his profile. "I've always found it interesting"—I tilt my head to the side and narrow my eyes—"how your god forgives the rapists and murderers and other atrocious people walking the earth, yet he can't accept homosexuality, individuality, or skepticism." I dizzy a little but hold my ground. "Thank the goddess my parents raised me to be a respectable, loving, nonjudgmental person."

Loud laughter rips through the air. "A lot of good that did you." He slams the small opening shut. "Doesn't change your fate."

His footsteps echo through the stairwell as he descends the lighthouse. And then silence takes over.

The burst of adrenaline that calmed my tremors evaporates from my bloodstream. My legs weaken and I collapse on the floor next to the tray of food—two slices of white bread, two slices of cheese, a banana, and a small carton of water.

I should eat to keep up my strength for when he returns. But what if the food is dosed? What if this is my last meal? What if they're giving me just enough to keep me alive, just to turn around and kill me?

Should I even try? I'd much rather go on my own terms rather than those of a mentally unstable individual.

I shove the tray away, lower myself to lie on my side and close my eyes.

My mind goes to my friends, to Phoebe. They must be out of their minds with worry right now. I would be if our roles were reversed.

Tears sting the backs of my eyes, but I don't let them fall.

"Find me, Phoebe," I whisper into the darkness. "If anyone can, it's you. Find me."

THIRTY-THREE

PHOEBE

"I don't give a fuck if the town is freaking out, Emerson." I slam a hand on the dining room table. "It's not *my* fault you all decided to keep this sadistic motherfucker from everyone for so long." With a quick sweep of my hand, papers fly off the table toward the police chief. "Maybe if you'd spoken up sooner, the bodies wouldn't be piling up. And maybe, just maybe, we wouldn't be on a massive manhunt for one of the Seven."

Within hours of Delilah going missing, her house—my temporary home—became command central. An officer is either inside mapping out their next moves or outside on guard or both. More often than not, Travis is here, directing other members of the force where to search. With the addition of one more K-9 unit, Travis is hopeful we will find her sooner.

Delilah's family takes turns checking in with me for updates, though they get information when I do. But it isn't just them asking for news on Delilah.

They also ask how I'm holding up, if I need anything— dinner or groceries or another set of eyes of the information

Delilah and I gathered. And when Delilah's mom swings by, she wraps me in her arms for a solid minute before we get to work.

Every officer is clocking twelve-plus hour days and on call when they're off the clock. Every founding family member, young and old, is scouring the town for one of their own. Even the Graves family.

We're exhausted and hungry and ready to rip each other in two. But we won't stop. We won't give up. Not until we find Delilah safe and whole and breathing.

"There's never a perfect way to handle a situation, Ms. Graves. I don't tell you how to do your job. Don't tell me how to do mine." He crosses his arms over his chest. "After the chaos with the first murder, we thought it best to keep the others quiet."

"We?" I ask, incredulous. "So you asked the entire police department for their input? You asked *all* of the Seven for their insight? And you got a unanimous *keep it quiet* vote? Bullshit." Barefoot in the same clothes I've worn for days, I step within inches of him. "*You* made the decision. *You* were wrong. Fucking own it."

Roger Emerson steps toe to toe with me, towers over me, and grinds his jaw. "I fucked up, Graves," he bites out. "But fighting about it now steals time from us. Time we don't have." He inhales and steps back. "Yell at me after we find her."

He's right. I hate to admit it, but he's right. Delilah should be our only focus until we find her.

I nod. "It's a date."

With as much information as we have from the previous victims and with the number of people actively searching for Delilah, I have hope we'll find her quickly. But it isn't long before two hours have turned into ten. And then ten turn into twenty-four.

By hour thirty, we've drawn a grid over a map of the town and are assigning people to search sectors, one zone at a time. The caffeine is on constant refill as we work until we pass out. Officers and founding family members call in with updates on cleared areas. Every time we mark off a zone on the map, anxiety roots itself deeper in my bones.

In a blink, one day turns into two. And as of six hours and eight minutes ago, we've hit day three.

Months ago, the search was about finding this killer and bringing them to justice. Now, it's so much more. Delilah's life is in our hands. If we don't find her soon…

My eyes burn as my throat swells for the hundredth time since her car and phone were found in the parking lot at RJ's.

I want to cry—for missing her, for wanting her safe, for wishing our last interaction had ended differently. I want to scream—at myself, for everything I said or did that led to her leaving the house three nights ago; at life for dealing me such a shitty hand and teaching me all the wrong ways to love someone; at the universe for taking away the one person that's always believed in me, that never gave up on me, no matter how poorly I treated her. I want to punch the walls until my knuckles bleed because then maybe I'll be worthy of someone as kindhearted and beautiful and magnificent as Delilah Fox.

But now isn't the time to cry, scream or punch walls. Now is the time to focus.

Emerson's radio goes off. "Zone C3 clear."

I grab the blue highlighter from the table and draw an X through the cleared area.

"Proceed to D3 and report back," Chief tells the officer.

"Affirmative."

I stare down at the map and the countless zones we still have yet to search.

Officers are scattered throughout town, most near the mountains and forestland. Members of the Seven are grouped together and sifting through more familiar places, such as the wooded areas closer to houses and businesses. But even with dozens of people in pursuit of this killer and on the lookout for Delilah, it doesn't feel like enough.

We need more help. We need to know this sick fuck's motives.

"There has to be something we're missing," I mutter as I trace the map with my fingers. "A clue we're not puzzling together correctly."

Chief Emerson shuffles papers around on the table. "All young women in their twenties. Some were flourishing in the community while others were starting to get their life back on track." He uncovers a piece of paper with a comparison chart on it. "All disrobed, physically assaulted and disfigured. We found sage at three of the four scenes, but it could be that we missed it at the first. And then there's the—"

I cut him off. "St. Agnes card."

He nods. "I spoke with the minister and he had nothing to offer other than prayers." With a shake of his head, he rolls his eyes.

"What about the nun?"

Straightening to his full height, he furrows his brow. "Sister Esther? She can't remember the day of the week, let alone answer questions without spacing out."

"No. Not Sister Esther." I sift through the piles of paper in search of my notes. The small slip of paper peeks out from under a stack of photos. I scan the page. "Sister Rebecca," I say and meet his eyes.

A ghostly expression takes over his face as he slowly

shakes his head. "I may not be a religious man, but I try to keep up with changes in town." His skin turns impossibly paler. "There's no Sister Rebecca."

For hour-long seconds, we stare at each other. And with each passing second, his admission sinks in.

There's no Sister Rebecca. She isn't a part of the church. All the religious and ceremonial ties to the crime scenes.

Holy. Fucking. Shit.

"I need to go," I blurt out. "To the church. Now. I need to go."

"Phoebe, it's the middle of the night." Emerson rests a hand on my shoulder. "You stay here. I'll handle this."

Glancing down at his hand, I arch a brow then meet his eyes. "No offense, Emerson, but I think I've pieced together more about this case than you. I'm going."

"You're not a cop," he says in an attempt to thwart me.

"But I am one of the Seven. And considering most of the town is now aware of what's happening, I doubt I'll have problems siphoning answers from the good minister." I step out of his hold. "Now, if you'll excuse me, I need to figure out where some deranged woman posing as a nun took my girlfriend."

White noise fills my ears and I pause mid-step toward the bedroom.

Girlfriend.

I snap out of my stupor and jog toward the bedroom. And as I lace up my heeled ass-kicking boots, I nod.

Yeah, Delilah Fox is mine. Girlfriend. Lover. Confidant. Champion. And after everything that's happened in the past seventy-two hours, it's damn time I own it.

"I'm coming, Fox. Hell or high water"—I tug one of her hoodies from its hanger and slip it over my head, inhaling her sandalwood scent—"I will find you."

After waiting hours in the lot for the doors to unlock, I enter the sky-high Gothic building with several others. The clap of my heels announces my arrival as I enter the nave of the church. A middle-aged man dressed in black with a white clerical collar peers up from the person he's speaking with and excuses himself. In a few long strides, we meet and he offers me his hand.

"Ms. Graves, so nice to see you on this fine Thursday. How may I be of service?"

It's been a while since I've tossed out my fuck-you smile, but his ray-of-sunshine attitude in the middle of a crisis brings it right out.

"It's not a fine day. My girlfriend is missing." Second admission feels better than the first. "Which is what brings me here."

Wrinkles form between his brows as they knit together. "Not sure I understand."

"Do you have a Sister Rebecca working here?"

"Sorry, no. Our clergy includes myself, Sister Esther, Brother Paul, and the music director, Grace-Marie. We have volunteers that work with the youth groups, bigger services, and events, but no one named Rebecca."

"Fuck," I hiss.

The minister jerks back slightly as several churchgoers gasp at my open profanity. He makes the sign of the cross over himself and hugs his Bible tighter to his chest.

I should probably apologize, but there are more important things to worry about than cursing in a church.

"Has anyone else mentioned seeing a new nun recently?"

"No one has brought it to my attention, but I will ask those who frequent for prayer."

I dig through my bag and locate my business card from the Gazette and a pen. I scribble my cell phone number on the back and hand it to him. "Please call with any information. No matter how small it may seem." I inhale a shaky breath. "The woman I met here last month gave the impression she was employed by the church. Now that I know otherwise, I can't help but believe she is a part of the recent carnage in town. She may be the one who took my girlfriend."

The minister reaches out and wraps a warm hand around my forearm. "I'll call with any information. You have my word."

I nod. "Thank you."

As quickly as I had entered the church, I exit. But not before pulling out my phone and calling Chief Emerson.

"What'd he say?"

"Never heard of her. He'll call after speaking with others."

"Fuck." A loud thump sounds in the background.

"Exactly. But it got me thinking."

"I'm all ears, Graves."

It isn't the time to gloat, but damn does it feel good to have the chief of police asking for my insight.

"If you came to town with some sick headspace and a mission to rid the world of people not following the word of God, you'd want to remain anonymous."

"No rentals or names on documents," he mutters.

"So, aside from the woods, where could someone go that may be abandoned or infrequently checked?"

Papers rustle in the background. "You headed back to the house?"

"Five minutes out."

"I'll order food and call Travis. And then we're mapping out every damn structure in this town."

My heart races as the determination in his voice hits my ears.

"We're going to find her." Alive, I want to add, but keep to myself.

"We'll find her, Phoebe."

Fight like hell, Fox. I'm coming.

THIRTY-FOUR

DELILAH

"We'll just throw her in the back of the car and leave," the growly man says. I have yet to see his face, but his voice haunts me every time I close my eyes.

"If it were that simple, don't you think I'd have already suggested as much," a woman says, obvious irritation in her voice.

Uncertain how long I passed out after he took me, I assume I've been here close to a week. Today marks the fifth day the sun has risen and lit up my temporary prison.

During my time trapped in this brick-and-steel cell, nine trays have slid across the floor from the door. The first two trays, I ignored. Still loopy from whatever he knocked me out with, I feared the food or water was drugged. An easy way for him to keep me dazed and confused but alive.

By the middle of day two, I'd thrown up four times. My lips chapped as my body begged for water and nutrition.

Still, I held off. I stood my ground, stared out the small window facing the Pacific, and invoked the goddess to help my loved ones find me.

When the sun set for the second time, I caved and drank a

carton of water. Devoured the measly slices of bread. It was nowhere near enough, but it curbed the twist in my belly and ache in my side.

Every tray since, I've waited until the man's feet descended the stairs and an echoing boom hit my ears before I slowly consumed enough scraps to keep me alive.

But as dawn glitters on the ocean's horizon, he doesn't descend the stairs today. Instead, he stands on the opposite side of the door and argues with a woman. A woman who has not been here, to my knowledge, since I was locked in this brick-and-steel tower.

"Then what *do* you suggest? She hasn't been here long enough to be cleansed."

Cleansed? What the hell is he talking about?

"Regardless, we're running out of time. We'll just have to pray she's searched her soul while under our mercy and asked God for repentance."

"Should we prepare to surrender her soul?"

I'm sorry, what? Surrender my fucking soul?

My hands tremble at my sides as ice seeps into my bloodstream. I back away from the door, never taking my eyes off of it. A shiver ripples through me from head to toe as my back hits the wall. I shake my head again and again and again, refusing to believe this is actually happening.

When I woke in this room and remembered being attacked in RJ's parking lot, every cell in my body knew what happened. What was going to happen. But instinct told me that Phoebe and my family would come to my rescue. Instinct told me not to give up.

So, I remained strong.

Until one day turned into two and two morphed into three.

I refuse to give up hope, but my optimism has been on a downward trend.

Phoebe is the smartest, most resourceful, persistent woman I've met. She won't give up looking. Ever. If she wouldn't concede with strangers, she sure as hell won't admit defeat when the person taken is someone close.

Our last conversation has played continuously in my head as I wither in this room. It has gnawed at my heart.

The anger, frustration and neglect simmering in my veins, those feelings were one-hundred-percent justifiable. Phoebe treated me with such disregard for days, as if I was a roommate in passing or a servant at her disposal. I tried to tell myself that it was decades of behavior drilled into her psyche. She didn't know any different. She was inattentive and inconsiderate of me and my needs because she's never had to concern herself with someone else's thoughts or desires.

But I despise how I left things.

I may have been upset, I may have needed space to clear my head, but I shouldn't have walked out the door so hotheaded. I should've taken a deep breath, acted more mature, and been more civil before I got in my car and left.

As it stands, all I see now is Phoebe's confused expression as I had demanded she figure out her future, as I had pressured her to figure out where I fit into it.

My stomach sours.

Please don't let that be the last conversation we share.

I need to apologize. I need to get down on my knees, clasp her hands in mine, and beg for her forgiveness. My behavior was childish, cruel and reprehensible. And it makes me sick to think I may not get the chance to take those last words back.

"We don't have time to perform the ritual," the woman declares. "We'll have to cut corners and pray God accepts our sacrifice just the same."

Did she say… *sacrifice*?

Fuck.

"Get the kit from the car," she commands. "Be quick about it."

I spin and face the window. In the past five days, I've tried to open it countless times without success. I've smacked it with the flimsy trays my food comes on and done more damage to the tray than the window. But I haven't had the strength to try much else.

Desperate times and all...

I shuffle back from the window, stand in a forward-facing lunge, crouch slightly, and then hurl the sole of my shoe at the window. It makes contact with a lackluster *thump*, not a crack or splinter in the glass. So I do it again. And again. And again.

Until the squeak of metal on metal hits my ears and the hinges of the steel door protest.

I whip around and plaster my back against the wall. Big Burly Man waltzes in and swallows the room with his sinister smile. Behind him, a woman with a familiar face stands at the threshold. Disgust fills her eyes as they rake up and down my body.

"Time to atone for your sins," the man says as he crosses the room, ready to pounce.

"You don't have to do this," I plead. "We can all walk away unharmed."

High-pitched laughter bounces around the room as the woman at the door throws her head back and cackles. When she levels me with her gaze, all I see is hostility and malice.

"This town is congested with greed and sin and abomina-tions." She takes a step into the room and I get a better view of her face. "It is my duty as a servant of God to rid the world of those who do not abide by his laws."

It's on the tip of my tongue to argue with her. To stall whatever it is she plans to do to and with me. To delay her sick and twisted plans, even if only by minutes, in the hopes someone might show up.

But I don't get the chance.

Burly Man lunges forward, clutches my arm with his meaty hand, and drags me toward the door.

I have no idea what happens once I leave my prison, and I refuse to leave this room willingly. I dig my heels into the floor, lean back, and tug on my arm in an attempt to free myself. And then I tug again. And again.

With a curl of his lip, he growls, tightens his hold on my arm, and crushes my bicep. In a blink, his lips morph into a wicked smile and my stomach plummets. "You know, I love it when they fight. Every single one of them. As if any of you sinful whores stand a chance." He yanks me toward the door. "You damned yourself." His eyes shift momentarily toward the woman. "And God sent us to rid this town of evildoers."

The woman walks ahead of us and descends the stairs. "Bring her to the most northern point of the cliff. I'll prepare." And then she disappears from view, the echo of her shoes on the metal stairs ricocheting off the walls.

I struggle against his pull and he picks me up off the floor. Facing forward, he crushes me to his chest and descends the stairwell. I thrash in his hold, kicking and screaming and doing my damnedest to elbow him in the ribs.

The sound of waves crashing against the rock face hits my ears as we reach the bottom floor of the lighthouse and step toward the open door.

I kick harder. Thrash more violently. Scream for help at deafening levels.

And he simply laughs as he exits the building.

I won't die here. I won't be another murder victim on this sick fuck's roster of supposed sinners. I won't leave this world at the hands of some deranged lunatic who claims to do God's work.

Fight fucking harder.

Kicking has been ineffective. My arms are practically pinned in place by his. I give a slight roll of my head and find I'm able to move it most. So I drop my chin to my chest, inhale of deep breath, and fling my head back as fast and hard as possible.

The back of my head screams in pain as he clutches me harder. "You'll pay for that, filthy fucking bitch."

To spite him, I do it again. His hold loosens and I flail. My feet hit the ground, but I only take one step before he fists my hair and yanks hard.

An ear-piercing scream leaves my lips as my legs lose strength. Rather than pick me up again, he drags me by my hair toward the woman at the cliff.

"Help!" I scream over and over as my throat turns raw and my voice grows weak. I yell and heave and squirm.

The pain doesn't matter. All that matters is escape. If I get away, I may survive this nightmare.

"Shut the fuck up!" *Thwack.* His fist collides with my cheek. "No one is coming. No one can save you except him."

We reach the woman near the cliff and my eyes meet hers. And it's when we're this close that I finally recognize her. The nun from the church.

A whimper escapes my lips as she brandishes a knife, the serrated teeth glinting in the early sunlight.

"You were born of him," she says as the man yanks my hair and exposes my throat. "But you have betrayed him."

The nun brings the tip of the knife to my forehead and draws a cross.

"And now, you must pay for your deviance. For lying with women. For tarnishing sacred, marital acts out of wedlock."

She rears back the knife and my heart thrashes in my rib cage.

"God sent me to earth to wipe away sin. And now it is time to cleanse the world of yours."

She slashes down with the knife and fire scorches my abdomen. A violent scream rips from my chest. The man twists his wrist and yanks. My scalp burns as he tears locks of my hair from the roots. He hoists me up until my shaky legs almost straighten.

"Repent for your sins," she demands as the blade sears my skin once more. "Beg for his mercy. Beg for mine." Another slice of the knife.

Blood saturates my clothes and chills my skin as the morning ocean breeze whips around us. Battered and scored, my body feels shredded as I sway in the man's grip. Pulse whooshing in my ears, my breaths come in small sips. The woman stares down at me, her face slowly blurring as my limbs grow heavy.

"Is it time?" the man asks.

She nods. "Yes. Bring her closer to the cliff."

Synapses fire in my head and scream at me to fight. They yell to push harder. To try one last time. To give it my all and survive this horror.

But I can't lift my arms. I don't have the strength. A constant tingle flits through my fingers, the tips going numb.

I want to live but can't survive this on my own.

Dragging me by my hair, the man stops when my feet teeter on the rocky cliff. He twists me to face her as she steps closer. She lifts a hand in front of my face and draws a cross in the air. Bible verses spill from her lips as my eyes drift over her shoulder.

For a moment, I get lost in the sight of the tall evergreens as they ruffle in the wind. I inhale one last deep breath, soaking up the pine-scented, salty air. The backs of my eyes sting as I take in the pink and orange painting the sky. A soft whimper vibrates my throat as I picture Phoebe and the first time her features softened. The first time her lips met mine.

My eyes fall shut, tears spilling down my cheeks as I imagine my fingers in her thick auburn hair. As I smell her sweet vanilla perfume with a hint of jasmine. As I get one last glimpse of her smile in my memory.

I open my eyes and stare at the trees, but something isn't right.

A flash of movement catches my attention. I can't make out what it is, but I pray it's a person and not an animal.

And then a shock of auburn hits my blurry vision.

My heart bangs beneath my sternum as hope floods my veins.

She's here. She found me.

"Sister," the man interrupts her spiel. "We've got company."

"Drop her."

Before her words register, I fall to the ground and slide down the rock face.

THIRTY-FIVE

PHOEBE

"Fox," I scream as Delilah disappears over the cliff. My calves burn as I charge forward. Ignoring everyone behind me telling me to stop.

The nun and her accomplice bolt from the cliff toward the car on the opposite side of the lighthouse. The car with four officers stationed on all sides, waiting.

I skid to a stop just before I reach the cliff, inching forward and peeking over the edge. Small trees jet out from the rock face and block my view. Careful of my footing, I ease forward and look for any sign of her. A shoe, her shirt, any article of clothing.

But I can't see a damn thing.

A demand for help rests on the tip of my tongue. I spin around, ready to bark orders and spot search and rescue with harnesses secure on their waists and lines being anchored. But they aren't moving fast enough.

"Hurry up."

Soft brown eyes meet my fiery gaze, a gentle tug at the corners of her mouth as she nods. "If our lines aren't secure, we can't pull her up." She tugs her rope and walks backward near the cliff. "We'll find her, Phoebe."

A skirmish sounds behind me, but I don't turn to witness the fight. With the number of police officers, founding family members, and SAR folk on scene, the nun and her henchman aren't going anywhere except a jail cell.

My pulse thrums in my ears as three people scale down the rock face, arm's length apart, with a rescue stretcher. I don't dare look away as they disappear beneath bristly evergreen limbs. I don't breathe as I wait for someone to announce they've found her.

Seconds pass in decades as I tap, tap, tap my thighs with my hands. *I can't take this*. I can't fucking stand here, waiting, doing absolutely nothing while Delilah is hurt and scared and who knows what else.

"Anything?" I yell down to the SAR team.

No response.

A hand lands on my shoulder and I jump back. "Fuck!"

"Sorry." Travis sidles up on my right. "Anything yet?"

I shake my head. "No one will fucking answer me," I yell toward the SAR team. And then my headshake turns into an all-over body shake. I wrap my arms around my middle as a shiver rolls up my spine.

"She'll be okay," Travis whispers as his arm bands around my shoulders and pulls me closer. "She has to be."

The backs of my eyes sting as my vision blurs. "I-I can't l-lose her." My heart spasms as the words leave my lips. "I c-can't."

Travis hugs me tighter. "You won't, Phoebe. *We* won't."

"How c-can you be certain?" Tears coat my cheeks.

"Delilah may be sweet and timid, but she's a fighter." He eases his hold on me, inches back, and waits until I meet his gaze. "She fought for you. Now it's time we all fight for her."

I open my mouth to tell him he is right. But as the words form, a shout from below hits my ears.

"Found her. Coming up."

I pace the edge of the cliff and look between the branches, anxious to lay eyes on her. I tap my thighs as I wear a new path along the cliffside, eager to see my Fox. Hour-long minutes tick by before fluorescent yellow peeks between the evergreen foliage.

Thank fuck.

As they steadily climb up, an ambulance darts through the trees, maneuvers so that the rear faces the cliff, and parks. The medics meet us near the edge and glance down as the crew inches their way toward us.

The moment Delilah crests the rock face, the medics swoop in with a gurney. In a matter of seconds, she is transferred from one backboard to another. The EMTs strap her down and wheel her into the ambulance. It all happens so fast I miss the chance to ride with her to the hospital. I don't get to ask questions before they speed away.

How bad are her injuries?

Blood. There was a lot of blood. Too much blood.

Is she breathing? Her lips had an undeniable blue hue to them. Blue lips mean only one thing—not enough oxygen in the blood.

"Is her heart…"

Travis takes my hand and hauls me away from the cliff toward the sea of officers dealing with the serial killer duo. "Come on," he says as we pass them. "I'll drive us to the hospital."

Too stunned to speak, I stumble in his wake. Get in his SUV as if I've done it countless times. Buckle my seat belt as my body goes numb.

Travis cranks the engine to life, flips his lights and siren on, and flies down the road toward Stone Bay Memorial.

"She'll be alright, Phoebe. She's in good hands now."

I want to believe him. Really, I do.

But I can't ignore the widening splinter in my chest as my world falls apart.

The nauseating blend of antiseptic and bleach singes my nasal passages. But I'd be willing to breathe the repulsive fumes every day of my life so long as Delilah's heart continues to beat.

It's been four hours and thirty-seven minutes since the ambulance sped away from the lighthouse cliff. Travis crushed the accelerator and drove twice the legal limit to get us to Stone Bay Memorial in a matter of minutes, calling Kirsten on the way and asking her to notify everyone else.

A menacing creature, the clock on the wall of the waiting room, continues to taunt me as time ticks on without answers or updates.

I just need to know she'll be okay. Please, let her be okay.

Within minutes of entering the hospital, the entire Fox clan descended. Hugs and tears were exchanged as August Fox spoke to the woman at the reception desk. Seconds later, he joined us in the waiting room, shaking Travis's hand before pulling me in for a long, warm hug.

"My little dove is strong, Phoebe," he'd said. "She just needs a boost of strength from us now."

Since entering the hospital hours ago, the only update her parents have received is the standard, *"We'll inform you of any updates as soon as we have them."*

I really want to punch the nurse at the counter for her detached etiquette. But then I remind myself that I have been equally indifferent toward everyone most of my life. Maybe apathy is how she copes with all the horrific things that come through the hospital doors.

An hour ago, Lawrence walked in with a large to-go box of coffee, cups, and all the add-ins. Appreciative of the dose of caffeine, we all filled a cup and gave him a hug before resuming our spots in the waiting room.

The Fox clan huddles together near the open doorway of the waiting room, speaking in hushed tones and consoling one another. A gray pallor has taken over Jet as June clings to his arm and rests their head on his shoulder. Skylar, Kirsten, Oliver, Lawrence, and Levi West swallow a corner of the room, Lawrence constantly reassuring Skylar that Delilah is getting the best care.

Fingers beating a constant rhythm on my thighs, I pace the length of the waiting room, the heels of my Dior boots chipping away at the marbled linoleum. I don't do well with waiting. Never have, never will.

The room quiets and I spin around to see what's garnered everyone's attention.

At the threshold of the waiting room, Tikaani Imala swallows the entrance, his expression unreadable and hands shoved in the pockets of his knee-length white lab coat.

August rushes him. "How is she?"

The corners of Dr. Imala's mouth tip up the slightest bit a beat before he rests a hand on August's shoulder. "Surgery went well. Her liver was nicked from one of the cuts, but we were able to stitch it in time. She suffered several broken bones from the fall but will heal with time and rest. Though most of her wounds were superficial and have been stitched and tended to, she lost a significant amount of blood." His expression turns solemn. "We did need to resuscitate her once."

I weave between the Fox crew. "She's breathing okay?" I roll my lips between my teeth. "Her lips were blue."

Dr. Imala gives a curt nod. "As I said, she lost a lot of blood. Because of that, her body was oxygen deprived." His lips curve into a gentle smile. "She's receiving oxygen while she recovers."

"Can we see her?" Jet asks.

Dr. Imala scans the crowd, his expression sheepish. "Give me a little longer and I'll set her up in a private suite."

Our collective sigh is audible.

"Appreciate it, Tikaani." August claps him on the back of his shoulder.

Another half hour passes before we're escorted to Delilah's room. Her family shuffles in first, tears on their cheeks as they take in the sight of her. Everyone else follows while I remain glued to the hallway floor.

A rhythmic beep echoes from the room and I close my eyes, listening to the strong cadence of her heartbeat. I let the sound vibrate over my skin and seep into my veins. Let it take over and replace every bleak thought I've had since Delilah didn't come home five days ago. I revel in the warmth finally taking up space in my chest again.

She's alive.

I unstick my feet and enter the room. Hands graze my arms. Murmured words fill my ears. But I pay them no attention as I move closer to the bed, my eyes waiting to catch sight of her. The one person blocking my view shifts to the side and I finally see her.

My Fox. Mine.

The room blurs as I stand at the foot of the bed. I reach out and clutch the rail as my legs give out. Arms wrap around me from behind as I collapse on the floor and a sob rips from my lips.

"Shh, shh, shh." Warmth and comfort surround me as I'm rocked side to side. "It's okay, Phoebe," Aurora coos in my ear. "Our girl will heal and be whole once more."

This only makes me cry harder, louder.

Aurora doesn't loosen her hold. If anything, she strengthens the embrace. And together, we sit on the floor and console one another—until my tears slow and heart settles.

I've never had an affectionate family. I've never had someone willing to fight for my heart and a goodness they see in me that I don't. In a matter of months, I have been gifted both.

I admit I have a long road ahead of me when it comes to love. But after experiencing a fraction of what it feels like to belong to someone, to have people care about you unconditionally, I'm willing to take the journey.

"Better?" Aurora whisper-asks and I nod. She rises and offers me her hand. "Time to see our girl."

I take her hand and we shuffle to the side of the bed. I stare down at my Fox, her face mottled with bruises.

Leaning over, I place gentle kisses to the bruises on her face, then I shift to her ear and lower my voice. "Come back to me, Fox." I close my eyes. "I still need you."

THIRTY-SIX

DELILAH

Beep. B-beep. Beep.

Black and yellow and a hint of red swirl my vision.

Whispered words from garbled voices hit my ears.

Beep. B-beep. Beep.

Fogginess clouds my thoughts and I'm unable to make sense of what's happening.

Heat wraps around my numb fingers. Soft. So warm.

Beep. B-beep. Beep.

A pungent smell wafts up my nose and settles on my tongue.

Stabbing pain in my side that just. Won't. End.

I want to scream.

Beep. B-beep. Beep.

Debilitating and endless. Please make it fucking stop.

Unintelligible words from a foreign, louder voice ripple in my ears as warmth flows through my veins.

No more pain.

No more fogginess.

No more voices.

Nothing.

Sharply whispered words blend with a constant *beep, beep, beep* as I lay like the dead in a coffin.

"Tomorrow will be a week," the voice hisses. "You aren't doing enough. She should be awake."

Sifting through memories, I try to put a face or name to the voice. The harder I try, the more my head aches.

I stop trying.

"She's been through a tremendous ordeal and her mind and body need to recover."

Weight shifts over my body.

"Her vitals look good. She'll wake up when her body is ready."

"Do you even have a degree to practice medicine? What the hell kind of answer is that?"

Lancing pain ripples through the center of my chest.

Mentally, I ball my fingers into fists and scream.

The beeping gets louder. Faster. And the voices fade away.

Fire spreads from my chest outward.

Spasming.

Pulsating.

Stealing my attention.

A different kind of heat hits my veins—this one tranquil and welcome—and the pain tapers from paralyzing to tolerable.

Every muscle in my body loosens. Every thought in my mind fizzles out. And the ounce of curiosity I had moments ago evaporates completely.

Heavy and weightless is all I feel.

As my mind starts to drift, one last thing filters through the fogginess.

"Come back to me, Fox. I need you to come back."

Cold air tickles my nose while heat blankets the entire right side of my body. Chemicals, vanilla and flowers swirl in the air as the repetitive beep I've heard on and off for days hits my ears and makes me wince.

I shift left in an attempt to alleviate some of the heat on my side. With the slightest movement, my muscles scream in protest and I stop. A groan rumbles deep in my chest but is muted as it leaves my lips.

One flutter, followed by another, I crack my eyes open. A dark, unfamiliar space fills my limited vision. I blink several times to clear my eyesight. Eyes wider, I do a slow scan of the dimly lit room.

Thick, long curtains are tugged together on the left wall. Between the bed and wall, soft light glows from a lamp behind a recliner, someone asleep in the chair. I squint to make out details of the profile and, after a moment, discern it's my mom.

"Momma?" I try to say, but my voice is dry and hollow and close to nonexistent.

I reach up and clutch my throat, wires and tubes moving with my hand. Ignoring my throat, I lift my hand in front of my face and stare at the IV line on the back of my hand and heart monitor on my finger.

I'm in the hospital.

I stare at the glowing red light from the finger clip as confusion sets in.

Why am I in the hospital?

Closing my eyes, I sift through my most recent memories.

Jumbled like a freshly opened puzzle, I can't make out

what's recent and what happened weeks or months ago. Flashes of Phoebe in my house, her clothes in the spare closet, her naked body in my bed. Lips and tongues and moans as Phoebe begs me for more. Dinner with my family. Jet telling us about an upcoming dance competition he and Shanti are participating in. Joking with June in the back room of Sage Whisperer. A night out with Skylar and Kirsten where the mood shifted from glum to less worrisome. A rush of excitement as Paige and I talk about expanding the romance section in the bookstore.

A hand slides up my belly and settles over my sternum.

I twist my head slightly and my eyes water when I catch sight of Phoebe. She curls closer to my side but doesn't give me her weight. The soft light edges her profile and calls attention to the dark circles under her eyes, ridge between her brows, and her disheveled, fiery locks.

The sight of her gives me pause.

In the years I've known Phoebe Graves, she has never appeared so unkempt and exhausted.

How long have I been here?

What the hell happened?

I gingerly lift a hand and rest it over hers. Before I exhale, Phoebe stirs at my side.

"Fox?" My last name scrapes her vocal cords.

"Firefly," I rasp, barely audible.

The mattress dips, the stiff sheets chafing my skin as she pushes up on an elbow to look me in the eyes. Inches from my face, her exhaustion is more evident. More pronounced, the dark half-moons under her eyes say she's barely slept in days. The ridge between her brows is as notable as the creases marring her forehead.

"What's wrong?" I lift a hand and cup her cheek.

Her eyes roll closed and she gently leans into my touch.

Twisting, she kisses the heart of my palm. "You almost d-died." The last word comes out strangled as a tear spills down her cheek.

A bizarre pang surges beneath my breastbone at the news. The backs of my eyes sting as the heart rate monitor beeps in quicker succession.

Died. I almost died.

I stroke her cheekbone with my thumb. Swallow past the expanding swell of emotion in my throat. "But I didn't," I choke out.

Piercing blue eyes meet mine and all I see is adoration. All I feel is warmth and love. All I know is I got a second chance at life and I won't waste it.

Before I second-guess myself, I pull her closer. "I love you, Phoebe. It may seem premature to say, but—"

Phoebe lowers her lips to mine and cuts me off with a soul-searing kiss. Unlike our previous kisses, this one is slow, charged and teeming with emotion. In this kiss, she tells me how scared she was that she'd lose me. She tells me I am more than just someone she spends time with. I am more than sex and lust. And it's in this kiss that she wordlessly says she is in love with me too.

She breaks the kiss, rests her forehead on mine, and trails the length of my nose with the tip of hers. "Love you too, Fox." Her lips caress mine in a chaste kiss. "And you're never allowed to scare me like that again. Got it?"

Tears roll down my cheeks as I nod. "Got it." I sniffle. "Now, tell me what happened."

And until a nurse enters the room hours later, Phoebe relays the last two weeks. The nightmare, the horror, and the waiting. Throughout it all, my stomach sours. When Phoebe mentions our fight the night of my abduction, guilt swims through my veins.

I did this—to myself and to us. In a single night, I fractured her heart and put myself in harm's way with one emotional outburst. Rather than spark a rational conversation and share how I feel—as I typically would—I got fired up and exploded.

Who am I anymore?

Phoebe talks in hushed tones and fills in her side of my disappearance. And as I listen to her frantic tale, I detach emotionally and berate myself mentally.

THIRTY-SEVEN

PHOEBE

She's shutting me out and I don't know why.

After extensive questions and an array of tests, Dr. Imala signed off on Delilah's release paperwork. She has weeks of therapy ahead of her—physical and psychological—but leaving the hospital is in her best interest for the remainder of her recovery.

When Dr. Imala delivered the news with a practiced smile, not a flicker of excitement danced across Delilah's face. I expected to see her face light up as she thanked him for all he did to save her. But the only acknowledgment Delilah gave was a clipped nod.

Uncertain how to process her reaction, I did my best to keep her distracted. And myself.

The two days before I wheeled her out of the hospital and drove us back to her place, she'd turned inward. Became quieter than normal. While I told her about half the town visiting, bringing her flowers, and offering love and support, Delilah built an invisible, unscalable wall around herself.

Maybe the splintered memories of her abduction came

back and she wasn't certain how to process what happened. Maybe she didn't understand her own feelings regarding the whole situation. More than that, maybe Delilah didn't know how to move forward.

However inconceivable, I want to help. I want to see that spark in her smoky blues again. I want back the woman who refused to give up on me regardless of my behavior. I want her affection, passion and light.

Her. I want her.

But the more she withdraws, the more I hesitate.

Delilah suffered unimaginable things for days. None of us can remotely comprehend what she went through, but we refuse to give up on helping her make it to the other side. Aside from me being the pesky, overly attentive girlfriend and nursemaid twenty-four-seven, she's had nonstop visitors every day. Between her family and friends, the house is never still, never quiet.

Yet, she remains despondent.

Filling two bowls with vegetable and barley soup, I load a plate with several slices of crusty bread. Soup and bread on a tray, I carry everything to the living room and set it on the coffee table before sitting on the couch beside her.

Curled in a blanket, Delilah stares unfocused at the movie on the television. "Thanks," she mutters, her gaze trained forward.

I reach for her hand, curling my fingers around hers, and she flinches. It's yet another blow to the solar plexus.

That flinch… it's my fault. I have yet to pinpoint the exact reason, but something I've said or done triggered her to recoil from my touch. And I fucking hate it.

"Sorry," I say and add more space between us.

A huff leaves her lips. "It's not you."

I peek over at her and see she's closed her eyes. And damn, it makes me want to wrap her in my arms. It makes me desperate to exorcise every last piece of traumatic shrapnel from her head and heart. To give her whatever she needs to feel safe and whole and fearless once more.

Inhaling a deep breath, I rein in my emotions and speak on the exhale. "It's okay if it is, you know."

At this, she meets my gaze. Her brows slowly tug together before she gives a slow shake of her head. Tears well in her eyes as she wrings the blanket in her hands. "Swear it's not you."

Heart beating chaotically in my rib cage, I test my luck and slowly reach for her hand again. This time, she doesn't jerk away from my touch. My whole body sighs in response.

"Talk to me, Fox." Desperation drips from every word, but I don't care. I *am* desperate. "Whatever it is, we'll get through it." I sweep my thumb over her knuckles. "But please, don't bottle it up. Let me help carry the weight."

Delilah drops her gaze to our joined hands as she flips her hand over and laces our fingers. Her brow creases as her eyes lose focus.

"It's strange." She swallows, then scoffs. "My brain feels like uncooked, scrambled eggs." She lifts her gaze and holds mine. "Gross and odd analogy, but that's the best way to describe it."

I chuckle softly. "However it works for you, Fox." So long as she shares the load, I don't care how she tells her story.

Her gaze returns to our hands. "There's so much swimming around in my head. Moments while I was in the lighthouse. The outlandish thoughts I had while I waited to see what would happen next." Her brows twitch briefly before her eyes meet mine. "You said I was gone five days."

I nod.

"For me, it felt like five weeks." Licking her lips, her gaze shifts to look over my shoulder. Eyes unfocused, she worries her bottom lip. "Realistically, I *knew* it'd been less than a week. There was a window in the room. I counted the sunrises and sunsets."

Her free hand picks at the blanket.

"And then I thought of the other women." Red, watery eyes flit to mine. "I wondered how long they'd been kept in similar circumstances—trapped in a room with very little human interaction, given just enough food and water to survive, scared over what would happen next, fighting for their lives as someone stole them from them."

As she shares, a sharp, scorching pain pierces my heart. A vicious cramp gnaws at my belly. I fight against the misery. I don't dare let it show on my face or reflect in my body language. My feelings are minuscule next to Delilah's experience and distress.

I asked her to unload what's been eating away at her soul. Now I need to remind myself that the agony I feel as she tells her story is barely a fraction of what she will endure for years to come. With this one thing, I can never be selfish.

Bitter laughter spills from her lips. "How fucking horrible am I for thanking every cosmic force I didn't end up like them?" Dropping her chin to her chest, she subtly shakes her head. "I got lucky. I had an army of people looking for me within hours." Her hand trembles in mine as she lifts her head. Tears stain her cheeks. "Those w-women…" She sniffles as her tears fall faster. "They were tortured longer and slower." She grips my hand with boundless force. "They w-wanted to make me hurt but knew they were short on time."

Flashes of Delilah near the cliff flit through my mind,

followed by images of the vile woman slashing a knife over Delilah's torso. The memory will haunt me until I take my last breath. But her version of the memory must be infinitely worse.

Every cell in my body feels compelled to console Delilah. To tell her that she is safe now, that I will never let anything happen to her again.

But how can I make such bold promises? How can I be everything at all times for her?

Simple… I can't. And that reality is a punch to the gut.

Delilah loosens her hold on my hand and then soothes the ache by tracing her fingers gently over my palm.

"Seconds before I slipped off the cliff, I thought, *This is it. Today, I'm going to die.*" She scoffs. "And in that moment, I was so angry at myself."

My gaze lifts from our hands to study her expression. "What? Why?"

Puffy red eyes dart between mine. "Because the last time we were together, I acted like a selfish brat. I yelled at you." She tips her head back, sniffles, then levels her gaze, her chin wobbly. "I've never spoken so harshly to anyone."

The corner of my mouth quirks up. "I have that effect on people." I stroke her hand with my thumb. "Sorry, Fox."

"Don't apologize." She shakes her head. "I'm as much at fault as you."

A shiver rolls through her body and echoes through mine where we're connected.

"On that cliff, I braced myself for the inevitable. But I hated that—" She swallows a beat before more tears spill down her cheeks.

I inch closer to her on the couch and wrap her hands in both of mine. "Whatever it is, you can tell me."

She sucks in a shaky breath. "I hated that I was so mad at

you that night when all I had wanted was to tell you I love you."

My pulse thrums beneath my ears and I stop breathing.

"If I'd acted more rationally that night, if I hadn't stormed out of the house, maybe none of this would've happened."

I erase every ounce of space between us. "No, Fox. Don't you dare shoulder the blame for what they did." Inching back, I cup her cheek and lift her chin, waiting for our eyes to lock. "What *they* did is *not* on you. Not now. Not ever. You hear me?"

A flood of tears rolls down her cheeks as she trembles in my hold. "But—"

"No." I vehemently shake my head. "No, Delilah. You will not take this on. Not for a single second. I won't allow it."

A fractured laugh leaves her lips. "Is that so?"

My thumb caresses her cheekbone. "It is."

With a slow, measured movement, I lean in and press my lips to hers in a chaste kiss. And thank fuck, she doesn't flinch.

"Couples disagree and fight and need space from time to time. We're so new, and I have a lot of demons to vanquish. Me messing up is inevitable." My fingers drift to her hair and tuck a lock behind her ear. "All I ask is for you to be patient." I trail my finger along her neck to her shoulder, following the action with my eyes. "And if you need to yell at me"—my gaze flits to hers—"yell at me. With you, I know it comes from a good place."

"Okay," she whispers.

"Okay," I parrot.

Her eyes dart to the coffee table as she rolls her lips between her teeth. Then her eyes are on me, a wince pulling at her expression.

"What?"

"Can we have something other than soup?"

At this, I laugh.

Since she's been home from the hospital, canned soup has been on the lunch and dinner menu daily. No one in their right mind wants me to cook. I'd burn down the house.

"Absolutely."

If only every predicament were so easily solved.

THIRTY-EIGHT

DELILAH

After our talk last night, some of the weight lifted from my shoulders.

For hours, we picked at enough takeout for four people and watched a rom-com. The movie isn't something I'd normally choose, but Phoebe knew I needed something light that would lift my spirits.

When the movie ended, we stowed the leftovers and went to bed. Phoebe molded her front to my back, slid her arm around my waist, mindful of my cast and bandages, and kissed the spot beneath my ear before sleep finally took us.

And for the first time in weeks, I slept like a rock. No dreams. No nightmares. Just sweet, blissful sleep.

As I rolled out of bed this morning, I felt more myself. A little more carefree. A slight smile on my lips.

Until Phoebe walked into the bathroom.

Yawning as she entered the bathroom, she paused inside the threshold. My eyes flicked to hers in the mirror and every ounce of bliss I'd felt was sucked from the room. Eyes fixed for several seconds on the faint yellow and green marks of my fading bruises, guilt and pity painted her face.

That look... I don't see our relationship lasting if all she sees are my bruises and scars.

Healing—emotionally, physically, psychologically—will take time. Acknowledging I survived will take time. Finding my happiness again will take time. Not feeling guilty for making it out alive while four other women died will take time. I know this. I accept this. And I will fight my self-reproach for many days to come.

But I won't be a pity case. I won't be gawked at with sympathetic stares.

And since I bolted from the bathroom half an hour ago and covered every possible inch of skin as I dressed, one question has rolled around in my head.

Will *we* survive this?

I want to believe it is possible to move past what happened with time. My optimistic heart says all things are within reach. That I just need to be patient and understanding.

Yes, I went through something atrocious. But so did Phoebe, just from a different perspective.

And what kind of asshole would I be if I gave up on Phoebe so easily?

Phoebe's whole life has been one traumatic experience after another. But seeing as she grew up with it, it was simply a part of daily life. What she has endured holds as much importance and significance as my abduction and near-death experience.

I want to say we will get past this—her pain and mine. I want to believe that love, real love, does heal.

But as she requested of me, I need her to not harbor all the guilt. If I give her some of my pain, I need her to do the same in return.

"Smells good."

I startle from my introspection. "Thanks."

"Sorry."

She sidles up to me at the stove as I cook scrambled eggs—which I've overcooked.

"Don't apologize." I turn off the burner, twist and rest a hip on the range, and reach for her hand. "I was in my head and didn't hear you come in."

Phoebe inches closer and ever so slowly drops her lips to mine. I love and hate that she has to tiptoe around my reflexive anxiety.

When she breaks the kiss, I grip her hand harder. Keep her close. "I want this, us, to work."

Brow furrowed, her head tilts slightly. "Me too." Confusion coats those two syllables.

I inhale deeply, hold it for a beat, then exhale a shaky breath. "I don't know how to say this without it coming out wrong."

Phoebe cups my jaw, caresses the apple of my cheek with her thumb, and locks her crystalline blues with my steely blues. "Whatever it is, Fox, just say it." Not an ounce of hurt or malice laces her words. Only reassurance.

You can do this, Delilah. You need to say this.

Digging deep for courage, I swallow then give my thoughts a voice.

"In the bathroom, the way you looked at me, my bruises. When you came in…" Nausea roils in my belly, but I mentally shove it down. "I need you to not look at me like that." I nibble at the corner of my bottom lip. "I get that it's hard, but I need you to not look at me like a charity case." I lift a hand to her face and trace the line of her jaw with a finger. "I need you to look beyond the bruises and scars." My fingers drift to her damp hair and toy with the ends. "To see *me* as you did before."

"I do see you." Her whispered words dance over my skin. "Sorry I stared. I blame my semiconscious brain." Phoebe rests her forehead on mine as her eyes close. "All I see is you, Fox," she confesses, her lips a breath from mine. Her eyes open and steal my breath. "Promise I'll be more cognizant going forward."

"Are you sure?" The question comes out before I stop myself.

Phoebe inches back and studies me with scrupulous eyes. "Am I sure of what, Fox?"

I hate this. I hate this. I hate this.

"Are you sure you want to do this? Be with m-me after..." The thought dies on my tongue as my heart wrenches painfully in my chest.

"Do I want to be with you?" Incredulity laces her tone. "Is that a serious question?"

"It's just..."

When I don't continue, Phoebe does. "What?"

"What if I'm broken? What if the old me never comes back? What if you have to approach me like a scared animal for the rest of my life?"

I suck in a sharp breath.

"Can you live like that?" The question comes out a hint hysterical as my heart thrashes in my chest. "I'm not sure I can."

Phoebe steps into me until our bodies are flush. She brings both of her hands to my face, tips my head back until our eyes hook, and nods.

"If you're broken, then I'm broken." She presses a chaste kiss to my lips. "I want your broken." She kisses between my eyebrows. "But only if you're okay living with my broken too." She kisses my forehead then meets my gaze. "Never wanted anyone until you, Delilah Fox." Her thumbs caress my cheeks. "I only want you."

A tear slips free and paints my cheek. "You're sure?"

I hate that I have to ask. I hate that I need reassurance. But after everything that's happened, I can't risk my heart.

I need her candor.

I need to know she isn't staying with me out of sympathy.

I need to know her love is real, true and lasting.

The hint of a smile tugs at the corner of her mouth. "Only if you are."

My whole body sags in relief. "Yeah, firefly." I wrap my fingers around her wrists and push up on my toes. "I'm sure."

And then I kiss her as though the world is ending.

EPILOGUE

PHOEBE

Three weeks later

I'VE COME TO TERMS WITH THE FACT THAT I WILL NEVER HAVE A loving relationship with my parents. A sad reality but one I accept.

The Graves lineage—and those they choose as life partners—isn't one built on kind words and gentle embraces. Though I can't speak for my siblings, I will no longer feed the callous behavior my family has perpetuated for generations.

In my own way, on my own terms, I love *some* of my family. Going forward, though, it will be from afar. I'll see my father at the Gazette frequently but have opted to work remotely more often.

As I put distance between myself and my family, the insistence that I pursue a relationship with Beau Langston disappeared completely. Last I heard, he was attempting to court Jasmine Kemp—the youngest in the Kemp family and newest addition to Calhoun-Kemp Industries, who own the wealthiest restaurants in Stone Bay.

I'll keep an eye on that development and be on standby if Jasmine needs help.

"The second bedroom may as well be your closet," Delilah teases as I walk in with the umpteenth box labeled *shoes*.

"Won't hear any complaints from me." I shrug and set the box in the corner.

My relationship with Delilah is far from perfect. She knows this as much as I do. But we are both willing to put in the work and do our damnedest to be transparent with our feelings before they spiral out of control.

Me moving into her place seemed inevitable. The amount of time we were together surpassed our time apart.

A few days ago, she offhandedly suggested I move more stuff in—clothes, toiletries, everyday items. For the briefest of seconds, I hesitated. But it had been long enough to make her wilt.

And fuck me... when sadness steals her smile, it rips me to shreds.

That simple suggestion morphed into an hour-long conversation. At least seventy-five percent of that hour was me seeking reassurances.

Did she really want me invading her space? Because that's what me moving my life into her house would be—an invasion.

For weeks, I fretted over Delilah—while she was missing and since she was found—and hadn't so much as touched cleansers, makeup, or haircare products. No one said a word about my appearance the entire time—that's what nice people do. When I caught my reflection for the first time in weeks, I winced. A troll had more appeal than I'd had.

Bringing day-to-day things from the Graves estate to her house made sense. Most people are turned off by others using their toothbrush and underwear. I figured she just wanted those things to herself.

But then my mind went off on a tangent.

Did she want me to move in? Or would she send me packing once she was more herself again?

The latter looped in my mind during our entire conversation. And then she took both my hands in hers and, as if reading my mind, said what I needed to hear.

"I want you to stay, Phoebe." Her thumbs caressed my knuckles in slow, steady strokes. "I want to do this with you. Live together." The corner of her mouth quirked up. "If that's something you want too."

Since that talk, we've been different.

Delilah is more herself—though I still glimpse a hint of darkness in her expression. Doctors say her mental scars will last longer than the physical, but both will heal with time. So long as she doesn't bottle up her pain or put on a brave face for others, she will recover when her body and mind are ready.

As for me, almost losing Delilah was this light bulb moment. After a lifetime of darkness, alienation, and disapproval, I got the wake-up call I so desperately needed.

Delilah is more than my girlfriend. With her big heart and relentless drive, she saved my life. She rescued me from becoming a worse version of the woman I despise most. For a time, I fought her subtle insistence. But she refused to give up trying.

If one person in Stone Bay is capable of thawing my ice-cold heart, it is Delilah Dove Fox.

And every time she gifts me her smile, her touch, her affection, I thank every star in the night sky for her tenacity.

We unload several more boxes from August's truck and put them in the appropriate room before breaking for lunch. August and Aurora suggest we relax while they pick up food.

Neither of us argues.

In less than an hour, Skylar, Lawrence, Kirsten, Travis, and Oliver will descend on the house for an unpacking party. Though most of my belongings are clothes and shoes, I do have some furniture and miscellaneous decorative pieces to find a new home for.

Minutes after the first bite of lunch, the house bustles with helping hands and eager smiles. While the Foxes and I finish lunch, Oliver drones on about his band playing at Dalton's tonight. His excitement is infectious.

They try to mask it, but everyone tiptoes around Delilah. And she isn't oblivious.

Not a single person has mentioned what happened to her captors—the tag team duo dubbed the St. Agnes killers.

After endless hours of interrogation—god, how I would've loved to be a fly on that wall—Rebecca Salt and Joseph Tinx were officially charged with five counts of false imprisonment, four counts of alleged homicide, one count of attempted homicide, one count of serious bodily harm, one count of misrepresentation, and one count of eluding an officer.

When Chief Emerson shared the news, I breathed a sigh of relief and thanked him profusely. As the two await trial, as they remain isolated in jail cells, Emerson continues to throw the book at them. Neither of them has requested legal representation. And according to Emerson, Rebecca has *faith* God will release her from prison and absolve her of all crimes. According to Rebecca, she was doing the Lord's work and he would be proud.

Some fucked-up shit, if you ask me.

I look forward to sitting front and center at the courthouse while her verdict and sentence are read.

Once they're permanent fixtures in Washington Corrections Center, we will all breathe easier. But none more than Delilah.

When their sentences are handed down, she will finally be free. She'll feel safe enough to be her whole self again.

"I envy your wardrobe," Kirsten says as she hangs a thigh-length, scrunched-sleeve, pale indigo denim dress in the closet.

"Don't get any ideas, sunshine," Travis grumbles.

I chuckle. "Thanks." Arching a brow, my eyes dart between Kirsten and Travis. "I may need to thin out my collection, though." I shrug as though getting rid of thousands of dollars' worth of clothes is no big deal. "Not sure everything will fit in here, even if we add more shelves and rods."

Kirsten removes another dress from a garment bag and all but drools at the sleek, curve-hugging, burnt-orange fabric. "Put me at the top of the donation list. I'll gladly take any of this off your hands."

Delilah laughs and the entire room stills. A second later, we resume our tasks, hopefully not making things any more uncomfortable for her. But I'm not the only one that's missed her laugh.

One by one, the bags and boxes empty. Before long, everyone says their goodbyes and gives us fierce hugs. After one last hug, Delilah promises her parents we'll be over for dinner on Sunday.

Skylar follows Lawrence out the front door, pausing just past the threshold. "See you at Dalton's later?"

With a slight fidget, Delilah lifts her hand and toys with the ends of her hair. "Yeah." She nods for emphasis. "Wouldn't miss Ollie's show."

Skylar steps into Delilah's space too quickly, causing her to flinch, and wraps her arms around Delilah. "Love you, Dee Dee. See you in a bit."

Fake smile firmly in place, Delilah nods as Skylar backs away. "We'll be there."

"If you're uncomfortable, we can leave."

Delilah shakes her head as we stand by the car and stare at the pub, loud music spilling from the open doors.

"My rational mind knows it's safe to be here. That no one will hurt me in the middle of the bar." She inhales an audible breath and swallows. "But my skittish, skeptical mind says to jump back in the car and go home."

"Whatever you want, Fox, I will support." I slip my hand in hers and lace our fingers. "Say the word."

The corner of her mouth twitches, the hint of a smile showing. Shifting her gaze from the bar to me, her smile widens.

"Thanks." She gives my hand a gentle squeeze. "I need to do this, though." Her gaze returns to the building. "I need to take back control of my life. I need…" Her hand shakes in mine. "I need to regain the power they ruthlessly stole."

Never in my life have I known a woman more brave, resilient and remarkable than Delilah. Proud doesn't remotely cover how I feel by her side.

"Whenever you're ready."

Several minutes pass, neither of us saying a word, before we enter Dalton's and find the rest of our group. And the addition of Levi West, another of the Seven. We slide onto stools at a tall table, order greasy food and drinks, and join in on the conversation. The entire time, Delilah holds my hand with delicate yet firm strength beneath the table.

A waiter refills our drinks, then signals to Oliver, Hailey, and Trip that it's time to take the stage.

Hailey and Trip head for the stage while Oliver finishes his drink. As he rises off his chair, Oliver leans into Levi and says something only for his ears. Levi nods.

Feeling like I'm missing something, I inch closer to Delilah and drop my voice. "What's up with them?" I jut my chin toward Oliver and Levi.

Delilah glances briefly in their direction before grabbing a fry and dunking it in barbecue sauce. "Best friends since Ollie was sixteen." Her eyes dart around the table to make sure no one pays us any attention. "Ollie's had feelings for Levi most of that time, but keeps it to himself."

A warm fizz bubbles in my chest. "Like you did with me?"

She swirls another fry in sauce, her lips tucked between her teeth to fight a smile. "Kind of." One of her shoulders lifts, then falls. "I wanted to be your friend. Over the years, the fondness I had for you slowly became a crush." Chin slightly tucked, she peeks at Levi from the corner of her eye. "Ollie's always wanted Levi as more but settles for being his friend."

My mind swirls with images of the West family.

Felicity West may be the middle child in her generation, but she carries the torch for the West name in Stone Bay. A matriarch in her own right, she refused to change her surname when she and Jefferson married. But with the power she possesses, Jefferson happily hyphenated his last name, adding hers. Having the West surname in Stone Bay is as equally influential as being a Graves, Fox, Langston, Emerson, Barron, or Imala.

The idea may be antiquated, but we still have pride in the small town our ancestors constructed.

Levi West, like Delilah and the Fox family, is quiet. Reserved. He mirrors Felicity in that respect. Were he more like his father, he'd puff out his chest and insist that people grant him unearned respect. Like my mother. Must be a thing for those with easily bruised egos that marry into the founding families.

And if there ever comes a day when Levi needs advice

from someone who's been in a similar situation, I'll nonchalantly offer. But until that day arrives, I'll mind my own business—something new I'm learning… and struggling with.

The loud boom of a bass drum fills the air as the jukebox cuts off. All heads in Dalton's swivel toward the makeshift stage a beat before boisterous applause echoes through the building.

"Hello, Stone Bay," Hailey hollers into the mic, guitar slung backward on her torso. "How the fuck are you on this fine Friday night?"

Wolf whistles and roars of excitement rip through the decent crowd packed inside the pub.

"You ready to kick off the weekend with some rocking fucking roll?"

The noise intensifies as people shuffle closer to the stage.

"Fucking hell," I mutter.

Delilah chuckles. "Hailey's a riot. I love her *take no shit and live life to the fullest* attitude."

I swivel in my seat and arch a brow. "Do you now?"

She gives a noncommittal shrug. "One of the things I love about you." Clamping down on her lips, she fights a smile. "I just happen to find you more attractive."

"Oh really?"

"Yep." She pops the *p*.

I lean forward, ghost the tip of my nose along the line of her jaw, then pause centimeters from her ear. "How much more attractive?"

A shiver ripples through her body. The simple response heats me head to toe. My panties dampen as I think of all the other things I want to do to make her shiver.

She licks her lips. "Everyone is mediocre next to you, firefly."

"Yeah?" I ease back so we're eye to eye, only a breath between us.

"Always."

And then she kisses me, unrestrained and as if the world doesn't exist.

BONUS CONTENT

DELILAH

Two Weeks Later

"Sure you want to read it?" Phoebe hugs the most recent copy of the Stone Bay Gazette to her chest.

I hold out my hand and wait for her to give me the newspaper. When she doesn't after a couple minutes, I huff out my annoyance.

"Come on, Phoebs," I whine. "I'll be fine."

"Phoebs?" Her lip curls at the impromptu, foreign nickname. "What happened to firefly?"

I shrug. "That's reserved for when you're being nice," I tease.

"Oh, I'll show you nice."

Phoebe lunges for me on the couch, frames my thighs with her knees, and digs her fingers into my sides.

For a moment, I squirm and try to evade her wiggly fingers. And then I turn things around on her. I shift and dig my fingers in a tickle spot that makes Phoebe squeal. She slaps my hand and the newspaper tucked beneath her arm, the one she obviously forgot about, falls onto my lap.

Phoebe's hands drop as she inches back. "Don't, Fox."

Crinkling fills the air as I tighten my hold on the paper and look her square in the eyes. "Please don't fight me on this. I need to do this. Please, firefly…" My voice is a visceral cut to the heart. "Let me close this chapter of my life so I can start the next."

Phoebe swings her leg over and off my lap and plops down beside me on the couch. "Fine," she huffs out. "But I'm glued to your side until *I'm* certain you're okay."

With a subtle nod, I whisper, "Thank you." And then I unfold the paper and start reading Phoebe's story in the Gazette.

Stone Bay Gazette
Monday, May 13, 2024

St. Agnes Killers Sentenced to Life in Prison
Town mourns the loss of well-loved residents
By Phoebe A. Graves

Residents of Stone Bay sighed with relief last Friday, May 10th, when Judge Beaufort Langston clapped his gavel for the last time in the case of The Town of Stone Bay, Washington vs. Rebecca Ann Salt and Joseph Jacob Tinx.

Last fall, the quiet and quaint town of Stone Bay was flipped upside down when a woman was discovered in the woods not far from a rental property off Fossil Mountain Highway. At the time, Stone Bay Police Chief Roger Emerson said the homicide was an isolated incident.

Regardless, the news wreaked havoc on Stone Bay and scared citizens into isolation for several weeks.

Tireless hours were spent on the case, and after an altercation with another resident, the Stone Bay Police Department believed they had captured the person responsible for the woman in the woods.

In the weeks that followed, the town and its protectors rested easier.

Until midwinter, when another woman, Margot Pierce, a beloved Stone Bay resident, was found in the woods near the Stone Bay Ski Resort. Police searched for clues to solve the case quickly and quietly but had limited evidence.

To aid them in their search, a Stone Bay founding family member, Phoebe Graves, joined forces with Stone Bay police and provided a unique outsider's perspective on the case. Days later, a Stone Bay founding family member, Delilah Fox, partnered with Ms. Graves.

A dynamic powerhouse, they helped piece together the case and bring the parties responsible to justice.

On Friday, justice was served.

The verdict?

Salt and Tinx were found guilty of all charges brought against them.

The sentence?

Salt was sentenced to life in prison at the Washington Corrections Center for Women without the possibility of parole. Salt will work within the prison system to pay fines and restitution to the town of Stone Bay, the state of Washington, and the only survivor, Delilah Fox.

Tinx was sentenced to life in prison at the Washington Corrections Center without the possibility of parole. Though Tinx continues to defend his innocence—a virtuous man who fell prey to a scorned woman's coercion —and states he never committed any wrongful acts. Tinx will work within the prison system to pay fines and restitution to the town of Stone Bay, the state of Washington, and the only survivor, Delilah Fox.

> *As the town grieves for the loss of Julia Quinn, Margot Pierce, Sabrina Harris, and Yuki Takahashi, the surviving family members ask that any flowers, gifts, or funds be donated to local shelters for domestic violence, local search and rescue teams, and community programs designed to protect residents, such as martial arts training and the Stone Bay Police Department's "Stay Vigilant, Stay Safe" initiative.*
>
> *A vigil will be held for Quinn, Pierce, Harris, and Takahashi at the Stone Bay Amphitheater on Wednesday, May 15th, at 5:30 p.m. All residents of Stone Bay are welcome and encouraged to attend.*

I fold the newspaper and gingerly set it on my lap as I inhale a cleansing, deep breath. Phoebe rests her hand on mine but remains silent at my side.

"It really is over," I say, twisting to meet her waiting gaze.

Phoebe brings her other hand to my cheek, her thumb stroking melodically back and forth. The corners of her mouth curve up the slightest bit as she nods. "Yeah, Fox, it really is."

Prepare your heart for Oliver and Levi's story, Fallen Stars, the next standalone novel in the Stone Bay series. I love their story with my whole damn chest and know you will too.

Also... Remember the short erotica story a customer was looking for in Page by Paige? Once I wrote about it, I had to write it! So, I present... In Knots For You! Due to content, it's only available in my online store.

GRAVES
family tree

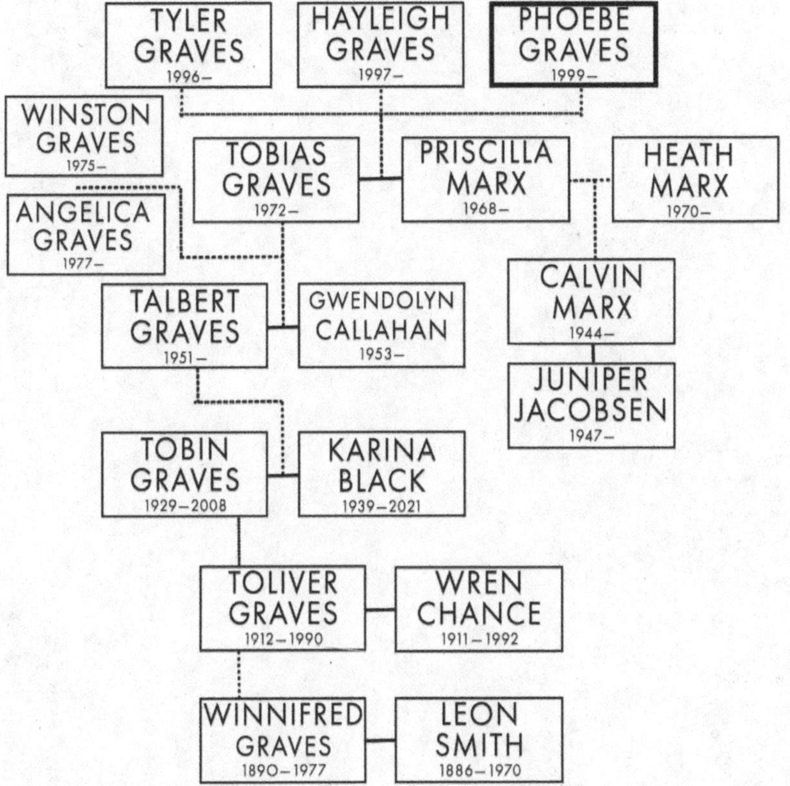

FOX
family tree

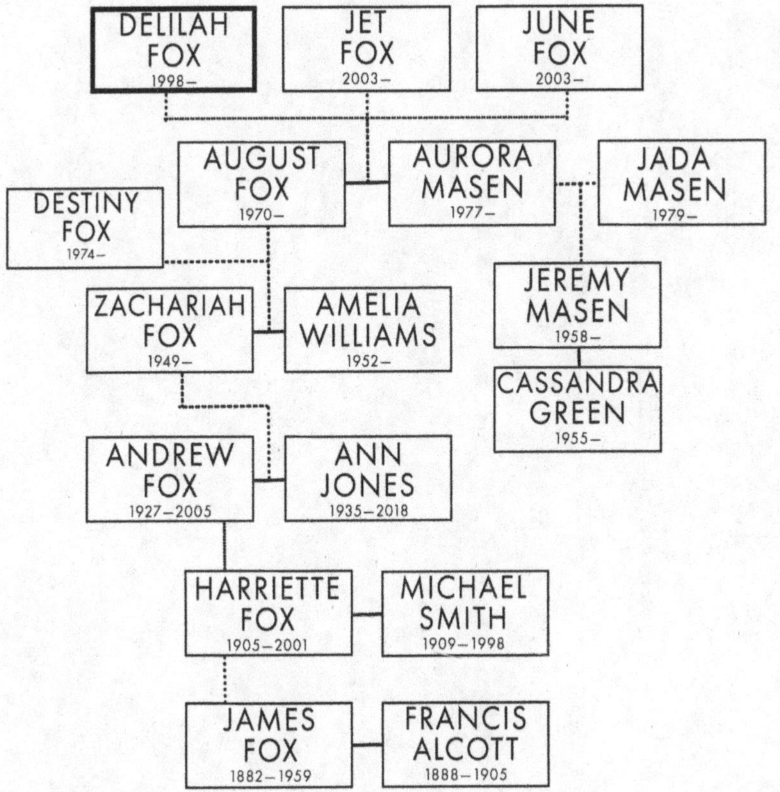

MORE BY PERSEPHONE

Broken Sky

Their eyes meet across the bar, but she looks away first. Does her best to give him zero attention. But when he crowds her on the dancefloor, she can't deny the instant chemistry. After one night together, he marks her as his. Unfortunately, another woman thinks he belongs to her.

Shattered Sun

When your heart is split in two, how do choose who to love more? While Ben—her childhood best friend—and Travis—the hottest cop in Stone Bay—fight for Kirsten's affection, someone else has their eye on her. When she questions everyone and everything, Ben and Travis vow to protect her. In the process, she falls for both men. Before it's too late, she needs to decide which man she loves more.

Depths Awakened

A small town romance which captivates you from the start. Mags and Geoff are two broken souls who have sworn off love. Vowed to never lose anyone else. But their undeniable attraction brings them together and refuses to let go.

One Night Forsaken

One night. No names. No romance. Just fun. Nothing more–at least, that's what she tells herself. Until he appears in her coffee shop months later with that addictive smile. She swore off commitment. He vows to never love again. But the more they fight it, the more life brings them together.

Every Thought Taken

As young children, an unshakable friendship brought them together. As teens, they discovered an undeniable love. Then life pulled them in different directions–into darkness and light–and slowly ripped them apart. Years later, he returns home in the hopes of a second chance with his first love and to conquer the demons of his past.

Distorted Devotion

Free-spirited Sarah lives life to the fullest. When a new love interest enters her life, she starts receiving strange gifts and letters. She doesn't want to relinquish her freedom or new love, but fears the consequences.

Beloved Devotion

Liz asks the love of her life, Tiffany, to marry her. When Tiffany hesitates, but says yes, Liz is determined to learn why. As the pieces start to fall in place, Liz discovers she doesn't know her fiancée at all.

Transcendental

A musician in search of his muse and a woman grieving the loss of her husband. Two weeks at an exclusive retreat and their connection rivals all others. Until she leaves early without notice. But he refuses to give up until he finds her again.

The Click Duet

High school sweethearts torn apart. When fate gives them a second chance, one doesn't trust they won't be hurt again. Through the Lens (Click Duet #1) and Time Exposure (Click Duet #2) is an angsty, second chance, friends to lovers romance with all the feels.

The Inked Duet

A man with a broken heart and a woman scared to put herself out there. Love is never easy. Sometimes love rips you apart. Fine Line (Inked Duet #1) and Love Buzz (Inked Duet #2) is a second chance at love, single parent romance with a pinch of angst and dash of suspense.

The Insomniac Duet

He was her high school bully. She was the outcast that secretly crushed on him. More than ten years later, he's her boss, completely oblivious to their shared past, and wants no one but her. More importantly, he doesn't understand her animosity toward him.

The Artist Duet

A tortured hero with the biggest heart and a charismatic heroine with the patience of a saint. Previous heartache has him fighting his desire to be more than friends with her. But she is everywhere, and he can't help but give in. The Artist Duet is an angsty, friends to lovers slow burn.

PLAYLIST

Here are some of the songs from the **Fractured Night** playlist.
You can find and listen to the entire playlist on Spotify!

Slip Away | UNSECRET, Ruelle
Umbrella | J2, JVZEL
Start of Time | Gabrielle Aplin
Island | SVRCINA
If Our Love Is Wrong | Calum Scott
Love and War | Fleurie
hoax | Taylor Swift

CONNECT WITH PERSEPHONE

<u>Connect with Persephone</u>
www.persephoneautumn.com

<u>Subscribe to Persephone's newsletter</u>
www.persephoneautumn.com/newsletter

<u>Join Persephone's reader's group</u>
Persephone's Playground

<u>Follow Persephone online</u>

instagram.com/persephoneautumn
facebook.com/persephoneautumnwrites
tiktok.com/@persephoneautumn
bookbub.com/authors/persephone-autumn
goodreads.com/persephoneautumn
amazon.com/author/persephoneautumn
pinterest.com/persephoneautumn
threads.net/@persephoneautumn

ACKNOWLEDGMENTS

To my family... I love you so much! Your endless support of this crazy, fulfilling dream makes my heart so full. I wouldn't be who I am without you and I wouldn't continue this author journey without your encouragement.

Rosa at Fairy Proofmother Proofreading! I am eternally grateful for your expertise and insight. My books wouldn't be as incredible (or correct) without your touch. Love you!!

Abi of Pink Elephant Designs! I promise I won't bug you to make extra changes after you've created files... again. But thank you for making my covers beautiful and addicting to look at. My stories wouldn't be the same without your artistry.

To all the bloggers and ARC readers that continuously promote my stories, get excited about books I'm terrified of putting out in the world, or read and love my words. I love you all so much!! Your support means more than you know. I love seeing your posts and joy about my books.

To everyone that picks up one of my books, I love you! Whether Fractured Night is your first Persephone Autumn book or your 20+ book, I never take a single one of you for granted. All the fucking hugs!!!!

ABOUT THE AUTHOR

USA Today Bestselling Author Persephone Autumn lives in Florida with her wife and psycho cat. A proud mom with a cuckoo grandpup. An ethnic food enthusiast who has fun discovering ways to vegan-ize her favorite non-vegan foods. Most days, you'll find her with a tea latte or fruity concoction in her hand. If given the opportunity, she would intentionally get lost in nature.

For years, Persephone did some form of writing; mostly journaling or poetry. After pairing her poetry with images and posting them online, she began the journey of writing her first novel.

She mainly writes romance and poetry, but on occasion dips her toes in other works. Look for her non-romance publications under P. Autumn.